BLAC

EMMA SILVER

"Keeps you turning to pages to uncover new clues. Horror fans will enjoy the almost Stephen King-like creepiness infusing the story."

Suzanne Cantrell

"phenomenal... witty, heartbreaking at times, and down right scary, Blackbrooke is a roller-coaster ride from its terrifying beginning to the jaw dropping finale."

Carmen Jenner, Book Me!

"Absolutely blew me away. I haven't stopped thinking about it for days."

Ellen Gault, Always YA at Heart

"A terrifying yet captivating debut... I enjoyed every minute of it."

Emmy, Sinfully Delicious Book Reviews

"WOW!"

Ali, Ginger-read Reviews

CROOKED CAT

Cover Artwork by Nicholas Raymond (http://freestock.ca/
horror_macabre_g66-bloody_hand_print_p1501.html),
Alica Blechova, Julie Saraceno and Yamamoto Ortiz
Design by Crooked Cat
Editorial Assistance: Sue McCaskill

Blackbrooke: 978-1-908910-47-9

Printed for Crooked Cat by Createspace

First Silver Line Edition, Crooked Cat Publishing Ltd. 2012

Discover us online:
www.crookedcatpublishing.com

Join us on facebook:
www.facebook.com/crookedcatpublishing

Mrs Hynes,
for noticing a spark
and nurturing it.

Eternally grateful.

The Author

Emma was born and raised in Manchester.

Blackbrooke is her debut young adult horror novel after spending many years honing her skills drafting short stories and devouring horror through the ages from R.L. Stine's Goosebumps collection through to Stephen King.

Emma is also the author of a semi-biographical account of her dad's years in a rock band in the 1970s, Driving Exile.

Outside of her day job in public relations, Emma has worked for a Manchester entertainment magazine, reviewing theatre shows gigs and movies.

She gets most of her ideas and is inspired by music and also the fighting spirit of young people who aren't afraid to challenge the norm and stand up for what they believe in.

This fleeting 'moment' in life is what she tries to capture in her writing.

Acknowledgements

Here's the part every writer dreams about – saying thank you to everyone who's influenced and helped create the book you're about to read.

I'll start with Crooked Cat Publishing who believed in Blackbrooke from the start. Laurence and Steph have been everything a writer could hope for and helped make Blackbrooke the best it can be. A special note of thanks goes to fellow Crooked Kitty, Rose McClelland, whose advice and support has been invaluable along the way.

My unofficial story editor, Candice Cooke who listened to Blackbrooke from concept to completion and wasn't afraid to challenge me along to way, which I didn't always like! However, it resulted in the piece of work I have today which I'm unspeakably proud of.

My personal literary critic, Rebecca Nelson. Fellow English graduate, book lover, red-brick-brain - you're quite possibly the most thoughtful and intelligent person I've ever met and your opinion means the world to me (as does my delicious godson, Lewis. Thanks for him too, Mr & Mrs Nelson!).

Guy Davies, for pushing me to write and believing in me throughout the ten years we were together and all of the years before that in high school.

My fabulous parents who, although now practically live on opposite sides of the world from one another, still feel like numbers one and two of the three musketeers. I love you both so very much and have always felt your pride in my achievements.

Thanks to my English teacher, Mrs Hynes whom the book is dedicated to. I was lucky to have you teach me through high school and by god, did you believe in me. Not every young person gets to experience being taught by someone like you and I think that's an absolute tragedy. Speaking of tragedy, your hatred of Romeo and Juliet still makes me chuckle…

Oh wow…James, Tim, Brian, Julian and Lou – I hope you'll find it in your heart to forgive me one day for this. I haven't forgotten my summer of love with Exile. How could I?

And finally, to all the young people out there who formed the inspiration for Liberty Connor. Don't step back from what you believe in. Believe me when I say, the fire that burns in your belly doesn't last very long if you don't fan the flames. Keep your spark, don't give in and remember everyday just how wonderful you are.

Emma Silver
November 2012

BLACKBROOKE

The Rules

1. No one is permitted outdoors after sunset.
2. All blinds must be shut at nightfall, and not opened until the morning klaxon is heard.
3. Triple glazing is required in all rooms.
4. No one should be invited into your home that you do not know.
5. When outdoors, children should be supervised at all times.
6. Dark woodland areas are strictly out of bounds.
7. Long hair must be worn in a tight bun at all times.
8. Young people are not permitted to fornicate until they have been sworn in all of the Rules at age 18.
9. Visitors to Blackbrooke must apply for a Visitor Pass and check in at the town border and check out upon exit.
10. Any Blackbrooke residents wishing to leave cannot, under any circumstances, return.

Prologue

I was seven when I saw my first Crit.

It was a balmy summer's day in Blackbrooke. The kind where it looked as though water had settled on the horizon. *Sweltering*, I'd overheard someone say.

Summer was the best time. The days stretched on for hours, which meant only one thing. The nights were shorter.

It granted the townspeople that extra dollop of freedom the winter so cruelly snatched away. In winter, we'd spend the majority of our day holed up, just waiting for the morning klaxon to signal the daylight. However, because this was the north of England, even when the electronic shutters covering the windows lifted, it was still dull outside. Blackbrooke was a town in the centre of vast woodland stretching for miles outside of the border and the trees did an excellent job of sucking all the light from the sky. Even when they were bare in the winter, they still seemed to close in on us.

Although the summertime was wonderful and I'd spend my days skipping in glee, it was dangerous. Of course, the Crits didn't come out during the day but it meant that when they finally did emerge, after the sun went down, they were famished.

In the height of the summer, the daylight stretched for just shy of seventeen hours, leaving the Crits with the remainder. They took no prisoners.

There was nothing physically stopping the Crits from wandering through Blackbrooke during the day. They weren't like monsters in folklore and horror stories that would burn up as soon as daylight hit them. Apparently, when the humans and the Crits used to mix centuries ago, it resulted in conflict and there were battles and death on both sides. So they reached an agreement. Humans got the day and the Crits got the night. Any party daring to break that rule was fair game. The Watchers were the only Crits allowed to roam around the town during the day, but no one cared about them. They were harmless.

Because the agreement was put in place so long ago, there was no record of how it happened. From what I learned about the Crits, I couldn't believe they were actually capable of any kind of negotiation. In my mind, it would be like trying to strike a deal with a hungry lion.

The day/night agreement was one thing, but the so-called 'agreement' to keep the Crits contained to one town wasn't so amicable. Blackbrooke was always their home, but one hard winter in the eighteenth century saw them starting to venture further afield. The Outsiders panicked, of course, and drove them back with fire, knives, arrows, guns, even cannons. Eventually they realised too much money and resource was being wasted on this pointless task, especially when Britain needed all of its weapons for war, so it was decided a fence would be erected around the town, keeping the Crits in. And us of course. Only there was one difference. We were allowed to leave once we turned eighteen, as long as we promised never to return. That was Rule Ten. There was no Rule Ten for the Crits. Outsiders liked to keep them where they could see them.

Ending your life was frighteningly simple in Blackbrooke. Forget using a noose, pills, blades. You simply had to open your door and walk out. Summer would be a good time of year to walk out. The Crits would have you straight away, they were so ravenous. However, Blackbrooke suffered the majority of walk outs in the winter when its residents were depressed and despairing of the long, dark nights.

Sometimes, when I was sitting in my bedroom, alternating between playing with my toys and just staring into space, I'd understand why people got so down. It never seemed fair, especially when Outsiders could roam around the streets whenever they wanted.

Well, maybe not whenever they wanted. After all, we remained in Blackbrooke because of the dangers. It always amazed me people could commit crime against one another on the Outside. In Blackbrooke, the Crits were the enemy. They were the ones we had to avoid. We didn't have that kind of crime in Blackbrooke and that's why more than ninety-five per cent of the population stayed put. Spending their lives happily Crit-dodging.

Monsters in the woodland were a piece of cake compared to a smiling, neighbourly assassin. It was black and white here whereas, on the Outside, the lines were blurred and the occasional story I caught between hushed conversations, rattled me to the core.

Rape.

Murder.

Terrorism.

The internet kept us up to speed with news from the Outside on one of the few websites we were actually able to view. The connection was poor as, in spite of all of the cosmetic work the Government carried out on the town, they couldn't complete anything that required too much disruption. Digging up the roads for something they called 'broadband' wasn't an option. It may have disturbed the Queens in their underground tunnels, and the Crits were likely to have destroyed any construction sites during the night. So, we had to settle for a dial up internet connection through our phone line, and it was because of this that we were only permitted to see certain websites. Despite there being a buzz several years ago when it was announced we could have internet in our homes, no one really wanted it. It was easier to remain in our little bubble, imagining everywhere was like Blackbrooke really.

Humans and Crits. Simple.

That's why it astounded me when I learned Outsiders felt sorry for us. They had a misconception we were imprisoned against our will in this creepy town forever. I'd see it in the eyes of the hoards of tourists that passed through, staring stupidly at us as though we were going to burst from our clothes and turn into Crits ourselves. The coach tours went by Blackbrooke Academy, and we barely batted an eyelid as some of them would nudge one another, pointing as we played in the schoolyard.

Poor kids.

That's what they were thinking. Sometimes I heard them say it. Even when I was in earshot, I'd scowl at a usually overweight Outsider in too-tight shorts and an 'I Heart Blackbrooke' t-shirt, while they cocked their head to one side and waved at me like I was simple.

On that particular hot summer's day, I crouched on the edge of the woodland near Blackbrooke Academy. My back was pressed against a thick oak tree and I didn't dare to breathe. My ice cream, now melted into a pink mess on the dry soil in front of me, was already swarming with ants. I couldn't bring myself to finish it as the constant slurping was making too much noise and threatening to give away my hiding place. I looked down at my yellow stripy t-shirt and grimaced at the pink stains where I'd smeared ice cream. Now my hands were sticky. Every time I touched the tree, dry bits of bark would stick to my clammy skin.

I licked around my mouth in nervous excitement, and a wasp buzzed around me but I barely flinched. Bugs hardly bothered anyone in Blackbrooke.

Spiders in my bath in the morning made me smile. "You were hiding from the Crits too," I'd grin, picking it up and letting it crawl up my arm, before depositing it into my school shirt pocket. They rarely remained there and occasionally one of my teachers would chuckle as I arrived to school with the critter crawling in my hair.

"Libby!"

I clamped a hand over my mouth to stifle a giggle. It was the unmistakable whine of my best friend, Cassius. I could tell he was angry from the quiver in his shout. He was the master at Hide and Seek, which was amazing given his brilliant white hair and skin which made him stand out more than anyone in town. He'd leave me wandering around for an age, muttering and cursing him mercilessly.

I bit my lip, listening to him shout. He wouldn't find me today. It was really rather clever of me to hide on the edge of the woodland. Technically, we weren't allowed this close to the trees as that's where the Crits reside. But on that day it was easy to forget they existed. I could hear the distant sound of music blasting from the cars of the older teenagers, and the school field was full of groups of friends and families, making the most of the bright weather on this lazy Sunday. The school field doubled up as a park as it was so large and whereas, it sat completely neglected in the winter, that day it was bustling.

Making me feel safe.

Lulling me into a false sense of security.

"Liberty! I give up! Where are you?"

His voice was further away now and I let out a small laugh, confident he wouldn't hear me. I leaned around the tree to see him walking away sulkily, kicking the heads off dandelions in his path.

I felt guilty for a moment.

Despite being five months older than me, Cassius was small. Too small for his age at barely four feet and weighing probably the equivalent of a bag of sugar. I examined him as he reached up a bony arm and pushed his yellow tinted glasses further up his nose. He had to wear the glasses to protect his eyes from the sun and usually wasn't seen out of them throughout the summer.

Whereas I wore t-shirts and denim cut-offs, Cassius was clothed head to toe. His translucent skin was too sensitive to be exposed, even when slathered in sun-block.

I smiled as he got further away. I'd always felt responsible for him, ever since our parents threw us together as toddlers.

I was a solid child – the type that people couldn't help but make comments about.

"When that puppy-fat disappears, she'll be a stunner," my dad's friends used to say.

I paid no attention to them. My weight didn't matter. Plus, the heavier I was, the more I could protect Cassius because, although the humans in Blackbrooke didn't commit crimes against one another, children could still be cruel. I rarely saw Cassius in school as boys and girls were kept in separate wings of the Academy but, on the occasions we shared the same air, I'd be constantly balling my hands into fists and stamping my feet in rage if anyone dared to mock the defenceless pale boy.

I was already a full head height taller than him and every night I'd kneel at the side of my bed and whisper a prayer that God could make Cassius grow. Just a little bit.

My mum said Cassius idolised me but I'd always scoff at the suggestion. I wasn't someone to look up to. There wasn't really an ounce of fun to me. I studied hard at school, even at the tender age of seven, and was never naughty. Mum taught me how to play chess when I was five and on those long winter nights, we'd play for hours, sometimes in silence. Me with my brow furrowed in concentration, and mum, her long red hair, free from its daytime bun, cascading over her shoulder.

I wasn't one of the cool kids at school. Not the loudest. Not the funniest. I just blended in and did as I was told.

That was until today, of course. Not wanting my friend to win yet another game, I'd done the one thing my parents warned me not to do when I ventured out to play.

"Whatever you do..." Dad would point as I was halfway out of the door.

I ducked my head back behind the tree and closed my eyes.

"...don't...."

I exhaled deeply.

"...go in..."

I opened my eyes.

"...the woodland."

That's when I saw it.

You would think a seven year old would scream at the top of her lungs, but I didn't flinch.

The Hunter was stood about ten feet from me, up an embankment, glowering down, red eyes flashing. Its tail twitched from side to side, like an excited dog, and it made a low growling sound as it lowered its head.

Crits were similar in a number of ways. But there were different types.

Four to be exact.

They were linked by features such as red eyes and thin S-shaped necks that made their heads bounce in perpetual motion. The demonic grins also bound them, with hundreds of tiny sharp teeth in several rows.

Hunters were wolf-like. Predators. They did exactly as the name suggested, finding food for themselves and the other Crits. They were easily the most bloodthirsty of all of them. Along with the Watchers, Hunters walked on four legs and possessed long snouts with nostrils the size of my fists.

The Hunter jumped down from the embankment to get closer to me. It now stood on the same level and I saw the highest part of its hunched back was the same height as me as I'd slowly slid up the tree so I was on my feet. I didn't take my eyes off it as it took another step, the sound of its old bones cracking so loudly that I was amazed one of the families I could still hear laughing on the grass didn't hear.

It was going to eat me, that I was sure of. That's what the

Crits did if they encountered a human. They took no pleasure in killing. There was no vendetta against humans. They were all just hungry and, in Blackbrooke, Crits were at the top of the food chain.

I pressed myself into the tree, hoping a small miracle would enable it to envelop me into its trunk and hide me there until the Hunter grew tired of waiting and walked away.

It shouldn't have been out during the day but I was on its land and I was alone. It probably smelled me as soon as I had the idea for the hiding place earlier in the day. The meat of a human would have been enough to rouse it from the deepest of sleeps, I was sure.

Trails of saliva now started to dribble from its mouth and it licked at them, curling its mouth into a snarl as it edged closer.

I closed my eyes when I started to feel its hot breath on my body, smelling of rotting flesh from the meat trapped between its teeth.

I waited for the first bite.

A hissing sound jolted me and I frowned in surprise as the Hunter looked up at the embankment it had just stepped down from at the dozen or so Watchers, sat on their backsides glaring at us.

No wait, not us. They were glaring at the Hunter. Hissing.

The Watchers were small and cat-like. The sight of them didn't frighten me as much as I was used to seeing them wander around Blackbrooke during the day. They were harmless, but no less disgusting to look at. Smaller than Hunters, they possessed the same appearance, but moved more slowly, lazily, sloth-like.

The Hunter turned back to me and another Watcher lifted its head to let out a piercing cry. The Hunter's ears flattened to its head like a frightened dog. It shook itself, as though soaking wet and then stepped away from me begrudgingly, stealing glances at the Watchers, lowering its head even further.

My whole body was now quivering. I didn't dare take my eyes off the Hunter. After all, it might have just been stepping back so it could take a run up and tear into me at speed.

Instead, the Hunter continued to back away from me, growling to itself. The Watchers didn't move, still staring at the larger Crit as it got further and further away, disappearing into the thick trees until all I could see were its ruby red eyes flashing at me.

"The Crits," Mum had said during one particular chess game, "are a lot like the pieces in chess."

I blinked at her, not understanding what she meant.

"The pawns," she picked one up and flashed a small smile, "they're the Watchers. Harmless. They're on the frontline. Merely pets doing the dirty work for their masters. Easily disposable." She nudged the piece one square along.

I did the same with one of my white pawns.

"The knights," her index finger touched the black horses head, "are the Hunters. Attacking with no real rhyme or reason. It's not sophisticated, but it's powerful and it can knock you sideways when you're least expecting it." She swiped one of my pawns.

I looked up at the Watchers as they started to disperse one at a time. They weren't as powerful as the Hunters, they were pawns.

So, how had they made it back off from a human meal with merely a look?

"The Lurkers," Mum pointed down at another piece. "They're the bishops. They look the most human of all of the Crits and they don't kill instantly. Like the Hunters, they take you by surprise when they attack but," she slid the piece diagonally and took one of my knights, "they're more refined."

I nodded seriously, drinking in every detail as I attempted to outsmart her with a feeble move.

"The Queens," she sighed, picking up the piece. "Protected by the Lurkers, fed by the Hunters and kept informed by their

Watcher pets. The Queens are the worst, Lib." She set it back on the board with a shaking hand. "They do as they please. Whatever they want, they get."

There was real venom in her voice and she didn't meet my eye.

"What are we?"

She frowned and I gestured to the game. "Which piece are we? The humans?"

Mum shook her head in dismay. "We're nothing but the squares on which they play. They move on us." She placed down the queen and picked up her bishop again, moving it to the edge of the board. "And we let them dance on our heads."

She completely lost my childish brain at that point and I sighed, fingers hovering over the pieces. My eyes flicked up as she reached out and took my fingers gently in her hand, lowering them down onto one. "You're not the board though, Liberty." She wrapped my fingers around the white queen and smiled. I looked at the piece in my hand, still not quite understanding but having the mature awareness that my mother was trying to tell me something.

I knew the queen would move around her king, protecting him at all costs. I cocked my head to one side at the white king, not able to stop the image of Cassius entering my head. I felt like a Queen on some days, put on earth to protect him.

"Now, Liberty." Mum waved her hand over the board. "Fight."

I thought hard for a moment before moving my queen over to her side of the board. "Check-mate," I grinned.

Once the last Watcher disappeared, I shot out from behind the tree, stumbling in panic and throwing glances over my shoulder. Sure the Hunter was going to be back to get me.

"Cassius!" I croaked, my dry throat barely making a sound like some kind of nightmare. I bolted onto the field, ignoring the strange looks families and groups of friends were throwing at me as I used all of my strength to propel myself faster.

Why didn't it just eat me? Why did it spare me?

"Cassius!" I found my voice and frantically looked around the field for my little friend.

I spotted him walking towards the gates to leave and raced over without stopping. I just grabbed the collar of his sweatshirt and dragged him along, like a dog. "We have to go."

"Libby! Where were you? I was looking every–"

"Shut up," I ordered, my mouth tight, looking behind me again. I knew the colour had drained from my face. "We just need to leave."

Cassius knew better than to argue with me and, lowering his head, let me drag him as he struggled to keep up. We continued that way through the town, until we reached the safety of my house.

I didn't tell him about my encounter in the woodland with the Hunter. I didn't tell anyone about it, scared the official Government people who sometimes visited the town would want to speak to me. They had always scared me with their black suits and too-serious faces.

I lay awake at night sometimes, constantly asking the same question.

Why was I still alive?

As the years rolled by, the question, along with the memory, made its way to the back of my mind. The Blackbrooke Rules as well as Blackbrooke's history became something of an obsession, and I devoured book after book on the subject. I knew and followed the Rules religiously and I became consumed with the idea that I'd be one of the five per cent of the town's population who would leave.

Just as soon as I turn eighteen, I'd scribble into my diary at eight years old, *I'm leaving this town and I'm taking little Cass with me.*

Exclamation mark.

Little did I know that in less than two years, Cassius and I would no longer be friends. We'd grow apart after I'd start to spend more time with another friend, leaving him to fend for himself in the cruel confines of Blackbrooke Academy.

I was seventeen when we finally spoke to one another again.

I was seventeen when my world turned upside down.

I was seventeen when I saw my next Crit.

Chapter I

"Oh my God, it's freezing."

My friend Gemma hopped from one foot to the other and leaned down to rub her bare legs, which were pink from the cold. "Be honest, are my legs hideous?"

I ignored her and craned my neck to look across the sports field.

"Can you see the boys?" she asked, following my gaze.

It was so cold that morning that a mist had settled on the field, making it difficult to see. I felt my body shudder from the chill.

"I hate that we have to wear t-shirts and skirts for sports," I muttered, watching my breath ascend as mist.

Gemma grinned. "It's worth it to see the boys, though, isn't it?"

I giggled and quickly cleared my throat as the sports coach, Mrs Tate, came jogging across to where Gemma and I, along with around twenty other girls from the class, were stood shivering.

"Okay ladies," she shrilled, clapping her hands and rubbing them together. "Let's get running," She started sprinting ahead, and turned to run backwards. "Stick to the track. And, Miss Jones?"

"Yep?" Gemma raised her hand.

"If I catch you over with the boys again, there'll be trouble."

"I promise I won't go over this week!" Gemma shouted back before turning to me and sticking her tongue out.

"Come on, let's go and see them."

She grabbed my hand so we could bolt straight off course. There were several large trees around the edge and we hid behind one, peering around it.

"Oh my God," she whispered, her cheeks pink from the run. "Noah looks amazing in those shorts."

I hit her on the arm. "You say that every week."

"Oh come on." She narrowed her big blue eyes at me. "Like you're not thinking the same thing about Angel Gabriel over there."

"Shut up," I muttered, kicking at the bottom of the tree.

"Excuse me, ladies!"

We looked up in shock at one of the snipers from the tower, staring down at us.

"I'm pretty sure you're not supposed to be over here."

Gemma and I exchanged glances and she stepped forward, hands on her hips. "Oh yeah? What are you going to do about it?"

The man was wearing a balaclava to disguise his face, which always made me nervous. It was protocol for them to hide their identity so we weren't encouraged to speak to them and put them off the task they were employed to. They dressed in black from head to toe and sat in the tiny tower all day behind a large gun, just watching for stray Crits wandering into the Academy. The sniper laughed heartily. "I'll tell the teachers."

Gemma reached down and ran her hand up her leg seductively. She used her other hand to take the bobble out of her hair, holding her bun in place. I watched in horror as her bright blonde hair cascaded forward and she flipped it back.

The sniper stared.

"Gem!" I hissed. "Put your hair back up."

She ignored me and cupped her hands over her mouth to shout to him. "Bet you've not seen your wife shake out her bun in years!"

He turned away quickly and she laughed, rejoining me.

I yanked her towards me. "Are you crazy?"

"Oh Lib." She started pulling her hair back into place, bobble clamped between her teeth. "Get a grip, the Crits aren't going to scalp me in the middle of the day. Besides, we all know the hair rule is complete crap. It's just a way to make us look less attractive so the boys aren't as tempted to jump our bones."

"So," I scowled, turning away. "You never know. It happened once, a little girl was scalped by a rogue Queen during the day in 199–"

"Relax," she interrupted, reaching up to squeeze my auburn bun. "You should shake it loose sometimes," She got to work rolling her gym skirt up at the waist so it was unspeakably short. "In more than one respect."

I let out an uncomfortable laugh. "Just because you've broken one of the golden rules doesn't mean I will."

"But Lib," she whined, turning me to face the boys and resting her chin on my shoulder. "It's so much fun."

"It won't be fun when the Hunters are tearing you and Noah limb from limb because you stink of sex."

I'd known Gemma for years and she was always vivacious. Petite, blonde, boobs.

What more could you want as a teenage girl? The boys loved her and she made the male teachers nervous.

I eyed her discreetly as she clapped and jumped up and down, watching Noah. I was too young to worry as much as I did about her but I couldn't help it.

She flouted the Rules whereas I followed them to almost biblical lengths, too afraid to deviate from them. The thought of seeing the Hunter in the woodland when I was a little girl popped into my head. Once bitten…

The boys would be finished with their sports lesson soon. I bit my lip, looking down at myself. Next to Gemma, I didn't really feel particularly sexy. In fact, I struggled to see what Gabriel even saw in me.

"But you're beautiful!" Gemma would wail whenever I complained.

I'd done as everyone predicted and lost the puppy fat, just *too* much of it. I was taller than Gemma but that wasn't difficult as she barely reached five feet and still found myself on the shorter end of the spectrum. Ironic, seeing as I was always one of the taller kids when I was younger. My breasts weren't even worth mentioning as any hint of them had melted away with the puppy fat two years ago.

My hair remained unchanged, thick and auburn which was scraped back in a bun through the day until I knew all of the shutters had closed for the night, and then I'd release it, letting it cascade down my back, feeling relief from the pressure of how tightly I pinned it.

The smattering of freckles that covered my nose and cheeks as a child was still there and made me look younger than my seventeen years. I hated them with a passion but according to Gabriel, they were 'adorable'.

If I were pushed I'd say I liked my green eyes as they were a nice almond shape sat either side of my small, pinched nose.

At best, I'd have said I was cute. Probably pretty if I was more masterful with make-up.

The whistle to signal the end of the football match sounded and Noah jogged over, breathless and pink in the cheek from exertion.

Gemma was pink-cheeked for a different reason and practically dived into his arms, wrapping her legs around him. I turned away and hummed to myself as he pushed her up against the tree, kissing her while she giggled wildly.

Gabriel spotted us and raised his hand in a friendly wave before making his way over.

I looked down.

Gabriel was, quite honestly, the most beautiful boy I'd ever seen in my life. He had dark, Mediterranean looks from the combination of a Spanish mother and Italian father. His hair was thick and overgrown in a cute mop that I loved to run my fingers through. His peanut coloured skin was flawless and his eyes were like chocolate pots with long, thick lashes framing them.

I never would have thought that he would be interested in quiet and serious Liberty Connor. But after passing several notes to me in the library over the course of a month, I conceded that he perhaps wasn't playing a trick on me after all. I let the possibility he actually did want to spend time with me enter my head. We continued to meet in the library and whisper to one another about our families and studies until one day we snuck into a quiet corner and I let him kiss me. My first kiss. I'd fallen hard and fast. It was love. That was, if love gave you butterflies in your stomach whenever you see that person and your skin prickles at the slightest touch. It snuck up on me when I was least expecting it. I never thought I'd be the type of person to fall for a boy as I'd never really been bothered before Gabriel. I always assumed it would be Gemma who would be the first of us to pair off. I did, for a while, feel suspicious of Gabriel's motives, wondering if it was actually Gemma he wanted to get to. That was soon dismissed when I'd look into his eyes and see his whole attention and adoration aimed squarely at me.

Part of me hated being that giggling girl who gazes adoringly at her boyfriend; it used to turn my stomach when I witnessed it from the other girls at the Academy. However, I soon learned that it's a rather different story when it happens to you.

I shivered as I tried not to eye Gabriel's solid body as he stood tall in front of me on the school field. "Hi." He placed a hand on my cheek. "Aren't you cold?"

I licked my lips. "Freezing."

It was particularly bitter on that November day and the fog continued to roll ominously over the sports field. Our sports kits now seemed even more obscene, especially as my teeth were chattering and legs were turning a rather unattractive shade of blue.

Gemma screamed and we looked as Noah had slung her over his shoulder so we had full view of her backside.

Noah and Gabriel were best friends and had been since they were small. Easily two of the best-looking boys in the whole school but not an ounce of arrogance.

Noah was tall and, what he lacked in the brain department, he made up for in brawn, making the coupling between him and my petite friend mildly amusing. He had sandy hair which had faded from bright blonde as a child. His skin was tanned and healthy and had huge blue eyes which almost matched Gemma's.

"Right then." He patted Gemma's bottom and walked backwards. "Tonight, I request you two join me and this little vixen for a movie marathon at my house."

I exchanged glances with Gabriel, who rolled his eyes.

"Are you two actually going to *watch* the film this time?" I asked, already mentally making my excuses.

He placed his index finger on his mouth as though deep in thought, swinging Gemma from side to side, causing her to scream more.

"Put me down!"

He obeyed and she wrapped her arms around him. "His mum is away." Her eyes sparkled. "Having dinner and drinks with *my* parents."

Gabriel looked at me and I jerked my head for him to come closer. "I'm not sure I fancy a night listening to those two get friendly again."

Our friends were once again kissing and running their hands over each other's bodies. "Good point. Listen," Gabriel took my elbow and guided me so we were stood on the other side of the tree. "My parents are heading to Gemma's as well."

I frowned and he laughed awkwardly. "I just thought…"

The penny dropped and I recoiled. "What? Tonight?"

He shrugged and picked up the locket on my necklace, playing with it in his fingers. "We've been talking about it a lot."

My mouth went dry. "Erm…I know but…"

"But what?" He looked through those damn eyelashes and I felt my heartbeat quicken.

"The Rules," I breathed as his lips brushed my neck.

"Forget the Rules!" His breath was hot and I shuddered, reaching up instinctively and grabbing the back of his neck. "Everyone's breaking the Rules these days."

I pushed him gently. "No, we can't. Not until we're eighteen."

He looked mildly disappointed but smiled and planted a kiss on my forehead. "Fine. Will you still come round though?"

I shrugged, non-committal.

We walked back to join our friends and Gemma had, once again, let her hair out of the bun. Noah was running his fingers through it as he kissed her hungrily.

"Okay Romeo." Gabriel slapped Noah's back. "Let's get inside. The girls are freezing."

"Put your hair up," I hissed to Gemma as she fell into stride with me, behind them. "I won't tell you again."

"He's so gorgeous," she whispered. "Honestly, I feel horny all the time."

I grimaced. "Seriously Gem, too much information."

We walked up the hill and bypassed the gym changing rooms, heading into the canteen. Sports wasn't compulsory so Gemma and I never really cared we were ditching it. In fact, the only reason we turned up was because the gym kit was slightly more appealing than our school uniform.

It consisted entirely of grey.

Skirt.

Jumper.

Grey socks or tights.

The only saving grace was the white shirt but even that was finished off with a grey tie. I always thought Outsiders were disappointed when they saw us, sure they expected us to be wearing straw hats and blazers and walk two-by-two.

The canteen was the only place boys and girls could socialise in the Academy, after many protests staged by the pupils over the years. Canteen was a down-market description. It was embarrassingly flashy, thanks to the constant redevelopment money the Government kept ploughing into the town. The room was large and airy and there were gigantic white sculptures hanging from the ceiling on wires. They'd been commissioned by some Turner prize-winning artist from the Outside, and the tables and chairs were strange offbeat designs. Everything reeked of expense and I could imagine the Government bods standing back with their arms folded, smugly surveying their handiwork. We called it 'Outsider Guilt', and it came back to those looks of pity we were used to seeing whenever Outsiders visited the town. I quickly learned that when the British Government felt guilty or helpless about something, they threw money at it.

Apparently, the security systems all around the Blackbrooke border were the most sophisticated in the world. It beat the White House and Buckingham Palace.

Not that we cared. Outsiders needed to feel confident the Crits wouldn't escape, I suppose. We knew that was the reason, nothing to do with protecting us from the Outside.

Honestly, they must have thought we were stupid.

No one in Blackbrooke batted at eyelid at the constant regeneration. We were so used to it that any novelty had worn off a while ago. It was only the churches that the Government weren't obsessed with knocking down and starting again, meaning they were the only buildings that retained character. Everything else was ultra-modern - strange shaped buildings and a hell of a lot of black glass. There was definitely an architectural trend in the 21st Century, and I can't say I was a fan.

I sat at one of the dazzlingly white tables and Gabriel slid onto the seat next to me, taking my hand discreetly, in case any passing teachers saw. We were under eighteen and yet to swear in the Rules, so any relationship was forbidden. It happened though. All around us were other couples, holding hands and stealing quick kisses. I'd occasionally catch eyes with another girl cuddling up to her boyfriend and we'd nod to one another in acknowledgement. It was like being part of a club.

"I love you, Lib," he whispered and I nuzzled into his shoulder quickly.

"I love you, too."

Gemma and Noah returned, carrying drinks.

"Hot chocolate all round," Gemma shrilled, placing the white paper cups down.

I wrapped my icy cold fingers around one, embracing the warmth, and inhaling the sickly sweet liquid. Despite how indulgent the room was, I liked the canteen. Because the older boys and girls were allowed to mix, there was always a constant buzz of conversation and laughter. I enjoyed the sounds of knives and forks clattering and the smells of whatever culinary delights the chefs had fixed for us.

"Oh Jesus." My eyes snapped opened as Gemma cursed and I followed her and Noah's glare.

"If it isn't Crit Boy." Noah placed his hands behind his head. "Isn't that the one who called you a whore the other day, Gem?"

Gemma nodded and scowled.

I swallowed and returned my eyes to the cup.

"Retard," Noah said through gritted teeth. "I'll deck the freak."

"Please do," Gemma purred, her hand rubbing his solid chest. "He needs a lesson."

Gabriel looked at the person in question and raised an

eyebrow. "You know what, I've been to school with him for years and I still don't know his real name."

I pressed my teeth together and felt Gemma's eyes burn into me. "Why don't you ask Lib?"

I shrugged awkwardly, watching the boy stalk up to the counter and order himself a drink before searching his pocket for change. He was wearing his usual attire that set him apart from everyone else – skinny black jeans, long grey woollen coat and black Converse. Defiantly shunning the school uniform almost everyday, as always.

Gabriel nudged me. "Go on then."

I licked my lips nervously. "That's Cassius."

"Cassius?!" Noah shouted loudly and I grimaced as Cassius looked over at our table. "More like Casper."

"Didn't he used to be your boyfriend?" Gemma kicked me lightly under the table and I flashed her a warning look.

"No." I felt my cheeks flush pink and couldn't meet anyone's eye. "We were friends when we were kids but…not anymore."

"Well." Noah curled his lip. "I don't know about anyone else, but he freaks me out. It's those eyes and that skin."

"He's an albino," Gemma said nonchalantly, inspecting her nails.

I felt a pang in my chest. The same one I used to feel as a child when someone made a cruel comment about him. "No, he isn't."

Gemma gestured over her shoulder in the direction of Cassius who was now reading the notice board on the other side of the canteen. "Of course he is. His hair is white and he's got funny eyes."

"There's something wrong with his skin, it's a condition called heterochromia and that's what makes his eyes two different colours as well," I snapped before lowering my voice. "They're not *funny*. One's blue and one's brown. That's all."

I looked at him again. Cassius turned eighteen a couple of

months ago, making him one of the oldest pupils in our year. He wasn't the same little boy I used to have to protect when things got tough. Not a jot.

Whereas I had barely grown since the age of ten, Cassius was a different story. Perhaps my prayers were answered as he now towered above almost everyone in the canteen at well over six feet. His limbs used to resemble pieces of string and he was always so weak and sickly, with me sometimes having to open a bag of crisps for him or remove the lid from a bottle of juice. No, he'd since filled out and, although still on the skinny side, now possessed broad shoulders and stood strong and solid.

I sighed, tearing my eyes away. "I don't even know him anymore."

Noah turned to Gemma. "Did he really call you a whore?"

She stuck out her bottom lip, sulkily.

"Right." Before anyone could react, Noah dived up and Gemma clapped her hands excitedly.

"Noah, no!" I made a grab for his t-shirt but Gabriel pulled me back down.

"Don't get involved," he warned.

I looked in horror as the big, bruising Noah strode up to Cassius and pushed him roughly.

"What the hell?!" Cassius demanded, recovering himself quickly.

The canteen grew quiet instantly and I ignored Gabriel's warning and dived from my seat, running to them. Noah shoved Cassius again, who staggered backwards, straightening the neck of his black t-shirt under his coat. He locked eyes with my appalled ones and tore them away, returning to Noah.

"Are you a Crit? You look like one."

"Get lost." Cassius made a move around him but Noah pushed him again.

"Calling my girlfriend a whore, eh?"

"What?" Cassius scrunched up his ghostly white nose and

boldly stepped towards Noah. "That's crap."

Cassius was taller but Noah was bigger and smacked his hand into his chest causing him to stumble again. His white hair fell over his eyes and he clenched his jaw in frustration.

"Noah, stop!" I begged. "Leave him alone!"

Gemma appeared at his side and folded her arms. "Apologise to me."

I stared at her in horror and Noah nodded. "Yeah, go on."

Cassius, now breathless, stood up straight. "I didn't call you that."

"Are you now calling her a liar?!" Noah bellowed.

"No." Cassius picked up his bag from the floor. I tried to catch his eye again but he refused to acknowledge me.

"Oh, forget it," Gemma declared, turning on her heel, nose in the air.

Sometimes you can be such a bitch, I thought, glaring after her.

"You *are* a whore," Cassius muttered under his breath. I winced as Noah turned back around and, before anyone could do anything, swung his fist back and right into Cassius' stomach, causing him to sink to the floor.

Everyone gasped and a few people clapped, prompting Noah to take a bow before draping his arm around a giggling Gemma to head back to the table.

Instinctively, I dashed to Cassius' side like I had on dozens of occasions when we were children. He used to blink back at me, his odd coloured eyes swimming with tears as his bottom lip would tremble, causing my heart to break in two.

"Cass." I reached out to touch his arm but he yanked it back roughly.

"Don't touch me," he snapped, his lip curled into a snarl. "Go back to your friends, Liberty."

He stalked past and I watched in dismay as he hurried out of the canteen.

***

"Dad?" I called, letting myself into the house later that day. The school day was shorter in the winter and this was the first three o'clock finish of the season. In December, it would be two, giving every child ample time to get home before it went dark. It all balanced out as, in the summer, our longest school day would be seven in the morning until eight at night.

I followed my dad's call and wandered into the kitchen of our modest family home. I smiled at my little brother, Oscar, sat at the small round wooden table, eating fish fingers and chips.

"Another nutritious meal." I ruffled his carrot coloured hair before reaching into the fridge for can of coke.

My dad stood, leaning on our never-used breakfast bar, reading a newspaper. It was his usual stance when I returned from school.

"Aren't you eating?" I asked, pulling myself up to sit on the kitchen work surface.

Dad snapped his fingers and pointed at the floor and I reluctantly slid back off.

"Can't be bothered cooking,"

He could never be bothered, which was why dinner usually consisted of a sandwich for both of us. Cooking wasn't my strong point so I rarely tried anything else. I wasn't even confident I knew how to switch on the oven.

"Libby?"

"Yes, Oscar?"

"Are you having fish fingers?" he asked, picking up one of his chips and dunking it in the pool of tomato sauce on his plate. Oscar was four years old and strikingly similar to my mother with his ginger hair and pale blue eyes. Both he and I had the same smudge of freckles across our nose and cheeks, but I'd inherited my dad's darker hair and green eyes.

I pulled out a chair and plonked myself down. "I'm not

having fish fingers, but I'll sit with you while you eat yours." I winked, and he beamed back, "How was school?"

Oscar launched excitedly into a story that didn't seem to make any sense, about a sandpit and bubbles. I scowled at Dad's back as Oscar prattled on. I knew Dad probably hadn't uttered a word to his son since picking him up from school.

Dad was definitely a man of few words unless there was a beer or two in his system. It wasn't that he was a drunk, he just spent so much time on his own during the day that I think he'd lost the ability and the confidence to hold a conversation.

I looked at Oscar again and felt a familiar pang of sadness. I reached out and rubbed his smooth cheek and he leaned his head onto my arm.

I forced a smile. "Right then, get that eaten so you can have a bath and then I'll read you a story."

"Yay!" he shouted, banging his fork down on the table. "Will you teach me about Crits?"

I frowned. "No. Not tonight."

He leaned his cheek on his hand, looking lost in his own little world while he continued to eat.

I stood. "Dad, I'm going to see Mum while Oscar finishes his tea."

Dad nodded and I touched his arm, causing him to jump. He flashed me a surprised look. "Please go and sit with Oscar. Just for a minute."

Dad begrudgingly obeyed, picking up his newspaper and pulling out a chair at the table.

"Daddeee!" Oscar cried in glee. "Do you want one of my chips?"

I sighed as I walked upstairs slowly towards Mum's room. I knocked lightly on the door but didn't wait for her to shout.

She was awake and lying on her side, staring at a spot on the floor.

"Hi Mum," I whispered, perching on the edge of the bed and stroking her forehead. "Was today a good day?"

I always asked her this although I wasn't quite sure why. She never answered.

I moved so I was cross-legged on the bed next to her.

The sound of the electronic blinds closing startled me and I watched the last part of the day disappearing between the slats. The blinds were on a timer which Dad had to reset almost every day as the winter nights drew in more quickly.

Satisfied they were closed, I pulled my long hair out of the bun and shook it out so it fell in big bouncing waves. "I was supposed to go to Gabriel's tonight, Mum. I didn't though," I whispered. "I don't want to break the Rules."

Mum blinked slowly.

"I mean, don't get me wrong," I sighed, staring at the wall ahead of me. "He's absolutely gorgeous and…I want to, but I'm just not really feeling ready. I don't know what it is, but I feel more frightened of the Crits whenever I think about…you know, being with Gabriel. I feel like I'll be putting us both in danger if I say yes." I played with my hair bobble in my hands. "You probably just want to scream and shout at me." My smile fell as I looked at her unmoving form. "Or maybe not. The thing is, Mum, you're the only one I can talk to and there's something really messed up about that because I might as well be talking to a tree." I swallowed and leaned closer. "Do you hear me?"

She didn't move.

I shifted so I was lying behind her and wrapped my arms around her stiff body, burying my head into her back.

"I love you, Mum," I breathed.

***

"Right," I clapped my hands as I walked into the living room, "Oscar's bathed and in bed, sleeping soundly."

"Thanks love." Dad didn't look up from the television.

I sat on the sofa, across from his armchair and curled my

legs under me. I felt tired now. This was usually how my nights turned out and I now understood why my mum used to be so exhausted all of the time.

Before she became an emotional vegetable.

Her depression had started before Oscar was born and was so subtle that neither dad or I noticed it at first. It was just mum being dramatic in my eyes. No, it started small, with her snapping at me more frequently or taking herself off for long walks in the summertime. It snowballed from there, and she'd often break down in floods of tears at random times. I remembered when I was taking part in a majorette competition with Gemma when we were both twelve and she fled the theatre, sobbing hysterically. I'd sat in the family car afterwards, still wearing my ridiculous leotard complete with sparkly tassels, watching out of the window as Dad tried to coax her back. I couldn't hear what they were shouting about, but I saw Mum gesture to me while she gripped at her hair and wailed uncontrollably. Once she finally did get in the car, she didn't say a word.

The silence was the next stage of her depression. It came in waves that got longer and longer, resulting in the mum I knew today. Not moving from her bed and never acknowledging the presence of another human being. Doctors had visited, including Gabriel's father who was the most well respected doctor in the whole of Blackbrooke but none could find anything physically wrong with her.

"She needs some time," Dr Moretti would say in his thick Italian accent, flashing a sad smile.

I always marvelled at how patient Dad was with her. He never lost his temper, not once.

I had. Several times.

Especially when she failed to show an interest in her young son who just desperately wanted some affection from his mummy. I'd felt guilty afterwards but her face didn't change, whether I was shouting and bawling or sobbing with regret, causing me to wonder whether she actually heard anything anymore.

"Mum seemed even further away today." I closed my eyes and played with the pom-pom on my slipper-socks.

Dad smiled sadly. "I know."

"Do you think it's the dark nights?"

He looked thoughtful, turning the remote control over and over in his hand. "Maybe."

I turned my attention to the wildlife documentary on the television, showing foxes hunting at night.

"It's coming up to the anniversary though."

My head snapped back. "Catherine?"

He nodded.

"Oh." I had forgotten it was at this time of the year Mum used to get really low. Easy to slip my mind as she was now low most days.

"Bloody tragic." Dad shook his head.

I looked down, feeling his eyes on me. I knew what was coming and I almost laughed out loud especially after the earlier events in the canteen.

"Do you see much of Cassius these days?"

I shrugged, not meeting his eye. "Sometimes. I…don't really know him anymore though. We stopped hanging out a few years ago."

Dad sucked in a sharp breath. "Poor kid."

On the television, a fox attacked a cat and shook it in its jaw.

"First his sister and then his mother," Dad continued. "I'm amazed he didn't walk out too."

I didn't say anything and inspected my nails, desperately wanting Dad to drop it. Noah's rough treatment of Cassius had played on my mind all the way home and I wasn't sure I'd be able to forget the look in his eye as he glared at me. I felt like a traitor. Particularly as Gemma was the friend I had ditched him for all of those years ago. Now, she and Noah were practically the ringleaders of his tormentors. That day was the first time they'd done it in front of me, but I knew they were always sniping behind his back and hollering insults down the corridor as he'd walk by.

Yes, there was no doubt Cassius hated me and my group of friends and I didn't blame him. He made it quite clear whenever I would catch him eyeing me in the corridors of the Academy. He'd look away quickly but I knew what he was thinking.

I hate you, Liberty Connor. You ditched me when I needed you.

"Still, his dad's alright, isn't he?" Dad's voice interrupted my thoughts.

I shrugged. "Not a clue."

"Does Cass still have that white hair?"

"Good Lord, Dad, what is this?!" I snapped and Dad shushed me, gesturing upstairs where Oscar's room was directly above us. "I just don't hang around with him anymore." I lowered my voice. "But yes, he does still have white hair."

Dad smiled. "You couldn't lose that kid if you tried. I remember you two wandering off in the supermarket and your mum was panicking. But I could spot him miles away."

I found myself returning the smile and tried to distract myself playing with the hem of my pyjama bottoms.

"There you both were," Dad reminisced. "Wandering off across the car park holding hands like an old married couple. Well, you half-dragging him anyway."

I closed my eyes. I could remember the day and I could still feel Cassius' clammy hand wrapped around mine as he looked at me with his odd coloured eyes, hanging on my every word. *"Let's run away, Cass."*

And we did.

Ran all the way across the car park before my parents caught up with us.

"Ah memories," Dad sighed. "Got to say though, Lib, I'm relieved you and him aren't still close. The Rules and all that."

"Dad!" I threw a cushion at him which he caught and launched back at me. "You're so embarrassing. Why do you have to even mention that?"

"It comes with the territory of having a teenage daughter, I'm afraid." He narrowed his eyes. "Wheezy at work said he saw you with the Moretti boy."

"Well, Wheezy's a liar," I said, too quickly.

"I'm just saying," his face turned serious, "be…mindful of the Rules, Lib. They're in place for a reason."

I nodded, feeling my cheeks grow even hotter. "I know."

When I looked up, Dad was back to being engrossed with the television, yawning and scratching his stomach through his bottle-green jumper.

He was a good man, really. A bit useless with Oscar and me at times but he was doing his best. Sometimes it would take the air out of my lungs as I thought about what he'd sacrificed because of Mum's condition. He'd once worked in the Labs where all of the research on the Crits was carried out.

Aside from the cattle carcasses strewn all over the streets in the morning after they'd fed, sometimes there would be the odd dead Crit. These would be bundled away and taken to the Labs for inspection. It was mainly for educational purposes for the town. They were never mutilated or cut up, and would be returned to the woodland by the time dusk came round again so as not to antagonise the Crits.

The opposite was true for humans that went missing.

We rarely saw the bodies again and nor would we want to.

Funerals contained no coffins, unless the family really insisted. But I never understood when it was empty.

Dad no longer worked in the Lab as he needed to be at home to look after Mum and make sure Oscar was picked up from school. So now he was in Clean Up. He'd rise at first dawn and head out in a van with several other colleagues to dispose of animal carcasses the Crits had fed on before the klaxon sounded and all of the kids went running out to school.

Basically, a bin-man.

I didn't care, but I felt like it must have been hard for him to go from scientist to labourer. However, the hours suited the new family set-up and the money was reasonable due to it not being the most appealing job in town.

I walked into the kitchen and make myself a cup of tea, returning with a bottle of beer for Dad.

"You're a good girl, Lib." He eyed the beer bottle and looked sad all of a sudden. "You've grown up too fast."

"It's okay, Dad," I whispered, getting the strangest sensation that he was about to cry and panicking at the thought of it.

"I know…I just love you very much." He looked at me. "Oscar, too."

"I know," I breathed.

With that, we both turned to the television and didn't utter another word.

Chapter 11

I took my seat and Gemma smiled at me. We sat together at a desk for two and were the worst possible combination. Mr Fuller, our teacher, pretended he hated it but I think our double act secretly amused him. Probably because Gemma was loud to the point of obnoxiousness and I'd scold her like a parent.

Blackbrooke was one of my favourite classes as it was the only one where the Academy allowed the boys and girls to mingle. We were never sure why exactly, but I think it had something to do with the subject matter being so gruesome that no one felt in the mood for flirting.

"You never guess what happened last night," Gemma whispered excitedly.

"Do I really want to know?"

She nodded quickly and glanced over her shoulder. "Noah and I were having sex and–"

I recoiled, not wanting to hear yet another sex story about her and Noah. I always found it near impossible to look him in the eye after she'd divulged details of positions and all manner of icky things. "I thought this was something I'd want to hear."

"Wait a sec, I'm not finished," she hissed.

The class was bustling with people talking excitedly to one another as we waited for Mr Fuller to arrive.

"We were having sex," she continued, looking pleased as punch. "And then we both…felt something." I squeezed my eyes shut and she playfully slapped my arm. "Anyway, we were in the basement room and we looked up and guess what we saw?"

My eyes widened in horror. "Gemma, please don't tell me there was a Crit watching you?"

She giggled. "Oh my God, it was the first time I've ever seen one in the flesh."

"How the hell did it see you?" I demanded, feeling the colour drain from my face. "Weren't the blinds closed?"

She licked her top lip. "We don't have blinds in the basement."

I groaned and lowered my head onto the table. "Dare I ask what it was?"

"A Hunter!" She clapped her hands and I winced. "You should have seen it, Lib! Its face was, like…grinning or something. Holy crap, it was insane."

I closed my eyes and counted to five. "Please tell me you stopped when you saw it."

"What do you mean?"

"Never mind. Just…be careful, Gem. These things are capable of all manner of–"

"I will," she interrupted in a singsong voice.

"Seriously, promise me."

She made a cross against her chest with her index finger. "I promise."

"Right, kiddiewinks!" Mr Fuller strode into the classroom, rubbing his hands together. "Sit down and shut up so we can get this over with."

We laughed and some pupils returned to their seats from their positions, perched on friends' desks.

I loved Mr Fuller. He was everything you hope for in a teacher – friendly, fair and knew what he was talking about. He usually taught the boys though so I only had this class with him.

I glanced at Gemma out of the corner of my eye to see her sucking on the end of her pencil.

She had a crush on Mr Fuller.

I cocked my head to one side as he picked up the Blackbrooke textbook from his desk. He was probably quite attractive with his dark skin and broad shoulders but I couldn't get past the fact the man was in his thirties.

And a teacher.

None of which mattered to the walking hormone that was my best friend.

"Hands down, the sexiest black man I've ever seen in my life," Gemma whispered.

"Shhh," I warned. "And change the record. I'm sick of hearing you say the same thing every week."

"Something to share, Miss Connor?"

I coloured and slid down in my seat. "No, sir."

"Great." He beamed. "Everyone open your textbooks to page fifty-seven. Today, we're going to look at…" He paused, a sparkle in his eye as he waited for us to get to the page. A collective groan sounded around the room. "Oh come on, the Hunters aren't that boring."

"Yes, they are!"

I turned in my chair to look at Gabriel sitting at the back and he winked.

We were always careful not to be seen chatting together too much in the class, just in case the teacher grew suspicious and called our parents in. Or some tattletale pupil decided to pipe up.

He was a welcome distraction from the torturous lesson that was about to begin on the type of Crit I knew all too well.

"Alright, alright." Mr Fuller raised his palms to us. "Fair enough. They rip you to shreds blah, blah, blah." He walked around his desk and opened one of the drawers, pulling out an object. "I wanted to try something a bit different in today's class anyway." He placed what looked like a large red button on his desk. "Right, I'm going to head outside for a cigarette break."

Everyone cheered and he shushed us, laughing.

"You lot will get me into trouble. Seriously, I'm heading for a smoke. Now," he eyed the room devilishly, "under no circumstances must any of you push this red button."

"Ooohhh," we chorused.

"I'm deadly serious here. They'll be terrible circumstances."

"Like what?"

I rolled my eyes. The unmistakeable voice of Noah from the table he was sat with Gabriel.

Mr Fuller shook his head. "It'll be awful. So don't do it. Have you all got that? Right, I'll be no more than five minutes."

He hurried out of the room and we sat in silence for a moment.

"Who's gonna push it?!" Noah shouted causing everyone to laugh.

"No one." I opened my textbook and flipped through the pages. I settled on an item about the Queens, the accompanying images causing me to shudder. One showed a woman's body completely hollowed out with all of her organs removed. I swallowed and slammed the book shut.

"I'll do it," Gemma whispered.

I flashed her a look. "Don't you dare."

"Oh come on, Lib. It's a bloody toy. What's the worst that can happen?"

Before I could say anything else, she got up from the seat and started walking slowly down the centre of the room between the desks.

"She's gonna do it!"

"Oh my God!"

The pupils whispered excitedly.

Gemma reached Mr Fuller's desk and pointed her finger over the button.

"Go on, baby!" Noah hollered.

She closed her eyes and pushed it.

We screamed at the loud horn sound and Gemma ducked under Mr Fuller's desk.

I took my hands away from my ears to see Mr Fuller stood in the doorway of the classroom laughing like a maniac and holding an air-horn in his hand.

"Classic!" He doubled over in laughter. "Might have known it'd be you, Jones."

Gemma slowly emerged from under the desk and straightened her skirt before stalking back to our desk.

She sat down roughly and glared at me. "It's not funny."

I pressed my lips together. "I know. I'm sorry."

After the class had recovered themselves from the shock, Mr Fuller stepped forward. "As funny as that was," he flashed a look at Gemma, "there's a point I'm trying to make. A very real point." He turned off the lights and walked to the back to switch on the projector.

Some statistics appeared on the whiteboard in front of us.

"Five thousand people in the UK try to take their own life every year," he declared, his voice serious and my brain immediately switched into action. I cleared my throat and sat up even straighter. "The scary thing is, that doesn't include any stats from Blackbrooke. Five thousand out of nearly sixty-five million people in the UK, that's about zero point zero zero something percent. Now," he flicked to another slide, "if we take Blackbrooke into account, the figures are more scary."

"We have around…two hundred walk outs a year. Out of a population of ten thousand, that means…" he flicked to the next slide, which was a pie chart illustrating his point, "...two point five percent of the population walks out every year." He paused while we digested it. "Doesn't sound like a lot as a figure but I can assure you, we're certainly trumping the national average. Go Blackbrooke!" he said sarcastically and a few people laughed nervously. "Now, out of that two point five percent…"

Next slide.

"A staggering eighty percent are aged seventeen."

I let out a shaky breath.

"The question is, why? Anyone got any suggestions?"

No one said anything.

"Erm…the winter?" I ventured quietly.

"Yes, Liberty," Mr Fuller acknowledged. "The winter plays a huge part. People get down in the dumps and there's an element of cabin fever because we're all locked in the house. Why do you all think my wife and I have four kids?"

People laughed and Noah made a howling noise.

"Yes, that's right, your teacher has sex – get over it. Anyway, the winter is a valid point but I wanted to talk about something else today. Something Gemma demonstrated wonderfully."

Gemma looked at the table and scowled.

"It's that dare devil attitude. The 'it won't happen to me' syndrome that's so wonderfully present in teenagers. I want to show you something."

He flicked to the next slide, which showed a group of teenagers at a party. The image looked like it was taken a while ago as the clothes and hairstyles were dated.

"You may or may not have heard about this bunch of kids," he started. "After watching one too many daft American films where teenagers have these wild pool parties at night, they decided they'd do it. Drunk, probably high…well, certainly high on life anyway, they had a garden party and invited some friends, barbeque, drinks," he paused. "You all know the drill."

"Sir?"

"Yes, Noah."

"Was there…fornication?"

Everyone laughed and Gemma clamped her tongue between her teeth, eyes still trained to the front of the classroom.

I wondered how she could feel such pride at going out with a complete prat.

Mr Fuller tried to hide a smile. "There might have been. Anyway, the sun went down and they carried on into the night, throwing caution to the wind."

My heart sank as I knew what was coming.

"One of the friends went into the kitchen to get another drink and when he returned…" He flicked to the next slide and some of the pupils gasped and while others looked away. The image was a police crime scene but there wasn't anything there that even resembled a human, just blood, flesh and bones scattered across the garden.

"Awful…" Mr Fuller flicked off the projector and walked to the front to turn on the lights.

Gemma had her hand over her mouth and looked dangerously close to being sick.

"Did the friend get away?" I breathed, not realising I was speaking out loud.

"Yes," Mr Fuller looked at me, "I did."

An even bigger collective gasp sounded.

He laughed sadly and shook his head. "Listen, it was awful, but it was a long time ago. It's fine. I'm telling you this because to the rest of Blackbrooke, this would have looked like a mass walk out. It was only down to me to tell everyone otherwise. And it happens a lot when…" Mr Fuller trailed off as the classroom door opened. He looked at his watch. "Ah Mr Godwin, nice of you to join us."

My head snapped up to see Cassius hurry into the room and plonk himself down at a desk near the front. His white hair fell over his eyes as he slouched down as though wanting to appear invisible.

"Yuck," Gemma whispered. "I hate that–"

"Enough," I hissed, thinking back to the conversation with Dad the night before. It was near the anniversary of the night Cassius' mother walked out, exactly one year after his older sister. "Leave him alone."

"Sorr-ee," Gemma muttered.

"As I was saying," Mr Fuller flashed Cassius a disapproving look, "a lot of teenagers feel invincible and might decide to take a chance and run out into the night to see their friend or perhaps their lover. Inevitably, they don't come back and the whole world and its dog see it as a walk out. Although we never say suicide in this town, that's what goes through everyone's head. So, I want all of you to stop and think before doing something crazy and running outside or sneaking out." He shook his head. "I bet a vast majority of teen walk outs are down to moments of madness."

I watched Cassius raise his hand slowly.

"Yes, Mr Godwin."

"The truth is, sir," he muttered, "with all due respect, you haven't got a clue."

Mr Fuller folded his arms and perched on the corner of his desk, eyeing Cassius with interest. "Well, no I don't. I don't claim to have any answers."

"I watched a film," Cassius blurted. I noticed he was colouring in a spot on his desk with his pen. "It was called The Village. Have you seen it?"

Mr Fuller shrugged. 'I don't know, maybe."

"It's about a town that lives in fear of monsters that roam around at night but it turns out to be the villagers who are in fact the monsters." He placed his pen down and looked at Mr Fuller. "They scared their own people witless so they wouldn't leave."

Mr Fuller narrowed his eyes. "Are you saying it reminded you of Blackbrooke? Because Cassius, I can assure you the Crits are very real."

"But what if they don't hurt people?" Cassius shrugged. "I mean, these things have lived with us for centuries. Maybe, they don't want to kill us anymore. Maybe we're free to go out at night."

"Then how do you explain walk outs, genius?" Gemma snapped.

He turned and curled his lip in disgust when he saw who it was addressing him. "I don't know, maybe they just get lost in the woods."

"Rubbish!" she laughed. "The Crits have you as soon as you walk out of the door, everyone knows that."

"How do you know?" Cassius' thin white eyebrows knitted together.

Gemma shrugged. "Everyone knows that."

"But how? Because that's what you've been told? I'm betting most of the Rules are complete bullshit, and it's a way of controlling us and making us afraid."

A few people giggled at Cassius' cursing. I felt my own lips curl upwards and I cleared my throat in an attempt to stop them.

Mr Fuller watched the debate with interest.

"Seriously, that fornication stuff has to be crap." Cassius laughed. "They just say it to limit the number of teenage pregnancies."

"No, it's been proven the Hunters can smell the pheromones we secrete after we've had sex," I piped up, without realising. "Sorry, it's just that my dad used to work in the Lab and…I got to hear about this stuff."

Cassius and I locked eyes and stared for a moment before he looked away.

"I hate the hair rule," Gemma complained and several girls nodded in agreement. "If it's daytime then why can't we wear our hair down?"

Mr Fuller shrugged. "I don't make the Rules."

"Can we please shake our hair out when we're in your class, sir?" Gemma asked sulkily.

Cassius rolled his eyes and turned back to the front.

"Absolutely not, Gemma," Mr Fuller chuckled. "I value my job."

The school intercom suddenly crackled into action and the familiar voice of the headmaster boomed into the room.

I glanced at Gemma, who shrugged. The headmaster was Mr Jones, Gemma's dad, which made her behaviour all the more amusing. My heart always shifted in my chest when I heard his voice. Mr Jones had always made me nervous and, even as Gemma's friend when I was invited round to their house for dinner and sleepovers, I never felt like he warmed to me. I told myself it was because he was still my headmaster and was trying hard not to let his crown slip, but there were times when I was quite sure I saw Gemma's mother flinch when he would raise his voice. Still, Gemma always seemed happy and at ease around him so I reasoned I was just being silly.

"Attention all staff and students, can you please make your way to the assembly hall immediately."

Mr Fuller sighed. "Okay, kids. You know the drill."

Several of us looked around the room but all of our class were accounted for.

I breathed a sigh of relief.

Mr Jones' booming voice interrupting every lesson in the Academy meant only one thing.

A pupil had walked out.

I picked up my bag as the rest of the class filtered past me. Noah pulled Gemma into a one-armed hug and I looked up at Gabriel hovering next to me. The colour had drained from his face and he touched the small of my back, as he guided me out into the busy corridor.

The mood was always subdued as everyone frantically looked around for their friends. I saw Cassius up ahead, walking alone. His gangly frame put him nearly a full head-height over the others and I found myself relieved he'd turned up to the class. If he hadn't, my heart would have been in my mouth for sure.

We filed into the hall and Gabriel squeezed my arm as he left me so he could go and sit on the boys' side. Gemma and I took a seat at the back with the other Year 13 girls. I looked towards the front at the eleven-year-old first-years. Their wide terrified eyes scanned all around them as they struggled to comprehend what was going on. I remembered what it was like to be at the front of this hall and look behind you, trying to seek some comfort from the giant pupils at the back. The ones who looked like grown ups. One small girl with a shiny black bun and delicate features locked eyes with me and I flashed her my best reassuring smile, hoping it helped prevent the tears that looked dangerously close to spilling from her eyes.

Gemma clutched my hand and I squeezed it back.

The room, which was filled with subdued chatter, fell silent as Gemma's dad came striding in. He was wearing his trademark grey suit and maroon tie and his weathered face was grave as it always was on these occasions.

"Good morning."

"Good morning, Mr Jones," we chorused quietly.

He looked down at the papers he'd put in the lectern in front of him. "It is with great regret to inform you," he said into the microphone, "that was have lost one of our brothers of Blackbrooke Academy."

Gemma and I exchanged glances and looked over to the boys' side and their anxious faces.

"Sixth former, Xiang Li, walked out last night."

"Who's that?" Gemma whispered.

My mouth dropped open but I didn't say anything. I craned my neck over to the boys' side.

"Holy crap," she hissed. "Did you know him?"

"No," I said, still looking at the sea of boys in grey uniforms, who had now started to shuffle in their seats in discomfort. The ones who knew him instantly paled and closed their eyes, whereas the ones who didn't shrugged to their friends clearly relieved. My throat felt dry and I licked my lips. "It was Cassius' friend."

"Oh right," Gemma leaned back in her seat, automatically

losing interest at the mention of my old friend.

I caught sight of Cassius sat on the back row, his head in his hands. There were empty seats either side of him and I suddenly felt the overwhelming urge to run over and comfort him, forgetting we were no longer friends. It was the same feeling I had when I attended his mother's funeral all of those years ago. He'd only just started to grow at that point but was still fragile looking as he stood next to his father, not taking his eyes off the simple empty coffin. Him and I weren't friends at that point, nor were we friends during his sister's funeral the year before, but I still felt a desperate need to be by his side. No, not at his side. In front of him, holding him, protecting him. Trying to make the pain go away.

Next to me in the school hall, Gemma was now inspecting her nails, looking bored.

"Xiang was a very talented pupil," Mr Jones continued. "He played the piano to grade 8 standard and had a keen interest in art. He loved to sketch and some of his work is currently displayed in the corridors near the art rooms."

I frowned as I listened to Mr Jones speaking. Drinking in every last detail of a boy I'd never know. I'd passed him a couple of times on the school corridors and would sometimes see him and Cassius studying together in the library, but we'd never even raised a smile in acknowledgement. In a strange way, I was glad. It made the news of his walk out a lot easier, knowing I'd never made a connection with him.

"He wanted to attend university in London and study History of Art. He is the eldest of three children and will be sorely missed by his family both at home and at Blackbrooke Academy."

I heard a sniff and saw one of the art teachers stood at the side of the room, crying quietly while another teacher placed a hand on her shoulder.

I lowered my head into a prayer with everyone.

It was only November. Less than a month since the clocks

went back an hour for daylight saving.
It was going to be a long winter.

Chapter III

"Sorry I'm late," I called, stalking into Tales from the Crits and throwing my bag behind the counter.

Denzil, who was leaning on the cash desk, raised an eyebrow. "Late? I didn't even know you were due in."

"Figures." I put on the red apron and wrapped the straps around my middle to tie in a bow at the front. "I'm doing an extra shift today because of the coach party. Remember?"

He stared at me blankly, his eyes bleary. "Nope."

"Bloody hell." I pulled out the glass cleaner from the cupboard at my feet along with a cloth. "Denzil, are you high?"

He grinned stupidly. "Might be."

I tutted and used my keys to open one of the jewellery cabinets so I could start polishing. It was always how I started my shift due to the thick layer of dust that settled on everything.

Denzil was in his late thirties and owned Tales from the Crits. Not that you'd know he was that old when you saw him. It was like he just couldn't get enough of his teen years and was reluctant to let go. His tattoos had been there for years and were now a faded greeny colour up his arms and covering his pale hands. He even had two tiny tattoos on his temples – one of a heart and one of a star.

He dressed like he was about to go on a protest march for green issues and the thick muddy brown dreadlocks didn't help negate the hippy image.

He was constantly draped in lots of tie-dye and multi-coloured knitwear, not exactly a popular look in Blackbrooke, which was quite straight-laced.

Denzil was a stoner and, although I disapproved of that greatly, I couldn't help but like him. He seemed to be the only adult in Blackbrooke who openly slated the Rules.

No one batted an eyelid at Denzil. Another victim of walk outs, Denzil didn't have parents or siblings and if one day he decided to walk out, I reckoned no one would notice.

I'd probably be the only person to know or care.

Tales from the Crits had been in his family for years and he now had it by default, although I knew he secretly loved it. Situated in the centre of the town, which admittedly only contained about a dozen shops, Tales from the Crits did a roaring trade whenever Outsiders would come rolling in. It would get so busy in there that we'd have to organise a one-in-one-out system to manage it. Denzil and I were the only staff as the shop was quite small and any more would be ridiculous. Plus, Denzil wasn't the most sociable. The only reason I worked there was down to one particular day that I still shuddered at the memory of.

***

"Go on!" Gemma had hissed as we stood across the road from the shop, eating sweets on the way home from school. *"I dare you to go in."*

We were twelve and severely bored. There had been a gas leak in the Academy on that particular day so we were dismissed hours early and found ourselves on the streets with nothing to do and nowhere to go.

I remember gulping as I glanced at the creepy shop which had all manner of articles hanging in the windows. Most of it was Crit memorabilia and there were replica Crit skulls hanging on strings. Horizontal blinds on the inside meant the view was limited, but it seemed dark and there was always a strange smell wafting out of the door at all times of the day.

Rumours of the shop's strange owner circulated through the Academy for years and the stories the kids used to tell one another about their Tales from the Crits experience were legendary. Some said his eyes turned red and he bared large Crit teeth at them. Others said he was actually a Queen in disguise and waited for children to enter the shop on their own before eating them whole.

I'd never seen him at that point. I had no reason to be purchasing Blackbrooke novelties. No one but the tourists did.

"Come on!" Gemma whined. "Please, Lib. I'll love you forever."

"Why don't you just go in?" I scowled at her, pulling a sugar mouse from my paper bag.

"Because," she blinked her big blue eyes at me, "he might tell my dad I went in on my own and I'll get into trouble. He doesn't know your dad. Everyone knows mine! Please, Lib!"

I bit my lip, not taking my eyes off the shop. I felt my heart start to quicken which was a sign I was actually considering it. "But what if he attacks me? What if he really is a Crit, Gem? What then?"

Gemma looked thoughtful for a moment and I watched her with interest as she rummaged in her sweet bag. Despite only being twelve, she already had flirtation licked, even with me. She held up a lollipop. "I knew I had one of these in here. It's a whistle-pop." She placed it between her rosebud lips with the wrapper still on to signal how it worked and I held out my hand to take it.

"Fine," I tried to sound nonchalant. Like I did this kind of thing everyday whereas in truth, I was petrified. I crossed the road, leaving Gemma clapping and giggling excitedly. I ripped the wrapper from the lollipop and placed it in my mouth, instantly rolling it around so it clattered against my teeth.

I threw one last look at Gemma before grabbing the door handle and letting myself into Tales from the Crits. The lollipop was now circling my mouth rapidly as my eyes darted around the dark shop. A bell jingled as the door opened, causing me to freeze.

Inside, the smell was worse. Almost sickly sweet but with the faint whiff of tobacco too. I looked around but couldn't see anyone. Aside from the smell, the shop wasn't as bad as I thought. It was actually quite pretty, with its various dream catchers and wind chimes hanging from the ceiling. Yes, there was Crit stuff which was off-putting, especially the porcelain replicas which sat in rows on the glass shelves, but amongst those articles, there were ornate candles, crystal balls, medieval glassware, chess sets. I span on the spot, trying to drink it all in and wondering why on earth I'd never thought to come in here before. I'd bet I could have gotten some cool items for my room or perhaps something unusual to wear in my hair to make my bun more interesting.

I'd been jealous when I saw Gemma that morning with two perfectly styled buns sat on top of her head. She'd been the talk of the Academy and I just knew every girl would be copying the cute do tomorrow. Gemma had that innate ability to lead where others followed. I didn't lead or follow. I just seemed to exist.

I sighed and walked to the turnstile of postcards, running my fingers on the wire and spinning it slowly. Some of the images were of various places in Blackbrooke and others were the Crits of course. Cartoons of them though. Outsiders could just about handle a cartoon. They even screamed and ran for their lives at the sight of a lowly Watcher. I thought back to my meeting with the Hunter and shuddered at its ghastly face, knowing there was no way Outsiders would flock to Blackbrooke like it was Disneyland if they knew the reality.

"Can I help you?"

I gasped and span around, dropping several postcards I'd pulled out, sending them scattering on the floor. One slid in front of the owner of Tales from the Crits.

My mouth dropped open as I backed away. I forgot all about the lollipop and that too fell to the floor.

The sight of him, stood tall and glowering at me from across the shop, took the wind out of my sails. In my awe of looking around the shop, I'd completely forgotten why I was in here in the first place. To actually see the owner for myself.

"What's the matter, kid? Crit got your tongue?" He walked around the counter and opened the till, throwing in the bags of change he'd been holding. He had a cigarette hanging out of the side of his mouth and ash dropped down the front of his grubby white t-shirt as he spoke.

I swallowed and edged closer to the door, ready to bolt. After all, I'd done what Gemma dared me to do. Surely I could leave now.

He looked up and sighed impatiently. "Listen, I know why you're here. You want to tell your friends I'm a monster or some shit. Well, tell them what you like, its no skin off my nose. I'll even feed you the lines if you like?"

"What?" I managed to croak, my hand now on the handle of the door.

He exhaled and looked to the heavens thoughtfully. "Tell them my hair turned into little snakes that were all trying to bite you. Or," he clapped excitedly, "tell them I'm a vampire and that's why the shop's so dark."

I curled my lip, stepping away from the door. "Are you telling me all of those stories aren't true?"

He eyed me as though I was simple, and started ripping open the plastic bags and depositing the coins in the correct drawers. "Sorry to disappoint you, kid."

I folded my arms, now feeling bold and slightly annoyed at the idiot in front of me. "My name is Liberty, not kid."

"Like the bell?"

"I'm sorry?"

"Liberty Bell." He slammed the cash drawer closed and walked around the front, mirroring my pose and folding his arms. "Never mind. Listen, isn't that why you're here? To get your little story?"

I was. Of course I was.

"No." I raised my nose in the air. "I'm here to shop and you,

quite frankly, have ruined the experience."

"Oh really?" I hated that he sounded amused. "How old are you, Liberty Bell? Because you speak like a thirty year old."

"Twelve," I shot back, turning back to the door. "And I'm so offended by your assumption of me that I'll be leaving now. I'll be sure to report you to the council for your rudeness." The words were spilling out of my mouth despite how ridiculous they were. "They'll make sure you get a punishment you deserve. Might even close you down."

He now looked like he was dying to laugh, which made me fume even more. I yanked open the door, the bell jangling loudly.

"It was good to meet you, Liberty Bell," he called as I left the shop. "You come back now!"

***

I'd scoffed at the idea of ever setting foot in the shop again and told Gemma as much as I filled her in on the strange dreadlocked man in weird clothes as we whiled away the rest of that afternoon. However, I couldn't shake Tales from the Crits from my head and all of its wonderful items so, less than a week later, I was back. Denzil didn't look at all surprised. I started visiting every week, spending my pocket money on little trinkets and books on Blackbrooke's history.

As soon as I turned sixteen, I begged Denzil for a job and he reluctantly agreed. It was partly due to my soft spot for the shop but, and I never told him this part, it was also so I could help Dad out with the bills after Mum became incoherent. I didn't get paid much but it helped. We could of course have asked the Government for money and they would have thrown it at us by the bucket-load (Outside Guilt again), but Dad was proud and I suppose I was too.

Over the years, the articles Tales from the Crits sold remained the same – a combination of lovely things that never sold and the Crit crap that flew off the shelves and into the hands of over-excited Outsiders. Best-sellers included 'Welcome to Blackbrooke!' postcards, Crit snow globes, and, my personal favourite, 'I Heart Crits' t-shirts. The book section was also popular and we would find the shelves bare after a coach party had descended. One of the more recent history books was written by Mr Fuller, so I'd always try to push this one if anyone enquired.

The irony was that most of the souvenirs were produced overseas and shipped across to us in unattractive brown cardboard boxes. Still, the Outsiders didn't care.

"Where did you get this batch of weed from then?" I nodded to the fat cigarette in his hand, while I polished the cabinet glass.

Denzil leaned over the counter. "Some Italians gave me some in exchange to see where the Crits live and hear some stories."

I gaped at him. "Are you saying you took some tourists into the woodland?"

"Nah, I just took them outside the shop to the trees. They believe anything. Also, told them about the night I wrestled a Hunter."

"Oh, for crying out loud."

"Hey," he raised his hands, "if they're stupid enough to believe an old stoner hippy, then it's their problem."

I shrugged. He had a point.

"Anyway," he blew out a perfect series of smoke rings, "speaking of Italians, are you still bumping uglies with that Machete kid?"

I flashed him a look. "It's Moretti, and if you're being rude then no, I'm not...bumping uglies."

"Yeah yeah."

I threw the cloth at him and he caught it and draped it over his shoulder. "How dare you. I'm not a rule breaker."

He rolled his brown eyes.

"What?" I demanded. "Are you encouraging me to play fast

and loose? I'll get eaten by the Crits. In fact," I raised my finger to the heavens, "I might as well just pour gravy all over myself and sit in the woodland waiting for sunset."

He smiled to himself and closed the cash drawer. "Did you see the newspaper this morning?"

I felt my heart sink at the possibility of another walk out. "No, why?"

He chuckled. "They found a bunch of Outsiders camping in the woods last night."

"Oh my God." I raised my hand to my mouth.

"Don't worry. The police got to them before the sun went down and they were escorted to the border."

I scowled and returned to the cabinet to straighten the displays inside. "Idiots."

"That's one word for them." He stretched his arms above his head, and his shoulders cracked. "I can't be bothered today."

"Nothing new," I muttered.

"So," he leaned on the glass I'd just polished, "are you and Machete saving yourselves until you're eighteen?"

I ignored him and pulled the cloth from his shoulder so I could get to work on the rest of the shelves. "Not that it's any of your business, but, like I always say, I follow the Rules."

"Christ, I don't know how you have the strength. I was at it from the age of sixteen."

"Yuck." I gave him a look of disgust. "Not a pretty thought."

"Thanks a lot." He straightened some of the postcards on the turnstile. "I think you should just go for it. You never know when your number's up."

I let out a laugh. "You can't really live by that mantra in Blackbrooke; it's the safest place to be. Aside from the Crits, of course."

He pulled at one of his dreadlocks that had come loose from the ponytail they were scraped up into. "Do you reckon you'll marry Machete?"

"Moretti!"

"I know. I'm just playing with you. So, do you think you will?"

I felt my face flush. "I don't know. I think so. We're looking at going travelling after school."

"Wow." Denzil's eyes widened and he looked sad for a second. "Do you want to leave for good?"

I picked up a ceramic Queen figurine, grimacing at it. "Not really, but I suppose that's what I'll have to do if I want to see the world. We'll see, I suppose."

"Indeed we will."

We were quiet and Denzil returned behind the counter to switch on the old and battered CD player. I curled my lip. I absolutely hated the music we played in the shop, it was so naff.

It was supposed to be dark and ominous but I just found it cringe worthy.

Sometimes, if we knew the Americans were coming, we'd put on the Harry Potter soundtrack and giggle at their mesmerised faces as they stepped through the door.

I really liked working in the shop. In Blackbrooke, you got so used to seeing the same faces day-in day-out so, although they were sometimes annoying, it was fun to meet the Outsiders just to get a change of scenery.

"Uh oh, here comes trouble…"

Denzil was looking over my shoulder and I turned just as the bell on the door rang and Gemma bounded in.

"Hey, my little worker." She stuck out her tongue. "Ready for a busy day?"

Denzil turned away to busy himself.

"What are you doing here?" I folded my arms and tried hard to look annoyed but felt secretly pleased to see her. "I'm working."

She strode up to the counter and unscrewed the lid on the

jar of bright orange pumpkin lollipops, helping herself. She hauled herself up so she was sat on top, swinging her legs. "I'm here to tell you that you're coming round to my house tonight – no arguments."

Denzil turned round. "Are you going to pay for that?"

She make a face before turning to him. "Hi Denzil," she said breathily. "How's it going?"

"Be a lot better if you paid for that lolly you're sucking on," he grumbled. "You'll put me out of business."

She removed it from her mouth and ran it over her lips as though kissing it. "This lolly?"

He looked away uncomfortably. "Yes. That very one."

Gemma raised her shoulder to her chin at me cheekily. She was convinced Denzil had a soft spot for her but I wasn't so sure. In fact, I always got the impression he couldn't stand her.

No, there was only one boy who had the patience to put up with Gem.

She got with Noah six months previously after being forced together due to the amount of time Gabriel and I were hanging out. They seemed to dislike one another at first but that changed as soon as they realised how much fun could be had without their clothes on. Now they were inseparable.

Gemma, for all her bravado, absolutely adored him. And I could tell the way he looked at her that he felt the same way.

It was a match made in heaven.

Or hell, depending on how you wanted to look at it.

"Sooo," Gemma purred, removing the lollipop from her mouth, "are you coming?"

I shrugged. "I don't see why not."

"Of course! Noah and Gabriel will be there and my parents…" she waved her tongue at me, "will not."

Denzil raised an eyebrow and leaned on the counter next to her. "So, does that mean you're going to have an orgy?"

She flashed him a disgusted look. "No, Swampy."

"It's Denzil, actually."

"Close enough." She winked and turned her attention back to me. "Are you in?"

I nodded, feeling a rush of excitement.

"Great." She slid off the counter and walked towards the door, her long white cardigan floating behind her. "My dad will pick you up at two today. That's okay, isn't it, Denzil?"

He shrugged, "Of course. The tourists will be long gone by then."

She pulled open the door causing the bell to ring again. "I know I don't need to tell you, but maybe don't mention our male visitors to Dad when he collects you."

"Puh-lease."

"See ya!"

"And with that," Denzil announced dramatically with a wave of his arm, "she was gone."

I smiled as I watched my friend bound over the road and into one of the few clothes shops in town. Probably to buy something slutty to change into tonight when the boys were round.

"Well, Liberty Bell," Denzil appeared at my side and clapped a hand on my shoulder, "if tonight's the night for you and Machete then may the force be with you."

"Denzil!" I pushed him away and laughed, although inside my stomach was performing somersaults.

***

"Right, is it going to be…" Gemma stood in the centre of the room, holding a DVD box in each hand, "horror or comedy?"

Noah leaned back on the sofa. "I'd say horror if it was actually scary."

Gemma frowned and inspected the boxes.

"I think maybe we should go for the comedy." I raised my hand and eyed Gabriel who had his arm draped around me.

"Twilight's pretty funny, isn't it? I mean, funny in a laughable kind of way." They blinked at me. "I mean, its not laugh out loud funny but its just that…its about as far way from our reality as you can get."

Gemma sighed and looked at the DVD box. "Can you imagine if the Crits were as fit as Robert Pattinson?"

Noah cleared his throat. "What's the horror about?"

Gemma turned her attention to the other one. "A psychopathic killer terrorizes a babysitter, then returns seven years later to menace her again. Could be good? No lame Crit imitations."

"Do you think it looks scary, babe?" Noah asked Gemma who shrugged.

"A bit."

"Great." He grinned. "Put that one on and get over here with me."

Gabriel shook his head at his friend. "Are you okay with this?" he whispered.

I nodded quickly.

I hated horror films. Especially ones that were about psychotic humans rather than monsters. It seemed so far removed from Blackbrooke where the monsters were very real and the humans were in it together. Gemma and I spent many evenings like this, but it was rare the boys joined us. It was reliant on someone's parents being out all night. And there was a lot of deception involved. My story was okay, I was staying over at Gemma's like I had so many times before. However, Gabriel was supposedly at Noah's and vice versa. It was risky and we relied on our parents never picking up the phone to one another. Gemma's parents were dining with Gabriel's parents tonight which always made me nervous. It just seemed to close for comfort.

Gemma flipped off the lights and hopped over the footrest to join Noah on the other sofa. He pulled her close so her legs were draped over his. We'd closed the blinds early before the sun had gone down which was something I usually hated to do as the days were so short anyway but we'd wanted to create an atmosphere. Also, we didn't want any neighbours who happened to be wandering by to look in and see two teenage couples hanging out.

I watched the opening scenes and felt my heart hammer in my chest. Gabriel squeezed me.

"Do you want a drink?" I whispered and he flashed his perfect white teeth at me.

"Are you really that scared?"

"No, I'm just thirsty."

"Then have some of my leftovers." He picked up his can of lemonade from the floor and handed to me.

"Fine." I took the can and pretended to have a drink.

My plan to escape the horror film for a few minutes, well and truly scuppered, I took to watching the television through narrowed eyes. When that got tiring, I focused on a spot just above the TV and tried to block out the noise.

One noise I couldn't block out was that of Gemma and Noah's lips smacking together.

"I don't know why they insist on watching a film," Gabriel muttered.

"I don't know why they insist on us coming over." I frowned in disapproval at my friend now lying on her back on the sofa and kissing Noah passionately as he lay on her.

"Do you think they want us to watch?" Gabriel whispered, and I sniggered loudly.

"Come on." I jumped up and took his hand. "Let's go and get that drink."

I pulled him out of the room and into the kitchen where we helped ourselves to another can from the fridge.

"I love this house," I sighed, eyeing the large country kitchen and running my fingers along the granite work surface. "Gemma's so lucky."

Gabriel shrugged. "Depends what you consider to be

lucky."

"What do you mean?"

"Well," he moved closer and wrapped an arm around my waist, "would you want Mr Jones as your dad?"

I laughed and placed my hand over my mouth to try and stop. He was right. Mr Jones was my idea of a nightmare parent. Gemma had enough strength of character to flourish but I was quite sure I would have been a frightened little mouse. Sometimes it surprised me that Gemma didn't hate him. I struggled to forget her eleventh birthday. Mr Jones had smiled warmly at his daughter and passed her a bigger box than usual. I was there, too. It was over breakfast, and I eyed the box with interest, wondering why there were holes cut out of the sides. Gemma squealed when she removed the lid to find the most beautiful little white kitten, sat looking up at her, meowing from fear of being shut in the box. She lifted it out and hugged the furball to her chest. Mrs Jones was nowhere to be seen which I thought was odd. There was a big pink bow around its neck and it had the brightest green eyes that Gemma joked looked like mine. Although it was cute, I automatically felt uneasy at the sight of the cat. Pets were a no-go in Blackbrooke. There was no law against having them but, spending a life Crit dodging meant people didn't exactly relish the idea of inviting a wild animal into their homes. Animals were unpredictable. You didn't know what they were thinking and, for that reason, they reminded me of Crits too much.

Word soon spread about Gemma's new pet, who she named Portia, and she even brought it to school on occasions where it nestled happily in her rucksack, until it was hungry and then it would cry loudly. I'd wince at every cry, thinking about the strangled sound the Watchers made to alert the Queens.

The story didn't have a happy ending. One morning Gemma awoke to find Portia was missing. She searched high and low and demanded I come round to help her look. It was useless. There was no sign of the kitten that usually spent every night curled up at the end of her bed. Mr Jones called her name and we raced downstairs, assuming he must have found her. He had, well, what was left of her. Gemma's screams of horror still echoed around my head at the sight of the mess of white fur and flesh that Mr Jones was holding up in front of her, a strange glint in his eye.

He held the dead kitten that way in the school assembly the next morning where horrified and disgusted gasps sounded around the hall. Gemma had stood at his side, humiliated and devastated, hiccupping on sobs.

"This," he'd pointed at the mess, *"is why no one is Blackbrooke should own a pet. It attracts the Crits to your home. So, next time you start pestering your parents for a four-legged friend, see this!"*

Even at the tender age of eleven, I knew Mr Jones had used his daughter in order to make an example of her to the other pupils. It was a cruel game and I disliked him even more from that day. Not only was he scary, but he wasn't to be trusted. No wonder Mrs Jones had cowered away on the morning he handed her the gift. She knew.

Despite this, Gemma never had a bad word to say about her father so I held my tongue, choosing instead to rant to Denzil whenever Mr Jones did or said something that irritated me. Denzil, for some reason, also hated the headmaster and Blackbrooke mayor, so he was my perfect ally.

Gabriel and I made our way into the main living room, leaving Gemma and Noah in the TV room. Gemma's house was so big, it had various living areas.

The living room was more formal with bookshelves covering most of the walls and a bottle-green Chesterfield suite that looked as old as the hills took pride of place in the centre of the room around the solid oak coffee table.

Gabriel closed the door behind us and pointed across the room. "Hey, look!"

I followed his gaze and saw an ornamental globe on one of the bookshelves.

We exchanged excited glances and skipped over to it. Gabriel carried it over the sofa. He patted the space next to him. "Come on, lets plan our trip."

I bit my lip. "Okay."

Leaving Blackbrooke to travel around the world was something we discussed constantly. From those whispered conversations in the library, to the lazy summer evenings lying on the grass of the school field, our fingers interlocked and my head resting on his stomach.

Leaving was a dream that most kids had but very few actually went through with it after getting spooked by the stories of crime on the Outside. I was determined, however, to get out as soon as I could. Ever since the encounter with the Crit in the woodland, I knew I'd never feel truly free as long as I was here.

Gabriel lay back on the sofa and extended his arm for me to lie down in front of him.

"Here," he pointed at Mexico, "I want to go here."

I span the globe to Europe. "I want to see Greece."

"What?" He nudged his shoulder into me. "Why Greece?"

"I don't know. Just the bits I've seen on the internet look amazing. All of the ancient ruins." I looked at the globe dreamily. "We don't have anything like that here, everything's new."

"Yeah," he sighed. "I love that the Government is slowly taking away any piece of history we have." He kissed my hair which was still scraped into a bun. "I think some of the souvenirs in your shop are older than the buildings."

I moved the globe around. "How about Australia?"

"Definitely," he said excitedly, running his finger across the length of the country. "And New Zealand."

"What do you think its like being in an aeroplane?"

"I can't wait," he blurted loudly. "I just want to hear those engines fire up and watch as we climb into the sky." He lowered his voice to a whisper. "When we got our pen friends from the Outside in the first year, the boy I spoke to said..."

I turned my head to him, feeling his breath on my cheek. "What?"

He whispered in my ear. "He said you soar through the sky and over the clouds like a bird. Free as a bird."

I smiled and looked at his dark fingers wrapped around my paler ones.

"Imagine, Lib."

I closed my eyes.

"Imagine sitting on a beach somewhere and watching the sunset over the sea and then being able to sit there all night, under the stars. Not afraid."

I licked my lips as I pictured what that must be like. "What else will we do?"

I felt his cheek, which was pressed against my temple, rise into a smile too. "We'll walk on the beach and look at the full moon and we'll find all of the constellations they talk about on the TV." He placed the globe down onto the coffee table so he could wrap both arms around me. "We'll live on the beach in a house that overlooks the sea and it'll be so warm that we have to keep the doors open all night." He planted a kiss on the side of my head. "We'll have lots of bedrooms so we can reserve some for Oscar and the twins when they grow up."

The twins were Gabriel's little brother and sister, Frank and Rosa. "Really?"

He nodded. "Yeah, they can come and meet their nieces and nephews."

I giggled and slapped him lightly on the arm.

"Before that, we'll get married."

I felt my heartbeat quicken in excitement. "Where?"

"Anywhere. Anywhere you want."

I turned my head and kissed him softly on the lips. "I love you."

"I love you too, Libby Connor."

I turned over so I was facing him. I could feel his heart hammering through his chest as I pressed myself into him. I reached up and pulled the bobble out from my bun and my hair fell over my shoulders.

Gabriel ran his hands up through it and pulled away, leaning his forehead on mine.

I looked into his dark brown eyes. "I think I'm ready."

His look turned from concern to surprise and he stroked my cheek. "Really? Right now?"

I nodded quickly and kissed him again.

All of a sudden, the Rules seemed so far away. I didn't care about them.

I cared about Gabriel. Right there at that moment, he was the only thing that mattered to me. Plus, in only a few months, we'd be out of Blackbrooke for good and wouldn't have to live by these Rules ever again. Just as soon as we turned eighteen, we could leave and go wherever we pleased. It wasn't long to wait but as I felt my body instinctively mould into his as we lay together, I knew I couldn't wait. Not one minute longer.

He moved so I was lying on my back, my legs either side of him as he kissed my neck softly.

"I'm nervous," I blurted.

"Me too." He let out a shaky breath, brushing a stray hair off my face. "I won't hurt you, I promise."

He sat up and peeled off his grey t-shirt to reveal his perfect body and I shifted so he could lift my own t-shirt up over my head. He looked down at me and I suddenly felt nervous at being so exposed. We'd never done anything more than kiss in the entire year we were together. However, over the last few months, the sight of Gemma and Noah practically devouring one another had stirred something in me that wouldn't go away and I found myself left wanting more.

I pulled him down onto me as we kissed, not daring to pull

away and look him in the eye in case I saw my nervous face reflected back.

I could feel Gabriel's entire body shaking and he reached down ran his hand up my leg, squeezing my thigh. I let out a gasp and he stopped.

"Sorry."

"No, it's okay," I whispered quickly. "It's…nice."

He kissed me again, edging his hand further up my skirt slowly. I leaned my head back in anticipation and let his lips move down to my neck as I clutched at his thick dark hair.

"What the hell?!"

The main light in the room flicked on and Gabriel and I jumped up to see Gemma's parents stood in the doorway, staring at us in horror.

"Oh my God," I whispered, grabbing my t-shirt and pulling it on.

Mr Jones looked like he was going to explode with anger while Mrs Jones was stood with her hand over her mouth in shock.

"What's going on here?" Mr Jones demanded, glaring from me to Gabriel. "Answer me!"

I opened my mouth but no sound came out. Gabriel was stood next to me, his chest heaving as he looked fearfully at our headmaster. I bent down and retrieved his t-shirt from the floor and passed it to him.

Mr Jones shook his head. "Gemma!" he bellowed, "wherever you are, get in here right now!"

I felt my body start to shake as the severity of the situation finally started to dawn on me. We were all in big trouble.

I heard footsteps coming towards the room and Gemma sheepishly let herself in with Noah close behind her. She took one look at me and then at Gabriel who was still stood clutching his t-shirt, his hair stood up in all different directions from where my hands had been in it.

I hastily pulled my hair up into a messy bun. It was funny

that I felt more of a harlot having my hair down than I did stood next to a shirtless boy.

Gemma was wearing the small cotton dress she'd secretly changed into when her parents left, and her hair was in a half-hearted, careless ponytail that she must have just pulled it into. She was stood barefooted, biting on her thumbnail.

Noah, although thankfully dressed, looked dishevelled. His lips were pink from kissing.

Mrs Jones looked like she was going to be sick.

"Sit down," Mr Jones ordered, "all of you." He flashed a look at Gabriel. "Put your shirt on."

Gabriel sprang into action, his cheeks flushing pink.

Gemma threw me a worried look and sat down on the sofa next to me. Thankfully the sofa was large so there was a gap between us and the boys, who had wisely chosen to keep their distance.

Mr Jones strode up and down in front of us, rubbing his chin in anger.

"Do the Rules mean absolutely nothing to you people?!" he shouted, startling us.

"Daddy, I–"

"Don't!" He pointed at his daughter, glaring in disgust. "I don't want to hear it."

Mrs Jones left the room and I could have sworn she was crying.

"Now," Mr Jones closed his eyes, "I'm going to have to hope we caught you before you actually did anything…"

I nodded and he snarled, causing me to shrink back.

"It's sunset, so you'll all have to stay here for the night," he said sternly. "In separate rooms." He turned to walk out. "I'll be calling your parents now and they'll come to collect you after the morning klaxon."

Noah buried his head in his hands and my heart sank at the thought of Dad knowing about this. He'd be so angry and embarrassed. I was likely to be grounded until my eighteenth birthday.

I looked at my friends. We all would be.

Gemma had paled and stared at a spot on the floor.

Mr Jones stalked out of the room and I let out a breath.

"We're in big trouble," Gabriel whispered. He leaned towards me quickly and whispered in my ear. "Remember, despite what happens – free as a bird, Lib."

I smiled and nodded. "Free as a bird."

***

"Do you have everything?" Dad asked awkwardly as he pulled up to the Academy gates. This was the first time he'd ever dropped me off at school and I could tell he didn't have a clue. "Did you pick up your lunch?"

"I don't take lunch."

"Oh…right. Well, have you got your bag?"

"It's on my knee."

"What about your–"

"Dad!" I cut him off. "I have everything."

Gabriel's words from several nights ago echoed around my head. Free as bird. I eyed Dad and pursed my lips. I certainly didn't feel very free now.

I turned to Oscar who was strapped in his car seat and blew a kiss. "Have a good day." I looked at Dad. "Are you expecting me to walk him in or are you going to drive round?"

Dad shook his head. "I'll drive round."

"See you later then."

"Three o'clock?" Dad called as I stepped out of the car.

I nodded and waved at Oscar who looked delighted to have accompanied his sister to her side of the school.

I had to hand it to Dad. I didn't think he'd follow through with the grounding and I certainly didn't think he was serious about being my personal chauffeur. I adjusted my bag on my shoulder as I walked into school.

He'd been angry. Angrier than I'd ever seen him before.

"Just imagine you're me for a minute, Liberty. Imagine!" he'd bellowed at me. *"I pick up the phone and I have to hear your headmaster tell me he's found you half-naked with the Moretti kid!"*

We'd yelled back and forth and I'd cried a thousand apologies, trying to tell him that I didn't get as far as he thought.

The grounding was for my own safety apparently. Dad said the Crits could probably smell the hormones raging in my body from miles away.

Several girls in the schoolyard turned to look as I made my way across the tarmac towards the school's main entrance. I felt my cheeks flush. The events of Saturday night had clearly made their way around the whole town.

Fabulous, I thought. That's ten thousand people who think I'm a whore. Quiet, clever Liberty Connor. It had most probably put me on the map if nothing else. Previously, I was only known as the best friend of Gemma Jones, daughter of the headmaster and much loved or feared by anyone who crossed her path.

I stalked into the building and to the canteen to get myself a hot drink before my dull history lesson. Why I picked history for A Level is beyond me. I just happened to be quite good at it.

I saw another group of pupils, whom I vaguely recognised as being part of Gabriel's football team in sports class, whispering and pointing at me and I sucked in my cheeks in annoyance. I wouldn't have minded if we did actually break a Rule, but we didn't. Not that it mattered to the Academy rumour-mill. If there was no walk out to gossip about then it would be focused on rule breakers.

I buried my face further down into my scarf as I hurried towards the exit after seeing a long queue and deciding I didn't want to stay there a moment longer.

"Attention students, can Liberty Connor please report to Mr Jones' office."

The canteen fell quiet as everyone looked at me. I knew what this was about. Gemma had warned me.

I was going to get kicked out of Mr Fuller's class.

And sports probably.

Anything that gave me the opportunity to mix with the boys.

Hell, I'd probably be banned from the canteen as well.

I might as well have worn a badge of shame on my chest like they did in the 17th Century. A scarlet letter.

My heart started to pound at the thought of not being in Mr Fuller's class. It was my absolute favourite.

I walked through a group of girls in the corridor leading to Mr Jones office and they stopped talking immediately.

I'm not having this, I thought after I'd walked past them. I turned back, outstretching my arms. "So what?" I called and they looked away uncomfortably. "So what if I supposedly had sex? What's it got to do with you?"

They couldn't meet my eye and I shook my head. "Spineless," I muttered, surprising myself with my own fiery attitude.

It was too early for Mr Jones' PA to be working so I strode up to his office door and knocked with a shaking hand. Any bravado I had in front of the group of girls, now well and truly diminished at the thought of coming face to face with Mr Jones again.

"Enter," came his stern voice from the other side of the glass.

I exhaled and turned the doorknob.

"Good morning, Mr Jones," I muttered, closing the door behind me. "Once again, I'm very sorry for…"

I trailed off as I saw Gemma sat on one of the chairs in front of him, sobbing. She looked up with her big sad eyes and her blotchy face crumpled into another cry.

My eyes flicked to Mr Jones nervously. "What's going on?"

"Please sit down," he gestured to the chair in front of him and I tentatively perched on the edge, placing my bag on the floor. "Now," he looked at his hands. "I don't usually do this but given the events of Saturday night…I thought it only fair…"

He's expelling me, I thought, feeling sick. I'm expelled.

No A Levels.

Nothing.

"Dad," Gemma croaked, "please…"

Mr Jones face registered a pained look as he glanced at his distraught daughter. "Fine," he said at last. "As you wish."

I was surprised to see him get up from his desk and walk out of the room, closing the door behind him.

"Gemma?" I looked at her, starting to feel panicked.

"I'm so sorry," she spluttered. "I'm so sorry, Lib."

I felt the colour drain from my face and I could hear the blood pumping around my body echoing in my ears.

She grabbed my hand. "I'm sorry but…Gabriel…he walked out last night."

Chapter IV

I felt my head snap backwards in shock. "No, he didn't." I stood abruptly and she recoiled in surprise.

"I'm so sorry."

My breathing quickened and I struggled to swallow. "That's impossible. We…we made plans. There must be some mistake."

Gemma made a grab for my hand again but I snatched it back.

There was no way. It was a lie.

I picked up my bag and ran out of the office and straight into Mr Jones waiting on the other side.

"Liberty, stop!" He had my arms clamped to my sides as I struggled to get away, hot tears now starting to flow down my cheeks.

"Let me go!" I screamed.

The same group of girls I'd shouted it only moment ago were watching the scene unfold, their hands over their mouths and shaking their heads in pity.

That's why everyone was looking at me and whispering as I walked into school.

They knew.

"No!" I cried, collapsing into Mr Jones' arms as he supported my weight. He walked me back into his office. This time I let Gemma comfort me.

"I'm so sorry," she whispered, stroking my hair as I slumped into her.

"It doesn't make sense," I wailed, my body going into

shock and my knees buckling. Gemma moved so she was kneeling in front of me and rubbed my legs.

I thought of Gabriel's perfect face.

His fingers entwined with mine.

His laugh.

"I'm going to be sick," I muttered.

"Dad!" Gemma stood up and Mr Jones passed her the waste paper bin from under his desk.

I took it and was immediately violently sick.

It tasted like the toast I'd shovelled down for breakfast.

Gemma rubbed my back and I hiccupped.

"Now, I know this is very difficult for both of you but I'm about to call an assembly to announce it." Mr Jones' eyes flicked from me to Gemma. "It's up to you whether or not you're there but seeing as Noah's taking some time off to come to terms with this..." Gemma let out a choked sob. "Well, I just think it would mean a lot to his memory if his other friends were present."

I wiped my eyes. "Of course."

"What?" Gemma asked, flashing her dad a worried look. "Are you sure?"

No, I wasn't sure. I wasn't sure about anything. None of this felt real. I couldn't grasp hold of the information long enough for it to stick in my head. It kept fluttering out like a butterfly. Or a bird.

Free as a bird.

I closed my eyes and thought about Saturday. Gabriel and I looking at the globe, planning our trip.

"I'll never get to do any of that," I said out loud, staring at a spot on the floor.

"What, Lib?" Gemma stroked my hand in both of hers.

"Any of it." I felt tears flow down my cheeks and my chin. I looked up and straight at Mr Jones. "I know what you saw on Saturday and how it must have looked but I loved him."

He nodded slowly.

I felt my face crumple. "I really did."

Mr Jones stood up, smoothing down his maroon tie. "I'm going to brief the staff and then I'll see you in the assembly hall."

He left the room again and I closed my eyes, feeling more tears pour down my face.

"It doesn't make any sense, Gem," I whispered. "We talked about the future. He even mentioned…marriage and kids."

Gemma bit her lip and took both of my hands in hers again. "Maybe he didn't walk out. Maybe he was on his way to see you or something…"

I shook my head. "He'd never risk it."

Gabriel was scared of the Crits. Sometimes, on the rare occasions we found ourselves alone, we'd talk about what scared us the most about them. It was always the Queens for me, despite coming face to face with a Hunter, it was the reclusive nature of them that made me nervous. I often wondered what their motives were, they seemed almost too sophisticated to operate as cattle bins like the others seemed to.

"The Lurkers," Gabriel would whisper. *"They're…vile."*

He was right. They absolutely were. Ripping strips off their victims until they passed out from the pain and eventually died.

I felt my stomach plummet at the thought of the Lurkers getting to Gabriel first.

I frowned. Did Dad know what had happened this morning when he dropped me at school? He was on Clean Up, surely he must have heard or perhaps even saw something and yet he didn't say anything.

Gemma and I sat in silence for another few moments just staring into space, the sound of the clock on the wall ticking loudly.

"Have you seen Noah?" I croaked eventually.

Gemma shook her head, fresh tears forming in her eyes.

"Dad won't let me near him."

"Even now?"

She nodded and wiped at her eyes with the sleeve of her jumper.

"Attention all staff and students, can you please make your way to the assembly hall immediately."

I looked at Gemma. "Come on. Let's go."

***

After the assembly announcing Gabriel's walk out, I had to get out of the Academy. Luckily, the guards on the gate didn't try to stop me as I bolted out, sobbing.

The whispers and nudges on the girls' side of the hall while Mr Jones talked about Gabriel's extensive list of achievements were too much to bear.

Gemma had taken herself to the toilets to wash her face which had become red from crying and I, selfishly, used the opportunity to run away.

It was another misty winter day where the sky had no clouds but appeared to be a grey seamless blanket. The cold air I sucked into my lungs was strangely comforting as I walked down the empty woodland road into the town.

I couldn't be around the other pupils. The idea of hearing laughter or seeing a smile on anyone's face was too much to bear.

Didn't they realise the sadness of today?

Did they realise how much of a hole Gabriel left in Blackbrooke?

Aside from my biased opinion, Gabriel was a popular pupil and that much was clear at the amount of boys who broke down in the assembly.

He played football, aced maths and was the model science student.

His parents were one of the few who'd successfully passed

all of the tests to get into Blackbrooke to live as a resident from the Outside. Blackbrooke was in desperate need of qualified doctors about twenty years ago as the Outsider GPs who travelled in weren't really working out, especially as they weren't allowed to stay overnight, even if there was an emergency.

Gabriel's father, fresh out of medical school and newly married, jumped at the chance. The reasons are unclear to me but I suspect it had something to do with the salary offered compared to the Outside.

In terms of ethnic minorities in the town – there weren't many. The original townspeople were white and because Outsiders had to go through such a rigorous and long application process to get in, there wasn't much variety.

The Government decided to step in around about the same time there was a call out for doctors and make the application process a bit easier for ethnic minorities in order to encourage them to apply and create a more 'mixed community' in Blackbrooke.

It worked.

Any other town would have probably seen a racist reaction to the new townspeople but, because humans were all on the same side, they were welcomed with open arms.

Gabriel was classed in the 'minority' category as his parents were Spanish and Italian, and he used to laugh when he told me about some of the bizarre counselling sessions held by Government Outsiders.

Like all kids, he didn't realise he was different until it was needlessly pointed out by an adult.

Those sessions weren't applicable anymore. We were a nice bunch in Blackbrooke and I think the Government just had a hard time understanding that when comparing us to the rest of the country.

No one was nicer than Gabriel though.

He was perfect in every way.

I stopped in my tracks and leaned my back against a telephone pole, sliding down it so I was crouched, my head in my hands.

The pain and confusion was too much to bear.

I let tears run down my hands and didn't brush them away.

"I love you, Gabriel," I sobbed.

I took a deep breath and looked up, right into the glowing red eyes of a Watcher.

I gasped and stood, scraping my back on the pole. I remained rooted to the spot in horror as it just stood inches from my feet looking up at me.

Its back was horribly hunched and its small head was stooped, like a hyena. I sucked in a shallow breath as its tail twitched and swished from side to side. Dribbles of saliva fell from its mouth in a steady stream and I kept hearing the sound of it trying to swallow and smacking its mouth together. The eyes were blood red and dull as they looked into my frightened ones. The highest part of its back reached halfway up my thigh.

"It can't hurt you, Lib," I whispered to myself, not taking my eyes off it. "It's just watching you."

It appeared to be chewing on its own spit.

"Did you see Gabriel?" I asked, my voice quivering. "Did you see him die?"

It continued to stare. Its fur looked like it was matted to its body with blood.

"Who was it?" I whispered, feeling my bottom lip wobble. "*What* was it?"

The Watcher moved quickly, causing me to jump, and licked and gnawed at a spot on its back.

The sound of a car engine made its ears prick and it looked up the road, grey tongue clamped between its teeth. I looked too and saw a familiar vehicle speeding towards us.

The Watcher stared as the van pulled up and Denzil reached over and threw open the passenger door. "Get in!"

I nodded, hastily picking up my bag and hurrying into the van, slamming the door behind me. I glanced over my shoulder as Denzil sped away and saw the Watcher wander into the middle of the road. I returned its look until it became a spec in the distance and turned to face the front. "Thanks," I muttered.

Denzil flashed me a worried look and glanced in his rear-view mirror. "I hate those things. They give me the creeps."

"Me too."

"Do you want me to take you home?"

I shrugged and looked out of the window so he couldn't see my tear-stained face. "Not really."

"Well," he leaned forward to turn up the heater, "I'm heading to the shop to unpack the stuff I've just collected from the border if you want to join me?"

I didn't respond.

He parked the van in the usual spot outside the shop and I got out and stood at the door as he fumbled with the keys while balancing one of the boxes.

"Tea?" he asked, setting the box down on the counter.

"Don't you need to get the rest of the boxes?"

"Ah, that can wait." He started pulling his dreadlocks into a ponytail. "I need a cuppa first."

"I don't want one," I mumbled, pulling out Mr Fuller's book from the shelf with my finger before deciding against it and putting it back.

"I heard about the Moretti kid," Denzil said eventually. I turned and he was scratching the back of his neck, looking awkward. "I'm sorry about that, Lib."

I nodded.

"It's always so sad when you know them."

"Hmmm." I picked up a children's picture book which explained the Crits as loveable creatures. I remembered the book from when I was a child as Mum used to read it to me. It was the same one I sometimes read to Oscar at night. It was supposed to be educational without being too frightening for the younger children. Easing them into the Crits gradually.

When I was small I became obsessed with the idea I'd end up with a Hunter as a friend and living in a pack with them.

Before I actually came face to face with one, of course.

I turned the pages and settled on the Queens. They were illustrated like fairytale witches complete with pointy hats and green, wart-covered skin. They looked funny and even loveable. The depictions of the Watchers were cute too.

I turned to look at the terrible drawings of the Lurkers who looked comical.

It was so far off the mark that it may as well not have bothered. Still, the Outsiders lapped it up and I imagined them reading it to their children and sitting it on a shelf between The Gruffalo and The Very Hungry Caterpillar.

"You should see the crap we've been sent in this delivery," Denzil interrupted my thoughts when he returned with a cup of tea for both of us, despite me not wanting one. "One of the things is supposed to be a replica Queens hand as an ashtray. Honestly, I feel embarrassed selling it. It's like that…" I listened as Denzil prattled on and continued turning the pages of the children's book. The last page was just a sentence.

"Be safe and don't go out at night because that's when the magical Crits come out to play!"

I couldn't take anymore. I was sick of inane chatter and sick of the Crits.

I stalked to the counter and smacked my fist onto it, making Denzil jump. "Gabriel wouldn't have just walked out. He wouldn't. Not in a million years."

Denzil sighed. "People do the strangest things when–"

"No!" I shouted, hitting my fist again. "I'm telling you now, he wouldn't have done it. There's been a mistake."

Denzil raised his sad eyes to me. "I'm afraid there's rarely a mistake in cases like this. I'm sorry to be blunt but your boyfriend is dead."

I shook my head. "He wouldn't commit suicide."

"We don't say that here."

"But that's what it is!" I cried, putting my hands on my head and walking away from the counter in exasperation. "A walk out is deliberate and I'm telling you that Gabriel would never do that."

"I'm really sorry, Lib."

"Don't be sorry." I picked up my bag. "I'll see you for my shift on Saturday. Thanks for the lift."

Denzil didn't say anything as I stalked out of the shop and made for home.

***

"You look pretty."

I ignored Dad as I made my way down the stairs in the house. Pretty wasn't really the look I was going for at Gabriel's funeral. I got to the bottom, smoothed down the black shift dress and absently reached my hand up to the back of my head to make sure the tight bun was in place.

Dad cleared his throat and straightened his black tie, looking severely uncomfortable.

"Are you sure you want to go?"

"Of course, I'm going." I looked in the small mirror on the wall at the bottom of the stairs and grimaced at my red, puffy eyes. Since I found out about Gabriel on Monday, I hadn't been back into school and spent the week holed up in my room staring at some goofy Polaroid pictures Gabriel and I took when we were together one day.

Polaroid cameras were popular with loved-up teenagers in Blackbrooke as it meant adults were less likely to see the pictures. Digital cameras meant the images sat on a computer which could easily be accessed and as for taking film to be developed...no way.

My favourite picture was when we'd been lying on the grass

on the school field. Gabriel was holding the camera above us and smiling widely while I nuzzled into his neck with my eyes closed.

It was now Friday and, each day as the horror of the situation sank in, I felt worse.

Dad was understandably worried, and I woke up a few times at night to find him sat at the top of the stairs reading the newspaper. There to stop me if I tried to walk out. He flashed me a wave and a self-conscious smile as I closed the door and climbed back into bed without a word.

Gemma had been round a few times after getting permission from her dad to check up on me. Her punishment was more severe than mine with Mr Jones, not surprisingly, coming down on her like a ton of bricks. No hanging out with friends (unless they were mourning), no television, no music and no pocket money. I couldn't help but think I'd gotten off lightly. She would step into my room silently and spend an hour sitting with me and stroking my hair as I sobbed into my pillow.

I didn't venture in to see Mum. She didn't need to see me like this in her state.

I might have been dreaming but I could have sworn I'd heard her crying over the last few nights. She usually remained silent so I reasoned it was just my imagination. After all, I'd done so much crying that I felt dizzy when I stood up so I wouldn't put my mind past hallucinating.

I picked up the small black clutch bag from the sideboard near the door. "Is Oscar with the neighbours?"

Dad nodded.

"Fine." I took a deep breath. "Let's go then."

We drove to the All Saints Church in silence. This was the church Gabriel and his family attended every week. It was a small, white chapel and I think it must have reminded his mother of Spain because, from what pictures I'd seen on the internet, it had a Mediterranean look to it.

My mouth was dry as I stepped out of the car and spotted Gemma and Noah clutching one another by the door.

"Dad…" I nodded towards them and he gestured for me to go ahead.

I approached slowly, feeling my legs grow weak. There were pupils from the Academy everywhere and some of them turned to stare at me as I walked over. I was starting to realise that my relationship with Gabriel wasn't actually as secret as we both thought it was.

Gemma took one look at me and ran over, pulling me into a tight hug. "I'm glad you're here."

I nodded, managing to prevent the tears from falling.

It was the first time I'd seen Noah since it had happened and he looked terrible.

He was pale and he had large dark circles under his pink, puffy eyes. I pulled away from Gemma and stepped towards him.

"Noah, I'm–" I gasped as he yanked me into a hug and squeezed me tightly. I could hear him crying. "I know," I croaked, rubbing his back. "I know."

He pulled back and rubbed his eyes with his thumb and forefinger. "I can't stop. I don't understand why he did it. I keep thinking about whether it was something I said or did…"

Gemma placed a comforting hand on his arm, tears running down her face.

We all exchanged glances before wrapping our arms around each other, leaning our heads together. We squeezed tightly, not wanting to let one another go.

The sun was shining brightly today which was a welcome change after the dull misty days we were getting used to. It was still bitterly cold though.

"Come on." I pulled back eventually and stood up straight. "Let's go in."

I caught eyes with Dad who was speaking intently to Mr

Jones and he raised a small, sad smile. I gripped the hands of my friends and we walked slowly into the church, our heads bowed.

"I'm not sitting away from you," Noah muttered. "I couldn't give a toss about the boy/girl thing."

"It's okay." I nodded. "I don't think that matters today."

We made our way to the middle of the room and filed into one of the rows.

I caught sight of Gabriel's parents and the twins at the front and closed my eyes, trying not to shed any more tears. Gabriel's mother looked distraught while his dad held onto her, trying to appear composed for the sake of the young twins who, at the age of three, had no idea what was going on.

I felt Gemma's hand grip mine and I wrapped my fingers around it.

I started to feel sick rising up into my throat as the hushed chatter in the church fell silent and the priest stepped to the lectern.

"Please be seated."

"I'm glad there's no coffin," Noah whispered from the other side of me. "I couldn't have coped with that."

My friends were either side of me, pressing in close, as though acting as boulders to hold me up.

"It's a truly sad occasion that brings us all together today," the priest started. "We're here to celebrate the life of Gabriel Vangelis Moretti."

His mum let out a wail and slumped into Dr Moretti.

The priest licked his bottom lip before continuing. "Gabriel was seventeen years old and lived life to the full. He had a keen interest in science and was a talented football player.

"Gabriel was close to his family. His mother Consuela, his father Guilo and his little brother and sister, Frank and Rosa, will sorely miss what they describe as their angel.

"A special mention at the request of Consuela goes to Noah

Hartmann who was Gabriel's best friend since they were small."

Noah choked on a cry and Gemma and I both instinctively reached to him to rub his arm. He looked down and tears fell down his nose and dropped onto the floor.

I took a breath and continued to listen to the priest talk about Gabriel and all of his achievements. It was obvious I wouldn't get a mention as our relationship was practically forbidden but it still hurt, as we were such a big part of each other's lives.

"Gabriel expressed an interest in seeing the world…"

My breath caught in my throat and it was now Gemma and Noah's turn to comfort me.

"He wanted to visit a number of places including Mexico, Australia and, according to a recent conversation with his mother, Greece…"

I felt my chest shake as I tried to take in a breath. Gabriel's mother turned in her seat and we locked eyes. She raised a small smile.

That was it.

That was the secret acknowledgement from Gabriel's parents.

"Thank you," I mouthed to her, my vision blurring from tears.

She nodded and returned facing the front.

I was now sobbing hard and hiccupping.

"Shhh," Gemma soothed, both of her arms around me. "It's okay."

"I need some fresh air." I whispered, feeling dangerously close to having an anxiety attack. I could feel my windpipe constricting and my breathing lost its natural rhythm, my lungs and throat feeling as though they were working against each other.

"I'll come outside with you."

"No," I said quickly. "Stay with Noah…he needs you."

I stood abruptly and edged out. Gemma slid over to him, and took his hand.

I lowered my head as I made my way to the exit, ignoring worried glances from people, including Dad as I hurried past. I pushed the heavy wooden church door open into the brilliant sunlight and gulped in a breath of air. I stood in the doorway for a moment, doubled over at the waist as my breathing regulated itself. There were more tears running down my face which I hadn't noticed.

There's a lot made of heartbreak in poetry, songs and movies but nothing can prepare you for it. It's indescribable, but the closest I can get is that its as though someone had reached into my chest and ripped out my heart. My quickened heart rate hadn't slowed since I found out the news so I constantly felt on the cusp of a heart attack. Food was a no-go too, everything I tried to eat just came back up again. And the black shift dress was a lot looser this time than the last occasion I wore it.

I walked around the side of the church and lowered myself onto one of the benches, staring across the rows of gravestones. I scowled at the sight of several Watchers roaming around outside the fence of the church.

Funerals always attracted them but they couldn't enter the gates of the church. No one knew whether it was a physical impossibility or whether they just respected the boundary in the same way they respected the Blackbrooke boundary.

I closed my eyes and concentrated on getting my breathing under control.

Gabriel would have a plaque in the 'Peace Garden' which was a small fenced off area of the graveyard housing young walk outs.

Children and teenagers.

My heart rate picked up speed again.

I opened my eyes as I felt the weight on the bench shift and glanced in surprise to see Cassius sit down on the other side.

He didn't say anything and we both just looked ahead at the gravestones. He must have been at the funeral service and I hadn't noticed him which is hard to believe as his skin looked especially brilliant white today and almost matched his shirt.

"I'm really sorry," he muttered eventually, leaning forward.

I managed a nod.

"I really liked Gabriel," he said quietly. "He seemed to be the only one who didn't take the mickey out of me."

I didn't say anything.

"Lib?"

I looked at Cassius who'd loosened his tie and untucked his shirt from his black jeans. His odd blue eye looked even brighter in the sun whereas his brown one was dull. "I know you have your friends, but I'm here if you need me."

"Thank you," I said softly. A breeze picked up some leaves in front of us and span them in a tiny cyclone. "I appreciate that, Cassius."

I noticed he was playing with a pen in his hands. I frowned wondering why he'd brought a pen to a funeral but then remembering that I rarely saw him without one, whether he was twirling it around his long white fingers, or resting behind his ear, it was there. "I know what it's like to lose someone you're close to."

I blinked at him. "I was in love with him."

Cassius looked down at the pen. "Yeah…I know."

I nodded, my eyes trance-like. "I don't know what I'll do now."

"Well," he shifted closer, "that's why I'm here for you if you need someone to talk to. It can be tempting to…"

"What?" I snapped. "Walk out? Is that what you're saying?"

Cassius shrugged.

I stood abruptly and brushed down my dress. "You don't need to worry about me when it comes to that."

Cassius stood too and his gangly frame loomed over me.

"That's just it, Lib. I do worry. You've not been in school, you're…"

I raised my eyes to his and he winced.

"You're…a mess."

I felt like I'd been slapped in the face. "Of course, I'm a mess. I've just lost my soulmate. You don't have a clue, Cassius." I shoved past him. "I'll tell you what," I called, walking backwards my arms outstretched, "you fall in love and then experience losing them and you might get an inkling of how I'm feeling."

I stepped straight into my dad who caught me in his arms.

"Lib." He turned me around so I was facing him. "What's the matter? Who are you shouting…"

Dad trailed off as Cassius walked over.

"Hi, Mr Connor."

"Jesus…" Dad whispered, staring in shock. "Cassius?"

Cassius flashed me a look and I folded my arms across my chest hotly. He shook hands with Dad who pulled him into a hug. He stood taller than Dad who looked practically petite in front of him.

"God, I can't believe how much you've grown," Dad beamed. "You're all grown-up. I've not since anything of you since…"

Cassius nodded and Dad looked away awkwardly. "How's your dad?"

"Erm…yeah, he's good." Cassius stuffed his hands into his pockets. "Still works on the market."

"Oh right," Dad sounded surprised. "I've not seen him."

Cassius let out a small laugh. "He looks a bit different these days, no hair."

"Oh," Dad nodded. "Bloody hell, I just can't get over *you* – I never thought you'd turn out such a handsome man."

"Dad!" I hit him on the arm. Despite being annoyed at Cassius, I was not about to hear Dad throw him a backhanded compliment.

"Sorry, Cass," Dad chuckled. "It's just that you were such a funny looking kid."

Cassius laughed heartily and I looked at him, wondering when the last time was that I heard him laugh. Probably when we were about nine years old and I fell out of the tree we were trying to climb. "It's okay, Mr Connor. I've seen pictures of myself. I know what I looked like. I'm amazed I didn't scare Lib off."

I shrugged and tried to hide a smile.

"How's Mrs Connor?" Cassius enquired innocently and I saw a shadow pass over Dad's face. He squirmed. "Oh you know…not good."

Cassius nodded in understanding. "And Oscar?"

"He's great," I jumped in, feeling my heart swell with pride at the mention of my brother. "He's doing really well."

"Good." Cassius smiled. "I've never even met him."

"What?" Dad asked, wide-eyed. "That won't do. Why don't you come round one night for some food? You and your dad? It'll be like old times."

"Oh Dad, I really don't–"

"That'd be great."

Cassius and I looked at one another and Dad's eyes flicked between us.

"Great," Dad said at last. "Shall we say Sunday? Lib can cook a nice roast dinner."

Cassius sniggered at my horrified expression.

"So, Cassius, are you still skateboarding?"

"Not since I was nine." Cassius laughed. "Are you still into fishing?"

"Too right!" Dad exclaimed and I looked around as he launched into a monologue about the sport. I caught sight of Gabriel's mum walking alone around the side of the church.

"Excuse me a moment." I touched Dad's arm.

I felt Cassius' eyes on me as I hurried away in the direction of Consuela. I caught up with her as she knelt next to a grave and frowned as I approached.

"Mrs Moretti?"

She looked up in surprise, and I had to look away as I saw Gabriel's eyes staring back at me. She stood and glanced at the grave. "I don't know that person." She laughed nervously. I'd always loved her Spanish accent. "I just noticed they lived to one hundred years old."

I licked my dry lips and forced a smile.

"I know how my son felt." She stared. "He was very deeply in love with you."

I felt my bottom lip wobble.

"Mama, el amor de mi vida." She laughed and looked up to the heavens, tears falling down her cheeks. "La chica más bella del mundo."

My body started to shake with sadness again.

She pulled me into a hug, stroking my hair. "Pobre chica," she whispered. "Demasiado rápido. No es justo."

"Consuela!" We both turned to see Gabriel's father looking at us both, concerned. He waved for her to join him.

Consuela nodded and took my face in her hands. Her eyes filled with tears again and she whispered so quietly. "Si confesamos nuestros pecados, él es fiel y justo para perdonar nuestros pecados y limpiarnos de toda maldad. Por favor, perdónanos. Por favor, perdónanos."

I shook my head. "I'm sorry, I-I don't understand you."

She took her hands away from my face and walked away.

I could hear her repeating the same words over and over again to herself.

"Por favor, perdónanos...Por favor, perdónanos."

***

"I'm worried about Noah," Gemma whispered as she was lying facing me in my bed.

I opened my eyes and frowned.

"I know I can't be there to keep an eye on him but..." she trailed off and rolled onto her back, staring up at the ceiling. "He's so upset."

I forced a small smile. "Noah won't walk out. He loves you."

"Gabriel loved you." She looked at me.

I rubbed my lips together. "I know...Just try not to think of the worst."

Gemma had taken it upon herself to stay over after the funeral. I knew it was Noah who she wanted to stay with the most. He was the worry. For me too. He'd looked so devastated that day, and we both knew his home life was a mess since his brother and father walked out in recent years. Our friend was definitely in a more emotionally precarious place right now but there was no way our parents would allow a visit. Even after losing Gabriel from our circle of friends, I could still tell in the mannerisms of my dad, and also Mr Jones when I encountered him, that they didn't yet forgive us.

"I've been so worried you're both going to walk." Gemma moved her long blonde hair so she wasn't leaning on it.

"Is that why you're here tonight?" I asked with a smile.

"No," she returned quickly. "I just didn't want to be home alone when my parents are staying with my grandmother for the weekend." She lowered her voice. "I couldn't stomach going with them. My grandmother looks at me like she knows I've had sex. She's worse than a Crit. She can smell it."

I forced a giggle to make her think I believed her excuse. In reality, she, along with my dad, thought I too was going to walk. I just knew it.

"It's a funny old town, isn't it?" Gemma whispered.

"Yes."

"But," she mused, "don't you think there's something beautiful about it? I mean, not the walk out thing or the Crits but..."

I looked at her in interest.

"I just don't think people on the Outside care about each other as much as we do. You, Noah and Gabe…well, that's my family." Her voice broke on the last word and I pulled her into a sideways hug. "Please don't walk out, Lib. I know you love him but…I promise, Noah and I will work really hard to make you happy again."

"I know you will." I smiled, stroking her hair.

"Promise me, Lib," she sniffed. "We'll get a house big enough for the three of us and we'll live together. People will think its weird and that Noah's some kind of bigamist but we'll be happy. You'll never have to be alone, Lib. Just promise me you won't walk."

I kissed her softly on the head and pulled the covers up around her chin like Mum used to do for me when I was a little girl. "I promise."

She nodded. "Good because I swear to God, I'll come looking for you and won't stop until I find every last little piece."

"That's disgusting."

"Well…let it be a warning."

"Okay. Gemma?"

"Mmm-hmm."

"Do you know any Spanish?"

She sighed. "No, I chose French. Don't know why because I don't plan on ever using it."

Gemma turned over and I wrapped my arms around her, spooning her.

Despite how different we both were, Gemma was like my sister. From the moment she waltzed up to me in the playground in primary school section of the Academy and demanded I play with her, I was enraptured. Her confidence and charm never ceased to amaze me and for a long time I felt like her shy, awkward friend.

We were 'school' friends for years as out of school I spent all of my time with Cassius but once I walked through the gates it was all about her.

My role in the friendship slotted more into place the older we got when we balanced one another out. She'd spiral out of control with worry or excitement, whereas I'd think things through and mull it over.

I also acted as a mouthpiece between her and the teachers a lot of the time. Because of all I'd been through with Mum, I'd learned to grow up fast and mature quickly, finding I had more in common with my teachers than fellow pupils most of the time. Gemma was the opposite and, although not afraid of flirting with adults, could never get past the 'us and them' mentality. I would often step between her and a teacher to make apologies for her bad language and inarticulate manner.

There was no doubt about it, Gemma was a firecracker. I smiled as I knew she and Noah would one day get married.

Noah was protective but fun loving and, believe it or not, Gemma had mellowed somewhat since being with him. She certainly didn't have as much of an attitude and wasn't afraid of being open about her feelings anymore.

I looked at her blonde hair spread across the pillow in front of me and smiled.

I ran my fingers through it and could smell the coconut of her favourite shampoo.

In about two days time, the girl who'd just told me she loved me like a family member, would hate my guts.

Yes, I knew it would take Gemma a long time to get over it and I doubted she'd ever really forgive me but I knew what I had to do.

On Sunday night, one week after losing the love of my life, I would be opening the front door of my house and walking out.

Chapter V

I pulled one of the silver trays out of the oven and coughed at the plumes of smoke that came bellowing out.

"Oh no, no, no." I dropped it on the side and used a dish towel to fan the black smoke. As it cleared, I saw my attempt at roast potatoes go well and truly out of the window. The fluffy uncooked spuds I'd lovingly drizzled oil and seasoning over only thirty minutes earlier were now a charred mess. "I don't understand." I coughed from the smoke hanging in the air.

I heard a giggle and looked over at the kitchen table where Oscar was watching me.

"Do you think this is funny?" I pushed my tongue into my cheek to try and hide my smile.

He laughed even harder.

"Right, that's it!"

He squealed as I scooped him up and lay him on the floor, tickling his belly.

"I'm going to blow a raspberry!"

"No!" he cried. "No, Libby!"

I pinned his little arms down gently. "Do you promise to stop laughing at my cooking?"

He shook his head and I lifted up his t-shirt and pressed my lips onto his milky skin while he tried to push me away. "No! It tickles!"

I started laughing and lay on my back trying to recover. Oscar clambered onto me and started trying to tickle me.

"Okay, okay! Stop!" I carried him to sit on the kitchen work surface. "I need your help." I pressed his nose. "I've made a mess of Sunday dinner."

"Are we having chicken?" Oscar asked, running his finger along the flour on the side from my failed attempt at Yorkshire puddings.

I bit my lip. "I'm hoping so. Depends how it turns out."

"Daddy told me to tell you about gibbets."

I eyed my brother. "What are gibbets?"

"Chicken guts."

The penny dropped and I felt my face fall. "Oh my God, the giblets!" I opened the oven door again and quickly pulled out the full chicken. I placed it down and stepped back. "Don't touch it, Osc."

He nodded and balled his hands into fists against his chest.

"Oh damn." I bent down to look at the chicken. "I wonder if I've ruined it."

It was at times like this I really missed Mum being lucid. I was way out of my depth and it annoyed me Dad just assumed I could do things like cook because I was female. Didn't he remember my last attempt at dinner when I almost poisoned us by cooking eggs more than two months out of date?

I grabbed two wooden spoons, flashing Oscar a look. "I'm not proud of what I'm about to do. Whatever you do," I used the spoons to prise apart the backside of the chicken, "don't burn this image of your sister into your brain for eternity."

I peered into the chicken. Sure enough, there was a plastic bag in there. Damnit! I knew this was going to go wrong just as soon as-

"Are you digging for gold?"

"Ahhhhhh!" I let out a rip-roaring scream at the voice right next to my face. I leapt back, holding up the wooden spoons like weapons, pointing them at a startled Cassius.

Oscar began laughing heartily. "Libby! Libby! He went like this…" Oscar put his index finger against his lips. "He-He went like this and said 'shhhhh' so he could creep up on you!"

I was still rooted to the spot as Cassius held his hands out defensively. His odd eyes were wide and I could see a hint of a smile on his lips. "Hi Lib."

"Hi...? Hi? That's all you're going to say when you scare me half to death?!" I slammed the spoons down and placed my hands on my hips.

Cassius looked at Oscar and grimaced. "Think I might be in trouble with your sister."

Oscar nodded knowingly.

"It's not funny," I fumed.

Oscar giggled again.

"Stop it," Cassius said out of the corner of his mouth to Oscar, "you're making it worse."

This made Oscar laugh even more and he clutched at his stomach, starting to become manic.

"Alright, that's enough, you crazy monkey." Cassius bent down so he was on eye level with Oscar. "Nice to meet you, I'm Cassius."

"Casp-ee-us," Oscar tried to repeat, looking unsure.

"Cassius," he laughed.

"Cap-leles."

I pressed my lips together.

"Okay." Cassius flashed me a look before returning to Oscar. "Repeat after me – Ca…"

"Ca.."

"Sea…"

"Ssssea."

"Us."

"Us!"

"Say it together – Ca-sea-us."

"Capsteus."

Cassius let out a loud laugh. "Call me Cass."

"Cass!" Oscar looked triumphant. "Can you get me down? No wait!" Oscar said. "You're big. Lift me up so I can touch the ceiling!"

I smiled and leaned on the counter, watching Oscar make friends. I always marveled at how at ease he was with strangers. I was never like that as a kid. If I hadn't been thrown together with Cassius as a toddler, if Gemma hadn't insisted I play, if Gabriel hadn't passed me the sweet note in the library, I was quite sure I wouldn't have had any friends at all. Oscar on the other hand was one of the most popular kids in his class, according to his teachers at a recent parents evening Dad and I attended.

Cassius lifted Oscar who clamped his tongue between his lips and reached his arm up to touch the ceiling. He then moved him to his hip, and high-fived him. "Good job!"

Oscar frowned. "Your eyes are funny."

"I know."

"What's wrong with them?"

"Oscar," I warned. "That not very–"

"It's okay." Cassius set Oscar down on the kitchen counter again, leaning his on his arms either side. "Well, something happened before I was born that made me like this."

Oscar continued to stare at Cassius, fascinated. "Are you old?"

"I'm the same age as your sister. My hair's just white."

"Only old people have white hair." He scrunched his nose. "You must be old."

"Nope, I'm eighteen. I swear. Look, my skin is white, too."

He rolled up the sleeve of his black jumper and laid his arm flat on the counter. Oscar scooched round and placed his arm down. Usually so milky looking, Oscar's arm looked pink and healthy next to Cassius' snow-white skin.

"Ooh! Is that why you're called Casper?!"

"No, my name's…" He eyed Oscar and shrugged in defeat. "Yeah, why not."

Oscar beamed and picked up his toy again as Cassius wandered over and eyed the spoiled food. "Wow. This looks…"

"A mess." I grimaced. "I can't cook. I don't know what my dad was thinking."

He peered into the tray containing the roast potatoes and turned his attention to the chicken. "What's the problem with that?"

"Giblets."

"Ah." He nodded in understanding. "Doesn't matter, what else do you have?"

I frowned. "Nothing really. There's a dish of vegetarian lasagna that one of the neighbours brought round in the freezer."

"Great," he said brightly. "Let's get to work defrosting that."

"But you were promised Sunday dinner."

"It's fine." He shrugged. "In fact, I hate to be the one to tell you this, but my dad and I don't eat chicken."

"Oh," my eyes widened in surprise, "I'm sorry, I never even thought to ask."

Cassius retrieved the glass dish containing the lasagna from the freezer. "It's okay. I know it's quite rare to not eat white meat but we went through a phase of keeping chickens for the Crits and once you've seen a raw carcass first thing in the morning that's enough."

"I understand." I removed my apron. "Where's your dad?"

Cassius jerked his thumb in the direction of the living room. "Catching up with your dad. It's funny they never stayed in touch. Just shows how much of a role our mums played in the group."

I chewed the inside of my cheek and looked at Oscar, not wanting him to overhear and start asking questions about Mum. I never knew how to answer. "Come on, you." I pulled him off the counter. "Go and sit with Daddy while we finish cooking and introduce yourself to the new guest. Remember how we discussed?"

Oscar stuck out his hand for me to shake.

"Good boy."

I stood back up as Oscar flew out of the room. Cassius was smiling at me. "He's cute."

"Yeah, he's amazing," I sighed, hoping I was playing some small part in how he was turning out. After all, I'd spent the last two years raising him as though I'd given birth to him myself.

"Right, I'm going to put this in the oven on a low heat for about an hour and then we'll have a look at it. So," Cassius turned back, towering over me, "how've you been?"

"Since Friday?" I laughed, moving away. "Erm, okay, I suppose."

"Listen, Lib, I'm really sorry if I insulted you were talking about walking out."

"It's fine." I opened the fridge. "Do you want a drink?"

"Yeah, great."

I threw him a can of coke and we both stood on opposite ends of the kitchen drinking and looking at the floor. We must have looked funny. I'd dressed smartly in a navy blue tea dress with a red trim, as I'd wanted to look presentable for our guests. It was a big deal for Dad to invite anyone round and I wanted to treat the occasion with some respect. Wearing my Sunday best seemed appropriate. I drew the line at shoes though and went barefoot. We were in my house after all, and I was slaving over a hot stove. For a short amount of time anyway.

Cassius, too, was dressed more smartly than I was used to, hinting that it wasn't everyday him and his dad got invited to places. His trademark black jeans were the same but his white shirt with black jumper over the top, complete with skinny black tie, made him look even more grown up than usual.

"Do you speak Spanish?"

"I'm sorry?"

"You." I pointed at him. "Do you speak any Spanish?"

"I'm afraid not. Why do you ask?"

I sighed. "No real reason, just something Gabriel's mum said to me at the funeral." I waved dismissively. "It's nothing."

"Why don't you just Google it?" He eyed me as though I was stupid.

"I have but..." I trailed off, "I can't remember exactly what it was and how to go about spelling it."

"Does it really matter what she said? Wouldn't it have just been the usual? 'Thank you for coming', 'isn't it sad' – that sort of thing?"

I looked away. "You're probably right."

"You seem better," Cassius observed, swigging from the can.

"Yeah, I feel a lot better, thanks."

In truth, I was feeling a combination of excited and scared. Tonight was the night I was going to walk out. I had never been more sure of something in my life and the idea of seeing Gabriel again on the other side was too exciting and heart wrenching to bear.

I'd thought about how exactly I wanted to do it. I was going to go out right at the start of the night because that's when the Hunters were at their most hungry so they were likely to get to me first.

I planned on having dinner with my family and our guests.

Bathe Oscar and put him to bed.

Speak to Mum.

Speak to Dad.

Walk out.

Dad was likely to still be up when I walked but all I had to do was pull the door open and bolt into the night.

And then it would be over.

All of the pain and anguish I'd felt over the last week would be over, and Gabriel and I would finally be free.

"Lib?" I blinked to see Cassius eyeing me. "Are you okay? You seemed miles away."

"I'm fine." I smiled, not meeting his eye.

I knew I had to be on the charm offensive today so as not to arouse suspicion. In the same way I'd had to look Gemma in the eye and make her a promise I didn't intend to keep.

As long as no one suspected anything, I was fine.

"You're going to walk out."

"What?!" I jumped away from Cassius who'd moved closer to me. "No, I'm not."

He pointed. "It's written all over your face, Lib."

"Cassius." I grabbed his finger and threw his arm to the side. "Please stop pretending you know who I am. We didn't even speak again until a couple of days ago."

He frowned. "I know you."

"No." I shook my head and lowered my voice. "You don't. You know nothing about me and do you know why?"

He raised an eyebrow.

"Because," I prodded him in the chest, "we were friends when we were children and then I moved on. I mean, I practically agreed to marry Gabriel. I-I've grown up. We talked about travelling and children and–"

"He walked out! He can't have cared about a future with you that much!" Cassius bellowed in my face.

I reached up and slapped him hard and he winced at the impact, raising his hand to his cheek. "How dare you, Cassius Godwin."

"Libby?"

We both turned in horror to see Oscar stood in the doorway, biting his fingers.

"Oh God," I moaned. "Oscar, I'm sorry I…"

He ran back out crying loudly.

"Oscar?" Dad called in concern from the living room.

"Shit." I exhaled, my cheeks pink. I looked back up at Cassius, his expression unreadable.

Dad came into the kitchen holding a crying Oscar who pointed at me. "Libby hit Casper."

I closed my eyes.

"We were just fooling around." Cassius let out a laugh. "We were playing a game and I said something rude and she hit me…that's what Oscar saw." He nodded at me. "Isn't that right, Lib?"

"Yes," I said eventually.

Dad turned his head to Oscar. "See? It's nothing bad. And it's Cassius, not Casper, young man." He looked at me, unimpressed. "How's dinner coming along? That chicken doesn't look anywhere near cooked."

"Change of plan. I ruined the food."

"It burned," Oscar declared, looking pleased as punch.

Dad turned to leave. "Just as long as there's something."

I sighed and felt Cassius' eyes burning into me.

"I'm going to say hello to your dad," I announced, turning on my heel. "Don't mention Gabriel to me again. In fact, don't even speak to me."

"No problem," I heard him mutter as I was already out of the door.

***

The dinner turned out to be quite pleasant, all things considering. I tried to push 'last supper' thoughts from my head throughout and, after an hour of avoiding each other's eyes, Cassius and I even managed some brief interaction.

Dad and Phil howled laughing at the memory of us trying to climb trees when we were little. Apparently, it was highly amusing to anyone observing. Me, surveying the tree and deciding whether it was too dangerous to attempt, and Cassius, too small and feeble to make it to the first branch.

I'd laughed heartily and occasionally glanced at Cassius when I knew he wasn't looking. It wasn't surprising the kids at school still hounded him for his appearance. The white hair was one thing but it was the white eyebrows and eyelashes that made him look alien. And his odd eyes made it difficult to focus when you spoke to him. It was like your own eyes got confused and darted between the blue and brown, unsure of where to settle.

In spite of these differences, Dad was right. He'd turned out to be really quite handsome. It was sad that people were quick to point out his unusual features without acknowledging just how striking he was. He was easily the tallest boy in the Academy and his smile was enough to light up a stadium. I'd never noticed his dimples when he was little. Probably because he was so skinny there was no fat on his face to highlight them but since he'd filled out ever-so-slightly, they were quite prominent.

On the occasions I'd be chatting away with Dad and Phil, I'd catch him stealing glances at me too. No doubt weighing me up, probably smug that I never grew tall like him. When I grew tired of his eyes on me, I'd deliberately and abruptly include him in the conversation, causing him to jump and quickly avert his eyes.

I was shocked at the sight of his father, Phil. He'd changed so much since the last time I saw him. When our parents used to hang out together, he was the life and soul of the party and used to make me explode into fits of giggles. He'd always reminded me of a rock star, with his long hair and trademark jeans and matching denim jacket. He'd play his guitar for Cassius and I and we'd sing and dance along. I always thought of him as one of the cool adults.

However, he no longer resembled that person. He was a broken shell of a man. He'd lost all of his hair, his unique style and his confident swagger. He sat in front of me like someone who sold insurance with his beige trousers and short-sleeved pin stripe shirt. I noticed his hand shook as he raised a fork to his mouth and wondered whether his nerves were shot to pieces after experiencing the loss of his daughter and then his wife.

Cassius and his father left shortly after we finished eating and I accepted an awkward embrace from both of them as they shuffled out of the door. I think Cassius was still suspicious of a potential walk out but I forced a bright smile and busied myself fussing over Oscar to make it look as though I was far too happy to do such a thing. Plus, I actually did have fun. It beat the usual night in with Dad and I staring at the TV while I brought him a beer at regular intervals until he fell asleep.

Once they'd left, I bathed Oscar and put him in bed as usual. The excitement of the day had clearly taken its toll on the little boy as he fell asleep before I could finish reading his bedtime story.

I'd sat with him for several moments longer than usual, stroking his hair and whispering my apologies.

You'll be fine, I kidded myself, smiling down at him. One day, when you fall in love, you'll understand.

He wouldn't, of course. He'd probably hate me for a really long time for leaving him alone with a useless father and comatose mother.

Or perhaps me walking out would be the wake up call Mum needed.

All I knew was that I had to walk out that night.

"Are you going to wash the dishes?" Dad asked, as I walked through the living room carrying several plates from the dining table.

"Yeah sure."

I placed the plates down on the counter and let out a shaky breath. A mundane conversation with Dad was good. It meant he wouldn't suspect anything untoward.

I glanced at the back door and bit my lip.

Now?

"Lib?"

I closed my eyes. "Yes, Dad?"

"Can you bring me a beer in?"

I took another longing look at the back door before retrieving a beer for him. I headed back into the living room and handed it to Dad before settling in my usual spot on the sofa. My heart was pounding and I was starting to feel sick.

I picked up a magazine and began flipping through it before throwing it back down when I realized my hands were shaking too much.

"Nice night," Dad declared.

I looked up. "Yes, it was."

We were quiet for a moment and stared at the TV showing a cheesy game show of some sort.

"It was good seeing Phil."

I smiled naturally, despite my nerves. "You should make more of an effort to see one another."

Dad nodded slowly. "You and Cass seemed to be getting on."

I shrugged. "I suppose so."

"Your mum thought you two would get married." He looked pained. "She wanted you to anyway."

I rolled my eyes in exasperation. "I was planning to marry Gabriel."

Dad's mouth turned up into a sad smile. "I know, sweetheart."

I closed my eyes and took a breath so deep that it hurt my lungs.

"I'm going to wash the dishes." I was trying to sound nonchalant, but I feared my voice didn't sound like my own anymore. It was strangled, like when you get an air bubble trapped in your throat.

Dad nodded and I stood, feeling the temptation to hug and squeeze him hard but I knew that would arise suspicion. I placed my hand on the back of his armchair to steady myself.

I'd purposely not been in work that weekend in case the sight of all of the Crit memorabilia made me chicken out. Also, I wasn't sure I'd be able to say goodbye to Denzil.

Despite the age difference and the fact he irritated the hell out of me most of the time, I'd grown close to him over the years. In a weird way, I probably trusted Denzil the most out of everyone I knew. There was no real reason for it, only that if I told him something, I knew for a fact he wouldn't tell another soul. I loved Gemma but part of me wondered how much she told Noah. She was an open-book so I presumed it was most things. My confidence in Denzil was partly because he had no friends or family granted, but still, I confided in him a lot. Always in a light hearted sort of way so as not to freak him out or make him feel uncomfortable. He was like my living breathing diary that I could rant and rave at whenever I needed to. He wasn't judgmental either, which made me feel ashamed of myself when I lectured him about his dependence on marijuana. However, I'm quite sure Denzil would have been hopping mad at the thought of me walking out.

"It's a coward's game," he'd spit, whenever news of a walk out would reach us.

I pressed my teeth together and leaned in the doorway of the kitchen, eyeing the back door.

The door wasn't a problem.

In Blackbrooke, we had to lock the doors and close the blinds, and that was it. The Crits couldn't get in and wouldn't even try. It's just not the way they worked and had been that way for centuries.

All I had to do was twist the key in the lock and then undo the top and bottom bolt, press down the handle and I was out.

Simple.

I walked slowly to the door.

"Think about Gabriel," I whispered to myself. "The sooner you get out, the sooner you'll see him again."

I took one last look over my shoulder, satisfied Dad was rooted in his seat for at least half an hour until he drained the contents of his can. He wouldn't notice I was gone until then. He'd think I was washing the dishes. I debated whether or not to turn on the tap to make it really convincing but I decided against it.

I was fine. He wouldn't come looking.

I'd put on a good show over the weekend and when I didn't go into work on Saturday, Dad and I took Oscar to the park and chatted about a number of inane subjects. He'd come away looking relieved I was 'back to normal'.

The guilt I felt wasn't as bad as I thought.

As soon as I got a flash of guilt, I thought of Gabriel.

Leaning his forehead against mine.

Rubbing my cheeks with his thumbs.

And that smile.

His walk out was still a mystery as he'd always seemed so happy, but I tried not to think about his motives. Instead, convincing myself Gemma could be right, that he was actually on his way to see me in a feverish moment. After all, I didn't know what his parents said to him after the debacle at the Joneses' house. Maybe they'd forbid him from ever seeing me again and that was enough to cause him to run. Maybe he was mid-argument and stalked out of the house without thinking about it. The truth was, I'd never know until I walked myself and found him on the other side. That would be my first question to him for sure.

I reached onto my tiptoes and carefully slid the top bolt on the back door across easily. I swallowed and knelt down. The bottom bolt would sometimes be difficult to move. I gripped my bottom lip with my teeth, wiggling the bolt slowly up and down to try and free it.

"Come on," I breathed, looking at the pressure points on my fingers going white from tension. "Please don't do this."

The bolt suddenly jerked open with a bang and I stood up abruptly, wincing and waiting for Dad to shout. I didn't dare to breathe, listening to the distant sound of the television from the living room.

The studio audience laughed at something the inane host

said.

I eventually exhaled and looked back at the door. The key was already in the lock.

Perhaps another indication Dad trusted me not to walk.

I slowly wrapped my fingers around the cold metal key and pushed against the wooden door at the same time as turning it.

"Come on, Lib," I whispered.

Free as a bird.

I nodded to myself and pressed the handle down, pulling the door open with a shaking hand. Before I could think about it too much, I slid outside and closed the door behind me.

My eyes were closed and my whole body was juddering.

What surprised me was how much colder it was outside. It took my breath away. I slowly opened my eyes and looked out across the garden.

It was nothing I'd ever seen before and no amount of movies or images could prepare me for what the nighttime looked like. I stared up, mesmirised at the moon. It was full and bright.

Brilliant white against a dark purple sky.

I felt my mouth open in wonder at the sight. I blinked several times and, as my eyes adjusted, I saw them.

Hundreds of tiny sparkling dots in the sky. Twinkling stars.

My eyes welled with tears and I let out a laugh, clamping my hand over my mouth.

"It's beautiful."

A slight breeze rustled through the trees and I took a tentative step down one of the stone stairs to the garden. I looked around me, savouring the moment, expecting to be bowled off my feet at any second by a Crit.

"Is this why you did it, Gabriel?" I outstretched my arms and leaned my head back.

Several leaves blew around my feet.

I couldn't get over the beauty of the sky. It was like looking directly into space. I had absolutely no idea it would look like that. I thought all images I'd seen had been enhanced in some way. I mean, there was no way you could actually see the stars.

But here they were in all their glory.

It was breathtaking.

The cold night air caused goosebumps to rise up all over my body.

I blinked and looked around me.

As beautiful as it was, I was surprised I wasn't dead yet. Perhaps it was unrealistic to expect the Crits to be roaming around my garden waiting for a walk out.

I looked back at the house.

There was a chance, if Dad realised what I'd done, that he'd open the door and drag me back in. If that happened there would be no chance I'd get the opportunity again.

No I had to get away from the house, and quickly.

I felt like my knees were knocking together as I shivered on the spot.

"Come on, Lib," I willed myself. "Move yourself."

I engaged my legs and edged quickly around to the front of the house.

The beauty of the night was one thing but what shocked me was how disorientating everything seemed. Even my house that was so familiar looked strange.

I moved to the front and walked down our path, onto the street.

My street consisted of a cluster of semi-detached houses facing into one another on a cul-de-sac. I was used to seeing the street alive with people coming and going but now I could barely see my hand in front of my face and the other houses were merely shadowy shapes.

On the Outside, the streets were lit with lamps which I always thought was quaint. However, I now realised how necessary it must have been.

A cloud shifted from over the moon and its white light returned, illuminating the large patch of grass in the centre of the cul-de-sac.

I started walking towards it, my head bowed.

A bird flew from one of the nearby trees and I gasped at how loud the sound echoed around the street.

I strode to the centre of the triangular patch of grass and lowered myself down onto my knees. Even though it hadn't been raining, the grass felt moist and I moved so I was lying down, flat on my back staring up at the stars.

The bun I was wearing made it uncomfortable so I reached round and slowly pulled out the bobble, letting my hair loose around me. It made me feel naked.

I closed my eyes and licked my lips, waiting.

"Just hurry up and happen." I frowned.

I'd played on this patch of grass hundreds of times as a child with Cassius when his mum used to come round and visit on Sunday afternoons for a coffee.

I remembered one particular day picking daisies to make a chain just as Gemma had taught me when we were both eight years old.

***

"What are you doing?" Cassius scowled.

I looked up at him, shielding my eyes from the sun. "Daisy chains. Come here."

He reluctantly sat down and leaned his chin on his hand, tearing out clumps of grass. "That's boring."

"No, it isn't." I frowned, carefully piercing the stem of one of the daisies with my thumbnail, tongue sticking out of my mouth in concentration. "Here." I scooted closer to him. "I'll show you. We'll decorate my hair."

"Bor-ing," he sighed.

Determined, I made Cassius learn how to make the perfect

daisy chain and he even let me put one around his head. We then had the bright idea to make the world's longest daisy chain.

We painstakingly spent hours making a chain that stretched from one end of the grass to the other.

"Okay!" I shouted to Cassius stood on the other side, cupping my hands over my mouth. "Be gentle when you pick it up!"

"We can't stretch it!" He shouted back. "Just lift up your end and let it stay on the floor in the middle!"

"Then what's the point in lifting it?!"

I spotted my dad walking towards the house, carrying his large medical bag along with his flask of coffee he took to work with him. I waved. "Daddy, come and look at this!"

Dad smiled widely and started making his way across the grass. He was wearing his trademark uniform of grey trousers and white shirt, finished off with the obligatory lab coat, which would go straight into the washing machine as soon as he stepped through the door.

Like clockwork.

It was ten years ago, and Dad was young and handsome. It was before everything started to unravel with Mum.

He removed his black-framed glasses and inspected the daisy chain, walking along the length of it. "What's she had you doing today eh, Cass?" he chuckled, rubbing his chin.

Cassius shrugged and ran his hand down the front of his overgrown, white hair awkwardly.

"Daddy, can you pick it up in the middle?" I called, nodding my head excitedly.

Dad sighed and placed his bag and flask down. "If I break this then don't cry, Lib."

"I won't," I shot back sulkily.

"Ready?" Cassius called.

I nodded.

"Daddy?" I stamped my foot.

"Sorry," Dad held up his hand apologetically, "I'm ready."

"Three... two... one..."

I giggled as we gently lifted the daisy chain which made a letter 'W' where Dad was holding it in the middle. "It's got to be a world record!"

Dad laughed. "Got to be. Are you done with it now?"

I placed it down and walked to join Dad, inspecting the handiwork stretching across the grass. "I think we should keep going and try and connect my house with yours," I said to Cassius who scampered over.

"That's a great idea." Dad ruffled our hair and retrieved his bag and flask. "Then you'll always find your way."

"Even in the dark?" Cassius enquired innocently, bending down to tie his shoelace.

"No." Dad shook his head and turned away to walk back to the house. "Never in the dark."

***

My eyes flicked open.

Dad.

If a Crit got me here then he'd be sure to find pieces of me strewn across this very lawn I used to play on as a child. All of the laughs, the games of football with him and Cassius, the frog hunting we used to do in the spring. All ruined and remembered from then on as the place his only daughter was killed.

Would he have to clean up pieces of me?

I sat up abruptly and looked around. There was still nothing I could see.

Nor could I hear anything.

The butterflies in my stomach were starting to get worse as I hadn't appreciated I'd be waiting so long. I picked myself up from the grass and glanced down the road.

I needed to get as far away as possible.

"I'll just run," I whispered as another light breeze whipped my hair into my face. "The Crits will hear me if I run."

I skidded on the grass as I started to bolt down the street, my breathing instantly becoming shallow and rising in thick mist into the air. The sound of my ballet pumps slapping onto the tarmac road echoed around the houses making a strange distorted noise that sounded like the bark of a dog.

Perhaps it's the Hunters, I thought glancing over my shoulder as I left the street.

I stopped when I reached the main road into the town.

Blackbrooke had one road in and one road out as you would imagine, and it was the same road I was stood on last week when the Watcher found me. It was lined with trees which arched so the branches joined together at the tips, as though holding hands.

I placed my hands on my head as I glanced up and down the road, debating which direction would be best.

The trees shook in the wind which whistled through the branches. Dry leaves scraped across the road behind me causing me to jump.

I looked down, now wishing I'd worn an outfit I actually liked. After all, I wouldn't have a real funeral so my dad wouldn't be able to dress my body nicely. After dinner, I'd changed out of my blue dress into my favourite jeans and a white vest with a large brown jumper over the top. The jumper used to be my dad's.

"You're probably scaring the Crits off with your terrible dress sense," I muttered to myself as I continued to glance up and down the road.

I was perplexed. I thought a Hunter wouldn't even allow me to step off the doorstep of the house before it devoured me.

"You will eat me, you damn Crits," I whispered before breaking into a run. I bolted down the dark road, which took a bend to the left. I glanced over my shoulder, thinking I heard a noise and when I returned my eyes to the front, I stopped abruptly.

“Oh my God.” I placed my hand over my mouth.

Watchers.

Hundreds of them.

Sat covering the road.

Some lying, some sitting, some standing. Others awkwardly cleaning and gnawing at their blood-matted fur and exposed flesh.

Still covering my mouth, I stepped backwards slowly, trying not to make any sound.

Don’t see me, I thought. Please don’t see me.

If the Watchers spotted me then they’d alert the Queens. They were the Queens messengers first and foremost. That was the worst kind of Crit I could come across. No one knew what the Queens did to their victims but some reports suggested death was slow and torturous, likening them to witches with broths and potions. No one really knew anything for sure, and there were no volunteers out there brave enough to find out.

I cursed the Hunters and the Lurkers for clearly choosing not to frequent this part of the town tonight. Why was it that I ran into a Hunter during the day, next to a busy field, whereas now I was out during their time and there wasn’t a single one to be seen? Maybe I just wasn’t to their taste. After all, the Hunter didn’t eat me that day in the woodland. Perhaps they were all watching me as I stood in the pitch black, edging away from the Watchers, wondering how long it would be before I gave up and went home.

Liberty Connor, not only did her boyfriend walk out but the Crits don’t even want her either.

One of the Watchers near to the front of the pack yawned and curled into a ball, licking its mouth and closing its eyes.

I took another step back onto something that felt a lot like a foot.

I let out a whimper. “This is it.”

I whirled around expecting to see the red eyes of a Queen staring back at me but I didn’t.

Instead the eyes were the familiar ones of Cassius.

I gaped at him in shock and he looked over my shoulder at the Watchers.

"Holy shit," he breathed.

My lips tried to form words. "What are you…"

A hissing noise sounded and we turned to see a Watcher stood about a foot from us, staring with dull red eyes. Its tail twitched.

I shook my head at it. "Shhhhh, there's a good–"

"I don't think that's going to work," Cassius whispered.

The Watcher sat down and raised its head to the sky, letting out the loudest, high-pitch scream I'd ever heard in my life. I clamped my hands over my ears.

All of the Watchers looked up from their spot on the road and narrowed their ruby eyes as they started to advance on us.

"Come on!" Cassius grabbed my hand and bolted down the street, around the Watchers and towards the centre of the town.

I looked over my shoulder to see them trotting after us, like hungry cats with their tails pointing up in the air.

Several sat down and screamed into the night.

"They're calling the Queens!" Cassius said, through gritted teeth. "We need to move!"

I ran as fast as I could, still clutching his hand.

"Quick, here!" He pulled me down the side of two of the towns shop buildings and we crouched down next to a skip. Our breathing shallow, we listened to the sound of the Watchers screams echoing into the night. Cassius was glaring at me, his brow furrowed. "I knew you were going to do this tonight."

My chest was burning from the run and the cold air in my lungs. "Why are you out here?"

His frown deepened. "Looking for you."

I sucked my cheeks in annoyance. "That's the most stupid thing I've ever heard in my life. Now we'll both die."

Cassius peered around the skip and then leaned back against the wall. "We need to try to get in somewhere."

I let out an unamused laugh. "Oh yeah? Where? Who the hell is going to let us in? Anyway, I don't want anyone to let me in. I walked out."

"Lib!" Cassius grabbed my shoulders and shook me. "Are you stupid? The Hunters and Lurkers will be feeding on the cattle for the next hour."

I stared at him, surprised at his anger. Not used to feeling his hands on me. When we were children, it was always me dragging him away from trouble and pointing in his face when he did something silly.

"The Queens walk the streets at the start of the night. Haven't you listened to anything in Blackbrooke class?"

My eyes searched his face and I shook my head slowly. "That's not right."

"Yes, it is!" He shook me again. "Is this what you want? Do you want the Queens to take you?"

We both looked around the skip at the sound of something scrapping across the floor.

It was a can blowing along the road in the wind.

We sat back in relief.

"I-I didn't know…" I looked away, feeling flustered. "I thought a Hunter…"

"No." Cassius leaned and looked out again. "Not for another forty minutes. And we'll have been taken before then."

I placed my palms on my forehead, rubbing it in exasperation.

"Now, I'm going to say it again – we need to try and get in somewhere."

I nodded, feeling truly afraid for the first time all night.

A loud scream ripped through the air and we exchanged terrified glances.

"It's too late," I cried, starting to panic. Forgetting to try and remain calm and strong in front of Cassius. "They're here."

Cassius' frightened expression was replaced with a shot of determination. "It's not over till it's over."

I heard another scream and made a move to look around the bin but Cassius grabbed my face in both of his hands. "Lib, listen. We need to just run."

I shook my head and looked away. Feeling tired all of a sudden.

"Lib!" Cassius moved my head so I was forced to look at him. "Come on, you're better than this."

"I want to die," I said, defeated. "I want the Hunters to–"

"Well, you can't," he snapped. "If you'd have waited a bit longer then…maybe. But not now."

I exhaled slowly and nodded.

He was right. It was either a slow, painful Queen-related death or we at least tried to run for our lives.

"If we run out into the street and head for my house we'll only have to run away from them for half a mile." He had a pained look on his face. "We might just make it."

I glanced around the skip and saw a shadow loom on the road and popped my head back quickly. "Wait a minute," I whispered. "Tales from the Crits is just across the street."

Cassius frowned.

"I work there." I nodded to explain. "Denzil, my boss, lives in a flat over the top. We can knock."

"He'll never answer the door."

"We don't know if we don't try," I said quickly. "We've more chance of Denzil letting us in than we have trying to out-run Crits for half a mile..."

Cassius buried his chin in his scarf.

"I think that's the only option," I said.

"Fine." He looked at me again. "Stay with me. Don't let go of my hand. If they make a grab for you, they'll take me as well."

In a feverish moment I almost laughed out loud at his seemingly brave words. He actually sounded like he meant them. "Vice versa."

"Yeah, sure," he said unconvincingly. "Are you ready? Let's go!" He grabbed my hand and pulled me to my feet. "Run!"

We bolted down the alley and back onto the street, which was bathed in bright white moonlight.

"Cassius!" I screamed and we both stopped, rooted to the spot.

We looked down the street, unable to tear our eyes away from the shadowy figures advancing towards us. They moved so fluidly they appeared to float off the ground, their long gowns of grey skin billowing behind them.

"Oh my God," I breathed.

The Queens.

There were a lot of them and they seemed so much taller than the six feet they were reported to be in books. Their necks were long and curled into an 'S' shape, like a vulture. Their heads were small with huge exaggerated features. The eyes were black with pinpricks of red and shaped like long feathers on either side of their head. Their mouths gaped open grotesquely. They pressed their hands together, as though in prayer, as they moved towards us slowly.

One cocked its head to one side, its long stringy hair falling onto its hunched shoulder.

Cassius stepped in front of me instinctively and pushed me back. "Run," he whispered over his shoulder. "Run while I distract them."

I glanced at Tales from the Crits, which was no more than thirty feet away from where we were standing. I looked back at the Queens who were getting closer by the second.

"We can both make it," I breathed.

Cassius locked frightened eyes with me and nodded. Despite how grown up he was now, I recognised that flash of panic from when we were children and he was frightened. I immediately started to run, my hand clasped around his tightly, pulling him towards the shop.

"They've stopped!" he called to me. "They've stopped coming."

"Then we might stand a chance," I called back to him. "Come on!"

We reached the door of the shop and I instantly started to hammer on it with such force that I saw the blinds on the other side of the glass shake.

"Denzil!" I screamed, hammering again. "Denzil, it's Lib, let me in!"

Cassius, still holding my other hand, was staring at the Queens who were in the same spot, staring back at us. I looked over at them between knocks and saw them all raise an arm and point a long, bony finger in our direction.

"Oh God!" I cried. "Denzil!" I choked, smacking the palm of my hand against the door. "Denzil, please!" Tears were now running down my face.

"They're coming," Cassius declared, sounding eerily calm. "Here we go."

I felt his arms wrap around me and we sank down on the spot. "No," I whispered into his chest, now not caring this was a boy I was no longer friends with. Not caring it was me who should be protecting him as I always used to, now just letting him envelope me in his arms.

I dared to look up and saw the Queens surrounding us, heads cocked in different directions. Now they were close I saw little red dots were their whole eye, the surrounding black was a gaping hole in their skulls. Their mouths hung about a foot open and they had thick, grey tongues that looked like oversized slugs, flicking around their mouths.

I squeezed my eyes shut again, waiting.

The door we were leaning against suddenly flew open and we slumped into the doorway of Tales from the Crits, onto the feet of Denzil.

"What the…" He took in at our startled faces before a look of horror and realisation passed over his features and he slowly raised his head to see the Queens' ghastly faces looming down. "Shit!" he shouted and grabbed the collar of my jumper, dragging me in while Cassius scrambled in on his hands and knees. Denzil slammed the door shut with force as though against a strong gust of wind and leaned himself against it. His whole body juddered as the Queens started to kick and hit at the door, their deafening screams piercing through the air.

Cassius sprang into action and pushed against the door, leaning his palms against it.

I stood and wrapped my arms around my middle, shaking from head to toe, watching Denzil and Cassius battle against the door, unable to move to help them.

"Stop!" Denzil shouted, turning his head towards the door to address the Queens.

Cassius was gritting his teeth from the strain of the door that looked as though it was about to buckle.

"I don't come into the woodland so you don't get to come in here!" Denzil bellowed.

The banging subsided and we put our hands over our ears to block out the sound of piercing screams as the Queens realised their efforts were in vain.

Denzil let out a shaky breath and placed his hands on his loose dreadlocks. I saw he was wearing baggy patterned pyjama bottoms and a holey white t-shirt as though he'd just got out of bed. He swallowed and slowly opened his horrified eyes to stare at me. "What. The hell. Was that?"

Cassius moved from the door and stood next to me as I eyed the floor. "I don't know."

"What on earth were you doing outside?" he demanded, flashing a look at Cassius. "Both of you."

I couldn't meet the eye of my friend, feeling ashamed. "I-I was going to walk out."

"What?" Denzil folded his arms, looking disgusted. "You?

Jesus Christ, Lib…" He looked at Cassius through narrowed eyes. "Is this some kind of pact? Who are you anyway?" He advanced on him menacingly. Cassius remained rooted to the spot and stared right back. "Did you put her up to this?"

"No!" I stepped forward and pushed Denzil back gently. "Cass was…Cass, he…"

"I was trying to stop her." Cassius stepped forward to Denzil. "I suspected she was going to do it so I went to find her."

Denzil rubbed between his eyebrows. "You're both stupid. You should be dead now."

I looked at my feet, bright pink from the cold in my pink ballet pumps which were now damp and dirty.

"How did you manage to escape without getting eaten?" he asked, looking from one to the other. "Seriously, how?"

Cassius shrugged, shifting to remove his grey woollen coat and black scarf, revealing an outfit of black jeans and a black jumper. "The Hunters are feeding on the cattle at this time…" He scowled. "Am I the only one who knows that?" He pointed at me. "You need to start listening in Mr Fuller's class, or read the book."

I squeezed my teeth together and felt my cheeks flush pink, annoyed at myself for not knowing a piece of vital information from a class I gained straight A's in.

Denzil was still shaking his head in disbelief. "Those Queens would have strung you up and tortured you for days. What if I hadn't been here? What then?"

I could feel myself start to get angry at the constant shouting.

Cassius shrugged. "We'd have been taken."

"Too right!" Denzil spluttered, letting out a laugh. "Of course you would! And all because Liberty Bell over here can't get over her boyfriend."

My head snapped up. "What?"

"You!" He stalked behind the counter. "The boyfriend

walks out and all of a sudden it's loves greatest tragedy and bloody…Juliet over here needs to end it all."

My cheeks now felt like they were scorching and I chewed the inside of my mouth.

"I mean, what the hell is your dad going to be thinking now? Were you even thinking about your brother in all of this? Isn't he about–"

"Enough!" I screamed, causing Denzil to jump. "Enough. I can't take anymore." I turned my head towards Cassius who stared back at me innocently. I now felt irrationally angry. "You."

"Me?" Cassius pointed at himself.

"You've ruined everything," I breathed, feeling my whole body quivering. "How dare you come out tonight trying to 'save' me. Just who do you think you are?" I strode over and jabbed him in the chest. "Do I look like a person who needs to be saved?"

He grabbed my hand, which was still prodding him after every syllable. "Yes, you do."

"Rubbish!" I spat. "You had no right to come out tonight!"

"You're my friend!" He leaned down so his face was at a level with mine. "You saved me more than a few times when we were kids. I care about you, Lib and–"

"We're not friends!" I screamed and he recoiled. "We're not friends anymore, Cassius! You hate me. My friends make your life hell. Tonight, I wanted to be with Gabriel and you should have let me!"

"He's dead!" he shouted. "Gabriel Moretti is dead and you need to accept it!"

I turned and picked up the first thing that came to hand which happened to be a snow globe with a Lurker figurine inside and, without thinking, hauled it at Cassius with a strangled scream. He ducked and it hit the wall behind, shattering into thousands of tiny pieces.

"Hey!" Denzil shouted from behind the counter, half

crouching in shock. "Not the merchandise!"

I picked up a Queen ornament and held it up, ready to throw at Cassius as we both circled around one another.

"You're nuts!" Cassius bellowed. "You're just as crazy as the day I met you. Chasing those kids around the sandpit that were calling me names."

"I'm not crazy!" I threw the ornament, which ricocheted off his arm and crashed onto the floor with a smash. "I'm angry!"

"Oh Christ," Denzil rubbed his temples and turned away, "I can't watch."

"Oh yeah?" Cassius raised his eyebrows and let out a mocking laugh. "You're not crazy, eh? Then what about that other time when you pulled on that girl's hair until she screamed all because she didn't choose me to play on her team?"

"Shut up!" I cried, picking up a glass paperweight with a replica Hunter tooth embedded inside.

"Or," Cassius circled the postcard turnstile with me around the other side, trying to get a clear shot, "the time when you threw a rock at Jacob Sterling on the school field because he pushed me off the slide?"

"I told you!" I hauled the paperweight which hit the wooden panelling on the counter with a loud bang, making a dent. "*That* was an accident!"

"Four stitches in his head!" Cassius' eyes flashed in what looked like feverish excitement. "When you hit Kat Culshaw's older brother with that wooden hammer you found in your dad's toolkit because he dared to ask why my eyes were different colours!"

"AHHHH!" I screamed and pushed the postcard turnstile onto him. He dodged it and it clattered onto the floor, sending the postcards scattering in different directions.

"That's it!" Denzil shouted, his hands cupped over his mouth. "Seriously, what the hell's going on here?!"

Cassius and I eyeballed each other, while I stood with my hands balled into fists at my sides. Cassius straightened his jumper and ran a shaking hand through his hair. He lowered his voice to a whisper. "I left my dad tonight so that I could come and find you because I wanted to have *your* back for once. I suppose a thank you is too much to ask, but you don't need to attack me."

I tore my eyes away from him, suddenly feeling embarrassed.

Maybe I was crazy after all.

Denzil looked with what can only be described as fear in his eyes. "Now I'm not surprised the Crits left you alone. You're a nut."

I slowly felt my lips curl into a smile and let out a laugh. Cassius shook his head and sniggered to himself.

"Well, I'm glad you find it funny," Denzil sighed, trying to look serious. "I'll be taking the cost of the damages out of your wages." He looked at Cassius. "I'm Denzil by the way."

Cassius strode over and shook his hand. "Cassius Godwin."

"Pleased to meet you…I think. Any friend of Lib's and all that…"

I stared at the broken slow globe. "My dad's never going to forgive me for tonight."

"Mine won't," Cassius muttered.

"And they bloody shouldn't!" Denzil spluttered. "I don't think *I'll* ever forgive you for this, Miss Liberty Bell."

"Sorry and…" I smiled self-consciously, "thanks for answering the door. And," I turned to Cassius, "I'm sorry about going mental. I just want to say…thank you, for coming to look for me."

Cassius scratched the back of his neck. "It's fine."

"Right then," Denzil clapped his hands together, "tea?" He frowned at Cassius and pointed to his own dreadlocks. "How do you keep up with the roots, mate? Bet that takes some dedication."

Cassius raised a questioning eyebrow.

"The hair." Denzil nodded. "The bleach."

I saw the merest hint of pink creep onto Cassius' pale cheeks. "No, I don't dye it. It's my…natural colour."

"Oh?" Denzil looked surprised. "Right…well, erm…tea?"

I watched Denzil disappear upstairs to the flat before turning back to Cassius. "I mean it, Cass. I'm…grateful."

"I know you're probably not." He looked away. "You wanted to be dead tonight."

I gulped at the finality of the words when they were spoken by someone else.

It would have been *my* assembly in school tomorrow.

"Lib?"

I looked up. "Yes."

He licked his lips. "I know that you wanted to join Gabriel but I just want you to know that…" he trailed off and we both frowned at each other as we heard the same noise.

A distant rumble getting louder.

"Is that…?"

We rushed to the window and listened, not moving the blinds to look outside.

"It sounds like a car," I whispered and we locked confused eyes.

"It can't be." He frowned.

The noise got louder and I heard Cassius' breathing get shallower. "Who could it be?"

I shook my head.

"I'm going to look," Cassius declared.

"No, Cass! Don't!" I grabbed his arm. "If the Queens see you, they might see it as an invitation."

"What, like your hair, you mean?" he shot back and I gasped and started to hastily pull my hair up into a bun, peeling the bobble from around my wrist.

Cassius parted the blinds with his fingers and I saw a strip of light pass over his face as a car zoomed past, causing him to squint.

"What the hell do you think you're doing?"

He let the blinds go and they clattered against the glass. Denzil, stood staring at us in horror whilst clutching two mugs of steaming tea. "Are you *trying* to rile up the Queens?"

"A car went past," I blurted, pointing towards the window. "Someone was out."

Denzil looked from me to Cassius who nodded. "So?"

"So?" I imitated him. "Someone's out just…driving."

He shrugged. "Probably another crazy kid looking to walk out."

"In a car?" I frowned.

Denzil shrugged again and pulled a dustpan and brush out from under the counter. "Here, clean up the mess."

I folded my arms across my chest, stepping towards him. "Denzil, do people usually drive up and down this road at night?"

Denzil blinked at me. "How should I know?"

I narrowed my eyes. "Aren't you surprised a car has just gone past outside at–"

"No, I'm not," Denzil spat. "Probably because two kids came bursting through my door at night. Forgive me if, following that episode, I'm not that shocked at the mention of a car on the road." He glared at me for another moment before looking at Cassius. "Are you quite sure it was a car?"

He nodded.

"Well," Denzil sighed, "I've got no idea. All I know is your tea's getting cold."

I reluctantly took my mug and Cassius picked up his with a smile. "Thanks for this."

Denzil leaned closer to Cassius. "Are your eyes two different colours?"

"Erm, yeah," Cassius looked down as though to try and hide them. "One's brown and one's blue."

"Right…" Denzil was still staring at him, nodding his head

slowly. "Are you…"

We both looked at Denzil. A pained look on Cassius' face and a warning look on mine. "Are you…an albino?"

"Denzil!" I scolded. "I don't think now's the time to be–"

"No," Cassius jumped in. "No, I'm not. I just have a skin condition."

"What is it?" Denzil probed.

"Right, that's it–"

"No, Lib, it's fine." Cassius held out his hand. "I don't care. It's heterochromia, if you want specifics."

Denzil raised both eyebrows. "Oh, I thought that was just something that affects the eyes."

"Well, no," Cassius scratched his arm, looking uncomfortable, "its skin and hair as well."

"Really?" Denzil persisted. "I'm not sure that's correct."

"Just what are you trying to say, Denzil?" I cut in, suddenly feeling anger. I'd had to listen to the same questions every time I introduced Cassius to someone.

"Nothing." Denzil shrugged. "I'm just…curious."

"Well, stop it," I snapped. "Heterochromia is what it's called. Is there a name for your ignorance?"

Denzil held up his hands. "Whoa, okay. Listen, on a side note, I think you both better call your parents."

Cassius and I exchanged glances.

I was not looking forward to that.

***

I blew on my second cup of tea and sat at the table in Denzil's flat, turning the pages of Mr Fuller's textbook. Despite his protests, I wouldn't accept Denzil's offer to give up his bedroom so instead there was a blanket folded up on the sofa and an airbed set up on the floor for Cassius.

I was ashamed to admit that I didn't want to sleep in Denzil's bed after he once told me that he never washed his dreadlocks.

The small lamp on the table cast enough light for me to read without disturbing Cassius and I swallowed as I read the chapter on the Hunters. Sure enough there was a passage on the times they roam the streets. Cassius was right. They fed on the cattle at the start of the night before taking to the streets halfway between dusk and dawn. I pursed my lips and sighed in disappointment at myself.

Mr Fuller would no longer think of me as a star pupil if he knew.

If I was ever allowed to go back to school, of course.

I grimaced. The phone call to Dad was as painful as I expected.

The rush of relief in his voice when I started to talk hit me like a bolt through the heart. The guilt was unbearable and my reasons just seemed so ridiculous when I tried to articulate them.

He didn't say much in return, just that he'd see me tomorrow when he picked me up to take me to school.

One positive that came out of it was Dad's reaction to Cassius the 'hero'. I'd rolled my eyes as Dad prattled on about how much of a man he'd become and how worried the 'poor lad' must have been about me in order to risk his life like that.

I conceded that it was quite brave, if a little stupid.

I was just looking forward to going to school. I hadn't expected to see Gemma and Noah ever again and now the reality of my failed walk out was upon me, I felt like I'd been granted another chance. I desperately wanted to pull them into a hug.

Oscar, too.

And Dad. Although I very much doubted he'd hug me back.

Mum was probably unaware of the whole situation. I hoped she was anyway. I couldn't imagine Dad offering the information.

I frowned, trying to focus on the text I was reading, stifling a yawn.

"Lib?" I heard Cassius' voice. "You need to sleep."

I looked in his direction, not able to see him because of the bright lamplight in my face. "Don't worry," I turned the page slowly, "I won't be walking out. You can relax."

"I know. I just think you need some rest."

I stared at the text, which was now seriously blurred and my eyes had started to sting. "Fair enough."

I peeled off the brown jumper and folded it over one of the chairs before turning off the lamp and carefully padding over to the sofa. Satisfied Cassius couldn't see anything, I removed my jeans and felt for the blanket, unfolding it and throwing it over myself as I lay down, shaking my hair free from its bun again.

I fluffed the paper-thin cushion as much as possible and snuggled down into it, closing my eyes.

"Lib?"

My eyes flicked open. "Yeah?"

"I'm glad we survived."

I blinked several times, my eyes starting to adjust to the darkness. I could make out the form of Cassius lying on the floor, parallel to me, on his back with one arm over his head.

"Me too," I whispered.

"You said the same thing to Gemma."

I frowned. "What?"

"All those years ago," I heard the smile in his voice and saw him lean up on his elbow facing me, "when you introduced me to her."

I thought for a moment. "I don't remember."

"We were on the grass outside your house," he started. I saw the brilliant white of his hair as he lowered his head. "We were seven, I think, and she came round to see you, but you were with me." He looked in my direction, even though we couldn't really see one another. "She took one look at me and nearly screamed."

I mirrored his pose, leaning my head over the sofa.

"She just stared at me and started asking about my eyes and hair and stuff. Calling me Milky…"

I shook my head. "She was such a cow."

"Still is," he blurted before lowering his voice. "Sorry."

I shrugged. "It's okay. You've not seen the best of her."

"You got so upset and stamped your feet," he laughed. "She went on and on that I was a freak and you said… 'its Heterochromia that makes him a freak-'"

"What's your excuse?" I finished my own line. "I'm the only person on earth who can insult someone while I'm trying to defend them."

He shook his head, still chuckling. "You didn't insult me at all."

"I hate it when people feel the need to ask you," I whispered.

"I know you do," he said. "Thank you for looking out for me. Even if I am bigger than you these days."

I lay on my back and fiddled with the blanket in my fingers. "I could still take you."

He sniggered. "After tonight's performance, I don't doubt that for a second."

My smile faded. "Will you be grounded forever?"

I saw him scrunch up his nose. "Nah, my dad just thinks I'm insane."

"That's nice." I closed my eyes and nuzzled my head into the cushions. I felt the weightlessness of sleep descend over me. "Goodnight, Cassius."

"Goodnight, Liberty Connor," he whispered.

Chapter VI

I tapped my pen on the desk and eyed the clock over Mr Fuller's desk. I glanced at Gemma's empty seat next to me once again.

Five minutes past nine.

I bit my lip.

Gemma was never late.

I turned and looked at Noah, whose jaw was clenched as he glared at the clock.

My heart was pounding. In all of my selfish haze of getting back to school to be reunited with my friends, I'd taken it for granted they'd just be here.

The door opened and I looked up hopefully, staring straight at Cassius. He frowned in confusion at my worried eyes as he removed the pen he was chewing from his mouth. His eyes flicked to Gemma's empty seat.

Come on, Gem, I willed in my head. Come on.

Mr Fuller strode into the classroom in his usual breezy manner. The sound of the door closing behind him seemed to echo around the whole room and I closed my eyes in dismay.

She wasn't here.

Gemma wasn't here.

In all the time I'd known her, she'd never once taken a day off school.

Mr Fuller clapped his hands together and smiled widely, scanning the classroom before settling on Cassius. "Too good for the Blackbrooke Academy uniform yet again, Mr Godwin?"

Cassius didn't look up and carried on colouring a doodle on his notepad. He was wearing the same outfit as last night as he'd gone straight from Denzil's to the Academy. "Sir, we live in a town with Crits, me wearing a shirt and tie isn't going to stop the world turning."

Mr Fuller shrugged. "Rules are rules, Cassius. I don't make them and I won't be the one to expel you," he pulled his battered textbook out of his bag, "but someone will."

I heard several whispers of disapproval echoing around the room between the other pupils.

I glanced at the clock again.

"Miss Connor?"

I blinked at Mr Fuller, startled.

He motioned to Gemma's empty seat. "Where's Jones today?"

I opened my mouth to talk and immediately felt tears prick my eyes. "I-I don't know."

His smile slipped and he looked beyond me, presumably to Noah. I glanced over my shoulder and saw he had his palms pressed either side of his head, staring at the table.

"Boo!"

The class uttered a collective gasp as Gemma popped her head around the door, a show-stopping smile on her face. She slinked into the room and winked at Mr Fuller. "Sorry I'm late."

"Take a seat," Mr Fuller looked a combination of relieved and angry.

Gemma quickly sat down, placing her bag under the table. She glanced at me. "What?"

"Where the hell have you been? Do you have any idea how worried I was?"

She pulled her bun loose, catching her blonde locks before they completely unravelled and starting again to tidy it up.

That show was for Noah, there was no doubt about it.

"Relax," she whispered when she'd finished, flashing a look

at Mr Fuller as he started writing something on the white board. "I was just running late. Dad couldn't find his keys."

I scowled and threw open the textbook. "You could have called me."

"I did." She leaned her face close to mine. "I did bloody ring, this morning. But your Dad said you'd stayed out last night."

I clenched my jaw and felt my cheeks flush red.

"Well?" she hissed, folding her arms. "Anything you want to tell me?"

I looked back at her accusing eyes, not sure where to start.

"Miss Jones!" Mr Fuller bellowed, causing us both to jump. "You interrupt my class by arriving late and you proceed to talk through it!" He pointed at the door. "Do you want to leave?"

"No, sir."

"Then shut up and listen." He chewed the inside of his cheek in annoyance and pointed at what he'd just written on the whiteboard. "God bless those who fall at their feet and may God have mercy. No soul shall be free and no freckle untouched…" he trailed off and faced the class. "Come on, people. Who said that, and what were they talking about?"

I swallowed and glanced at everyone's blank faces. I slowly raised my hand and Mr Fuller smiled, and rubbed his chin in amusement. "Yes, Ms Connor."

"Erm," I cleared my throat. "It was Blackbrooke's third mayor Henry Waterhouse in 1782 and he was…" I looked at the desk, "talking about the Queens."

"Yes!" Mr Fuller pointed at me. "Henry Waterhouse was the first mayor of Blackbrooke who spoke about the Crits with real venom. He hated them. Had people bring him mountains of books from the Outside which he devoured at a rapid rate to try and figure out how to defeat them. Or so the story goes anyway." Mr Fuller walked down the middle of the room, throwing the white board marker up and catching it. "Anyone know what happened to Mr Waterhouse?"

Once again the class was quiet. I knew the answer. I'd read it one day during a particularly boring shift at Tales from the Crits.

I rolled my eyes and raised my hand.

"Yes…Liberty." I could hear the smile in Mr Fuller's voice.

I opened my mouth to speak but he shot me down.

"In fact," he strode up to my desk and placed the marker pen down in front of me, "go to the front."

"I'm sorry?"

He pointed. "I'll take your seat and you go to the front and tell us about Mr Waterhouse."

I frowned and stared at the marker pen, rocking back and forth on the wooden desk. "I-I haven't done anything wrong," I said pathetically.

"No!" Mr Fuller stepped in front of my desk as the rest of the class watched in interest. "I'm not trying to embarrass you. I just think you could teach the class a thing or two about our town." He looked around the room. "It's them who should be embarrassed."

I slowly stood up, my chair scraping loudly on the floor. I picked up the pen and made my way to the front, feeling overwhelmed at the dozens of eyes staring back at me.

Gemma looked positively gleeful to have Mr Fuller sat next to her in my place. "Erm…" I croaked. "I…erm…."

I glanced at Cassius, chewing his blue pen. He winked and nodded in encouragement. I looked down at my ballet pumps, which were still dirty from last night and looked ridiculous with my grey school uniform. Dad hadn't thought to bring my school shoes with my uniform when he came round to Denzil's before school. He hadn't said a word to me during the journey and I had a feeling my punishment was going to be more severe. He was just biding his time.

"Okay," I said trying to sound resolute. "Henry Waterhouse was mayor of Blackbrooke from 1781 to 1789 and, as Mr Fuller said, was the first political figure to voice his opinion on the Crits. Not only that, he actively encouraged the townspeople to fight." I took the lid off the pen and turned to the board, standing on my tip toes to make the best use of the space. "In 1782, Waterhouse built an army who he'd sent out on patrol every night. The army consisted of…" I scribbled the numbers and the dates, "...three thousand five hundred young boys, including his eldest son. By 1783, that army was down to around one thousand and Blackbrooke wasn't happy." I drew an unhappy face and a few people laughed. "Waterhouse clung on to power for another few years and became increasingly deranged and determined to take on the Crits." I scanned my eyes over the class. "His obsession culminated in the most atrocious crime in Blackbrooke's history which occurred in the October of 1789. Waterhouse took the remaining members of his army which was down to less than five hundred at this point, as well as some young boys who'd been brainwashed by him and his eldest son. He took them into the woodland…" I looked at Mr Fuller who nodded his head slowly. "He took them to the woods at dusk," I repeated, "and up to where the Queens slept. He then spoke to the Queens and allegedly offered all of his army as a sacrifice in order to grant him eternal life." I perched on the edge of Mr Fuller's desk. "No one knows why he even tried as the Queens had never been known to strike a deal before but people suspect it may have been something to do with the children's books on folklore that he became obsessed with. It's then," I frowned to myself in thought, "a bit fuzzy as to what happened with the Queens when he tried to strike the deal but…basically, he started to sacrifice the children in the army himself. They were scared and he-he was the mayor and…he did horrendous things to them in a way to prove himself as serious to the Queens."

Noah raised his hand from the back.

I blinked at him, feeling a weird about being a teacher.

"Yes?"

He grinned. "What did he do?"

"Well, he burnt some alive, he tried to eat the flesh or others, he…" I felt my cheeks burn, "he sodomised some. Despite him taking them to the Queens as a sacrifice, he killed a large number of them in a sheer act of madness and desperation." I shrugged. "I told you it was atrocious. His madness is evident as he killed his own son. The Queens took some but we don't know how many they took and how many Henry Waterhouse killed himself."

Mr Fuller stood and walked to the front, indicating for me to sit down. "Thank you, Liberty."

I sat in my seat and Gemma nudged me. "Smarty pants."

"The story of Waterhouse might sound more like it belongs in a history class rather than Blackbrooke, but," Mr Fuller raised his index finger in the air, "it sparked off a chain of events which culminated in…"

"The Rules," everyone chorused, sounding bored.

"Yes, indeed," Mr Fuller chuckled. "Now, I want all of you to follow exercises one and two on page fifty-nine of your–"

"I have a question."

Mr Fuller looked wryly at Cassius whose hand was raised in the air. "That Waterhouse bloke, he killed all of those kids and young lads?"

Mr Fuller nodded. "Sadly, yes."

"In front of the Queens?"

"Yes."

Cassius straightened up. "And the Queens…they just… watched?"

Mr Fuller licked his bottom lip as he eyed Cassius.

"It's just," Cassius persisted and Gemma rolled her eyes and pretended to shoot herself in the head, "I thought Crits were programmed to attack, yet…these Queens just watched an old man murder a bunch of kids."

Mr Fuller folded his arms and I noticed he looked

awkward as though he didn't know what to say.

"That would have taken hours," Cassius exhaled. "They watched for hours, doing nothing. Why?"

I felt goosebumps rise up onto my skin as I thought about the grotesque faces of the Queens from the night before. I knew what Cassius was getting at. He was voicing the thing we both avoided talking about after it happened. Why didn't the Queens kill us right there and then? It was as though they were taking their time, advancing slowly. They just watched Cassius and I. Stared at us.

But why?

It was like they were playing with us.

Mr Fuller shrugged. "It's a good question, Cassius. I suppose we'll never know. Right everyone, page–"

"But don't you think it's odd no one's ever tried to find out?" Cassius persisted. "I mean, we tar all of the Crits with the same brush but maybe it's not all about food. Maybe it's something else, maybe–"

"Enough, Cassius!" Mr Fuller shouted, looking flustered. "We'll never know unless someone goes out and tries to find out and no one's about to do that. Now, seriously everyone, page fifty-nine, exercise one and two."

A faint buzz of chatter sounded as everyone reached for their pads and pens.

"Why's he so weird?" Gemma whispered, pointing in the direction of Cassius.

I shrugged, ignoring her.

"Anyway," she hit me lightly on the arm and flashed a look in Mr Fuller's direction to make sure he wasn't paying attention, "where the hell were you last night if you weren't at home?"

"I..." My brain searched for something quickly. I looked at the back of Cassius' head as he leaned it on his fist, reading the textbook. "I-I fell asleep at Denzil's."

Gemma recoiled. "Denzil? Please tell me you didn't..."

"Don't insult me," I shot back. "I went over to help him with a delivery and it got late and I fell asleep."

"Attention staff and students, can you please make your way to the assembly hall immediately."

Mr Fuller sighed. "We're destined to never have this class. Alright everyone, let's go."

Gemma stood up and glanced around the class, tucking her chair under the table. "Everyone here's accounted for," she shrugged. "God knows."

Noah sidled up to our table, his brown bag slung across his body. He stood next to Gemma and walked his fingers around her stomach.

She pecked him quickly on the lips before turning back to me. "Come on, let's go."

As all of the pupils filed out, I looked at Mr Fuller packing his things into his bag and turned back to my friends. "I'll catch you up. I just need to speak to Mr Fuller a sec."

"You sure?" Gemma walked backwards with Noah's arms now completely wrapped around her. "I'll save you a seat."

They turned and left. I stalled for time, packing up my bag, waiting for the last pupil to leave. "Sir?"

He looked up and smiled brightly. "Miss Connor, that was very impressive today. Thank you for allowing me to have a break from my teaching duties."

I shrugged, hauling my bag further onto my shoulder as it slipped. "It's fine. I find that story quite…interesting."

He raised an eyebrow. "If your essays are anything to go by, you find everything to do with Blackbrooke interesting."

I felt my cheeks burn, and I tucked a non-existent strand of hair behind my ear. "I…erm, want to ask you something."

"Shoot." He smiled and slid his bag to the other side of his desk so I had his full attention.

"Do you teach Spanish to the boys?"

"Si, senorita." He nodded, his chocolate brown eyes twinkling.

"I wondered if you could translate something for me?"

He gestured for me to continue.

"I may get this wrong…" I fumbled in the front zip section of my bag and reached in for the folded up piece of paper I'd been carrying around since the day of Gabriel's funeral. "Erm…" I cleared my throat feeling embarrassed. "Por favor…"

"That means 'please'." Mr Fuller looked amused at my attempt of a Spanish accent.

"It was 'por favor, perrrrr-don-anos'?" I winced. "I think."

"Por favor, perdónanos…." he repeated after me. "That means 'please, forgive us'."

I felt my brow crease into a frown. "Oh…"

He blinked at me expectantly. "Is that it?"

"Oh!" I snapped out of my trance. "Yes. I mean, thank you. That's great."

He grabbed his bag. "We should go to the hall."

I nodded, still confused by the translation.

"Where did you hear them?"

My head snapped around as I made my way to the door. "Sorry?"

Mr Fuller put on his jacket. "The Spanish words."

I shrugged. "Oh, it was Gabriel's mum actually. At his funeral. We were looking at a grave and she said it as she–"

"What else did she say?" Mr Fuller interrupted, his face instantly serious.

I shrugged. "I don't know. A bunch of things in Spanish that I couldn't understand."

Mr Fuller surprised me by striding over and grabbing my arm. "Think, Lib!" he shouted, shaking me.

"Stop it!" I cried, trying to pull away. "I-I can't remember what it was–"

"Think!" His face was inches away from mine now contorted with anger. "This is very important, Lib. Think!"

"I told you, I don't know. I-I can't remember–"

"*Think*!"

"Lucas!"

Mr Fuller let go of me instantly, a look of horror on his face as he saw Mr Jones stood in the doorway.

"I assume there was a damn good reason you were manhandling one of our students," Mr Jones snapped.

Mr Fuller shook his head and rubbed his temples. "I'm sorry, I don't know what came over me, I–"

"Get to the assembly hall," he snapped, still glaring. "Get to the assembly hall and then head to my office afterwards." He looked at me, his eyes narrowed. "Liberty, go to the hall."

I nodded, throwing a frightened look at Mr Fuller as I left the room, not understanding what on earth just happened. Although, Mr Jones had come to my aid, I didn't like the way I could feel his eyes boring into my back as I hurried to the assembly hall.

***

"All of the kitchen, and I mean, all of it. Let's see…the oven needs a good scrub as well. Oh! The fridge. I can't remember the last time the fridge was cleaned…What else?…"

I watched Dad walk around the kitchen rubbing his chin and looking positively gleeful as he dished out my punishment.

"Dad," I closed my eyes and slowly opened them, "trust me, I'll clean the kitchen top to bottom."

It was a relief he was speaking to me again as I didn't deal well with silent treatment. I had too much experience of that living with Mum. Instead, he was making sure I paid for my failed walk out with chores. It was clear that he was stuck between feeling angry at me, and relieved that I was still here.

He folded his arms, looking pained. "Lib, is it really that bad living here?"

I'd been dreading a question like this from the moment I

saw Dad again. The hurt registering on his features made the guilt of my selfish actions come rushing back.

"No," I said softly. "I told you, I just…miss Gabriel."

My words were so pathetic and feeble.

"I know what it's like to be in love," he smiled sadly, "but…and please hear me out here…"

I nodded.

"Although Gabriel was a nice lad," he winced at his own words, "he was in your life for what? About a year?"

"I've known him forever," I snapped, feeling my face flush red.

"I told you to hear me out." He moved so he was stood next to me, leaning against the table. His arm brushed against mine. "I just wanted to say that…we're your family. We love you."

I looked away.

"You're my daughter." He nudged me. "You've been my daughter for seventeen years and I love you more everyday."

"I know," I whispered. "I love you, too. I'm…sorry."

"It's okay." He pulled me into a hug and I felt tears prick my eyes as he squeezed me tight. "I know I'm not as good as Mum with this stuff," he rubbed my back, "but know that I'm trying."

I pulled away, quickly wiping a tear that had escaped from the corner of my eye. "I know you are."

He stepped away and tapped my arm. "Better get started on the kitchen, love. Sooner you do, the sooner you'll be done. Then you can make some supper for me and Oscar," he added with a wink.

I groaned and watched him walk out, chuckling to himself. I surveyed the kitchen.

It looked exactly as you would imagine a kitchen would look that's currently being used as a four-year-olds playroom and making beans on toast.

It was a mess.

I picked up a plastic tub containing some of Oscar's toys from the corner of the room and started collecting his stray action figures, scattered everywhere, throwing them in.

I placed the tub back and moved over to the counter to where Dad had let a stack of newspapers build up. I curled my lip and lifted the pile to look at the one at the bottom.

"Bloody hell, Dad," I said out loud, "there's a month's worth of newspapers here."

I sighed and picked up the stack in both arms, walking to the back door to put them in the large bin outside. I shifted so they were resting awkwardly on one arm and reached out for the key in the lock. I frowned as my fingers gripped thin air and I looked to see it wasn't in its usual place in the door.

"Great." I placed the papers back down on the counter and put my hands on my hips.

Dad.

Of course, he wasn't going to leave the key in the back door.

I'd lost my right to be trusted.

"Fine." I drummed my fingers onto my waist and looked in disgust at the pile of washing up. I hauled myself over and turned on the tap, emptying the bowl before cleaning it and starting to pile the dishes back in.

I hummed as I started to wash each dish and looked at the dusk outside. The sky was a brilliant pink.

I closed my eyes and rested my hands in the warm water, recalling the images of the sky the night before and the splendour of the twinkling stars.

I gasped and jumped back at the sound of the blinds jerking into action and closing for the night. My smile faded and I dried my hands and switched the lights on.

I hadn't expected to clap eyes on this room again and now I felt alien stood in it. It was as though I'd been away for a hundred years.

Aside from the mountain of chores, Dad had played a

trump card with my punishment.

That morning when he picked me up from Denzil's, Oscar wasn't in the car because he said he was taking him to the dentist. And when I got home from school, I found out Oscar was staying over at one of his friends' houses. It meant I hadn't clapped eyes on my brother since I'd tucked him into bed before the failed walk out.

Dad knew what Oscar meant to me and distance was the worst punishment he could dish out.

I opened the washing machine and pulled out the damp clothes into the plastic basket on the floor.

Growing up, I never thought I had a maternal bone in my body. I wasn't even bothered when Mum fell pregnant but as she started to withdraw from us, Oscar needed a mum and automatically turned to me. It was strange at first when he used to cuddle up to me on the sofa when we were watching television. I'd stiffen and remain sat in the same position unsure of what to do. As time went by, I grew to enjoy the closeness and looked forward to him falling asleep in my arms, sucking his thumb.

I looked at the floor, still crouched down at the clothes airer. There was a split in the linoleum and I ran my finger over it absently.

I was trying not to think about the events of the day. Another boy had walked. His name was Abram, and I vaguely remembered him from a presentation evening in the first year of moving into the Academy's high school from primary. I was called to the front of the hall and presented with a certificate for outstanding achievements in my first year. Abram was one of the other kids called to the front and the memory stayed with me because he stuck his tongue out at me playfully as he walked to join me at the front. I'd instantly gone red, of course, and for the rest of that day, I was quite sure I had my first crush on this boy with the mousy, unruly curls. That was all it lasted though as I was soon distracted by everything that came with being an eleven year old, which for me consisted entirely of getting good grades, devouring sweets and spending time with Gemma.

I didn't move from the spot on the floor as my eyebrows knitted together in thought. What had made Abram's walk out worse was that it had happened last night. At the same time as my failed attempt. I couldn't help but wonder whether the other Crits weren't busy in the cattle fields after all. Perhaps they were tearing Abram to pieces in another part of the town.

Or maybe that's why the Queens spared Cassius and me. They'd probably had their fill for one night.

My fingers, still tracing on the line on the floor, closed into a fist. I knew I should have been thinking about Abram but there was only one person who kept creeping into my thoughts.

Gabriel, I miss you, I thought. Even when I'm trying not to think about you, I miss you.

The cold from the floor penetrated my black leggings through to my knees. I at least hoped that, wherever Gabriel was, he was happy.

Free as a bird.

"Dear God," I started, tentatively pressing my palms together, "please…look after him and….erm…." I opened one eye and exhaled in defeat. "Forget it, I'm rubbish at this."

I rose to my feet and glanced around. Praying wasn't the only thing I was terrible at. The kitchen was now full of half-finished jobs. The dishes. The washing. The newspapers.

I flicked on the kettle, pulling myself onto one of the stools at the breakfast bar.

I had all night to sort the kitchen after all. No rush.

I half-heartedly picked up one of the newspapers which detailed some story about record numbers of tourists in Blackbrooke throughout the month of November. I leaned my chin on my hand letting my eyes scan over the inane words.

Seriously, why the hell did Dad insist on reading this crap

every single day?

It was either something about tourists, or money being ploughed into Blackbrooke for a new community centre or something, or it was doom and gloom.

It wasn't even as if there was much they could say on the sports front because our teams had to just play one another seeing as other teams on the Outside couldn't travel into Blackbrooke and if our team travelled out they wouldn't be allowed to return due to the Rules.

It meant there were two major football teams in the town that played one another every week. It just seemed like a ridiculous waste of time to me.

I frowned at a story about the number of shopping days until Christmas and stopped dead in my tracks. I eyed the pile of newspapers again.

Gabriel would be in here somewhere.

The story of his walk out. Probably a picture of his beautiful smiling face.

I swallowed and reached out, flipping slowly through the spines of the newspapers until I found the one dated last Monday.

He walked on Sunday so the Monday newspaper must have been the one.

I pulled it free from the pile and winced, preparing myself for what was going to be emblazoned on the cover.

I frowned.

It was a story about one of Blackbrooke's football players breaking his leg, meaning he was out of action for an entire season.

My chest tightened. How dare they put this garbage on the cover on that day.

I snatched open the first page and my eyes darted over each of the stories.

New library opening.

Big chill expected over the next fortnight.

I flicked to the next page.

Robbery in the town.

Goodbye to the Green family.

I snatched up the next page and ripped it in vigour.

Nothing.

Next page.

Nothing.

Next page.

Nothing.

I closed the newspaper and threw it onto the other side of the counter, rubbing my temples with my fingers. I reached over for Tuesday's edition.

Maybe they missed the chance to put it in for Monday's.

I did the same with this one which contained a cover story about a group of people killing Watchers and an urgent appeal to whoever it was to stop it as not to antagonise the other Crits.

Once again, I flicked through the pages angrily but there was nothing there.

My breathing grew shallow and I suddenly felt unspeakably angry.

"What's up, Lib?"

My head snapped up to see Dad open the fridge for a beer. He glanced around the kitchen and raised an eyebrow. "Taking a break, are you? I can see you've been…busy."

I ignored him. "Why isn't Gabriel in here?"

"What?" Dad looked confused.

"In here." I picked up the newspaper and smacked it with the back of my hand. "There's nothing in here about him. Nothing at all."

Dad looked at the newspaper and then back at me. "Lib, they never print anything about walk outs in there."

"What?" I asked in shock. "What do you mean?"

He leaned against the fridge, pulling on the ring-pull of his can which hissed loudly. "They just never have. Don't want to report them in case it's seen to glorify it."

"Are you being serious?"

He rubbed his chin in thought. "Yes, I think that's what I heard someone say once."

"But that's..." I shook my head searching for the right word, "ludicrous! Why wouldn't they write about a young person, a talented bright young person, whose life ended so abruptly?"

"Because," he shrugged, swigging his drink, "it's not exactly news. It's...private."

"It *is* news! It's bigger news than..." I trailed off and started to furiously flip through the pages, "Mr bloody Walker's prized turnips!" I threw it back down and Dad looked bewildered at my reaction.

"What do you want me to say, Lib? I don't write the paper. That's just the way it's always been," he called over his shoulder as he left the room.

I scowled at the newspaper again.

That was crap.

I wasn't buying it.

I walked to the kitchen door and closed it so Dad wouldn't hear me as I picked up the phone off the wall and stretched the cord back to where I was sitting. I looked at the dirty number pad on the receiver, wondering when the last time was it had been wiped clean. In fact, I couldn't even remember the last time it had been used to make a call.

I sighed and tapped in a number I'd committed to memory a long time ago.

People rarely changed their numbers in Blackbrooke and house phones were all we had. Mobiles were still a pipedream seeing as the Crits kept tearing down the masts whenever they were erected.

I cleared my throat and put the phone to my ear, listening to it ring.

"Godwin residence."

"Do you always answer the phone like that?"

"Lib, is that you?" Cassius sounded surprised. "Is everything okay?"

"Not really."

"What's the matter?" he asked, his voice serious.

"Nothing. It's nothing…urgent. It's just…" I licked the corner of my mouth. "Do you read the Blackbrooke Chronicle?"

"Not if I can help it," came his flat reply. "It's awful."

"Yeah." I curled my lip at a story about a little girl winning a drawing competition. "You're right there. Tell me something," I rested the phone between my chin and shoulder while I reached for another copy, "have you ever noticed it doesn't feature walk outs?"

Cassius was quiet for a moment as though thinking about it. "I can't say I ever have."

"Well," I shook my head at yet another terrible edition, "it doesn't. I asked my dad and apparently it never has."

"Why?"

"I don't know. But don't you think that's a little bit weird?"

"Hmmm," Cassius pondered. "I suppose so, but this town is off the chart so I'm not wholly surprised."

"Okay," I said slowly, looking at the dates of the papers before pulling out the one I was looking for. I flicked through it before closing it triumphantly. "So, you're not surprised that the day after Xiang walked out, the newspaper decided to dedicate four pages to Blackbrooke's Cutest Baby competition with absolutely zero mention of your friend?"

Cassius didn't say anything and I winced, wondering whether I'd pushed him too far.

"That's crap," he whispered at last.

I felt my heart pound in relief. "I know! Why wouldn't they honour people who've walked out? What's the reason? Dad said something about not wanting to spark copycat walk outs but–"

"Bullshit," Cassius interrupted. "Sorry…but that's…"

"Bullshit." I smiled. "I thought so, too." I started to bite on my thumbnail. "Something…weird happened today. With Mr Fuller."

"What?"

"I asked him to translate something for me and–"

"Is this the Spanish thing you were asking me about?"

"Mmm-hmm," I hurried on, glancing over my shoulder to make sure Dad wasn't stood listening in. "Anyway, when I told him it was Gabriel's mum who said the words, he totally freaked out and…grabbed me."

"He grabbed you?" Cassius voice filled with concern. "Did he hurt you?"

"No, not really. It was just…strange."

"So, humour me with specifics, what did the words translate to?"

"Oh, sorry. Of course. The words were 'please forgive us'."

"Please forgive us…" Cassius repeated. "And it was Gabriel's mum who said that?"

"Yes."

"When did she say it to you?" Cassius now sounded intrigued. "Put it in context."

"Erm…" I thought back to the moment I was trying to forget. "We were outside, after I spoke to you, and…she hugged me and said a bunch of things in Spanish." I frowned in frustration. "I could only remember a couple of words."

"Please forgive us."

"Yes."

"That's weird." Cassius sounded like he shifted the phone. "Do you think it was because they didn't mention you at the funeral?"

"I don't think so." I sighed. "I don't know, maybe…I haven't got a clue. All I know is, Mr Fuller completely lost it."

"I won't be able to look at him in the next class now I know that," Cassius muttered, more to himself than to me, I guessed.

"*You* won't?!" I let out a laugh. "I'm going to have to listen to Gem go on about how gorgeous he is."

"Poor you," he mumbled. "Hey, can I tell *you* something… weird?"

"Of course," I whispered.

"Abram. The kid that walked last night."

"Yeah? Did you know him?"

Cassius sighed. "He was in my biology class but I didn't really speak to him. He was a bit of a clown."

I felt my lips curl into a smile as I remembered him sticking his tongue out at me when we were kids.

"Anyway, Abram's family own one of those big Dodge van things. They're the only ones in the town with one because his dad's apparently obsessed with America and had one shipped in about a year ago. Abram went on and on about it for weeks, drove everyone mad."

He paused and I didn't say anything, unsure of whether I'd missed something.

"It's just that," he lowered his voice, "I'm pretty sure…I'm positive that was the car I saw drive past Denzil's last night."

I put my hand on my mouth and checked over my shoulder again. "Sooo…what? Do you think Abram flipped and took the car? Maybe he left town? If he's eighteen then he could go. He might have had enough."

"That's what I thought at first. But when I went to the supermarket earlier for my dad, I saw Abram's parents in there buying groceries and the car was parked outside." He sounded like his was biting on a pen as I kept hearing it tap against the phone. "And Lib, I can't describe it but they looked…haunted or something. I mean, they looked traumatised. I know they must be upset but this…was something different."

"What are you thinking?" I breathed.

"I don't know, Lib. There's probably a really simple explanation but there's just something that doesn't add up with this."

"Oooh!" I jumped, hitting my hand on the counter. "I bet when Abram walked out, his parents got in the car and went looking for him. That'll be it."

Cassius didn't say anything.

"Don't you think?" I said, less confidently this time. I twirled the grubby phone cord between my fingers nervously.

"You're probably right," Cassius said reluctantly. He yawned loudly and sounded as though he stretched. "I'm just thinking about it too much I suppose."

I bit my lip. He wasn't at all. Although my theory about the grief-stricken parents trawling the streets of Blackbrooke was feasible, I had a strange feeling in the pit of my stomach that told me I was wrong. That there was perhaps a more sinister reason but my brain wouldn't let me grasp onto those thoughts. It had taken enough trauma over the last week and I was quite sure one more thing would tip me over the edge.

I flicked over another page of the newspaper, deciding to change the subject. "I quite honestly feel like ditching school and marching down to the Chronicle office and demanding why they don't honour walk outs. And telling the staff their writing abilities are shameful."

Cassius chuckled. "Why would I not be surprised if you did that?"

I smiled. "Because you know what I'm like."

"I do indeed."

We fell quiet and I listened to the sound of him breathing.

"Lib?"

"Yeah."

"Why me?"

"What do you mean?"

He laughed but more nervously this time. "Why did you ring me tonight? Instead of Gemma or Noah?"

"I'm not sure actually," I said honestly, turning another page. "Although I think Gemma would just think I was insane and then proceed to talk to me about having sex with Noah."

Cassius coughed as soon as I said sex and I had to stifle a giggle so as not to embarrass him further. "And as for Noah…" I trailed off scrunching up my nose. "Well, he's like a brother and I love him, but I don't actually think he and I have had a one-to-one conversation in the entire time we've known one another."

"Figures." Cassius lowered his voice. "They won't like you speaking to me."

"I know, but…" I thought back to Dad's words to me earlier. "You came first."

"Yeah, I suppose I did." He shifted the phone again. "It's been really good to talk again. I don't want to sound like an idiot but…I missed you."

I felt my cheeks flush red and I was thankful he couldn't see me. It had been rather odd that I instinctively picked up the phone and dialled his number, especially as I hadn't done that since I was nine years old. And then I said the first words that entered my mind. "I missed you, too."

"Okay, well, I'll catch you in school," he said brightly. "Don't worry about hanging out or anything, I know those two would make your life hell and–"

"I'll see you tomorrow," I interrupted, smiling.

***

I sat in the kitchen the following morning, admiring my handiwork. After getting off the phone to Cassius, I'd sprung into action, whistling merrily to myself as I finished the jobs I started.

Dad had been impressed and did the typical adult thing where he pretended I still deserved to be punished so I could get to work on the living and dining room tonight.

In truth, I didn't mind. It had taken my mind off the thousands of things whizzing around it over the last week. I'd felt sick when I'd finished and realised I hadn't thought about Gabriel in about an hour.

I hated to admit that it was also a relief as well.

I eyed the clock ticking loudly on the kitchen wall.

Dad would be back from Clean Up in about fifteen minutes and then he'd be taking me to school. I turned the page of the Blackbrooke textbook in front of me and started reading about the Lurkers.

Not as intelligent and inconspicuous as appearance would have you believe, Lurkers are no more sophisticated than Hunters. Feeding is their secondary aim after protecting the Queens, but whereas the Hunters work in packs, similar to wolves in appearance and behaviour, Lurkers are solitary and hunt alone.

The origins of the Lurkers, as with any of the Creatures, is unknown. Several studies have claimed they have been around since the dinosaurs roamed the earth and numbers have dwindled due to their inclination to starve themselves. Quite opposite to the Hunters, Lurkers do not feel hunger as a physical sensation and will go for months without feeding if they do not 'stumble' upon food. They can live for approximately six months without a meal before they die.

Referred to as the laziest of the Creatures, we are likely to see the complete extinction of the Lurkers in Blackbrooke in the next 100 years, especially if plans to reduce cattle numbers goes through council as they are unlikely to overpower the Hunters.

I stopped reading as the doorbell sounded. I closed the textbook, and placed my spoon into the bowl.

The morning klaxon had sounded so I wasn't concerned. I remembered one night when I was little and sat watching the television with Mum and Dad and the doorbell rang. It was dark outside and my parents told me to ignore it. It rang three times and then stopped. Dad told me years later that the Crits had started going door-to-door like bad salesmen to get their meals. It was around the time there was a breakout of Mad Cow disease and we had to slaughter a lot of cattle.

I'd never understand why they did that.

So what if the Crits ate infected cattle? As long as we weren't eating it.

I looked through the peephole as I got to work tying my school tie, which had been draped around my neck, and pulled it open.

"Hi Libby," the young woman smiled brightly, "I'm sorry to call so early but Oscar wasn't very well last night."

I looked down at my little brother stood in front of her. I knelt and stroked his cheek and he practically dived into my arms. I lifted him up. "Thanks, Hope."

Hope cocked her head to one side and rubbed Oscar's back as he clung to me. "I was going to take him straight to school with Adam but he was quite upset and wanted to see you."

I kissed his hair and inhaled his scent, never wanting to let him go. "I appreciate that."

Hope smiled warmly, still looking at Oscar. I looked around her and saw Oscar's friend Adam sat in her car, waving furiously. I juggled Oscar and waved back.

"So, how are you, Lib?" Hope enquired.

"Good thanks." I placed Oscar down onto his feet and patted his backside. "Get inside, you. It's cold and if you're poorly, you'll make it worse." I stood, smoothing down my school skirt. "How are you? How's Caleb?"

Her grin spread even wider.

I always liked Hope. She was doing her A Levels when I started in first year of high school and she would volunteer to tutor me. Because I expressed a keen interest in history, she spent time with me and nurtured it. She would sometimes baby-sit as well, when my parents went to stay with friends on occasions. She and I would sit and chat for hours about various things and I always remember feeling like a grown up because she never talked down to me, despite the seven year age gap.

Hope and Caleb, one of the town's football stars, got married as soon as they turned eighteen and swore in the Rules. Adam was born soon after which was weird because I never thought Hope was the type to have kids so quickly. She and I would talk about our dreams, and I distinctly remember her saying she was going to leave Blackbrooke and attend University. "History of art," she'd say in her soft voice, her grey eyes twinkling. She would sit on the back doorstep, smoking cherry tobacco while I gazed at her from my spot at the breakfast counter. "And you, Ms Connor," she'd point her cigarette at me, "are going to come and live with me as soon as you turn eighteen. We'll head to London and party through the night."

Even at eleven, the image sounded too fantastical for me to consider it a possibility. Plus, eighteen was a lifetime away then.

It was her bohemian attitude, coupled with the long velvet dresses and pierced nose, making her stand out, that made her new life of domestic bliss in Blackbrooke all the more surprising.

Still, I couldn't exactly make any such comments. After all, if Gabriel hadn't walked, I would have been following Hope down that route.

"We're all good, thanks." Hope folded her arms and shifted on the spot, looking down at her sheepskin boots. "How's your mum doing?"

I shrugged, which had become my standard response whenever someone asked me about Mum these days. "Okay. Getting a bit better…I think."

I noticed Hope swallow and she looked at me with sad eyes. "It can't be easy."

"No," I agreed, wondering how much Hope knew about

my mum, "it isn't."

"How…old are you now?" She didn't meet my eye and rubbed her arms with her gloved hands. Her outfit was so ordinary, white duffle coat over jeans. Any hint of her old personality well and truly washed away along with the years.

"Seventeen." I nodded. "Eighteen in January."

"Oh," she smiled, eyes now in a trance as she stared at a spot on the floor, "it's flown. I-It's flying with Adam. I feel like I blink and another year has rolled by." She snapped herself out of her trance. "I'm pregnant again. They said that usually happens…"

I frowned, feeling confused. "I'm not sure I–"

"No, of course not," she interrupted, her cheeks flushing. "Sorry, I'm just feeling a bit faint."

"Oh," I felt a wave of panic that she might faint on my doorstep with her son looking on from the car, "do you want to come in and–"

"No!" she blurted, stepping backwards and forcing another friendly smile. "I mean, no it's fine. I just need to get Adam to school."

"Of course. Erm…congratulations on the pregnancy."

She stared for a second and surprised me by stepping back and yanking me into a tight hug. I slowly returned the embrace and patted her on the back.

"You've been a good kid, Libby," she croaked.

"Thanks," I said slowly, trying to pull away but not able to budge from her tight grip on me.

She eventually moved back and I saw her wipe a stray tear from her eye. "Thanks for the kind words. We're very excited about the new baby."

I now felt like I was staring at her as though she was an alien.

She reached out and rubbed my arm. "It's been nice…" she trailed off and shook her head. "I mean…you take care, Libby."

She turned and jogged down the garden path to her car. Adam waved at me again and I raised my hand to acknowledge him, not taking my eyes off his mum as she fumbled with the gear stick and sped away, wiping tears from her eyes.

"What the hell?" I whispered to myself, narrowing my eyes as I watched the car drive away. "What's going on in this–"

"Libbbeeeeeee!" The unmistakeable voice of Oscar bellowed from the kitchen and I smiled, instantly forgetting my strange exchange with Hope.

"What?" I walked to the kitchen and saw him, finishing off my now soggy cereal. He grinned at me and some milk dribbled out of the side of his mouth.

"You're not looking very ill to me, young man."

"I *am* ill," he said brightly, digging the spoon into the mush of cornflakes.

"Hmmm." I snatched up the bowl. "You will be ill if you sit there eating leftovers. I'll make you something proper."

Oscar giggled. "Can I stay in my pyjamas all day?"

"No," I said, pulling eggs out of the fridge and examining the box. "Do these come with instructions?"

"You can't cook," Oscar said matter-of-factly, licking some bits of cereal mush from his fingers.

"I know that," I shot back, pulling a pan from one of the cupboards, "but I really don't think I can go wrong with a boiled egg."

"Can I have toasty soldiers, please?"

My smile fell. "Okay, maybe I can go wrong."

The last time I'd made toast, I'd set the fire alarm off and we had to buy a new toaster.

"When's Daddy back?"

I eyed the clock. "Any minute now. Osc, are you actually ill? How do you feel?"

"Better."

I looked at the pan of water I'd placed on the hob and

when it started to bubble, dropped two eggs in. Might as well make Dad some breakfast, although he'd probably drop dead in surprise if I presented him with cooked food given the track record.

"Come and play with me, Lib." Oscar grinned, holding up a dinosaur toy. "You can be the chy-sarah-top."

I raised an eyebrow. "I don't want to be that one. I'll *eat* that one!"

He squealed as I strode over and scooped him off his seat. "I'll eat all of them! I'm the Libby-saurus!"

Oscar laughed loudly and I slung him over my shoulder, walking around the kitchen. "I'm going to put you in the pan and have you for breakfast! Yum yum!"

"No, Libeeee!" he cried between hysterical laughter. "Don't eat meeeeeeeeeeeee! I won't taste nice!"

"Yum yum! You're mine! Muhahahahahaha!"

"Lib."

I span around, Oscar still over my shoulder and saw Dad stood in the doorway of the kitchen.

"Oh hey, Dad." I smiled, breathless from spinning Oscar round. "I'm just about to eat your only son, you don't mind, do you? I think he'll taste like slugs and snails and–"

"Lib," Dad swallowed and I noticed his face was pale, "put Oscar down."

My smile faded and I leaned and placed Oscar on his feet.

"Come on, Libby-saurus!" Oscar frowned up at me, oblivious to the shift in mood. "I thought I was going to be your breakfast."

I didn't take my eyes off Dad and felt my breathing grow shallow. It was as though a cloud moved over the sun and, although I had no idea what was going on, I knew it was bad.

"Oscar, please go upstairs," Dad said quietly.

Oscar looked from me to Dad before nodding and running out of the room. It wasn't often Dad dished out orders and when he did, neither of us argued. Not even an over-excited four year old.

I watched Oscar disappear and looked at Dad. "What's going on?"

"Come into the living room."

I opened my mouth to speak but Dad had already turned to walk away, rubbing his jaw. I followed him, feeling like my legs were dead weights. The floor seemed to tilt under my feet and I reached out to steady myself on the wall.

Where was Mum? I thought, panicked. I hadn't heard her this morning which was nothing unusual but perhaps she'd got up in the night and…

I couldn't even think about it.

Dad held the door open to the living room and I followed, watching him as he closed it behind us.

"Dad?" I said, my voice quivering.

Dad lowered his head and I heard movement from behind me.

"Liberty."

I span and looked in horror as Mr Jones rose to his feet from our sofa. In all of the years I'd been friends with Gemma, Mr Jones had never once set foot in my house. In fact, I think the only time he ever spoke to my parents was when he'd call up and demand they come and collect me after Gemma had answered back and got herself instantly grounded with no visitor privileges. That, or the night he caught Gabriel and I on his sofa.

"What is this?" I looked from him back to Dad who couldn't meet my eye. "Dad, please."

"Liberty," Mr Jones said again, placing a hand on my shoulder. I noticed he wasn't wearing his trademark suit but beige jeans and a green jumper. Also, was it my imagination or did he look like he'd been crying. He squeezed my shoulder and I shuddered at his touch. "There's no easy way to tell you this…"

I closed my eyes.

"It's Gemma," he breathed. "I'm afraid she…"

I shook my head quickly.

"She walked out."

I remained rooted to the spot, staring at the garish patterned carpet wondering why the hell my parents had ever chosen it.

"Marie and I were sat in the living room reading and…" he looked up at my dad and shrugged sadly, "we both heard the front door open and close and…we knew."

"Had she said anything beforehand?" Dad enquired, sensing I'd lost the ability to speak.

"No," Mr Jones, still holding my shoulder, sighed, "not a word. She seemed a little withdrawn over dinner but… nothing to concern us."

I tried to swallow but my throat constricted. My mind started to reel. When did I see her last? Everyone had been excused from classes for the rest of the day after the news of Abram's walk out. What then?

I closed my eyes and felt like my whole body was being sucked back into the day before.

***

"Noah, don't you think Lib would look amazing as a redhead?"

I looked up to see Gemma hold up her palms at me, thumbs touching and one eye closed as she visualised her masterpiece.

"Seriously, Lib, I'm so right about this. Let me loose on the mop."

"Never going to happen," I sighed, returning my eyes to the table. I really wasn't in the mood today. "Plus what on earth would you dye it with? Hair dye's forbidden in this town. Everything's forbidden," I added glumly.

Gemma let out a laugh. "Well, Mum highlights mine for me. Noah's football friend gets the bleach from the Outside."

I looked at Noah, who mouthed 'Conrad' at me. The merest recollection of the heavy set, dark-haired boy entered my head but I didn't care enough to probe my memory further. Instead I shrugged and returned my eyes to the table.

"Are you okay?" Gemma lightly kicked me.

"Fine," I said softly without conviction. My nails were chewed to the wick and I knew I was more jumpy than usual. Every time I closed my eyes, all I could see were the dull red eyes of the Queens. I was amazed I'd managed to sleep at all at Denzil's and was quite sure I wouldn't, had it not been for Cassius on the floor at my side.

"Lib, we were thinking," Gemma flashed a look at Noah, and leaned closer, "how about we get out of here, acquire some booze and have a drink at Gabe's grave."

I recoiled at her suggestion. "Are you kidding? How are you going to 'acquire' alcohol? Is that from your little football friend as well."

She rummaged in her bag for her compact mirror. "No, but can't Denzil get us some? He's got to come in handy for something."

"He does come in handy, Gem," I snapped. "He's my boss and pays me. So, no, he can't get us booze."

"I think Gem's just saying," Noah rolled his eyes at his girlfriend, arm draped lazily on the back of her chair, "it'd be nice for the four of us to hang out. I mean, I know he's…not there but we didn't really get a minute at the funeral and I don't know…" he looked away sadly, "I just want to…talk to him or something."

Being in a creepy graveyard wasn't my idea of fun. Plus, I always felt quite bitter about walk outs in the graveyard, it's not like the bodies were actually there. It all just felt hollow and fake to me. "I'll pass."

"How about coming back to mine then?" Gemma folded her arms and narrowed her eyes. I could tell instantly that my comment about Denzil had irritated her.

I shifted uncomfortably, knowing full well I'd never in a

million years be allowed to do anything that resembled fun without facing the music at home first. My heart sank whenever I thought about seeing Dad and I just wanted to get it over with. "No, I can't."

"This is how it starts," she muttered. I could tell she was jiggling her leg up and down under the table, which she always did when she was starting to lose her temper.

I sighed, really not feeling in the mood to take her on. I was too drained. "What are you talking about, Gem?"

Not even my calmest voice worked to defuse the bomb that was about to go off. "This!" she spat. "This is how it starts. Soon you won't even want to know us."

I curled my lip and made the mistake of letting out a laugh at her words. "That's ridiculous, Gem."

"Is it?"

My eyes darted to Noah, looking for some help in taming the beast.

He frowned and shifted in his seat to face her. "Babe, calm down. She just doesn't want to hang out today. Cut her some slack. It just means we can hang out."

He planted a kiss on her jaw and another on her neck but she didn't take her eyes off me. Noah pulled back and noticed her glare, exhaling in defeat. "Whatever."

Now she glanced at him. She flashed him a strange look as though deep in thought, chewing the inside of her mouth. Slowly, she lifted her eyes to me again and I swallowed at the snide smile dancing on her lips.

"You're right, Noah. We should cut her some slack. After all, I'm sure she's tired after playing little housewife to Crit boy yesterday." She pinched her chin. "It was yesterday you cooked for him, wasn't it? And then, weirdly, you end up out for the night and your dad doesn't know where you are."

I knew Gemma's eyes would be sparkling in glee but it wasn't her I was looking at. My eyes were on Noah who first of all let out a laugh as though she was making a joke, but was now serious, his jaw clenched.

"So," she drummed her fingers on her lips, "I can't help but think this grand reunion, barely a week after the supposed love of your life walks out, may I remind you, got off to a very good start and you took the party somewhere else."

I felt my breathing start to grow shallow.

"Tell me, Lib, what does a Crit taste like?" She picked up her half-eaten banana and moved it in her mouth suggestively.

"Shut up, Gemma," I hissed. "You don't know what you're talking about."

"And what I'm dying to know," she leaned across the table, now well and truly in Mr Hyde mode, "does he have white pubes?"

"Enough!" I shouted and several people turned to look.

Gemma giggled and sat back in her seat.

Noah closed his eyes and when he opened them, they rested squarely on me. "What's she talking about?"

His voice was quieter than I'd ever heard before.

I couldn't tell them I'd tried to walk out. It would hurt them far more than any Cassius related tale. "I told you. I was at Denzil's shop, helping unpack. Call him if you want."

Gemma sniggered and I threw her a look that must have been one of my fiercer ones because I could have sworn she gulped.

"Lib," Noah started, unable to stop his lip from curling into a snarl, "mark my words, if I ever see you exchanging anything more than polite hello with that freak, I'll personally see to it that it's his assembly everyone's squawking their eyes out at next. Do you understand?"

Gemma took a swig of her hot chocolate, eyes on me.

"Cassius is a friend. I've known him since–"

"No." Noah pointed and shook his head, like a parent would to a petulant child. "If it was Gem who walked and there was a girl sniffing around me a week later, I'm sure you'd be the same."

Trump card. Noah had placed me in an impossible position. I sighed. "I suppose so, but it's not like Cassius is…sniffing around me, he's more like my brother or–"

"Open your eyes, Lib," Noah interrupted. "I've seen the way he looks at you. Gabriel didn't care, made him feel good that he was the one who had you, or some shit like that. I never liked it, though. And now I've not got Gabriel to talk me out of kicking the crap out of him."

"Got it, Noah." I lowered my eyes, feeling even more exhausted. In the short time I'd known him, I'd learned he was like Gem. When he got a bee in his bonnet, there was no point fighting your corner. Not until he was calmer.

"Well, on that note," I stood and pulled my bag on my shoulder, "I'm going to head home and catch up on the coursework. Have fun, you two."

I was barely out of the canteen doors when I heard the familiar sound of Gemma's footsteps jogging after me. "Lib!" she called. "Lib, wait!"

I begrudgingly turned seeing the familiar expression on her face that quickly followed her outbursts. Remorse.

"I'm sorry." She grimaced, looking as sweet as pie in front of me with her two French braids knotted either side of her head. "I just got angry because I wanted to see you today and…I was jealous you hung out with Cassius."

"Our dads are friends," I said, now feeling like I was addressing a child.

"I know," she whined. "I didn't mean it. Listen, I'll calm down Noah, he'll be fine with it honestly and I think he's only half serious about killing Cassius."

"Great," I muttered.

"Well," she glanced over her shoulder to look back into the canteen, "I better get back, you get yourself home quickly. It's cold out there."

I smiled. She was trying desperately to compensate for her venomous words. "I will. And, if you do go to Gabriel's grave, give him a kiss from me."

She brightened at this and nodded. "That's just the kind of thing Noah wants to hear you say. I'll tell him."

I rolled my eyes. Noah was officially turning into my dad. Only a younger, less intelligent and more bad tempered version. "I'll see you tomorrow."

"Bye, Lib." She pecked me on the cheek and pulled me into a quick embrace which I returned. "Do some coursework for me." She winked, before heading back to the canteen, throwing me one last look and small wave.

***

"Liberty."

I blinked and returned my eyes to Mr Jones.

"You're of course excused from school today. As am I actually…" He shook his head and flipped back into headmaster mode. "I know how terrible and shocking this news must be for you."

I didn't move. My mind replaying the images of Gemma planting that soft kiss on my cheek, almost having to stand on her tip-toes.

It played in slow motion. Her walking away.

The last wave.

"Lib," Dad approached and rubbed my arm, "I'm so sorry. You can take as much time as you need."

Both of their concerned faces peered at me.

She was happy. She was her usual self. Fiery. Cheeky. In love with the sandy-haired boy staring adoringly at her as always.

Oh God, Noah.

"Are you sure?" I breathed.

Dad pulled me to one side and lowered his voice to a whisper. "We found some…things on Clean Up."

I closed my eyes and moved my head away.

Gemma.

My beautiful vivacious friend.

"Lib?" Dad's eyes searched my face which I was sure was ashen.

I blinked and felt my mouth curl into a bright smile. "Eggs. I have eggs cooking."

"Lib, that doesn't matter–"

"Yes, it does." I moved away from him quickly. "I…erm… made them for you and Oscar. I just need to check on them."

Dad reached for my hand but I snatched it back.

"It's fine." I laughed flatly. "I need to get back to breakfast. It'll burn."

"Eggs won't burn. Please leave them."

"I'd just like to finish making breakfast," I snapped, stalking out of the room. "Shit!" I saw the pan boiling over and ran to turn down the heat. I watched as the bubbles subsided and the eggs became visible again, dancing around the bottom of the pan, clanging into one another. I took it off the stove, placing it on one of the cork heat mats on the kitchen side. I reached into the bread bin and pulled out two slices and placed them into the toaster.

"Don't worry." I tore my eyes away from the toaster as I sensed Dad's presence. "I won't burn it this time, I know we can't afford to replace it."

He sighed. "Please can you leave the breakfast and just go and have five minutes to yourself? You need to think about what you've just been told."

"I don't need to." I pulled some plates out of the cupboard. "I'm a veteran at this now. I can handle it."

"It's not a request," Dad muttered.

We looked at one another. He was right. Parents always had a knack for being right in these situations.

"I'll be in my room."

I reached the top of the stairs and sank to the floor, sitting outside the bathroom with my back pressed against the wall. I wanted tears to flow but they didn't.

I'd cried when I'd heard about Gabriel but that had a lot to do with Gemma's concern and her own tear stained face.

I didn't see the point of crying when I knew her arms wouldn't wrap around me.

She'd dried so many of my tears for as long as I could remember. True, I ended up mopping hers most of the time but she cared so deeply about me. When I hurt, so did she.

Instead, I just blinked and stared at the wall straight ahead.

"....since the notice went out, it's gotten a bit out of hand, I admit..."

I wrapped my arms around my knees as I heard the voice of Mr Jones in the hall downstairs.

"Too right," I heard Dad snap under his breath. "How much more can one girl take?"

"That's why I'm here."

I frowned and strained to listen to their hushed voices.

"It needs to be sooner rather than later." Mr Jones sounded as though he was speaking through gritted teeth. "You need to just get it done...before she takes matters into her own hands."

"I know," Dad sighed. "I'm just not...ready."

"Do you think I was?" Mr Jones snapped.

"Ssh, she's not a million miles away. Keep your voice down."

Definitely talking about me.

"I had to do it." Mr Jones sounded on the brink of tears. "She was spending to much time with the Hartmann kid."

"Noah?" I whispered, shifting to crawl on my hands and knees so I was closer to the top of the stairs.

"It was alright for him," he carried on. "There wasn't consequences for that boy."

"How was it?" Dad's voice was so quiet I could barely hear him.

"Awful. That's all I can say, you know I'm not allowed to speak of it."

"I know. And you say there's been another?"

"Yes," Mr Jones sighed, "the Martins took Abram."

I gasped and clamped my hand over my mouth, my eyes wide in horror. I felt my body start to shake as I recalled the conversation with Cassius the night before.

The Martins took Abram.

Took Abram.

"Gemma will be announced today in school. I've been granted time off but I don't want to be at home…"

"I can understand that." Dad sounded awkward.

"Like I said, it needs to be soon. She's high risk after losing her friends and you need to take her. If she walks then…well, we'll be paying for it a long time."

My whole body was now shaking in fear, and I stood up slowly and as quietly as possible. Being careful not to tread on any loose floorboards, I turned around to make for my room and found myself almost nose to nose with Mum.

I gasped and she covered my mouth with her hand.

We both stood still for a minute making sure Dad and Mr Jones hadn't heard anything.

They were still talking in hushed tones.

My frightened eyes flicked back to Mum, who stared back at me.

Slowly she removed her hand from over my mouth and stroked my cheek, a dreamy look on her face.

I closed my eyes as she moved her mouth to my ear.

"Liberty," she whispered and I let out a quiet whimper at hearing Mum's voice for the first time in more than a year. "I called you that for a reason." She moved back and pressed her forehead against mine. I hadn't realised we were the same height before.

"Mum," I mouthed but no sound came out.

I looked up and her blue eyes were boring into mine. I saw a flash of fire dance in them.

In that moment, I caught a glimpse of the woman I remembered. The one I played chess with for hours on end and who used to wrestle me to the floor like I did with Oscar, while we laughed wildly.

"Liberty?"

I nodded but couldn't respond.

The corner of her mouth turned upwards into a smile, and she said just one word to me.

The word jolted through my heart like a fire.

Just one word that would change everything in a single moment.

"Fight."

Chapter VII

"Denzil!" I called, letting myself into the shop. "Denzil, where are you?"

The Harry Potter soundtrack was playing and I immediately went behind the counter to switch it off. I drummed my fingers on the surface, wondering where he was.

Trust. A feeling so greatly under-appreciated. It's amazing the shift both mentally and physically when you realise you have no idea who to trust anymore. Mum hadn't said another word after my run-in with her on the landing and instead merely shuffled back to her room and back into oblivion. I'd remained rooted to the spot, staring after her, until Oscar popped his head out of his room asking for a drink.

Oscar. I trusted him.

Dad was a different story. The thought of being in the same room as him caused a ball that felt the size of an apple form in my dry throat.

"...it needs to be soon....she's high risk... you need to take her...If she walks we'll be paying for it a long time..."

It was as plain as day something was going on. I wasn't a stupid girl. Nor did I ever follow the mantra that ignorance is bliss. I certainly couldn't now because wherever Dad was told to 'take' me, it had to be soon according to Mr Jones.

I had no lock on my bedroom door but I did have a wooden chair at my dressing table that I could, and did, wedge under the handle.

I hadn't been to school which I was now regretting deeply as the hours spent sat in my room, listening to Dad move around the house, had made me more jumpy and paranoid. I'd snuck in to see Mum on several occasions but despite my desperate whispers, she had no answers for my questions. Just unblinking blue eyes, staring through me. She made me angrier. She clearly knew exactly what was going on but didn't tell me. It made me hate her.

No, not hate. I just didn't trust her either.

Whenever the clock told me it was early afternoon, I'd sigh in boredom and wish I was in Blackbrooke class, but then I remembered I no longer had Gemma. Plus, Mr Jones had been the one who told Dad to take me, and Mr Fuller had been so rough in his panic about Consuela's Spanish words.

I'd ventured downstairs so rarely that I hadn't spoken to Cassius on the phone, not wanting to be in the kitchen for long periods of time with Dad. I'd attempted to call Noah, deciding he needed to hear from me more than Cassius. I couldn't have been more wrong. On all three occasions, his mother said he didn't want to talk.

So, that just left one person and I couldn't wait until my next scheduled shift. My solid, dependable friend who I needed to share my theory on Gemma with.

"And so that concludes the tour of…" I saw Denzil and a young woman emerge from the back of the shop, his hand on her back, guiding her. "Erm…" he floundered at the sight of me and shot a look at the woman who was clearly a tourist given the 'I heart Crits' t-shirt she was wearing. Plus, she looked far too excited to be a Blackbrooke resident.

"Come on, Denzil," I folded my arms, feeling amused despite the ominous turn of events, "concludes the tour of what exactly?"

He ran his hand over his dreadlocked ponytail. "I was just showing Courtney the first building the Lurkers settled in."

I didn't mean to snigger and put on my best serious face as Courtney nodded excitedly.

"Denver said the first Lurker settlers used to live in this

very building, is that correct?" Her squeaky American accent grated on me.

"Erm…it's Denzil, actually," he said, wincing at my eyes burning into him.

Courtney was now looking at me, demanding an answer.

"Well…yes, as a matter of fact, the Lurkers did settle in this very building hundreds of years ago." I nodded, enjoying watching Denzil squirm. "They used to sit in this very spot around a small table where they'd take their tea every afternoon before they'd retire to the drawing room for a gay old game of charades."

Courtney clapped her hands together. "Oh my God, that's so British! Well, I really must go now. The rest of the group are waiting for me. It was good to meet you, thanks for the special tour."

"No problem." Denzil waved, looking like a lovesick puppy. "Oh, and call me if you want anymore information on Blackbrooke!" he called but the bell on the door had already rung as she skipped out. "How amazing was she?!"

"Enthralling," I replied, deadpan.

"Did you see the size of her boobs?" Denzil was still staring out of the window after her.

I threw my folded up apron at him. "That's vile. You do realise who you're speaking to."

He caught the apron and leaned on the cashdesk. "With what do I owe this pleasure anyway? Shouldn't you be in school?"

I avoided his eye. "I haven't been in for the last few days. Gemma walked out."

Denzil recoiled in shock. "What? Are you serious?"

I bent down to inspect the CD stack so he didn't see my face colour and my eyes fill with tears.

Aside from trying to fathom what the hell was going on, I'd obviously spent a lot of time thinking about Gemma since I heard the news. Without her, it felt like my world had gone quiet. I knew for a fact that I'd probably end up getting through entire school days from now on without uttering a single word now that I didn't have my little partner in crime.

I scattered the CDs, inspecting them closely. "I'm afraid I'm very serious. Her funeral's tomorrow."

"Shit," Denzil breathed, moving around to where I was standing. "I can't believe that. She was only in here the other week…" he trailed off. "How are her parents dealing with this?"

I shrugged. "Okay, I suppose….I don't really know to be honest."

Nor do I care, I thought, but didn't say out loud.

"And what about that boyfriend of hers?"

My breath caught in my throat as I thought of Noah who was refusing to speak to me. It was to be expected but I had to admit that I was hurt. Him and I were both in the same boat after all. We'd both lost our best friend and the love of our life.

"He's okay," I said quietly.

Denzil peered down with concerned eyes. "And what about you, Lib? How are you dealing with this? It's been a…crazy couple of weeks."

"Actually," I shot a look at him and he automatically stepped back, "I'm fine. I…came here to speak to you and have a look through some of the books if that's okay."

"Of course. What's up?"

"Well…"

His eyes widened in anticipation.

I took a deep breath, about to say the words my mind had been grappling with over the last few days. They came tumbling out of my mouth before I could regain any kind of composure and I gesticulated wildly as I told Denzil about the car driving past the shop belonging to Abram's family, my strange exchange with Hope, Dad and Mr Jones' hushed conversation, my mothers order at the top of the stairs. Once I'd finished I stepped back expectantly. "So…" I had to admit, it was a lot more damning in my head, "what do you think that means?"

Denzil looked thoughtful. "It means…"

I leaned closer.

"It means I've had far too much pot today."

"I'm serious!"

He laughed heartily. "Jesus Lib, that's some real conspiracy theory stuff. What's next? You're going to tell me Marilyn Monroe was murdered by Kennedy's people? Elvis hasn't really left the building?"

"Fine," I stomped to the bookshelves and pulled out several textbooks, "but I'm telling you, Denzil, something's going on. Gemma would never have walked. She hated those Crits, she wouldn't have given them the satisfaction. Mr Jones mentioned being 'taken' and I really think that means something so we–"

"Maybe she bailed."

"What do you mean?"

"She might have decided this town wasn't big enough for her head and did a midnight flit. In fact," he raised his index finger in the air, "she's probably kicking back with a pina colada as we speak."

"Pina colada?"

"What? They were very popular in the eighties." He picked up his 'I heart eighties' CD and sighed at my unimpressed face. "We never know the story behind walk outs, Lib. It could have been anything. She might have been on her way to see her boyfriend."

"I think her parents took her somewhere," I blurted. "I think she's on the Outside."

There. I said it. At first I thought she was dead without a doubt, but there was something about the way Mr Jones was speaking that made me question it. And once my mind gripped onto the idea, it refused to let go. Plus if there was a slight chance Gemma was alive then that meant someone else dear to me could be alive, too.

"Why would her parents take her out?"

"I don't know for sure," I snapped, flicking through one of the books. "I've just got a feeling about it. Plus, Blackbrooke Chronicle doesn't report on walk outs."

"And what's that got to do with anything?"

I exhaled impatiently. "Maybe they don't report on walk outs because they're not actually walk outs. Maybe some families take their kids over the border so they can get a shot at a normal life."

"That doesn't make sense." Denzil pulled a cigarette tin out of his back pocket and popped the lid. "Why would they just take their kids and dump them on the Outside? It's not like we're at war in Blackbrooke."

I scowled at the text in front of me and started reading about the Hunters. This particular book contained a lot of biological information on the Crits with anatomical drawings. It was one of the few books that actually went into a bit more detail rather than just containing anecdotal information.

The bell on the door sounded and I looked up excitedly.

My heart sank as I realised I'd expected Gemma to come bounding in.

Never again, Lib.

Unless she's not actually dead and just hiding out somewhere. Or perhaps clinking glasses with Gabriel on a beach, waiting for Noah and I to arrive.

No, it wasn't Gemma who strode into the shop, but Cassius, who didn't so much stride in, but half-stumbled. He placed his hands on his knees and bent double at the waist, desperately trying to catch his breath.

"I…ran all the…way…from school," he managed between gulping in air. His ghostly white skin had a hint of pink on his face and he peeled off his scarf and woolly hat. "Are you okay?"

"Of course, I'm okay. Why wouldn't I be?"

"It's just that..." he gained control of his breathing, "I called your dad and he said–"

"You rang my dad?" I recoiled firstly in surprise and then suspicion. "Why?"

He dismissed me with a wave. "I've called him everyday since I found out about Gemma. I just wanted to see how you were doing."

Denzil looked from him to me, amused.

"I'm okay," I said awkwardly. I instantly relaxed. Cassius wasn't the enemy here. I could tell by his concerned features and the look of relief in his eyes at the sight of me. "You didn't need to come down here."

"I just wanted to see you and check for myself. I ditched my afternoon classes."

"My hero..." Denzil mocked in a girly, dreamy voice.

I shot him a look and Cassius went even redder. Or as red as his skin would allow.

"Tea?" Denzil asked brightly, grinning like an idiot.

I nodded distractedly and turned back to Cassius. "I'm glad you're here actually. I have to talk to you about something." I carried a pile of books to the counter. "I need you to take half of these and try to find out anything you can about a secret place where people take their kids."

"Erm...what?"

"Come on, Cass!" I waved him over. "You need to hurry, we only have a couple of hours before my dad comes to get me."

I ignored his eyes on me as I skipped through the pages and didn't look up until Denzil returned, artfully carrying three steaming cups of tea.

"Now," I picked up Mr Fuller's book, "anything you read about people being 'taken' somewhere, flag it up. Denzil, do you have post-its?"

Cassius took a tentative step towards me. "Lib, are you feeling okay?"

"Of course."

"How are you feeling about tomorrow?" I could tell he was choosing his words carefully.

"Fine." I shrugged, squinting to read the small print at the bottom of one of the pages. "I'm thinking there might be a secret way out of town. Maybe in the woodland and then you can bypass border control. This map of Blackbrooke gets a bit vague and the fact the woodland is pretty much forbidden makes me think there's some secret–"

"Lib," Cassius took another step towards me, "are you okay? I mean, seriously..."

"You sound like Dad. I don't need your concern, I just need your help." I flipped several more pages and felt one rip in my hand. "Damn!" I muttered. "Take it out of my wages, Denzil. Hey!" I scowled at Cassius as he took the book out of my hands. I made a grab for it but he raised his arm up in the air.

I realised it would be futile to try to jump.

"Lib," he said softly, "I'm sorry to be the one to remind you but...you lost your best friend. You need to chill."

I frowned. "Gemma's not dead."

"What?" His eyes darted to the side. Denzil cleared his throat and turned away.

I raised my nose in the air. "She's not. I just know it."

"Then....where is she?"

"I don't know that yet, do I?" I snapped again, glancing at the books. "That's what I need your help with. She's not dead. I can feel it." I pointed at my heart. "This would be broken if she was dead but it isn't. So, are you going to help me, or are you going to just stand there looking at me like I've lost it?"

He placed his hands on his head. "You know I'm your friend..."

I narrowed my eyes.

"But," this time I didn't move away as he put his hands on my shoulders, "Gemma's dead." His voice was resolute. "I'm sorry, Lib, but she–"

"Not until I have proof." I returned his look. "Until then… grab a book. I'll fill you in about everything later, there's no time."

"It's a waste of time."

I'd had just about enough of his defeatist attitude. "Then leave!" I pushed past and gestured to the door.

He picked up his bag. "You're setting yourself up for disappointment."

"Really?" The bell rang loudly as I yanked the door open. "Get out."

"Don't worry," he muttered.

I glared as he stopped in front of me. "You need to face up to this, Lib."

"Just go home, Cass."

"I…" he glanced at Denzil, lowering his voice, "I care about you. I'm worried. I feel like you spent your childhood being there for me and now it's my turn. I just want you to be…" he trailed off and we both frowned at one another and slowly turned to look at Denzil.

The familiar chords of *It Must Be Love* by Madness blasted from the CD player.

Denzil raised his eyebrows suggestively.

"I hate you," I mouthed to him.

Cassius' mouth twitched in amusement and I felt myself start to smile as well. Despite the badly timed joke from my boss, I couldn't deny that Cass was just looking out for my best interests. Of course, he was worried. I sounded like a crazy woman – even to myself. On some of the nights when I sat on the floor next to my bed, clutching a knife I'd smuggled from the kitchen in case Dad broke the door down, I wondered whether the loss of my friends had actually made me insane. That I'd imagined the conversation between Dad and Mr Jones, along with the confrontation with Mum in the hall.

And just how strange was my exchange with Hope? Wasn't she just getting sentimental that I'd grown up so fast? Especially now she was a mother herself.

Just when I started to dismiss my thoughts as flights of whimsy, I remembered the one thing that made my mind reel this way in the first place.

Two of my friends were dead.

Supposedly anyway.

"Cass?"

"Yes."

I rubbed my arms from the cold coming in from outside. "Do you want to stay and we'll…drink tea with a dried up old hippy."

His smile widened. "I'd love to."

"Great. And maybe we can just have a look through a few books in the process…" I muttered to myself, as I closed the door again. This time I turned the sign on the door to 'closed' and turned the key in the lock.

We grabbed our mugs and made for the small narrow staircase up to Denzil's flat. It was as you would expect, full of little knick-knacks he'd collected from tourists. He had a collection of postcards stuck on his fridge and all over his kitchen cupboards from people who'd written when they returned back to their homes on the Outside. When I was last in the flat after my walk out it was the first time I'd been up there in more than a year. Not because I didn't like it, just because it never seemed appropriate and I think Denzil was already conscious about how our friendship was perceived in the town. No one said anything to me directly but I'd sometimes catch the occasional comment in the Academy.

"Just the two of them in that creepy shop…"

"Wonder what her boyfriend makes of that…"

I never told Denzil about it because I know it would have annoyed him. Probably embarrassed him as well.

Denzil threw himself onto the sofa as I pulled out a chair

at the small wooden table and Cassius did the same. I smiled as I noticed he'd brought the pile of books up with him. He saw me looking. "We'll look through them but I don't want you getting carried away."

"Yes, *Dad*," I said sarcastically, grabbing the book I was reading earlier. "Denzil, please can you open your blinds, it's like a dungeon in here."

"Mmmm." Denzil's smile widened and he looked on the cusp of sleep. "I like it."

I tutted and took a quick sip of my tea before turning to Cassius. It was only fair I filled him in on recent events. I repeated the same story I told Denzil only with more control this time, taking special care not to let my voice rise in anger. I didn't tear my eyes from him throughout and his expression remained the perfect combination of thoughtful and concerned and he'd nod occasionally. Perhaps he was merely appeasing me but he was making all of the right noises so I didn't stop. I could sense Denzil was listening again, obviously seeing whether it sounded less insane this time around. "So, all of that, coupled with my run-in with Mr Fuller about the Spanish words just makes me think…" I trailed off, not sure how to conclude my story.

"You think they've been taken somewhere against their will?' Cassius ventured, picking up his cup before placing it down when he realised he'd already drained its contents. "And that you might be heading the same way?"

I blinked at him. He got it. "Yes."

He exhaled slowly and leaned back. "And Mr Jones said what about Noah?"

"That there are no consequences for him. Whatever that means."

"Okay," he said slowly, "so, whatever's going on, we can assume your parents, Mr Jones, Mr Fuller and erm…"

"Hope?" I ventured.

"Yep, that's the one. They all know something." His last

sentence wasn't a question nor a statement. It was more like Cassius was thinking out loud.

"Make me another brew, Lib," Denzil called, sounding bored. "I can't move."

I turned in my seat. "Denzil, you're an adult, you must know what's going on."

Cassius followed my gaze to Denzil's sleepy form. The use of the word 'adult' was a stretch, I know, but it was technically true.

He chuckled. "I'm a child of the revolution, baby!"

"What?" I asked, already not amused by whatever naff joke he was bound to come out with. I'd heard them all before.

He sat up, pulling his ponytail free so the muddy dreadlocks fell forward. "I'm a Lost Boy."

"Jesus Christ," I muttered, giving up and turning back to the book in front of me.

"Kids," Denzil turned his palms upwards as though performing a magic trick, "your good friend, Denzil…is invisible."

"You need to lay off the pot," I mumbled as Cassius eyed him with interest.

"No, I'm serious." He walked to the table, leaning his hands on the back of Cass's chair. "In the eyes of Blackbrooke, I don't exist."

The confused looks on both of our faces prompted him to sit down. "Lib, you kinda know the story…" He grimaced and flashed an apologetic look at Cassius. "Both of my parents walked out when I was a teenager…"

I did know the story. Albeit, I knew of it anyway. Denzil rarely spoke about his family as it made him angry. Angry at them for walking out and ending their lives, angry about the Crits, angry about the Rules, but ultimately, I think he was just upset he was left to fend for himself.

Denzil chewed the inside of his mouth. "They walked together when I was sixteen and I ended up living with my

Gran but…then *she* died," he let out an uncomfortable laugh, "I stayed living there, turned eighteen, and sort of…got forgotten I suppose." He stood up and flicked on the kettle. I stopped reading so as not to appear rude and disrespectful as he spoke about his family. "No one came knocking at the door and because I had no guardian…I never swore in the Rules."

"What?!" Cassius and I cried in unison.

That was a new one.

Denzil raised his hands defensively. "I know, but they never came looking and I wasn't about to offer myself on a plate."

"So," I leaned closer, fascinated, "you don't know all of the Rules?"

He shook his head. "Not a clue. Asked some friends along the way but they never told me. One of the Rules I do know is that you're not allowed to talk about the Rules."

"Like *Fight Club*," I said, now frowning at the table.

I felt both pairs of eyes on me and shrugged. "What? I like that film."

Denzil laughed. "Yes, Liberty Bell, just like *Fight Club*. I'll tell you one other thing I know about the Rules…"

We leaned closer again.

"I know it's a two day event and the friends I've seen come out of there…they look traumatised. Like their whole world has come crashing down."

I knew my features were registering horror.

"So," he clapped his hands together, "enjoy yourselves, not long now!"

"Denzil!" I scolded.

"Sorry." He yawned, pouring another cup of tea. I tapped Cassius on the arm and held out my empty mug for him to pass to Denzil. "But I'm afraid to say it's the truth."

"When do you go?" I asked Cassius, my voice quiet.

"January 20th," he said without hesitation.

I nodded, feeling somewhat relived that I'd also be at that ceremony as I turned eighteen the week before it. They only did two Rules ceremonies a year, one in the winter and one in the summer. Because Gabriel didn't turn eighteen until June and Gemma in April, I thought I was going to be alone. Well, not completely alone. Noah had turned eighteen in November but the thought of Noah and I going to the ceremony together, clasping hands nervously, and soothing each other, didn't really ring true in my brain. He was my boyfriend's best friend, and my best friend's boyfriend, yet nothing to me really.

I'd have Cassius though and that was a great comfort.

We remained quiet for a while, just the sound of pages turning and Denzil shlurping his tea echoing around the room.

"I don't even know what I'm supposed to be looking for," Cassius muttered eventually, gesturing to the book in his hand.

"Just look for anything that might offer some clue as to where Gemma is. Anything at all." I had no idea either. All I was armed with was a vague idea that something wasn't right. Beyond that, I was completely lost.

Instead of lingering on feeling completely useless, I frowned in concentration at the page in front of me, eyes scouring for any clues as to what could be going on.

Not a lot is known about the environment the Queens live as it is forbidden to venture that far into the woodland but excavations over the last hundred years on the outskirts suggests they have formed a series of tunnels.

In 1979, a group of young people entered the woodland where one of the group fell through the ground into a large hole. Geologists found it to be an abandoned den of some kind but was too big for a typical woodland animal. Also due to its sophisticated engravings on its wall, Hunters and Lurkers were ruled out.

Deforestation over the last few centuries caused the woodland to draw back, so the Queens had to abandon this particular den. Aside from the engravings (See fig. 1), there was nothing for the experts to find.

I frowned at the image of the engravings and stifled a yawn, internally cursing Denzil for having it so dark in here during the day. Plus, I had had another sleepless night sat on my bedroom floor, knife in hand, which wasn't helping.

I blinked and widened my eyes in an effort to make myself more alert before continuing to read.

There are certain Rules the townspeople of Blackbrooke need to adhere to which have descended over generations. These Rules suggest the Queens may do more than simply eat their prey. The fixation on hair prompted the rule of females having to wear their hair in a bun, even throughout the day. This came from the incident at Blackbrooke Academy when a young pupil was scalped during the day by a rogue Queen.

Despite there being no confirmed sightings of the Queens in the daylight since this date, the hair Rule was adopted. Blackbrooke Academy also erected security fencing and employed the Watchmen to operate in the four corners of the school to ensure they cannot roam where the children play.

As with most Creature incidents, it is unclear what the Queens did with the hair they took that day and Outsiders with a keen interest in Blackbrooke as well as researchers have said it is naïve to think it was related to food. Some have claimed the hair is merely a keepsake whereas others have linked the Queens to witchcraft and black magic practices, However, as nothing resulted from the occurrence, it has to be attributed to a freak accident.

Alongside wearing their hair in a bun, the females of Blackbrooke are not permitted to dye their hair and must keep it natural. This Rule was introduced after Dr Brian White of UCSD claimed the scents of the chemicals in hair dye could be detected by dogs up to three miles away. In a speech delivered to Blackbrooke residents in 1982, White said: "For the sake of vanity, risking one's life just isn't worth it. Even if a female wears dyed hair in a tight bun, the smell can be detected from the heat given off from the scalp. Furthermore, the temptation to wear hair loose when it has been dyed in order to provoke a reaction is paramount – this will not do when the Queens have been known to scalp females. In conclusion, I urge Blackbrooke to create a new Rule against women dyeing their hair."

Although the Rule was never officially adopted, all hair dye was removed from Blackbrooke and the townspeople embraced the unofficial Rule.

"Gemma highlighted her hair," I said to myself smiling. "Denzil, I bet you've…"

I frowned. The light from the lamp was shining brightly in my face and I moved it to one side to see Cassius' seat empty and no sign of Denzil.

"Guys?" I enquired, looking around the room.

I stood slowly. "Is this a joke?"

Hearing nothing, I walked across the living room to Denzil's bedroom, pushed open the door with my fingertips and glanced in. The bed was untouched and I closed it again.

I turned back and gasped, shielding my eyes. The lamp was turned so it was shining in my face again. "Who's there?"

I heard a giggle and froze.

"Who is that?"

Another giggle.

I heard the sound of a page turning and noticed a shadowy figure sat behind the lamp. I pressed my back against the door.

"You look like a little rabbit," the voice rasped. "No need

to be so scared."

It turned another page.

My eyes darted. "Where did Cass and Denzil go?"

"I thought you'd be more upset, Lib." The voice was sing-song. "Hey ho, what can ya do?"

I tried to control my breathing which was getting more shallow. "Where are they?"

"Don't worry." The chair scraped loudly on the floor and I saw the person shift so their legs were crossed. "You'll be back soon."

"I'll be back? Where am I?"

They sniggered. "You're dreaming, of course."

I frowned. It felt pretty real to me. "I-I want to wake up."

"Relax, you will." It slammed the book closed. "I can't believe you don't recognise my voice."

"I'm sorry, I don't–"

It laughed again. "Here's a clue, you're right, I *do* highlight my hair."

My mouth dropped open and I took a step forward instinctively. "Gemma?"

"Don't come any closer!" she shouted in a raspy voice as I stepped forward again.

I shielded my eyes from the light. "Can you at least move the lamp from shining in my face?"

She positioned herself behind the lamp. I saw her hair was loose in big, bouncing curls falling over her shoulders but I couldn't make out her face. "Can't do that, Lib. I'm not… looking my best."

I rolled my eyes. "Come on, Gem. I don't care about that. You're my best friend. Plus, isn't this a dream anyway? Isn't this *my* dream?"

She returned to her seat. "Yes, it is."

I shuffled on the spot nervously. I felt like I was going to get shot by a firing squad any second.

"Lib," she sighed, "you're making them nervous."

"Who?" I frowned. "The Crits?"

She didn't reply.

I closed my eyes and then opened them again, expecting to be awake but still finding myself in the dream, looking at the shadowy outline of Gemma. "Where are you, Gem? Where are they keeping you?"

Nothing.

"Please, Gem…"

She let out a sad laugh. "You'll figure it out. I have faith."

I stepped forward and she stood up abruptly causing the chair to topple backwards and clatter on the floor nosily. Once again, I was surprised it didn't jolt me out of the dream because I jumped out of my skin. "I'm sorry, I didn't mean to do that. Just tell me where they have you or…tell me where you were taken." I felt tears prick my eyes. "Tell me where *I'm* going to be taken."

"I can't, Lib," she said softly. "I'm in *your* dream, remember? Just know this…"

I leaned closer still, managing to keep my distance.

"Just know that they're watching, All the time. And know you have the answer."

"That doesn't make sense, Gem," I whispered, feeling a tear slide down my face. "Please help me. I know you're alive. I'll come and get you, I promise. Please don't leave me."

She didn't move.

I clenched my jaw and dived over to the lamp before she could stop me. I turned it around so I could see my friend again.

I had to see her face.

She dived for it too but the fingers that wrapped around mine weren't Gemma's.

They were long, grey and bony.

I looked at them in horror before raising my eyes to look into the hollow empty eye sockets of a Queen, its mouth hanging open into a twisted smile.

I screamed.

***

"Lib!"

I jolted awake to Cassius peering at me. "Are you okay? I think you were having a nightmare."

I felt breathless and noticed I was sweating, heat prickling my body.

Denzil was now asleep on the sofa, arm draped over his face. I could see orange light coming in from around the blinds.

"You fell asleep and I didn't want to wake you up." Cassius removed his hand from my shoulder. "Your dad will be here soon."

He pulled the books into a stack and hauled them into his arms as we descended the stairs.

My legs were shaking.

I felt like I was actually in the same room as Gemma.

Well, Gemma before it turned out to be a…

I sucked in a breath of air and leaned on the banister.

Cassius turned around awkwardly, his chin resting on the pile of books. "Lib?"

I straightened. "I'm fine."

We walked on to the shop floor and I stood rooted to the spot watching Cassius stride to the shelves and start returning the books in the right places.

The nightmare I just had stirred something that I was hoping wouldn't happen.

A single thought that I wanted to ignore.

"She might be dead," I blurted.

Cassius stopped what he was doing but didn't turn around.

I started to shake and my eyes filled with tears, quickly spilling onto my cheeks. "She might be dead after all. Maybe it wasn't just clothes my dad found, maybe it was bits of her and he just didn't want to tell me. I know how silly I've sounded and you think I'm mental but…you see…"

Cassius slowly turned.

A sob threatened to erupt from deep down in my throat. "If she's dead…I really am alone. And I don't want to be. I-I don't trust anyone. I think I might be…" My mouth moved as I tried to articulate what I wanted to say but the words couldn't form. I wiped the tears with the sleeves of my jumper. "I'm scared, Cass."

I'd never said any such thing to Cassius. Liberty Connor, his big strong friend who protected him from the bullies. She didn't get scared.

Before I could start mumbling my apologies for sounding so weak, he pulled me into an embrace, squeezing me tight and stroking my hair. I let tears flow freely into his chest, and soak into his t-shirt.

"You can trust me, Lib. We'll figure this out, I promise," he whispered.

I closed my eyes. He smelt the same as the day I met him. A homely, comforting smell that I struggled to describe.

"I'm pretty sure you can trust Denzil, too, so if it gets too much or you get scared, then you need to come here. Then you call me, and I'll be right over."

His seemingly innocent comment spoke volumes to me. It meant he didn't trust his father or he would have offered his own home as refuge. "I'm sure there's got to be a really simple and innocent explanation to all of this but until then," he pulled back, holding my face in his hands, "we'll come here everyday and go through those books in case we can find something."

I frowned and shook my head. "There's nothing in those books. It's useless."

"Hey," he bent down so I was forced to look at him, "I don't remember you ever giving up, Miss Liberty Connor."

"I gave up on you," I surprised myself with the words and

his smile wavered. "No, you didn't. It was just a…friend sabbatical."

I laughed into his chest and he squeezed me tighter. "I'm not going anywhere. Now, will you be okay tomorrow?"

"Will you be there?" It was more of a request than a question. Otherwise, if Noah didn't show up, I'd be surrounded by people I either didn't know or didn't trust.

"Of course." He didn't flinch, as though he was planning on coming anyway.

I opened my mouth to speak but closed it again abruptly as I heard Dad honking the horn of the car outside.

Cassius rubbed the tops of my arms before picking up his bag from the floor.

"After the funeral," he said, reaching for the door, "do you want to come here and do some research?"

I wiped my eyes and stood up straight in an effort to look normal. "Yes, I think that might help."

"Great. Promise you'll call me tonight if you need to talk."

I nodded, knowing that what he really meant. *"Call me if there's trouble."*

***

I stepped out of the car and looked up at the gloomy Catholic church. A gust of wind blew my dress around my legs causing me to shiver.

Here I was saying goodbye to someone I loved.

Twice in as many weeks.

Don't think about it, Lib. Just concentrate on how you'll find her. Think about her alive and needing your help.

The thought was so overwhelming that I almost turned around and bolted in the other direction. I felt Dad's fingers wrap gently around my upper arm. "Come on, sweetheart. Gemma would appreciate you being here."

Not if she's still alive, I thought. If she's still alive then the thought of her friends and family at her funeral would fill her with fear.

Dad's hand made me flinch and it didn't go unnoticed. His sad eyes did little to comfort me, only confirming he was hiding something.

As it had the previous few nights, the chair in my room was wedged under the door handle and I curled in a ball on the floor, shivering but refusing to put the blanket over me in case I fell into a deep sleep. The more groggy I was, the less chance I'd have in putting up a fight if Dad came bursting into my room to take me wherever Gemma, Abram and most probably Gabriel had been taken.

My knees buckled as we approached the church doors and Dad sprang into action and grabbed my arm. I didn't attempt to stop him, comforted he wouldn't try anything untoward due to the dozens of people around us.

He placed both arms around me as we walked towards Mr and Mrs Jones who were stood sombrely, greeting people in the entrance of the church.

Mr Jones smoothed down his tie awkwardly, clearly struggling with straddling the role of grieving father and school headmaster. He looked tired and paler than I was used to, the strain of the day already looking like it was taking its toll. I couldn't stop my eyes from narrowing as he took my hand in both of his, unable to shake the thought that we wouldn't even be attending a funeral if it wasn't for him taking her somewhere. Wherever that was. "Thank you for coming, Liberty," he cleared his throat, "she would…"

Mrs Jones let out a sob and I turned to her, my face softening. It was like looking at Gemma in twenty years time. Her blonde hair was scraped back and her eye make-up was already streaked down her face. Mrs Jones didn't struggle with her role in front of me and pulled me into a tight hug. More importantly, her pain seemed genuine and not tinged with something more sinister in the way Mr Jones' was. Mrs Jones and I hadn't spoken all that much over the years, but I always felt more comfortable in her presence than I did in her husband's. I got the feeling she felt the same way. When she was in the company of Gemma and I alone, it was the only time I ever saw her smile. Whenever she was with Mr Jones, her eyes remained downcast and she'd become jittery. "Oh Lib," she was the same height as Gemma and for a moment, I closed my eyes and pretended I was hugging my friend, "I miss her so much."

I nodded. "Me too."

"I think you should take your seats," Mr Jones interrupted and flashed a loaded look at Dad. I tore my eyes away from Mrs Jones as Dad placed his hands on my shoulders and guided me into the church. She raised her hand into a feeble wave and I tried my best to flash her a reassuring smile, promising I'd make the effort to see her after the funeral. If it wasn't too painful for her of course.

The church was teeming with Blackbrooke pupils, further confirming Gemma's popularity. I very much doubt anyone would have noticed if I'd have walked on the night I attempted to and failed miserably. I recognised several faces in the crowd including several of Noah's friends on the football team who I'd sometimes see Gemma laughing heartily with in the canteen. Girls from our sports class who she would swap hair tips with. Even some of the teachers she thoroughly enjoyed answering back to, were stood dabbing their eyes and shaking their heads in disbelief.

I scanned the faces as Dad and I filed into a row close to the front. I couldn't see Noah anywhere and felt my heart sink to my stomach.

"Please, not you as well," I whispered to myself.

"Here's Cass," Dad said and I looked around to see Cassius slide into a row at the back. He locked eyes with me and nodded. Seeing him overwhelmed me, I hadn't realised how frightened I'd felt until I practically folded in two in relief. He wore the same outfit as Gabriel's funeral of black jeans and white shirt and skinny black tie. I looked down at my own outfit, also a repeat from the funeral the week before, and promised to burn it as soon as I got home.

Dad tentatively clasped my hand and I felt a rush of emotion as I remembered Gemma doing that very thing at Gabriel's funeral. Forgetting I didn't trust him, I squeezed his hand and let out a loud sob causing several people to turn and look at me.

"I know it's hard," he whispered. "Try not to look at it."

The casket at the front hadn't even entered my mind as I'd purposefully ignored it but now I couldn't prevent my eyes from rising to look to the front.

The coffin was white with ornate handles and covered in pink flowers.

"Dad..." I couldn't tear my eyes from it, "I'm struggling...."

"Me too." His face was ashen and he looked into my eyes. "I don't think I'll be able to do it."

My heart started to pound in my chest. "Then don't," I whispered eventually.

"If we could all please stand."

The voice of the vicar interrupted whatever Dad was going to say and he focused his attention elsewhere. I couldn't stop staring at him, wondering whether he was on the cusp of telling me that I was right to feel suspicious and mistrustful of him.

"Turn to page fifty-seven in the hymnbook," the vicar ordered and I reached a shaking hand to the book in front of me. "All Things Bright and Beautiful. One of Gemma's favourite hymns."

"When she was seven," I muttered. Did her parents know her at all?

I listened to the lyrics and shook my head in disgust, not even attempting to open the hymnbook. I could hear Dad mumbling his way through it and turned around to see Cassius roll his eyes and gesture to the book in his hand. I was surprised that Denzil was now stood by his side, and he raised a tentative smile in between singing.

They couldn't have chosen a more inappropriate song, judging by the look of horror that descended on the face of Mrs Jones as she sang.

All things bright and beautiful,
All creatures great and small,
All things wise and wonderful
The Lord God made them all

As the hymn drew to a long overdue close, I took the opportunity as everyone sat down to take another look around to try and spot Noah.

He definitely wasn't there.

I closed my eyes. I hadn't realised how much I'd miss him. And just how much I'd hoped he'd be there. I remembered him, Gemma and I wrapping our arms around one another at Gabriel's funeral and now I needed to embrace him. Show him I was still there if he needed me. I certainly needed him.

I was just hoping to God he hadn't walked.

I would have understood if he did, though. It's not like I managed to resist the urge. The only reason I wasn't dead was because of Cassius' bloody mindedness and stupidity in risking his own life to find me.

"Gemma was a vibrant happy girl and the only child of Jonathan and Marie. She loved life and lived it to the fullest. Her parents describe her as their beautiful, precious jewel whose time on earth, although inevitably short, was…"

I frowned.

Inevitably?

A few people coughed and shifted in their seats and the vicar looked momentarily shocked at his own words.

"My apologies," he said quickly, looking down at the paper in front of him. "I meant, although her time on earth was unfairly short," he flashed a nervous look at Mr Jones who glared back, "she made a huge impact on all of those around her, especially her best friend, Liberty Connor."

It felt as though all eyes were on me and Dad took my hand again. I couldn't concentrate on this tribute to my friend, instead I heard only one thing.

Inevitably.

Her life was inevitably short.

"Gemma and Liberty shared an unspeakable bond that could not and will not be broken," he continued. "They referred to one another as sisters and may our thoughts and prayers also be with Liberty during this sad time."

Inevitably short.

Stop it, I willed myself. Stop thinking like that. Just remember that she night be alive. *She's alive, she's alive, she's alive,* I mentally repeated over and over again as I struggled to keep control of my breathing.

"...a keen drama and art student, Gemma excelled..."

No mention of Noah.

I flashed a look at the back of Mr and Mrs Jones' heads.

No surprises there. I knew Mr Jones wouldn't have been as gracious as Gabriel's parents.

I rolled my shoulders and closed my eyes to try and keep focus. I could feel myself drifting away. All I wanted to do was get to the shop and see if I could find anything in the stacks of books there. Just like Cassius and I had agreed to do yesterday.

It was a long shot. If there were some kind of secret place then I imagined readily available books would be heavily censored anyway. Plus, I had absolutely no idea, if there was any kind of place, *what* it was. The minutes were ticking by and I couldn't shake the idea of an egg timer from my head with Gemma's life being the grains of sand draining away rapidly.

Dad swallowed and shifted his weight from one foot to the other, no doubt sensing my suspicious eyes on him.

"...as we prepare to lay Gemma's body into the ground..."

What body? I scowled at the vicar. *There is no body, you fool.*

"...we remember, not this sad occasion, but the bright and wonderful short life of our dear sister Gemma, who..."

The vicar trailed off and I jumped at the sound of the church doors as they flew open and clattered loudly against the wall. Everyone turned to see the latecomer and someone at the back let out a cry.

The vicar's mouth dropped open as he looked in horror at whoever walked in.

I craned my neck trying to see who it was and why they'd provoked such a reaction.

In-between the heads of people, I saw him.

Messy mop of sandy hair.

Sad blue eyes.

"Noah," I whispered, not being able to stop my mouth from curling into a smile. He was alive after all. Relief swept through me in one big rush and I shuffled to the end of the row as fast as I could so I could beckon him to stand with us. The whole room erupted into nervous chatter and gasps sounded. Several people had moved so they were stood in the aisle, blocking my view of him.

"Move!" I hissed in annoyance at the sea of backs. I stood on my tiptoes to try and glance between people's shoulders. "Let him in!"

The people in front turned to acknowledge me and I recoiled at their horrified faces. Eyes trained on me, they parted and let me move forward.

One woman had her hand over her mouth, shaking her head and I couldn't peel my angry eyes off her as I passed through.

"Pathetic," I whispered, losing my temper at their judgemental attitudes, "it's only her boyfriend, you sad bunch of–"

I stopped dead in my tracks several feet away from Noah.

My eyes went to his face first. Grey, shell-shocked, horrified.

But that wasn't what made everyone stare in terror.

It was what Noah was holding in his arms that provoked the extreme reaction.

I shook my head and I stepped back in fear.

Noah took a step forward.

Held in his arms, limp and lifeless, was a body.

The love of his life.

My best friend.

Gemma.

Chapter VIII

I felt my legs go weak again and leaned on one of the wooden pews to steady myself.

Noah, his eyes staring at a spot in front of him, as though in a trance, took another step forward and the crowd recoiled.

The gasps, screams and cries had stopped and an eerie silence had descended over the room.

My whole body was shaking as I watched him take another step.

I forced myself to look at her in his arms.

She was covered in dried blood. Matted into her hair. All over her face.

Her clothes were torn to pieces and bits of cloth hung down as though she'd been in a fight with some razor wire. She'd been wearing her favourite denim jacket. It looked like black leggings and a t-shirt but I couldn't be sure.

Her head flopped over Noah's arm as though her neck was broken as he carried her like a man would carry his new wife over the threshold.

He took another step forward.

There was a mass of blood on her abdomen. Dark blood.

I noticed the skin on her torso and up one side of her face was missing, exposing her skull and making it look as though her face was stuck in a deranged smile. Her left eyeball was completely visible.

I grasped onto the seat in front of me. My knees hit the cold stone floor with a thud as I looked up as Noah walked past me.

Vomit rose up into my mouth as I noticed, among the torn strips of clothing hanging down from her body, there was parts of her. I wasn't an expert in human biology but it didn't tale a genius to figure out it was her intestines.

Hanging down.

Hitting Noah's legs as he walked.

I fell forward onto my hands and crawled to the aisle to see Noah continue his walk slowly to the front of the church.

I caught sight of Mr and Mrs Jones staring at their poor daughter in the arms of her traumatised boyfriend.

Noah's white t-shirt and blue jeans were streaked in blood. There was blood smeared on one of his cheeks. He staggered and stopped to hoist her up further. I watched him lean his head down as he squeezed her tight, seeming to whisper something in her ear, his eyes closed. A tear fell down his face as he kissed her before standing up straight again and continuing his walk.

Still on my hands and knees, I watched, my mouth open in a silent cry.

"Noah," I choked.

The vicar stumbled out of the way like a coward as Noah approached.

Mrs Jones had fallen to the floor in shock while Mr Jones glared in horror at his daughters stripped body with exposed flesh, shaking his head manically.

Someone from the other side of the aisle made a retching sound which broke the strange silence.

I leaned forward even more to see but quickly shrank back with a gasp as a Watcher trotted past me, running to catch up with Noah. I edged back into the row and clamped my hand over my mouth.

Another Watcher ran past.

"Impossible," I whispered to myself. They weren't supposed to be able to get into churches.

I peered around the aisle again as Noah ascended the steps

to Gemma's casket and gently placed her body on top of it. Several pink flowers drifted down to the floor.

Her arm hung down and Noah took it and placed her hand over her heart.

I couldn't breathe as I watched. The side of Gemma I could see looked almost perfect.

All of the thoughts about research.

Finding out where she was taken.

Pointless.

Another Watcher ran past, brushing my face. I let out a small cry and shrank back. They all gathered at the front, sitting on their backsides, soundlessly watching Noah.

Noah pulled his lips away from what was his last kiss with his dead girlfriend and slowly turned around to face everyone. He stood straight, his hands balled into fists at his sides as he glared at a spot on the floor.

"She was on my doorstep," he said, loud enough for everyone to hear, "this morning."

My tears splashed onto the tiled floor as I watched him wrench himself away from the alter and make his way back down the aisle.

The half dozen Watchers that had followed him into the church, trotted after him and I watched, feeling sheer terror at the sight of their blood soaked coats. One stopped at the row I was crouched in and looked at me with its dead, red eyes.

I swallowed in fear and backed away slowly.

It looked at the other Watchers following Noah before turning and starting to walk towards me, its head bowed like it was about to pounce.

I crawled backwards, faster. "Go away," I whispered, kicking out my leg in a feeble attempt to scare it. "Get away from me."

Its paws which were bigger than my fists were either side of my legs and its dribbling and contorted face loomed in mine. It bared its teeth and I looked away, grimacing at the smell of flesh coming from its hot breath. Globules of spit dropped onto my legs and I whimpered, squeezing my eyes shut and braced myself for its bite.

Hands suddenly grabbed under my arms and I opened my eyes in surprise as I felt someone drag me away. A man from the crowd, who I didn't know, kicked at the Watcher which slinked away, out of the door to follow Noah.

"Those bloody Watchers," I heard Denzil's voice over my shoulder as he pulled me to my feet. "Are you okay?"

I started to nod but then shook my head.

"Everyone! Please move outside!" the vicar shouted, his voice high in fear. "Please move outside immediately!"

Some ran for the door, wanting to get away from the body at the alter. Mr Jones sped past, clutching his hysterical wife. Denzil watched them leave, his lip curled in anger.

Cassius approached, glancing over his shoulder watching the church rapidly empty. "Lib, I'm sorry. Someone was in my way and I couldn't get to you."

Dad sped over, looking panicked. "Lib, we need to leave right now."

I yanked my arm away as he went to grab it. "I want to see her."

"You don't," Dad shot back quickly. "You don't, Lib."

I ignored him and pushed past, running in the opposite direction to everyone else. It felt as though I was approaching her in slow motion. The white coffin, now streaked with blood, looming ahead of me. I felt my bottom lip tremble as I ascended the two steps to where she was.

I looked up at the ornate wooden carvings on the roof beams and took a deep breath before looking down at her.

Up close, it was more horrific than I could have imagined. I couldn't take my eyes off the exposed flesh on her face. I could see facial muscles, jagged edges of skin, her exposed eyeball looking grotesquely frightened. The other side of her face was covered in scratches but I could still make out her beautiful features. One half of her rosebud lips that I used to admire so much.

I reached a shaking hand out to stroke the hair remaining on her head.

An image shot into my head of spending hours brushing it when we were children and she'd giggled and tipped her head back as I ran the brush through it slowly.

I closed my eyes and tore them open again to look at the rest of her.

It was clear there were organs missing and the flesh that remained in her stomach looked so soft that I could bet I could have reached straight in and wrapped my fingers around her spine. The bottom of her rib cage was visible. Brilliant white bone against the backdrop of red and pink.

Her leggings were torn and covered with dried blood. One black ballet pump remained on her foot and the other was covered in dirt as though she'd been running barefoot at some point.

I picked up the hand that Noah had laid on her heart and saw her fingernails were full of dirt and blood.

"If anyone attacks me, I'll fight like hell."

Her words whenever we watched a horror film. I believed her as well. I almost used to feel sorry for anyone who ever tried to attack Gemma.

I replaced her hand.

"Okay," I whispered, "I'm done now." I bent down and planted a kiss on her tiny fingers. "Don't worry, I won't remember you like this. And I'll kill them." I looked at her dead face, imagining the pain and the fear she must have experienced. "I'll kill them all."

I turned around slowly, now dangerously close to fainting. My vision started to fill with hundreds of black spots and I ignored the worried faces of Cassius, Denzil and Dad looking at me from the bottom of the steps. I couldn't find any words so I just stepped down, stumbling on my weak legs. Dad made a move to grab me but I held up my hands for him to back-off.

I shuffled to the exit, needing fresh air in my lungs.

Mr Jones was stood talking to the vicar, shaking his head and clutching his grey hair in desperation. I stopped in my tracks at the sight of him and for a moment we just stared at one another. Forgetting he was Mr Jones, the man who shouldn't be trusted, the one who may have taken Gemma to her death, I opened my mouth to whisper how sorry I was. However, I didn't get the chance as he strode over, clasping a rough hand on my shoulder, causing me to lose my balance.

"Why didn't you say something?" he barked, shaking me roughly. "Why didn't you tell us that night? Answer me! Why didn't you tell me my daughter wasn't a virgin?"

I stared at him in horror unable to function as he shook me again, spit showering my face as he bellowed. "Tell me! Why wouldn't you say something?"

"Get your hands off her!" Dad shouted from behind us. "Step away from my daughter, John. You know better than anyone she doesn't have a clue."

Mr Jones pushed me away and placed his hands on his head again. "She knew all along!"

Dad stepped in front of me. "Shut your mouth. She's been through enough."

"She needs to start being honest!" Mr Jones moved quickly before Dad could react and wrapped his hands around my neck.

It took me a moment to react before I started clawing at his face trying to escape the clammy grasp tightening around my neck. He glared at me, his grey eyes bulging. I could see his mouth moving as though he was shouting but a loud ringing sounding in my ears made everything muffled, like I was under water. As his grip tightened, my eyelids fluttered, trying to stop the black spots from multiplying.

A woman's voice joined in with the muffled shouting and

there now felt as though a lead weight had been placed around my neck. It was at that point, I realised I could no longer see anything at all. My eyes started to roll to the back of my head as the oxygen supply to my brain cut off.

"You'll die like that!"

I made out those words as my mouth opened and closed like a fish, feebly attempting to gulp in air.

I saw Gemma in that moment. Stood in front of me outside the canteen.

"Do some studying for me…"

The kiss on the cheek.

The wave goodbye.

Only now she didn't skip away like I remembered. Instead she planted her hands on my chest and pushed me roughly. My eyes snapped open as I realised I was now on the stone floor of the church entrance. I groaned and looked up to see Denzil and Cassius pulling a writhing Mr Jones away from me, with Dad stood in front of him, gesticulating wildly.

I felt hands on me and let Mrs Jones move me so I was slumped against the wall. I felt like my windpipe had been crushed and she took my face in her hands. I blinked and could tell she was speaking to me but I still couldn't hear a thing.

"Liberty!" I winced as my hearing came back in a rush, the sudden wall of noise hitting me like a juggernaut. "Can you hear me? I'm so sorry, Liberty. I'm sorry about him."

"It's okay," I croaked, pulling myself to my feet.

The vicar was nowhere to be seen as though he'd fled at the first sight of trouble. Probably turning a blind eye to the town's mayor and headmaster using violence against a teenage girl.

I saw Cassius was trying to calm down my dad who looked as though he was going to kill Mr Jones with his bare hands. However, that seemed to be covered by Denzil who had Mr Jones by the throat, looming taller than him, as he pushed him against the wall. His lip curled in rage. "Just who the hell do you think you are doing that to a young girl? You're disgusting."

Instead of looking scared at the younger and stronger Denzil threatening him, Mr Jones laughed in his face. "I'd be careful if I were you. You know who I am and what I can do. I'll have your shop closed down before dawn."

Denzil tightened his grip and pulled Mr Jones so they were nose to nose. "Using money and status to get your way? There's a surprise."

Mr Jones managed a shrug in Denzil's grasp. "I suppose I'm just the better man."

This seemingly innocuous comment threw Denzil into a deeper rage and he pushed Mr Jones into the wall, raising his fist to hit him.

"Stop!" Mrs Jones immediately dived from my side and pulled on Denzil's arm. "Please stop!"

Denzil glanced at her and reluctantly let go of her husband whose face was now bright red with a combination of anger and fear.

Dad took my arm and pulled me away from the wall, taking my weight as I struggled to take a step on my shaky legs.

Mr Jones sank down so he was crouching, his hands over his face. Mrs Jones looked at him, tears flowing down her face, before turning to Denzil. "I'm sorry."

Denzil waved dismissively and I noticed he didn't meet her eye and jerked his arm away when she placed her hand on it. Mrs Jones stepped back towards her husband, cheeks flushing pink. "I'm sorry," she said again. I wasn't sure who the apology was for.

"Come on," Dad said to me quietly, "let's go."

Cassius looked shell-shocked as he fell into step with us on the gravel path, leading away from the church. I was still rubbing my neck, sure I could feel the moulding of Mr Jones' fingers imprinted in my skin.

"Remember what I said!" Mr Jones piped up from the heap he was in on the floor. We turned on the path and eyed him. "You'll die like her! You should have told me she was a whore!"

I covered my ears and turned away, squeezing my eyes shut. "Make him stop."

"Not a problem," Denzil muttered, stalking back up to the church.

This time Mrs Jones moved to one side and let him pass.

He yanked Mr Jones up onto his feet and swiftly punched him square in the jaw, sending him falling backwards. I heard his head hit the stone wall and didn't even flinch. At last, he fell silent. No more vile words that made no sense.

Denzil grimaced at the impact, shaking and flexing his hand. He turned to Mrs Jones before he walked away. "That was long overdue."

She gulped and didn't take her eyes off the floor.

"Let's get home," Dad muttered as we reached the car. He yanked open the door and frowned as I made no move to get in. "Come on, Lib."

I'd climbed into our trusty, if a little battered, station wagon on countless occasions beforehand. I never thought about it, never questioned it. I just got in and let Dad drive me home. Now, as I reached for the door handle, I felt an electric shock of fear rush through my body. I withdrew my hand and shook my head. "No."

I could sense Cassius and Denzil stood behind me and knew Denzil's van was parked next to us.

"What do you mean?" Dad asked impatiently. "Get in the car. You need some rest after that..."

I took a step backwards. "I don't want to be around you, right now."

"Lib…" Dad closed the car door and leaned his arm on the roof. "Come on, this is *me*."

"I…" My voice was quiet and I cleared my throat to try

and sound more assertive. "I don't trust you, Dad."

His mouth fell open in surprise and he moved so he was stood in front of me. I had to look away, unable to stand his hurt expression. "Please don't say that…"

"I want to go with Denzil."

His eyes widened. "And you trust *him*? But not me?"

I nodded and felt Denzil's hand on my shoulder.

Dad looked at the three of us before lowering his head in defeat. "Lib, you're making a mistake..."

"Just don't hurt Oscar," I croaked. "I can stand you plotting to hurt me but if you so much as lay a finger–"

"I'd never hurt that boy," he said evenly. "You have my word. I-I don't want to hurt you either…"

But you will, I thought, my eyes challenging him.

He looked away, unable to make any kind of denial. Dad wasn't a liar, I had to give him that. Whatever was going on, he couldn't tell me but he also couldn't find it within himself to assure me of my safety.

"Bye, Dad." I turned away, pushing past Denzil and Cassius who watched. I turned back to see Dad place his hand on Denzil's arm. "Listen," he looked pained, "do I need to be worried about…*this*?"

Denzil eyed my dad's hand on him. "No, dude. It's not like that. I'm her friend."

Cassius and I climbed in the front of the van with Denzil, crammed onto the long seat next to the driver.

Denzil put the key in the ignition and I noticed his knuckles were bloody from hitting Mr Jones. He sighed and moved his head in our direction but not meeting our eye. "Let's go and figure out what the hell's going on in this craphole."

As he backed the van out of the space, I tried not to look at Dad who was leaning on the car, shoulders shaking from crying.

Chapter IX

"Maybe we should have called his house," Cassius muttered. "He might have gone home."

"No," I looked out of the windscreen at the dark trees lining the road, "I know him. He'll be out somewhere."

It was an unspoken assumption that we would look for Noah before heading to the shop for the night. We hadn't spoken much and my eyes remained trained on the street and the surrounding woodland for my friend.

Mr Jones' words kept creeping back into my head but I couldn't concentrate on trying to decipher what he was trying to accuse me of.

Whore.

He'd used that word to describe his own daughter.

His only daughter whose ravaged body had been dumped on the doorstep of her boyfriend on the morning of her funeral. Bodies never turned up after a walk out. Humans were eaten whole so this didn't make any sense.

"Why didn't you tell me my daughter wasn't a virgin?"

As if…

I blinked at the road ahead of us.

As if *sex* had gotten her killed.

Placed on the doorstep of the boy who'd taken her virginity. It was a message but from who? And why?

"I had to do it…she was spending too much time with the Hartmann kid."

I closed my eyes as I thought back to the conversation between him and Dad as I crouched at the top of the stairs but quickly dispelled it.

I had to think about finding Noah in case he too was in danger.

"Do you have any idea where he might be?" Denzil asked me casually but I could tell by his voice that he was giving up hope. We'd been driving up and down the same road for the last hour. Dusk was rapidly setting in and the sky was starting to get a hint of orange as the sun disappeared into the trees.

"Let's just keep looking," I said tightly.

In truth, he could be anywhere and potentially covered a lot of ground since the funeral. I just prayed he hadn't decided to walk into the woodland as I knew there was no way Denzil and Cassius would let me venture in there so close to sundown.

I felt ashamed that I didn't know him better but the truth was, we were never close. I wasn't lying to Cassius on the phone several nights ago when I said I doubted Noah and I had ever had a one-to-one conversation in the entire time we knew each another. We hadn't needed to, and I also got the distinct sense he didn't like me very much. Well, not that he didn't like me but there was an unspoken awareness that we had very little in common. He didn't concentrate in any of his lessons whereas I was a straight A student. I followed the Rules intensely whereas he could barely recite them. We both loved Gemma and Gabriel and that, in all truth, was the only thing that bonded us.

I gulped as I wondered how he'd react even if I did find him that evening.

Cassius reached to switch down the heater in the van as the air had become stifling.

I couldn't help but remember Noah's warning to me the day before Gemma walked.

What was it again? Something about killing Cassius if there was anything more than a hello exchanged. Yet here was Cass, pressed up next to me in Denzil's van, occasionally taking my hand and whispering that everything was going to be okay.

That was one thing I did know about Noah, he had always been hot headed. When Gemma and I used to sneak and watch them play football we'd witness him losing his temper whenever his team would lose, taking it out on the cones outside of the pitch or on one of the other players. Gemma found it adorable, of course, whereas I would roll my eyes, wondering just what it was he was trying to prove.

Despite having little time for him, I couldn't fault his adoration for my best friend. I closed my eyes and leaned my head back into the battered leather car seat, thinking back to the summer time when they first started going out.

***

"Noah Hartmann! Noah freakin' Hartmann!"

Gemma tossed several articles around her room, causing me to flinch. She yanked open the door to her large mirrored wardrobe and reached inside, pulling a jumper I recognised as Noah's from one of the hangers. With a frustrated cry she tossed it towards the door and the hanger clattered loudly. I grabbed one of the dozens of pink scatter cushions on her bed and hugged it to my chest while I waited for the one-woman cyclone to stop.

She moved to her chest of drawers and started rummaging around before pulling what looked like a shoebox decorated in pictures of hearts and flowers that she'd cut out of magazines. Before I could admire it, she launched that at the door too and I sighed to myself.

Gemma, her face now red, grabbed her hair in frustration and stamped her feet. "I HATE Noah Hartmann!"

I ran my tongue over my teeth and winced at my words before I even said them. "Gem…what's happened?"

"What's happened?" she repeated, her eyes filled with rage and her hair now wild after tugging it from its bun. She looked like a cave woman, complete with flaring nostrils and predator-like

stance. "I'll tell you what's happened, Liberty!" she spat, waving her finger at me. "Noah-aren't-I-amazing-feel-my-muscles-Hartmann was caught red-handed by yours truly."

She looked at me expectantly but I shrugged, not having a clue what she was talking about.

She made a growling noise of annoyance and stalked over to the box on the floor, its contents now scattered everywhere. She picked up a Polaroid of her and Noah and feebly started trying to rip it in two.

"Gemma!" I shouted, kneeling up on her bed and grabbing the photo from her hands. "What's going on?"

"I caught him..." she closed her eyes, "flirting with Violet Thomas!"

I raised an eyebrow. "Is that it?"

"Have you seen Violet Thomas?" she demanded, hands on hips.

I had to be honest, I couldn't place her at all. I'd heard the name a few times and knew she was in our year but had no idea what she looked like.

The anger then seemed to leave Gemma's body in a big rush and my sweet and loving friend returned. She looked at her feet, her voice starting to quiver as she spoke. "She's tall and has jet black hair and she's...really pretty. Much prettier than me."

I cocked my head to one side. "I very much doubt that."

"She is!" Gemma cried, throwing a distracted look to her collection of Noah memorabilia strewn on the floor. "I knew it, Lib! I knew Noah was only with me because Gabriel's with you. I was an easy target! He's had his blonde fix now, he can move on to someone like-like her!"

I stood now, knowing that my extra bit of height served as an advantage sometimes with my hysterical friend. I pulled her into a hug, "Listen, maybe you were mistaken–"

"He was leaning his hand on the wall behind her and she was laughing at something he said," she fumed, accepting the hug, albeit stiffly. "He went out with Lucille Roderick and she's a redhead, then me, and now that cow Violet with the black hair.

He's looking for a full-set, Lib! How could I have been so stupid?!"

"Well," I pulled back and rubbed the tops of her arms, "if that's the case, then let Violet what's-her-face have him. Let her break Rule Eight and risk her life while you watch on smugly."

"Mmm-hmm." She didn't meet my eye.

I ducked my head down. "Gem?"

Slowly her eyes raised and she bit her lip. I felt my mouth drop open. "You didn't..."

Her silence spoke volumes and I turned away, placing my hands on my cheeks. "Oh Gem, what were you thinking?"

"I wasn't!" she shouted, angry at me and also at herself causing her voice to wobble. "It just...happened. I was going to tell you but every time I tried, you always seemed to make some comment about the Rules and I chickened out. I knew you'd judge me."

I let out a shaky breath and rubbed between my eyebrows. Aside from the fact my friend had broken one of the golden Rules which could endanger her, I was trying to hide the fact I was hurt that she didn't think she could tell me and also the thing I didn't want to admit.

I was a little jealous she'd experienced it.

"It doesn't matter now." She kicked the box and sent more articles flying across the room. There were notes in there that they'd passed to one another in school, flowers he'd presented to her on the field that had now dried, receipts from dates they'd been on. "Forget Noah Hartmann! I don't need him! I wish I'd never met him."

That last statement was an in adverted dig at me I was quite sure. If I hadn't started going out with Gabriel, then Gemma wouldn't have met Noah.

"Gemma, listen..." I plonked myself back down on the bed, unsure of what to say to make her feel better about possibly getting the boot from the boy she'd broken Rule Eight for.

However, I was saved by the bell. Or not so much the bell, but the sound of a shower of dirt and stones hitting her bedroom window. We locked eyes and I saw her brow crease into a frown of confusion.

Another shower of stones.

Gemma dashed to the sash window and pushed it open, kneeling on her pink padded window seat. "What the hell do you want?" she demanded.

I joined her and peered out to see Noah stood in her back garden, hands in the pockets of his grey school trousers and the sleeves of his white shirt rolled to the elbows.

"I need to talk to you," he hollered up. "Erm..hiya Lib."

I wiggled my fingers in an awkward wave and debated going back inside but deciding I too wanted to hear what he had to say for himself.

"Gemma, let me explain–"

"Explain?!" she shot back, leaning even further out of the window. I instinctively reached out and clasped a handful of her school shirt. "Explain what? That Violet Thomas is your new girlfriend?"

He leaned his head back in frustration. "Gem! Violet's going out with Conrad. I was talking to her about the birthday party his folks are throwing for him."

Gemma pressed her lips together as though considering this for a moment. "You were right in her face and she was laughing."

Noah unfastened his tie and pulled it off, rolling it around his fist. "Yeah, she was laughing because I said she should break Rule Eight for his birthday and she said she already had." He was talking more quietly now and Gemma and I both strained to hear him. He ran a hand through his hair and looked panicked all of a sudden. "Did you mean it when you said it was over?"

"Yes," Gemma said haughtily, folding her arms.

Noah nodded and looked down. "I love you, Gem."

I heard her breath catch in her throat and she cleared it. "I don't believe you, Noah. I don't believe your little story about Violet. I think you were flirting and I don't like it. And I certainly don't believe you love me."

She stepped back triumphantly and grabbed my arm so she

could slam the window closed. She was no doubt about to launch into a self-righteous monologue about how sorry he'd be whilst also justifying why the hell she'd broken Rule Eight within two months of dating Noah when I'd been with Gabriel three times as long and all we had done is kiss.

However, before she could open her mouth, the sound of Noah's voice resonated through the glass window.

"Gemma Jones!"

Her eyes widened.

"I love you, Gemma Jones!"

Her mouth dropped open. "Shit!"

We both raced to the window again and Gemma snatched it open.

"Gemma Jones, I'd die for you! I love–"

"Shut up!" she hissed down to him. "Are you mental? My parents will hear you!"

He outstretched his arms. "I don't care. I want the world to know."

"Well, you should care," she scolded, eyes darting to me in worry. "My dad will kill you if he hears."

"Let him!" Noah cupped his hands over his mouth. "I'm hopelessly in love with Gemma Jones! Does everyone hear me?! I love–"

"Noah!" she barked, but there was now a smile in her voice as she clamped a hand over her mouth. "You'll get me into trouble. Do you want me to be grounded forever?"

He grinned up at her. "Whatever it takes to convince you that I'm serious." He turned around on the spot. "I asked a question, Blackbrooke! Do you hear? I'm in love with Gemma Jones!"

"He's lost it," I muttered, shaking my head. "Noah, go home before it goes dark!"

"Ah, there's another hour of daylight," he dismissed me, not taking his eyes off his girlfriend. "Plus, I'm not going anywhere until you say you believe me and tell me we're back on again. Let the Crits eat me. I don't care."

Gemma sat in the window seat again, playing with her hair which she'd gathered over one shoulder. "My dad will get to you before the Crits do if you carry on bellowing."

Noah looked towards the house and shrugged. "So? If he comes out here, then I'll ask for his daughter's hand in marriage."

"Noah! NO!" Gemma was laughing now and it was my turn to fold my arms and look unimpressed. If Mr Jones did hear him shouting sweet nothings up to her window, then I was quite sure I'd have to go home as part of her punishment. Plus, I was not sure I could forgive him yet for the revelation that he'd taken my friend's virginity.

"Yep, that's what I'm going to do," Noah called up. "I'll ask him for your hand in marriage, and then in April we'll marry under the oak tree on the school field."

Gemma giggled. "Shut up, Noah!"

"What?" He laughed, too. "We'll marry in the place I first asked you out, the place we had our first kiss, remember?"

Gemma nodded quickly.

"And I," he pointed at himself and started walking backwards, "will head there right now and wait patiently for my bride to show up."

She leaned out of the window a little further. "So you'll wait under that tree until I turn eighteen next April?"

"Yes, I will. My best man, Gabriel, will bring me supplies and I'm sure your lovely maid of honour will make sure no Crits get me. She does a good job looking after you." He winked and I rolled my eyes, unimpressed. "So, all that's left to say is..."

Gemma bit her lip.

"Gemma Jones..."

"Oh for the love of God..." I turned away.

"Will you do me the honour..."

"Why didn't he do this before he talked you into bed?"

"Shhhh!" Gemma hissed. "Don't ruin the moment, Lib!"

"...of becoming...."

I begrudgingly joined her at the window again and groaned to see Noah on one knee, hands over his heart as he gazed up.

"Yes?" Gemma breathed, willing him to speak the words she'd been longing someone to say for as long as I'd known her.

Even I held my breath.

"What's going on?"

"Ahhhh!" Gemma and I screamed and jumped out of the window, slamming it shut.

Mrs Jones was leaning in the doorway to Gemma's room, her tongue pushed into her cheek as she eyed us.

"Mum!" Gemma said, overly-brightly. "Isn't it just lovely? Lib and I were just saying what a lovely day it is outside and admiring the garden. Your roses are really starting to come out now and I love the way they catch the light in the evening, it's quite exquisite and–"

"Were you talking to someone?" She pointed to the window. There was a martini glass containing clear liquid in her hand which was a common sight as her and Mr Jones had what he referred to as 'cocktail hour'. It sounded more exciting than it was as the pair would just sit in silence in the main living room and sip a drink before having dinner.

"No," I jumped in quickly, stepping in front of Gemma, "we were just getting a little excited…about the roses."

"Mmm-hmm." She narrowed her eyes and advanced. Gemma and I instinctively stepped back, our backs pressed against the window. "May I?" She grinned, pushing a stray blonde hair from her face. "I'd quite like to admire my roses, too."

Gemma was shaking her head, and I flashed her a look which I hoped told her she was looking far too guilty.

"Sure," I said, pulling Gemma out of the way of the window. Noah wasn't exactly in my good books but I'd hoped he'd have had the good grace to get the hell out of there as soon as we slammed the window closed.

Mrs Jones cleared her throat and walked to the window. She opened it and rested her palms on the outside of the frame to get a good look.

Gemma winced and took a deep breath.

Mrs Jones eventually popped her head back in and smiled brightly. "You're right, the roses do look good from up here. Good job too, they take a lot of work, you know."

We nodded, not daring to do anything else.

"Yes, not really for the faint-hearted and not to be entered into lightly," a hint of a smile was dancing on her lips, "you need to think long and hard before you enter into such a…commitment." She walked to the door, swilling her drink around the glass. Before she left, Mrs Jones turned back to us, a wicked glint in her eye. "They are very attractive though."

We waited until we heard her footsteps on the stairs and rushed back to the window. Noah was still stood in the exact spot, his hands in his pockets. He shrugged and smiled when he saw us again.

Gemma's mouth hung open in a laugh and she shook her head. "I'm going to kill you,"

He started walking away, towards the loose piece of fence in the Joneses' vast garden that he'd climbed through. "I'll see you at the oak tree, Mrs Hartmann."

We watched him disappear before Gemma threw herself onto her bed. "Oh my God!' she shrieked, placing one of her cushions over her red face.

***

My eyes flicked open and I turned to Denzil. "I know where Noah is."

As we approached Blackbrooke Academy, I grimaced at the sight of the locked gates. School had been closed that day for the funeral so we were locked out. Aside from the locks, the gates, along with the fence around the Academy was about ten feet high. Even if we decided to do the action movie manoeuvre and drive the van into them, Denzil's battered van was likely to disintegrate on impact.

Cassius was clearly thinking the same as me as he leaned forward to eye them. "I very much doubt Noah's in there. Not a chance he'd have been able to climb those gates or the fence."

I unclipped my seatbelt and clambered over Cassius, throwing the door open. "Noah is on the football team, athletics team, as well as having a black belt in kickboxing. If anyone's getting over those gates, it's him."

"Erm Lib," Denzil scratched his head, "that doesn't help *us* though."

I narrowed my eyes at the gates. "If I get a leg up from one of you then I'll be able to haul myself over."

They exchanged doubtful glances.

"Come on," I said impatiently. "It's dusk, we don't have much time."

"Exactly!" Cassius jumped out of the van and loomed in front of me. "If we throw you over the gates and Noah's not there, how are you going to get back over?"

"He is here. I'll bet my life on it."

Denzil honked on the horn, and half hung out of the van, cupping a hand over his mouth. "Noah!" he bellowed and then stopped to listen. "Noah! Lib's here! We're here to bring you home!" He shrugged hopelessly. "I don't think he's there. If he is, he can't hear me."

"The Crits will though," Cassius grumbled.

I walked around the van and pulled Denzil's arm down before he could bellow again. "Listen, if Noah is there then I very much doubt he's going to respond. He's on a revenge mission, he doesn't want to go home."

"Revenge?" Denzil raised an eyebrow. "It's more like suicide."

"That's why I have to get him." I wrapped my fingers around the gate poles. "Okay, one of you give me a leg-up."

"Lib," Cassius leaned on the gate next to me, "let me go over. You stay here with Denzil."

I let out a laugh. "You have to be kidding me, Cass. Noah

isn't your biggest fan. Do you reckon you'll be able to persuade him to come back?"

Cassius opened his mouth but I shot him down.

"No, you won't. Now," I hauled myself up, stepping onto the horizontal rung at the bottom of the gate, "help me up."

Denzil was now at my other side and shrugged at Cassius in defeat. "She's going whether we like it or not."

I smiled. Denzil knew how bloody minded I was.

Cassius sighed and looked up at the pink and orange sky. "Ten minutes. I reckon that's all you've got."

I stepped onto Denzil's interlocked hands and reached up to the bar at the top, using all of my strength to haul myself up. "All of those tree climbing sessions," I shouted down to Cassius breathlessly, "really came in handy in the end."

"Yeah, but you always ended up getting hurt!" Before Cassius had even finished his sentence, I lost my footing and dropped to the floor on the other side, landing on the right side of my body with a thud. Momentarily winded, I lay facing away from them just blinking into space.

"Lib!" Cassius shouted.

I coughed and rolled over to see their worried faces. "I'm okay." I picked myself up and dusted off my clothes. "I hope no one looked up my dress just then."

"Urgh," Denzil curled his lips, "don't be disgusting, I'm not a pervert."

Cassius shook his head. "You don't need to worry anyway, you're wearing tights. It's not like we could see anything."

Denzil and I blinked at him and I saw a faint hint of pink creep onto his cheeks.

"Not that I was looking."

Denzil held up his index finger for me to wait a second and jogged back to his van. I frowned as I watched him open the passenger door and reach into the glove compartment. "Here," he said when he returned, "take this with you."

I reached through the gate and wrapped my fingers around

the cold metal of the gun, eyeing it in fascination.

Cassius let out a laugh and shook his head. "If she gets caught out there in the dark a gun isn't going to protect her against Crits, there'll be dozens of them and there's probably what? Six, eight bullets at the most?"

Neither Denzil or I responded and just looked at one another. I nodded in understanding. The bullets weren't for the Crits. They were for me in case I couldn't make it back in time.

"We'll wait." Denzil's words were loaded. "We'll wait as long as we possibly can for you to come back."

"We'll wait until she's back," Cassius snapped, glaring at Denzil. "Lib, we're not going anywhere, just…please don't do anything stupid."

I didn't hesitate anymore and took off as fast as my legs could carry me. I wasn't wearing my coat, just the black dress from Gemma's funeral, tights and black ballet pumps. Similar to the ones Gemma had died in. It was freezing as the sky had remained clear all day. To anyone indoors it would have looked like a beautiful summer's day but the sub zero temperature and the hardened iced ground underfoot confirmed that it was one of the coldest Novembers in Blackbrooke for a long time.

The playing field sloped downwards and I skidded and fell hard onto my backside with a cry, sliding the rest of the way down. I lost grip of the gun and it bounced down the hill next to me. I quickly retrieved it and was instantly back on my feet, running as fast as my legs would carry me towards the centre of the field where the oak tree was. The cold air started to burn my lungs as I gulped in more. My heart, not used to such physical exertion, was hammering in my chest and for a horrible moment I started to wonder whether I was wrong after all. Maybe Noah had gone home after the funeral and here I was running around Blackbrooke at dusk trying to find him.

I slowed as I got to the tree and placed my hands on my knees to try and steady my breath.

That's when I saw him.

Sat on the other side, out of view from the school, his back pressed against the trees trunk and eyes staring straight ahead.

I stopped, afraid of scaring him, aware I was still holding the gun in my hand.

"Noah?" I said softly.

He didn't even glance up as I stood in front of him. "Go away."

There was a shotgun leaning against the tree and I noticed a huge hunting knife lying on the floor next to him.

I knelt down. "I can't do that."

Now he looked at me. His blue eyes, usually sparkling and full of life and fire, were dead. Tear-stained and empty. His face was red from crying and he wiped his nose.

"Get out of here, Lib. It's nearly time."

"I know." I swallowed nervously. "I'm here to come and get you."

He didn't say anything but shook his head.

"Noah," I started, choosing my words carefully, "you need to come with me. Something…really bad is going on and I'm going to figure out. I need your help though."

He didn't respond.

I glanced around the field which was now bathed in pink light. The sun was nearly down.

"Noah, please." My voice quivered in fear and I reached out and placed my hand on one of his knees drawn up to his chest. Parts of his sandy hair looked pink from where he'd ran a bloodied hand through it. He was still in the clothes from earlier and I noticed that where Gemma's body was pressed into him, the patch of blood was a dark purple colour. It looked like it was him who'd been bleeding. My eyes returned to his face and I recoiled in surprise to see he was now looking at me.

He touched the stain. "Wouldn't have bled like this."

"What?" I frowned.

He closed his eyes and tears fell down his face. One fell onto his lips and he wiped it impatiently. "If she'd been dead a while, she wouldn't have bled like this."

I felt my breath become shallow as Noah let out a sob.

"When I found her…" he cried and had to stop for a moment to catch his breath before lowering his voice to a whisper, "she was still warm, Lib."

Now it was my turn to cry. I felt my face crumple.

Gemma had been away for days.

Tortured.

Freshly dead this morning with most of her organs gone.

If I didn't think it was the work of the Queens before, then we were certain now. Any of the other Crits would have devoured her straight away. There would be nothing left.

Taken our beautiful friend apart, piece by piece, like a puzzle while she probably screamed and cried, begging for her life.

"Noah," I took him into my arms, his head buried into my shoulder as he clutched tightly, "please come with me. We're going to figure out what's going on."

He was shaking as he pulled back from me. He picked up the knife and looked across the field.

The same view four friends used to look out at.

Two down.

Noah and I wouldn't have argued that it was the best two who weren't here right now.

"I'm not going anywhere," he whispered. "I'm armed and I'm going to take as many as I can."

I shook my head, taking his face in my hands and forcing him to look at me. "No, you can't. It's pointless Noah. It'll be the Hunters and the Lurkers that get to you first. We're next to the cattle fields here."

"So?" he spat, more tears running down his face. "They're

all the same."

"No," I moved my face closer to his, "you know as well as I do that what happened to Gemma wasn't the work of them. It was the Queens. You'll die out here, Noah, and the Queens will carry on." I shook him as I saw his gaze slip away. "Please listen! Gemma's not the first and she won't be the last if we just give up."

He looked away. "I've got nothing left."

"You have me!" I cried, hearing the desperation in my voice. "I need you, Noah."

The light around us started to dim and my heart began to pound again in fear.

At this rate, I'd be using the gun.

"No one needs me anymore," Noah said. "She needed me. We were going to get married under this tree."

"I remember." I hiccupped a sob. "She was so excited."

"You don't understand…" He shook his head. "Gabriel… now her….I've lost everything."

I stopped crying immediately, feeling a shot of anger in my veins. "Of course, I understand. How dare you say that to me!"

He blinked up at me.

"How-How could you?" I screamed. "I've lost everything, too. We've both lost everything! Why can't you see that, Noah? I'm still here!" I looked at him, my chest heaving and tears I didn't think I had left were rolling down my cheeks. "I'm still here and I need you, but you don't care!"

"Don't say that!" he wailed. "I just want it to be over…"

"Me, too." In a feverish moment, I raised Denzil's gun and pressed the barrel against my temple. My palm was sweaty and my hand was shaking.

Noah was on his feet straight away and held his hands out in front of him. "What are you doing?"

I shook my head. "You won't come with me so what's the point? I'd rather kill myself than live on this earth knowing the last of my friends is dead."

"Lib," he stepped closer, panic in his eyes, "there's no point in you doing this. You've got your family. You need to be there for your brother."

I wrapped my finger around the trigger. "None of that matters."

"Please," he sank to his knees in front of me, "don't do this. Get out of here and live."

"Not without you."

Noah exhaled and shrugged hopelessly. "It's too late. It's dusk. We'll never be able to get anywhere in time."

I considered putting the gun down but decided he still wasn't completely sold. "My boss is waiting in the van at the school gates. We'll make it if we run and then you can come back to the shop with me. You don't need to go home. You can help me."

Noah looked back at the shotgun.

"Noah," I appealed again, trying desperately to keep his attention, "leave it. Let's go and figure this out together so we can get vengeance on the ones who actually deserve it. Even, if we die doing that, it'll be worth it. *This* isn't worth it though. It's the wrong time…for both of us."

He nodded slowly and my breath caught in my throat in anticipation. "Okay," he whispered, "but we're going to need to run."

He grabbed my hand which was still holding the gun and yanked me in the direction of the gates. They now seemed so far away and the hill I fell down loomed up ahead.

"Faster Lib!" Noah shouted, pulling me up the hill as I struggled to gain any traction on the frozen ground with my ballet pumps.

It was now almost dark as we bolted across the grass. I felt like we were deer in a meadow during hunting season. Ripe for killing.

A low howl sounded in the distance.

"Oh shit." I clutched Noah's hand even tighter.

"Come on!" he cried, panic bubbling in his throat.

I threw a glance over my shoulder and saw large black figures appear at the edge of the field.

Hunters.

They were far away but would be on us in a matter of seconds.

"They're here!" I shouted and Noah picked up even more speed and I concentrated on not falling again as he pulled me along. In that moment, I wondered whether the Hunter I encountered as a child was amongst them, finally ready to claim its meal after ten years of regret for letting me go free.

I saw Denzil and Cassius at the gates, shouting and beckoning us in panic.

"Come on!" Denzil bellowed. "Hurry! We can hear them!"

We smashed into the gates as we reached them and Noah hoisted me up without hesitation. My arms felt like jelly as I mustered up the strength to haul myself over at the top.

"Just jump, Lib!" Cassius called, "Just jump and get in the van!"

I looked down and saw Denzil reach his interlocked hands through the fence for Noah to step up on. I looked back over the field and, from my vantage point at the top of the gate, saw Hunters running, getting closer. I could hear the rumble of their feet hitting the grass. Everything slowed in that moment, the sounds of my friends shouting for me to drop down now muffled and I blinked slowly at the magnificent sight of the sea of wolf-like Crits stampeding towards us.

"Come on, Lib!" Cassius cried, bringing me back to reality.

I sprang into action and jumped down and on top of Cassius who broke my fall.

"Sorry," I mumbled, picking myself up off him.

We dived into the van as Noah pulled himself over the fence. Denzil was beckoning him to jump. The Hunters were just beyond him, running on four legs. Their eyes bright red and flashing with hunger and their breath was mist rising into the cold air.

"Come on!" Cassius and I shouted, honking the horn frantically.

Noah jumped down and stumbled as he tried to land on his feet, recovering and running straight to the van. We pulled him in by the collar of his t-shirt and Denzil jumped into the drivers seat, slamming the door.

The Hunters reached the gates as Denzil started the van and slammed it in reverse.

The first one jumped over the gates with ease and shook itself like a dog before glaring up at the van which was flying down the road leading to the school.

Cassius, Noah and I watched in horror as the Hunter started to bolt towards us.

Denzil was looking out of the back window. "Come on you piece of shit!" he cursed at the van. He threw it around when we got onto the road and quickly changed gear. "Let's see how fast this thing can go."

We changed position to turn in our seats and look out of the back window as the Hunter emerged onto the road. It looked up and down in a moment of confusion before clocking the van and starting to bolt after us. Several others appeared behind it and also started to pursue us.

"Oh God." I turned to the front and threw a panicked glance at Denzil who was glaring in the rear-view mirror.

"Come on then, you useless Crits. Give it a try."

The accelerator was pressed to the floor and at last the Hunters started to get further away.

"Right kids," Denzil shouted, "when we get to the shop, straight in. As fast as you can."

We nodded, eyes wide in fear.

Noah let out a shaky breath and leaned his head back, placing his hands on his face and running them down it.

"Did you leave my gun behind?" Denzil asked me quietly.

I smiled and held it up for him to see. I'd thrown it under the gates before I jumped over.

"Thank God." He grinned. "It belonged to my granddad."

It was almost completely pitch black but Denzil didn't turn the headlights on in fear of more Crits seeing us. It was bad enough the van ran on diesel so made a racket anyway.

"Dive!" Denzil shouted at us before he'd even stopped the van. We piled into the shop without seeing or hearing another Crit and stood for a moment, catching our breath. Denzil locked the door and pushed all of the bolts into place. "I'm heading up."

We didn't say a word but followed him, our heads bowed. I was now feeling exhausted and my brain couldn't function properly. Noah and I had come very close to being devoured on the school field.

Cassius and Denzil had put themselves in danger too by waiting for us.

I had grand plans of getting back to Denzil's and us researching through the night to try and get some answers but, looking around at our tired faces, that wasn't a realistic option.

Denzil flicked on the kettle and gestured to Noah's blood stained clothes. "I think we all need to get changed."

I rubbed the tops of my arms, realising none of us had clothes here and we were all still wearing our outfits from the funeral.

Denzil headed for his bedroom, starting to unbutton his white shirt. "We'll look like a bunch of hippies together."

The three of us stood while the kettle boiled and switched off, leaving the room quiet except for the sound of Denzil opening and closing drawers.

Cassius sat on the sofa and pressed his palms together. He looked so tall and thin in comparison to the shorter and more athletic Noah. "I need to sleep."

I nodded. "Me too."

"You can take the sofa, Lib." Cassius turned to me. "Unless

Denzil will give up his bed for the evening."

"The sofa's fine."

"Are you okay?" He frowned at me. "Do you want some water? You're looking a bit…ill."

"It's just catching up on me." I glanced at Noah who was glaring at a spot on the floor. "It's been a tough day all round."

"Sure." Cassius stifled a yawn. "I know what you mean. We'll look into this more in the morning."

Noah's head flicked to him. "What?"

My heart sank at his expression. It was the same one from the canteen that day when he practically spat Cassius' name.

Cassius was leaning his cheek on his hand. "I was just agreeing that it's been a tough day all round."

"Oh yeah?" Noah stepped closer. "What the hell has it got to do with you, freak boy? I mean, what are you doing here anyway?"

To my surprise, Cassius stood up. "I'm here because my friend needs me."

"*I'm* her friend!" Noah pointed at himself. "She doesn't need anyone but me!"

"Noah!" I stepped forward but Cassius held up his hand, not taking his eyes off him.

"You will never be Gabriel!" Noah bellowed. "You'll never take his place. So you need to get the hell out of her life and leave her alone. Do you understand?"

Cassius rubbed his jaw, mulling over Noah's words. "I'm very sorry for your loss. Both of them."

Noah narrowed his eyes.

"However," Cassius stood up straight, "I'm getting sick of your poor as shit attitude towards me."

I gasped, instantly wondering just how hard Noah was going to hit him.

"I've been Lib's friend since we were babies," Cassius continued, calm and collected. "She was, is, and always will be my friend. Whether it's the same for her is irrelevant. As are your feelings towards any relationship I have with her."

Noah swallowed and eyed Cassius, more with interest than venom, much to my relief.

"I don't claim to be Gabriel." Cassius shook his head. "I don't even come close and I know I'll never replace him."

I looked at the floor, shifting my weight from one foot to the other uncomfortably.

"But I'm her friend. Do you understand?"

Noah looked as though the one thing he wanted more than anything was to get angry. However, Cassius spoke so softly and commanded such a presence that he couldn't. "Fine," he said eventually, "but seriously, if I catch you trying to put the moves on her then I'll kill you."

"Right!" Denzil emerged, carrying a pile of clothes. "Here we go. So, what did I miss?"

"Nothing," we all replied in unison.

***

I blinked up at the ceiling and listened to the rhythmic breathing of Noah on the floor next to me and Cassius who was asleep on the armchair. Noah was having a restless sleep as he kept twitching and moving around. I reached down and felt his forehead, which was covered in sweat.

"It's okay, you're safe here," I whispered. Earlier in the evening there had been no way on earth he *wasn't* going to sleep on the floor next to me. It was as though he saw himself as a guard dog protecting me against the pale, white-haired boy who wanted to have his wicked way. The two of them didn't speak for the rest of the night. No one did really. There was nothing left to say, and I desperately needed to rest so I could try and organise my thoughts into some order and sense.

However, as it was at home, sleep seemed to elude me and I sat up and stretched my arms over my head.

About twenty minutes earlier, I'd listened to Denzil make himself a cup of tea and head downstairs to the shop. Clearly, I wasn't the only one struggling to sleep so I decided to join him. I stood and looked down at the ridiculous outfit he'd given me to wear: purple tie-dye board shorts that finished halfway between my knee and ankle and a baggy Pink Floyd t-shirt.

I think Noah liked how hideous I looked seeing as he was now relishing the role of protector. Not that I minded. The pink Woodstock t-shirt and pale blue flares on him meant we were even. Cassius was given too-short jeans and a stripy jumper in all the colours of the rainbow that was covered in holes.

I tiptoed out of the room and made my way downstairs towards the faint light of the shop. Denzil was sat on the chair behind the counter, reading through some books, deep in thought.

"Hey," I yawned, leaning my elbows on the counter, "couldn't sleep."

"Not surprising." He turned a page before glancing up at me. He was now wearing his tortoiseshell-framed glasses which he was rarely seen in as he wore contact lenses throughout the day. I thought they suited him but he hated them as they made him feel 'old' apparently. "Do you want a drink?"

"No," I said quickly, "it might wake the others up if you put the kettle on again."

His lips curled into a smile. "Not talking about a hot one, Lib…"

I frowned and looked at his empty mug on the counter. Next to it was a small shot glass with brown liquid inside. He reached down the side of the chair and pulled out a bottle of whiskey, shaking it. "Want some?"

"I really don't think that's the best…" I trailed off as Denzil flashed me a look over his glasses.

"Please don't tell me you're going to go on about the Rules now, Lib."

I didn't make a move for the bottle and he shrugged and set it back on the floor. "I'm just seeing if there's anything here." He gestured to the book. "Highly doubtful."

"That's what I was thinking earlier. I think we're going to be alone in figuring this one out."

Denzil shrugged. "I've got nothing better to do. So," he pointed upstairs, "how's the love triangle panning out?"

I reached over the counter and slapped his hand. "Have some respect, that's Gemma's boyfriend."

Denzil grinned and turned a page. "Doesn't like Cassius much, does he?"

"No, he doesn't," I said quietly. "Noah was Gabriel's best friend and thinks Cass is…sniffing around me apparently."

Denzil watched me as I picked one of the pens for sale at the till. They had bobbing skulls on the end and lit up when you started to write with them. "Hmmm."

I clicked the pen and narrowed my eyes. "That was loaded."

Denzil shrugged and pinched his chin as though reading an interesting part of the book when in reality I recognised he was mocking me. "He is, though, isn't he? Sniffing around? He likes you, I can tell."

"He's my friend!" I said, exasperated. "You're as bad as Noah. Can't a girl have friends without there being an ulterior motive? Christ, Denzil, I buried my boyfriend last week, give me some credit."

"Okay, Liberty Bell," he conceded and placed the book down so he could give me his full attention, "but have you ever thought the boy might quite like you?"

I shook my head without hesitation. "I ditched him. I'm just amazed and grateful he doesn't hate me. Besides," I folded my arms, "who are you to make a comment like that? Have you ever even had a girlfriend?"

To my surprise, he let out a loud laugh as though I'd said the funniest thing in the world. He grabbed the glass of whiskey and downed it in one, waving a finger at me as he swallowed. "What a question. Today of all days…"

He'd lost me and I think my face said it all.

He sighed. "If I tell you something, will you promise not to freak out or use it against me in the future?"

I nodded.

He lowered his head and mirrored my pose, leaning on the counter. "To answer your question, yes, I have had girlfriends. Well, singular. Just the one girlfriend." He winced. "This might be a bit of a shock but I used to go out with Marie Jones."

My eyes widened. "Gemma's mum?!"

He nodded and looked dreamy for a moment. "Yep, back when she was Marie Picton. Or just Maz…I suppose you could call her the love of my life."

I frowned. "But Mrs Jones just seems so much…older."

"She isn't," he said quickly as though leaping to her defence. "She's thirty-eight like me. Just married that old man. We were soul-mates when were about your age. I adored her."

"Then what went wrong? You must have done something really bad for her to marry Mr Jones," I reasoned, more to myself than to him. I couldn't imagine anyone falling in love with Mr Jones, especially not a woman as attractive as Mrs Jones.

He sighed sadly. "It all changed when she went away to swear in the Rules. She came back a different person. And things just…ended. Then she got with that arsehole who was about ten years older and a complete arrogant prick, got married and had a baby." He smiled apologetically. "But that baby turned out to be Gem so I suppose something good came out of it." He picked up the book he'd placed on the chair and fiddled with it in his hands, turning the pages but not reading anything. "Gem was so like Maz. It was like being back in time."

"So, is that why you punched Mr Jones today?"

He laughed again. "One of the reasons. But mainly, I was just pissed off that he hurt little Liberty Bell."

"Thanks," I nodded, "for everything, I mean. It's really good of you to let me stay."

He flashed me a determined look. "It's the least I can do. I'm not exactly proud to call myself an adult in this town right now. There's too many secrets and I'm in the same boat as you." He lightly slapped my arm affectionately. "I promise you that, Lib. You can trust me to help in any way I can."

"I know," I inhaled deeply, "but until then…"

He raised his eyebrows expectantly.

"Pass me that whiskey and tell me all about this love affair with Mrs Jones."

***

I yawned and rubbed my temples.

Noah set a cup of tea in front of me. "Are you not feeling well?"

"I think I'm still tired."

Nothing to do with the shots of whiskey I knocked back with Denzil last night. I grimaced.

Cassius exhaled loudly and closed another book. "Has Denzil got his computer up and running yet? This is useless."

Despite the whiskey, I still hadn't slept well which irritated the hell out of me. Especially when Dad once told me that the only reason he drank in the evening was so he was able to fall asleep easily. Instead, I spent the night tossing and turning from dehydration and the occasional nightmare featuring Gemma's ravaged body.

At about five in the morning I'd given up and pulled myself to the bathroom to find Noah sat leaning against the bath, sobbing. I hadn't even noticed he was missing. After spending the best part of two hours holding one another and crying for our friends, we were forced to emerge after Denzil nearly knocked the door down.

Noah hadn't said anything when he cried. He didn't need to. I had to keep reminding myself that the two of us had been through more than most people have to experience in a lifetime.

Noah pulled out a chair at the table and flashed a disdainful look at Cassius. Clearly, the crying earlier had done nothing to dispel his prejudice for my friend. "Have you found anything, Lib?"

"Nothing," I admitted, staring at an image of a dead Hunter on one of the pages. I shuddered, remembering the sound of their feet hammering on the ground the night before as they chased us.

"I was thinking," Noah said and I ignored Cassius raise a sarcastic eyebrow, "all of the stuff you told me about earlier, the strange things you overheard, maybe you should write everything down, see if there's any clues when we see it in front of us."

Noah had reacted just as I suspected when I told him about everything that had happened, particularly the things to do with Mr Jones. In fact, Denzil now had a large hole in one of his kitchen cupboards when the penny dropped with him that Gemma's father may have been behind her death. He lost his temper and we'd been spending the best part of the morning trying to bring him back down from the ceiling.

Denzil was holed up in his room trying to get his computer working so we could at least attempt to get online to try and find any clues from the Outside. It was a long shot as the internet was not only slow but hit and miss as to whether you could actually make a connection.

"I still think we should go and get Consuela and bring her here." Noah jerked his thumb in the direction of the door. "She practically admitted she killed Gabriel."

"Well, not quite," I tried to reason, even though Noah echoed my thoughts exactly.

Please forgive us.

The image of Consuela saying those words to me at the funeral were quickly superseded with the thought of us kidnapping her and holding her hostage at Denzil's until she was persuaded to speak.

I shook my head. "We'll figure it out ourselves. We can't trust anyone outside of this place at the moment."

Noah curled his lip and nodded his head towards Cassius. "Are you sure you can trust him?"

"Erm, hello. You can speak to me, you know."

"I know I can," Noah shot Cassius a look, "I don't want to."

The pair exchanged dirty looks.

I sucked in my cheeks in annoyance. "Okay, I've seriously had enough of you two sniping at each other."

"He started it," Cassius whispered.

"You started it by just being here."

"I thought I made myself clear last night," Cassius shot back.

I cleared my throat loudly and they both blinked at me.

"You two are hilarious." I shook my head. "Okay, forget everything you think you know about one another, throw out all of the perceptions and let's start again." I walked behind Cassius, placing my hands on his shoulders. "Noah, this is Cassius, he's eighteen years old and has a condition called heterochromia which is why his eyes are different colours and his hair and skin is white. He lives with his dad on Springside and tragically, his older sister walked out when he was very young, followed by his mother who couldn't deal with the loss. If that wasn't enough to deal with, he then has to go to school and get picked on by people who don't understand, and don't even make an effort to understand, his condition."

Noah looked away and his cheeks coloured.

I took a breath. "To add insult to injury, his best friend ditched him to go and hang out with some of the kids who bullied him." I moved around the table so I was stood behind Noah and rubbed the top of his arms as his eyes remained fixed to the same spot. "Cassius, this is Noah, he's eighteen years old and works harder than any other person I know when it comes to the things he's passionate about. He's a superstar sportsman. He's lives on Ridgeway which is a couple of streets along from you, with his mum. His big brother walked out when he was little and then his dad. He's having a really hard time at the minute because his mum seems to, wrongfully, take this out on him. Not to mention the fact he's lost his best friend and his girlfriend."

Cassius nodded and looked at Noah with concern.

"So you see," I returned to my seat, "underneath it all, you have quite similar backgrounds. Plus, you're both my friend so that's another thing you have in common."

They looked uncomfortable and shifted in their seats.

"Oh Christ."

We turned to see Denzil eyeing us as though we'd lost our minds. "Did I just wake up in a cheesy American teen flick?"

I returned my eyes to the book in front of me. "Shut up, Denzil."

He chuckled to himself and gestured to the bedroom. "The internet won't work."

"Of course, it won't." I closed my eyes, thinking about where we could find more information. Suddenly my eyes flicked open. "Hang on a second, what day is it?"

"Saturday."

"What's the time?"

"Eleven," Cassius frowned, "why?"

I looked at Noah who blinked at me cluelessly. "It's around this time Mr and Mrs Jones visit his mother, isn't it?"

He nodded sadly. "Yeah, it's when I'd go round and see Gem for a few hours."

"What are you saying?"

I felt a shot of determination. "I'm saying we break into their house and look for clues."

"Clues about what exactly?" Denzil looked unconvinced. "If there's something going on where kids are getting killed and the parents know about it then I very much doubt there will be a paper trail. We've been over this."

I wracked my brain trying to remember the conversation I'd overheard between Mr Jones and Dad.

"....since the notice went out, it's gotten a bit out of hand, I admit..."

I narrowed my eyes. "There's something. Mr Jones talked about a notice. He's the headmaster and the mayor, he must have an office in his house where he keeps everything. Or a computer with working internet."

"Yeah, that's probably password protected." Denzil folded his arms. "It's a long shot."

"We have to try," I pointed at Cassius, "and I want you to come with me."

"What about me?" Noah stepped up. "If you need someone to break in to somewhere then I'm going to be more use than–"

"Noah, we're going to break into Gemma's house." I nodded slowly as I spoke. "*Gemma.*"

He winced every time I said her name.

"You're not ready to be in there." I looked at Cassius again. "He's the only one I can trust who won't get distracted. Denzil, I'm afraid I need a getaway driver and someone to try and alert us if the Joneses come back earlier, which, let's face it," I smiled at Noah in a feeble attempt at humour, "they have a tendency to do."

"So I'm just supposed to sit here and wait?" Noah demanded hotly.

"Yes," I nodded. "Keep trying the internet and going through the books. Anything at all you can find." I turned to

Cassius and Denzil who were already at the door. "Let's go and keep up with the Joneses."

"Oh God, you're not going to start with lame one-liners are you, Lib?"

"Shut up, Denzil."

***

We pulled up in front of the Joneses' house and looked up at it. It appeared more imposing than ever. It was a symmetrical house that had a black front door in the centre and windows either side, it reached up four stories high and I couldn't help but think it was a waste, especially now it was just Mr and Mrs Jones living there.

"They're out." I observed the empty driveway. "Let's go."

"Wait!" Denzil grabbed my arm. "What am I supposed to do if they come back?"

I exchanged glances with Cassius who shrugged.

"Honk the horn."

"Honk the horn?" he repeated, his eyes wide. "Are you kidding? That won't go unnoticed."

"Well," I said slowly, "just...distract them."

"You could punch Mr Jones again," Cassius piped up, trying to be helpful.

Denzil lowered his head onto the steering wheel and groaned. "I love it when a plan comes together."

"Oh, hush." I patted him on the back before jumping out of the van. "You'll figure it out." I looked down at the horrendous hippy outfit and grimaced. "We really need to stop at my house for clothes when my dad's out getting Oscar from school."

"My house too," Cassius grumbled gesturing to the overly long sleeves of the jumper which had holes to put your thumbs through.

We left Denzil sitting in the van further down the street

and jogged up the long gravel drive to the house.

"Shall we ring the doorbell first?" Cassius enquired from behind me.

"I hope you're kidding."

"What?" he asked, watching me as I cupped my hands over my eyes and stood on my tiptoes to peer through the window to the main living room. "There's no point breaking in if someone's at home."

"Trust me," I walked around the side of the house, "they're not here. Relax."

"I am relaxed," he mumbled.

I never would have told him but the crazy jumper suited him. It reminded me of when he was a little boy and his mum would put her jumper on him when he got cold.

I drummed my fingers on my waist as I looked around the floor near the back door.

There it was.

In the stone planter was an oversized and too-perfect pebble.

I picked it up and turned it over.

"Bingo." I popped open the little hatch on the plastic stone and pulled out the key.

"I can't believe he was right," Cassius whispered, as I turned the key in the lock, hoping the Joneses hadn't installed an intruder alarm since Gemma's death.

Noah told us about the key before we left. It was apparently planted there by Gemma so Noah could sneak in whenever he wanted. I tried not to feel hurt that Gemma had never told me about the key.

Cassius and I tentatively stepped into the small utility room and looked at one another worriedly. It then dawned on us we were officially trespassing.

"Okay," I exhaled, "let's start looking. The sooner we find something, the sooner we can get the hell out."

We walked through the amazing kitchen and I could sense

Cassius marvelling at it from behind me in the same way I had on every other occasion before. I strode towards the room next to the main living room that Mr Jones used as his office and pushed the door.

I'd expected it not to budge. I thought my shoulder would bang against it and we'd have to look elsewhere.

However, I was wrong and it opened easily.

My eyes scanned the bottle green and dark-wood room and landed on the desk, covered in papers.

"I've got you, you son of a bitch," I muttered, stalking over.

"Lib, just be careful. Don't make it obvious someone's been in here," Cassius appealed, stood nervously in the doorway.

"Do you think I care about that?" I sat down on the large green leather chair at the desk and picked up a pile of documents. "Are you going to help me or not?"

Cassius slowly wandered over but made no move to help. He just watched me frantically look through what turned out to be student essays. "Why the hell does he have to take his work home with him? Talk about a red herring…" I plonked them down and frowned at the computer, pressing the power button.

"Lib," Cassius moaned, "there's no way you're getting onto the computer."

"I bet he's got broadband in this bloody house, just like Outsiders do," I said to myself bitterly, ignoring Cassius.

The screen pinged into action and asked for a password straight away.

GEMMA

I hit enter.

Incorrect password!

I let out a laugh and shook my head. "Of course it's not

that."

MARIE

Enter.

Incorrect password!

"Shit," I narrowed my eyes in thought.

"It's not going to be obvious," Cassius reasoned, perching on the edge of the desk and picking up a stray pen, starting to chew on it.

"Thanks for your input," I spat. "What does Mr Jones love more than anything?" I leaned my cheek on my fist, my other hand hovering over the keyboard. "He loves that pigging school, this crappy town…"

BLACKBROOKE

I winced.

Enter.

Incorrect password! You have had too many incorrect attempts. Please contact your system administrator.

"Oh no." I flicked off the computer in a moment of panic. I looked at Cassius guiltily.

"You got locked out, didn't you?" He raised an eyebrow.

"Maybe."

"Bloody hell, Lib," he folded his arms, "he's going to know someone's been in here."

"No way." I headed across the room to the writers bureau, pulling down the door. "People can access computers remotely. He'll just think it's hackers."

"Yeah," Cassius looked at me as though I'd lost my mind, "teenage hackers who currently hate him. The most intelligent girl in Blackbrooke Academy..."

I ignored him and pulled out a stack of letters, flipping through them quickly. They looked like bills and wage slips. A massive collection he'd hoarded from over the years.

"I can't believe he ended up with Gemma as his daughter." Cassius walked around the desk running his fingers along the wood. "She seemed quite…fun."

"She was," I said distractedly, eyeing one of the letters and puling it out of the pile.

Cassius nodded and looked out of the window. "I mean, she was a bitch to me but I could tell she was funny."

"Mmm-hmm."

"I liked that she made you laugh," he continued, "even when we weren't talking, I'd hear your laugh from the other end of the corridor in school and…it was just nice."

"That's great," I said half-heartedly, my eyes scanning the letter in my hands.

"Lib…I just wanted to say that when we get through all of this…well, I'd quite like to talk to you about some stuff…"

"Holy crap," I breathed.

"No, don't worry," he plonked himself down on the chair, "I'm not going to make you embarrassed or anything but…I suppose just wanted to say–"

"You *need* to read this letter," I interrupted him and waved it in the air. "It's from a couple of years ago."

A wave of disappointment flashed over his face before he snapped out of it and strode over, taking the letter from me. I stood on my tiptoes to try and read it again over his shoulder but settled on leaning around his arm.

It was addressed to Mr Jones and appeared to be sent from an official Government body.

The paper was thick and expensive.

I swallowed as I read over the words again.

Dear Mr Jones,

I am pleased to inform you that your application to become a Guardian of Blackbrooke has been successful. You will begin to undertake the role as of 1st February.

As outlined in the training session and covered in the study materials for the exam, it will be your responsibility in part to ensure the your fellow townspeople adhere to the Rules at all times.

There have been several incidents in recent months due to disclosure of the Rules to minors. Mr Jones, you have been appointed in this role to ensure this does not happen again.

Here at the Blackbrooke Agency, we do not tolerate premature loss of life but understand that should an incident occur where a minor is exposed too early, matters must be passed to the parent or guardian. Although it is not always possible, we ask that you work hard to ensure anyone looking to complete Rule Twenty earlier than expected should be reported to us beforehand so we can make a record and ask the relevant questions.

You will be measured on how successful you manage and safeguard the Rules of Blackbrooke to ensure they do not fall into the wrong hands.

Blackbrooke is an inspirational model for the rest of the country which the outside should aspire to. We are very proud to offer you this position, Mr Jones, and hope you relish in this new role.

Yours truly,
Carl Evans
Chief Executive
Government Blackbrooke Agency

I pointed to the line about premature loss of life and looked up at Cassius. "I'm liking this town less and less."

"What's Rule Twenty?" he whispered, not able to take his eyes off the letter.

"I don't know but we need to find out." I sighed. "Waiting until January to swear in the Rules isn't my preferred option. There has to be a way we can find out the rest of the Rules. They have to be in this house somewhere."

"Was there anything else in there?" He nodded to the paperwork overflowing from the cabinet.

"I don't know. I'll tell you what, you stay here and look through this and I'm going to look in their bedroom."

"Bedroom?" He narrowed his eyes. "What the hell could you possibly find in there?"

I was already at the door and outstretching my arms. "I don't know. Maybe they've both got a Rule book tucked under their pillow, like a bible."

Before Cassius could argue, I shot out of the room and raced up the stairs. Instinctively, I made for Gemma's room like I had done on hundreds of occasions previously. I stopped in my tracks, remembering what I was actually there for.

I turned to Mr and Mrs Jones' room. When I pushed open the door I realised I'd never been in there before. As children, we were forbidden from setting foot over the threshold. Mr Jones wasn't one to argue with, or risk the wrath, so we never really bothered to push it. I remembered Gemma starting to tell me that her and Noah had done it in there one time and I'd clamped my hands over my ears, unable to listen.

I felt my mouth curl into a sad smile as I thought about my friend again. I inhaled and raised my head high in defiance.

I need those Rules, I thought.

I sat on the bed and pulled open the small drawer on one of the white bedside tables. The whole room was white and stark. I'd always thought this room would reflect Mrs Jones and be decorated in quite a feminine way, especially since the rest of the house was so corporate.

I frowned when I thought back to the conversation with Denzil last night about Mrs Jones. I couldn't imagine them as a couple.

Denzil with his hippy clothes, tattoos and dreadlocks and Mrs Jones with her sensible dresses and flat shoes, her hair always scraped back into a perfect bun.

It seemed so impossible. However, the dreamy look in his eyes not only confirmed he was telling the truth but also heavily hinted that he still held a candle for her. Almost twenty years later. I shuddered as I imagined always feeling that way about Gabriel, even if I married someone else.

I glanced in the drawer and saw a pot of expensive looking face cream and a hair brush. Clearly Mrs Jones' side of the bed.

I raised my legs up and scooted onto the other side of the bed, pulling open the matching drawer which just contained a rather boring looking book on how to be a successful leader. I picked it up and flicked through the pages in case there was anything tucked away in there.

I threw it back in the drawer and slammed it closed.

There were built-in wardrobes all along the wall facing the end of the bed. The doors were mirrored like the ones in Gemma's room and I walked over to them to look at my reflection.

I pulled my hair loose from the messy bun and shook it out over my shoulders.

My face was pale and my cheekbones jutted out further than I remembered. I wondered when the last time was that I actually ate something or had a good night's sleep.

I turned to the side and took in a breath of air pushing my cheeks out, before exhaling in defeat. I looked so colourless as though my fire had been extinguished along with my friends.

Who was I kidding?

Here I was, breaking into the house of my dead friend's parents, looking for what exactly? An answer? What good would it do anyway?

Even if I found something damning, who would I tell? Mr Jones practically ruled this town anyway. And looking at me now, people would just tut and shake their heads at the sallow, slip of a girl.

Poor Liberty Connor. She lost everything. Even her mind. Just look at her face. Poor, weak girl…

I narrowed my eyes at myself. I'd tackle my broken image later. Until then, I needed those Rules.

I tentatively opened one of the wardrobe doors.

This one contained Mrs Jones clothes and a smell of vanilla instantly hit my nostrils. She always smelt this way. I remembered when I was at her house one night when I was about eight and upset after having a nightmare. Mrs Jones had taken me downstairs and made me a hot chocolate. When she'd comforted me, I'd smelt vanilla on her skin and her hair.

I cocked my head to one side and ran my fingers over some of her dresses hanging in front of me. It was only now, I realised how young she was. The thought of her being the same age as Denzil was bizarre. On that night when she'd made me hot chocolate and cuddled me, she would have still been in her twenties.

I looked up and saw several shoe boxes on the shelf above. I reached to pull one down and set it on the bed and removed the lid, seeing that it was dozens of images of Gemma as a baby and young child.

I smiled and pulled them out. It hadn't occurred to me before that there weren't any photographs of Gemma in the house.

I felt my throat grow tight and stopped at a picture of her and I as little girls. We were sat on the sofa in the main living room and appeared to be giggling wildly at something. I ran my finger over her face. Whereas I was a chubby kid with unruly hair, Gemma was cute as a button. I flipped through the rest of the images before hastily returning them and fumbling with the lid, before I started crying again. I put the box back in its place and pulled down another one.

This one contained Gemma's old school books and some pictures she'd painted as a toddler. I returned them with a sigh when I saw they weren't going to offer any more clues.

There was another box I could see but it was set back further from the others. I jumped up to try and retrieve it, my tongue sticking out of the side of my mouth in concentration.

"Yes!" I whispered as I managed to knock it and catch it awkwardly in my arms.

I hurried to the bed and snatched open the lid impatiently.

I could tell this box was different straight away.

It was full of newspaper clippings and old photographs, as well as pages ripped out of notepads containing long lists of names. At the very bottom I noticed pink coloured paper and pulled out a heart-shaped card that was handmade. The writing on it was messy and I squinted to try and read the writing.

I know I need to stop sending you these but I can't. Please meet me in our place. Please just talk to me.

A photograph fell out of the inside of the card onto my lap and I frowned, inspecting it.

It showed Mrs Jones, looking around sixteen years old and the spitting image of Gemma, wearing high-waisted white shorts with a belt and a small red halter-neck top, finished with white tennis pumps. Her petite, slender frame was bronzed from the summer sun and she was smiling widely. I struggled to remember whether I'd actually seen Mrs Jones smile like that in all the time I'd known her.

She was turned to the side and stood on her tip-toes, her

arms thrown around the neck of a boy who looked the same age as her. He had his lips on her cheek which was turned to look at the camera.

I cocked my head to one side and inspected the boy. His hands were clutching her waist as though he never wanted to let go. His dark brown hair was outgrown and fallen over his face.

I looked closer.

No.

It couldn't be…

The sound of a car horn beeping outside blasted through the air.

"Denzil," I whispered in panic, standing up abruptly and sending the box and its articles scattering all over the floor. "Oh no," I bent down and started trying to pick it up, stuffing it back in the box.

I heard footsteps hammering up the stairs and a breathless Cassius appeared at the door. "Lib, they're back!"

He rushed to help me and I replaced the lid on the box just as the front door opened and closed.

My eyes were wide with terror and Cassius raised a finger to his lips, turning his head to try and listen to the conversation going on downstairs.

"I just don't know why you had to snap like that," I heard Mr Jones say sternly.

"She was being unfair." Mrs Jones voice, always quiet and timid. "I lost my daughter."

"We both have!"

"I know…I just can't get my head around all of that 'greater good' stuff yet. It's too soon."

"Well, you need to get a grip," he snapped, "because this is what everyone has to do. You've known it from the start. No use crying over spilt milk."

Cassius eyed me with concern, sensing the anger from Mr Jones' words boiling up in my body. I willed myself to commit his words to memory.

It went quiet and we remained unmoved, still crouching on their bedroom floor in front of the wardrobe.

"Where are you going?" Mr Jones demanded.

"Getting changed."

We exchanged horrified glances as Mrs Jones' footsteps started on the stairs.

"The wardrobe," Cassius whispered, pulling me up and inside.

I was still clutching the box as we squeezed into the small space between the clothes, closing the doors.

"Sshh," Cassius warned.

I was pressed up into him while his back was against the wall.

The sound of the bath running could be heard and I prayed Mrs Jones wouldn't need anything from this particular wardrobe. The bedroom door opened and I drew back into Cassius even more and he placed his hand on my stomach and pulled me back into him. A carpet of goosebumps suddenly covered my body.

"Shhh." He leaned his chin to rest on my shoulder. I turned my head to him. "Stay quiet, Lib." His lips practically brushed mine as he spoke, and I nodded quickly, feeling my quivering start to subside. I could feel his heart hammering in his chest, resonating through my back.

We heard Mrs Jones open and close several drawers and yawn.

My own heart was now pounding so loudly that I could have sworn she must be able to hear it.

"Marie!" Mr Jones shouted. He was coming up the stairs and I almost whimpered. "I've got a meeting in an hour." He was stood in the doorway. "Do you want to come with me?"

"Not if I don't have to," she answered quietly.

"Fine."

The sound of him turning and walking away.

Cassius and I both slumped in relief.

Just at that moment, Mrs Jones threw open the doors of the wardrobe.

She recoiled and gasped at the sight of us, gripping the top of her silk robe.

Cassius and I also drew back even more.

"Marie?" Mr Jones called. "Are you alright?"

Mrs Jones couldn't remove her horror-struck eyes from us and stood, unblinking with one hand still on the door.

"Marie?" Mr Jones footsteps were getting closer to the bedroom again.

I looked at her with pleading eyes and shook my head.

She glanced down and I felt my cheeks colour as I realised I was still clutching the box filled with all of her personal possessions.

She frowned in confusion.

"Marie!" Mr Jones bellowed and I saw a mild flash of panic in her eyes as she closed the doors on us.

"Yes?"

"What did you yell out about? And why didn't you answer me?"

"Oh, I…I thought I saw a spider." She let out a nervous laugh.

They were both quiet and I imagined he was probably looking at her as though she'd lost her mind.

"Erm, did you say you had a meeting?" she asked overly brightly.

"Yes."

"Great, on second thoughts, I'll come with you. In fact," I heard her swallow nervously, "why don't we pick up a bite to eat on the way? I'm hungry."

"Would be good to see you eat something," he said reluctantly after what felt like the longest pause in history. "Fine. Get dressed and I'll see you downstairs in a couple of minutes."

***

"Do you want to just run it by me one more time, *why* you ignored me honking the horn in the van like a mad man?"

I rolled my eyes at Denzil's exasperated question as we walked back into the shop.

After the Joneses left the house, Cassius and I waited in silence until we were sure they'd definitely left. I couldn't understand why Mrs Jones would protect us. After all, she owed us nothing. I'd been clutching her possessions in the wardrobe of her home. I was surprised she hadn't dropped dead with a heart attack at the sight of our startled faces. Or screamed for her husband to kick us out.

Noah looked up at us from his seat at the kitchen table as we entered the flat. He gestured to our normal clothes and frowned.

"We went to our houses to get some stuff," I shrugged. "Cassius brought extra in case you didn't want to go home."

Noah looked Cassius up and down. "His stuff won't fit me, he's a bag of bones."

Cassius ignored him and plonked himself on the sofa. He'd looked perplexed since leaving the Joneses' and I put it down to shock.

I sighed in disappointment at not bringing the box with me. I'd decided that seeing as Mrs Jones had let us get away, stealing from her probably wasn't the best idea.

"Did you find anything?" Noah enquired.

I pulled the letter I'd been reading from Mr Jones' pile of things from my pocket and passed it to him.

"Jesus," Denzil uttered, reading it over Noah's shoulder.

"I know." I turned to Cassius. "Did you find anything else while I was upstairs?"

"No," Cassius shot back quickly, "nothing at all."

I flashed a suspicious look but he avoided my eye.

"And you're telling me Maz actually saw you?" Denzil

asked again. "Nothing like stealth, kids."

"Hey," I protested, flicking on the kettle. "We were in the wardrobe."

"Oh great, because she was never going to look in the wardrobe of her own house."

"You hid in the wardrobe?" Noah looked amused.

I closed my eyes, picturing the look on her face when she saw us. "Yes, and she opened it, saw us and then got Mr Jones out of the house so we could escape–"

"All the while," Denzil cut in, "I'm sat in the van and…in fact," he moved so he was sat facing Noah at the table, "picture the scene, Moses."

"It's Noah, actually."

Denzil eyed him for a moment before waving his hand dismissively. "Same thing. Anyway, picture this, I wave them off while they break into someone's house. The Joneses turn up, head into the house and then come back out after five minutes and there's no sign of the kids. What would you be thinking?"

"Erm…I don't know."

"Well," Denzil clicked his fingers, "I'll tell you what you'd be thinking! You'd be thinking the Joneses had just murdered them both and fled out of town!"

I let out a laugh and looked at Cassius, expecting him to join in but instead he stood up and walked towards the door to Denzil's room. "I'm just going to see if I can get any joy with the internet."

I frowned and made a mental note to check on him. I turned to Noah. "Did you find anything?"

He curled his lip. "Nothing major. Got online for fifteen minutes and managed to find some references to Blackbrooke in articles claiming the Queens are into witchcraft or something but it was pretty general." He shrugged. "I'll carry on as soon as freak boy's done."

I flashed him an unimpressed look at the nickname.

"She definitely saw you?"

"Bloody hell, Denzil!" I shouted. "Yes, definitely."

He took the cup of tea I offered him. "Was she okay?"

"Well, I think she was quite surprised to find two teenagers in her wardrobe but other than that," I shrugged, "I don't know really."

"How did she look?" he asked, picking up a book from the table, trying to appear nonchalant.

"Just like Mrs Jones, I suppose."

He nodded slowly. "Sure."

Noah looked momentarily confused at the exchange before standing and stretching. "Right, I'm going to walk back to my house and get some stuff."

"You're not going alone, are you?" I asked worriedly. "I'll go with you."

"Lib, it's the middle of the day." He chuckled. "Mum's at work so I'll be straight back in less than an hour."

I folded my arms in a huff.

"Seriously." He placed a hand on my shoulder.

I bit my lip. "Okay, well if you're not back in an hour, we're coming to look for you."

"He'll be fine," Denzil said, as I peeled my eyes from the door Noah had walked out of.

"I know, I just…can't lose another one."

"You won't," he said resolutely. "Not on my watch."

I sat on the sofa, turning to look at him. "I saw a photo of you today…in Mrs Jones' wardrobe. There was a box full of old pictures that I didn't get the chance to look through properly, but you were in there. You were wearing jeans and a white t-shirt and your hair was really short." I frowned and closed my eyes, recalling the image. "It was near some trees and it was really sunny. Mrs Jones had on a red top and–"

"White shorts."

I opened my eyes to see him staring at a spot on the coffee table. "I remember the day that photo was taken. God, I loved those shorts. She had the best legs. She hated them, though. Went on about being fat..." He was suddenly animated. "I remember she was paranoid about a birthmark on her thigh – I don't know whether you saw it on the picture – but I thought it was amazing. It was shaped like a heart and I used to kiss it..." he trailed off and flashed an apologetic look. "But you probably don't want to hear that...I can't believe she kept that picture. What else did you find in the box?"

I shrugged, not wanting to mention the card which I presumed was from him. It seemed too personal. "I didn't get chance to look."

He nodded thoughtfully.

"Denzil?"

"Yeah."

"Maybe you need to open the shop. Isn't there a coach party due?"

He stood up, stretching his arms above his head. "No, that's tomorrow."

"Oh...Is it too late to make a request...from the Outside?"

He frowned. "Listen, you might live under my roof at the moment but I don't condone drug use and–"

"No," I said quickly, "it's not drugs. It's..." I picked up a pen and piece of paper from the table and scribbled something down that I'd memorised from a magazine. I held it up and he frowned in confusion.

"What the hell is that? Is it even..." he lowered his voice, "legal?"

"Yes, it's readily available from the Outside," I said matter-of-factly.

"Fine." He pursed his lips in disapproval as he snatched the paper off me. "It's not to do with feminine hygiene, is it?"

I ignored him. "I'm going to see if Cass is okay. I think the thing at the Joneses' really shook him up."

"Fine." He nodded. "I'll go down to the shop and unpack the rest of the delivery. Feel free to join me if you get bored."

"Noted."

I found Cassius hunched over the keyboard of the computer in Denzil's room, rubbing his jaw and clicking the mouse furiously.

"Hey," I sat down on the bed behind him, "you managed to get online then?"

"Denzil was right," Cassius blurted, not looking at me. "They've all been right all along."

"What?" I leaned around him to try and see what he was looking at but the text on the webpage was too small to read.

"All of them." He picked up several pieces of paper off the printer and inspected them.

"Are you going to tell me what you're talking about?" I leaned back on my hands. "I'm not very good at guessing, I'm afraid."

His eyes were wide with fear. "I found something at the Joneses' house." He shifted to reach into his back pocket and pulled out a folded up piece of paper. "Read it."

I did as instructed and took the paper from his shaking hand, my eyes scanning over the words. It was dated ten years ago.

Dear Mr Jones,

As you are already aware, we will write to you bi-annually with any results or additional research for you to communicate to council members.

We have been working with UCNA to identify any anomalies in the way your town follows the Rules. Although the Creatures abide by the Rules which have been in place for centuries, it appears there are several groups or individuals who may be more at risk at falling victim.

Using the research we have and analysing the last Blackbrooke census, we have pulled together a list of those we believe extra effort should be made to keep them from being seen by a Creature. As you will see, there are a variety of reasons and we have kept the explanations to a minimum in this initial correspondence, however if you wish to see the full report on this study then please inform us and it will be sent immediately.

In terms of action to be taken, there is not anything you need to do directly but just have an awareness and please consider including it in future Rules ceremonies for the ultimate transparency.

As ever, if you have any questions please do not hesitate to contact us.

Yours truly,
Carl Evans
Chief Executive
Government Blackbrooke Agency

I looked at Cassius and he nodded for me to continue and I turned over the page to see a list.

Ethnic minorities
Mr Lucas Fuller
Mrs Edwina Fuller
Mr David Lawlor
Mrs Jean Lawlor
Miss Angel Lawlor
Mr Christopher Lawlor
Mr Guilo Moretti
Mrs Consuela Moretti
Mr Gabriel Moretti
Mr Chi Li
Mrs Mai Li

Mr Xiang Li
Miss Su Li

Twins
Miss Jessica White & Mr Tobin White
Mrs Katie Brown & Miss Jane Layton
Mr Ryan Cornwell & Mr Jason Cornwell

Triplets
Miss Jane Wright, Mr Carl Wright & Mrs Amanda Brown

Dwarfism
Miss Caroline Anderson

Cleft Palate
Mr Jackson Moody
Miss Catriona Hurley
Mrs Anna White
Mr Adrian Sutcliffe
Mr Kevin George

Down syndrome
Miss Katie Parker
Mr Andrew Wellham
Mr John Cornwell

I read the next few words and I felt my heart sink. I looked at Cassius before returning my eyes to the paper.

Albinism
Mr Cassius Godwin

Chapter X

"They lied to me," Cassius said for the hundredth time since reading the letter. We were now sat downstairs in the shop, after I persuaded him to tear himself away from the computer.

Denzil was unpacking a box near the bookshelves and kept throwing sympathetic looks in our direction. Noah had returned and remained tight-lipped, choosing to sit on the small stepladder on the other side of the shop. I could tell all of the talk about Cassius actually being an albino was making him uncomfortable because that was one of the insults Gemma and him used to band around to upset him.

Cassius clasped his hands together in front of him as he sat forward on the chair behind the counter. "I can't believe it. After all those years arguing with people who called me an albino," he ran his hands through his snowy hair, "I feel stupid. Why the hell wouldn't they tell me?"

I shrugged and looked down at my cup of tea. "I don't know why they didn't tell you, maybe because you're 'high risk' and they didn't want you to know it." I flashed a searching look at Denzil for him to help me out. "Maybe they were doing it to protect you."

Cassius was bouncing his leg up and down with nerves as he chewed on the skin on his thumb. "Heterochromia. I mean, at risk or not, there's no need to lie about who I am."

"Being an albino doesn't determine who you are, Cass," I said softly, "it's just a condition you happen to have. And, I agree with you, I don't think they should have kept it from you but I think they were probably just doing what they thought was best at the time."

Denzil cleared his throat. "If they'd been told you were at risk then I imagine they wouldn't want the town to have the opportunity to gossip." He looked at me and I nodded in agreement. "Those Watchers are always wandering around as the eyes and ears of the other Crits. God knows how much they pick up on and whether they report back."

"Why am I at risk?" Cassius raised his eyes to address us and I saw a flash of anger. "At risk of *what* exactly?"

"I have no idea," I sighed and reached for one of the skull bobble-head pens. "Right, lets do what Noah suggested and write down what we know."

Noah walked over, sensing he might be able to help.

I started scribbling some notes on the tissue paper we used to wrap the ornaments in. I wrote down in a bullet-point list all of the strange things that have happened recently. I read them out to the others.

Consuela's words at Gabriel's funeral.
Strange exchange with Hope.
Abram's family car spotted on the night of his walk out.
Conversation between Mr Jones and Dad.
Mr Fuller's reaction to Consuela's words.
Gemma's body.
Mr Jones' attack at the funeral.
Letter about Rule Twenty at the Joneses'.
Cassius – albinism, high-risk.

I sucked in a breath and looked up expectantly.

"You're in danger, Lib," Denzil nodded, "there's no doubt about that. Your dad practically said as much as the funeral."

I chewed the inside of my mouth. "If only we knew the rest of those bloody Rules. I know I need to be afraid; I just have no idea what I need to be afraid of."

I started making another list of all of the walk outs I could remember. "Who was before Xiang?" I muttered to myself, casting my mind back. It was a girl. "Kayla Smith!" I said triumphantly. I cocked my head to one side. "Kayla, Xiang, Gabriel, Abram, Gemma – what do they all have in common?"

The others were silent.

"Come on, guys," I appealed, "anything at all you can think of, even if it's silly."

I inspected the list again.

"They were all seventeen," Cassius ventured.

I nodded and wrote that down, feeling like we were having one of those brainstorm sessions in the Academy.

"That could be a good point, actually." Denzil rubbed his chin and leaned on the counter in front of me. "Didn't Mr Jones say there were no consequences for Noah, or something like that, when he was talking to your Dad? Maybe because Noah's eighteen."

I considered the point before shaking my head. "But that doesn't make sense. If it were seventeen year olds getting killed or being 'taken' or whatever they call it, then the entire population of Blackbrooke would die out soon enough. We're all seventeen at one point."

"Virgins, then." Cassius stepped forward and Noah shot him a look of warning. "I mean, we saw…what we saw yesterday at the funeral. And you heard Mr Jones, it was like he was blaming her death on the fact she wasn't a virgin. Maybe he thought she was and…it backfired somehow and that's why she ended up in that state."

Noah cheeks flushed red and he caught my eye.

"It's okay," I mouthed to him.

I nodded slowly. "Just for the sake of argument, let's consider that for a second. Seventeen year old virgins are, for want of a better word, killed." I cast my eyes over the list. "Did anyone know Kayla?"

"She lived on my street," Cassius said.

"Would you say she was a virgin?" I knew how ridiculous my question was but I didn't know how else to approach it.

Cassius shrugged. "I don't know. She was quiet though and I never saw any friends round at her house. She didn't go around with any boys in school to my knowledge."

"Let's assume she was, then." I drew a 'v' next to her name. "And what about Xiang?"

Cassius nodded quickly. "He was my friend and never had a girlfriend."

A 'v' went next to his name.

I clenched my jaw as I saw the next name was Gabriel. "Um…to my knowledge, I can write a 'v' next to the next one. Unless he was dishonest."

Noah shook his head and flashed me a sad smile. "Only had eyes for you, Connor."

"Definitely a virgin, then." My cheeks flushed, and was it my imagination or did Cassius let out a relieved sigh?

"Abram?"

"If we're going off his face then I'd say he definitely was."

"Noah, that's harsh."

Noah shrugged. "Sorry, he just wasn't a looker. I never saw him with a girl."

Another 'v'.

That took us to Gemma and I didn't labour the point and lifted the pen from the paper. "It'd stack up seeing as I'm in danger and I'm still a virgin. It also makes sense that Mr Jones insinuated Noah was safe as it's common knowledge he was seeing that Lucille girl before Gemma."

Noah clenched his jaw. "Yeah, I'm not proud of that."

I shrugged in an attempt not to judge him despite remembering clearly that I hit the roof when I found out that not only had Noah deflowered my best friend but he wasn't even a virgin himself.

"Wait a sec," Denzil raised his hand, "doesn't stack up

already. Cass is eighteen and he's still a virgin, aren't you?"

"What?" Cassius spluttered, letting out a laugh. "You don't know that."

All eyes were on him now and I was surprised to feel a pang of jealousy, resisting the strong urge to demand who she was. Instead, Cassius blushed and didn't meet our eyes. "No, you're right. I am."

Relief rushed through me and I tried not to show it. "To be honest, I'm not sure that theory stacks up because I'm quite sure that most young people in Blackbrooke follow Rule Eight; it's the minority who break the Rule early. So, if it were seventeen year old virgins who were at risk then I think we'd see a whole lot more."

I felt perplexed and placed the pen down.

Noah and Cassius sighed in defeat, both still clearly deep in thought. I cocked my head to one side looking at the two very different boys in front of me.

If Mr Jones was correct, then Noah was safe. And if our assumption it was seventeen year olds was right then eighteen-year-old Cassius was also safe. I thought back to earlier in the day when I spoke to them both about how similar they were really. It was supposed to be an exercise to get them to stop bickering but I now wondered if there were common anomalies that granted their safety.

"This is Cassius…he's eighteen years old… lives with his dad on Springside… older sister walked…followed by mother… bullied at school…ditched by his only friend…"

I could feel my lips moving soundlessly as I repeated my earlier words to myself.

"This is Noah…he's eighteen years old….works harder than any other person I know …superstar sportsman…lives on Ridgeway with his mum…big brother walked…then dad…mum takes this out on him….lost his best friend and his girlfriend…."

I scanned the list of recent walk outs with wide eyes and pressed the tip of the pen into the paper, so hard it ripped.

"Oh my God…"

"Lib?" Cassius stepped towards the counter. "What's the matter?"

Names flew through my head, spinning around like an out of control carousel.

Noah…Cassius…Oscar…Frank…Rosa…Su…Jessica

I raised my hand to my mouth. "I think I know what's going on."

Denzil and Cassius exchanged glances.

My whole body started to shake at the realisation. "Noah, Cassius, you're safe because your elder siblings walked. Just like Frank and Rosa are safe because Gabriel walked, and Oscar will be safe. And Xiang's sister Su is safe."

They didn't say anything.

"It's the eldest child of every family," I blurted, "the first-born."

I felt Cassius' eyes search mine in disbelief.

"And they have to be virgins." I lowered myself on to the chair behind the counter. "It's the Queens. It has to be the Queens." I blinked in an attempt to focus. My voice sounded distant and alien as though the words were choking me. "Henry Waterhouse, Blackbrooke's first mayor…"

"The one that killed the kids?" Noah asked.

I nodded, my eyes trance-like as I thought back. "He sacrificed his eldest son. He was obsessed with those vile Queens. His son was killed and he stayed in power and the Crits retreated like he was some kind of hero, even though he'd committed such crimes. And then the Rules were born." I looked up at their unblinking faces. "Henry Waterhouse sacrificed his son and struck a deal with the Crits…he was desperate for power and youth. It was ludicrous, the man was mad…he offered the sacrifice."

Noah sniggered and we eyed him in surprise. "Oh…come on, that's some weird shit." His smile fell as he absorbed the information. "Are you serious?"

"It's a theory." I didn't meet his eye. "It's one theory and we can't discount it."

"She's right."

We span around in shock to see Mrs Jones stood in the middle of the shop, clutching the box I'd been looking through in the wardrobe earlier. She shuffled awkwardly and reached up to smooth the piece of honey coloured hair hanging down from her bun.

"Liberty's right," she said again, her voice quiet.

Denzil stared in surprise. "How the hell did you get in here? That door was locked."

She let out a nervous laugh. "I used to sneak in here plenty of times when we were younger. I became a master of picking the lock and opening the door without letting the bell ring."

Denzil narrowed his eyes. "What do you want?"

She looked at her feet and I saw her bottom lip tremble.

I couldn't get over how much Gemma had looked like her, even down to her mannerisms. She too was petite and was stood dressed in black from head to toe in a dress with tights and flat shoes and a trench coat over the top. She looked ready for another funeral.

"I wanted to bring you this." She held up the box and stepped towards the counter to set it down. "I saw you had it earlier…in my house."

"Listen," I appealed, "I'm really sorry about that. We crossed the line and–"

"You did." She nodded in agreement, her blue eyes burning into mine. "But I'm glad you did…I'm done with this town and its Rules. I want to help in any way I can."

I nodded slowly.

"No way." Denzil was stood with his arms folded, shaking his head. "We don't need your help."

"Really?" She raised an eyebrow. "I seem to recall you didn't swear in the Rules, Denzil, so I imagine I'd be quite a handy person to know."

He pressed his tongue into his cheek. "I'm presuming the bag by the door means you're expecting to stay here?"

We all looked over at the brown leather overnight bag Mrs Jones must have placed down as she walked into the shop. She looked embarrassed. "Yes, I was hoping to if that's okay."

"Hmmm," Denzil walked around her, like a vulture, "I really don't think your husband would be happy with that, would he?"

Her mouth twitched into a sad smile and she looked at Cassius and I. "Did you go on his computer in the house?"

I felt my cheeks burn. "Yes."

"Well…I managed to convince him it was me."

Denzil moved in front of her and she blinked up at him.

"But he wasn't very happy about it…" She moved the piece of blonde hair that hung over her face and tucked it behind her ear. I gasped at the sight of a huge purple bruise around her eye. Cassius shook his head, flashing me a guilty look.

She looked dangerously close to tears as Denzil tilted her chin upwards so he could inspect it more closely. "Lib, where did you put the gun?"

"Forget it," Mrs Jones wiped away a stray tear that escaped from her injured eye, wincing at her own touch, "what's done is done. I just…don't want to go back there."

Denzil looked even angrier. "You won't go back. You can stay here at the bloody youth hostel, everyone else is."

I felt a wave of sadness as I returned Mrs Jones tentative smile.

"What were you saying?" Cassius interrupted my thoughts as he gestured to Mrs Jones. "When you walked in, you said Lib was right…"

She nodded quickly. "It's forbidden to talk about the Rules but you got there yourselves and plus…I don't care anymore. You're right, everyone in Blackbrooke has to sacrifice their first-born in order to retain order and ensure the Crits stick to their side of the bargain and leave us alone."

We fell silent and she carried on, not moving from her spot in the centre of the shop.

"It's been going on for centuries apparently. You find out when you swear in the Rules and that's when they tell you all about the history, about this Waterhouse man. He was a sick fool but he at least managed to control the killings apparently. His feud with his son was unknown by the Queens who thought he was handing over the most precious thing in the world to him at the time. In truth, it did him a favour as he kept his power, and it was an effective way to restore harmony in the town." She let out a nervous laugh. "I'm sorry, it's a rather brainwashing affair. I remember the Rule ceremony like it was yesterday. I-I felt like my world fell apart."

Mrs Jones shot a look at Denzil but he wasn't looking at her, instead, his eyes trained on the floor.

"There was of course uproar in the town when Waterhouse announced Rule Twenty. It was unfair and they took some convincing that it was for the 'greater good'."

My breath caught in my throat at the memory of Mrs Jones saying those words to her husband when we were in her house earlier that day.

"I know…I just can't get my head around all of that 'greater good' stuff yet. It's too soon."

"You have to sign a contract when you swear in the Rules," she hurried on. "We're not told what happens to them once they go but…well, you can only imagine."

All colour had now drained from Denzil's face. "Why the hell does everyone do it? Why don't they just…stop?"

She shook her head, looking scared. "We can't. The consequences would be too great. The Crits would be able to roam the streets whenever they wanted. They could attack us in our homes. We all die. And if a family refuses to hand over their child before their eighteenth birthday, the Queens claim the entire family as punishment."

I instantly thought of Oscar.

Cassius, now stood next to me, edged closer so our arms were touching. I felt myself prickle in fear as he slowly and gently took my hand and wrapped his fingers around it, out of sight from the others behind the counter.

"It's all so confusing," she said, wiping a tear, "they take you to swear in the Rules and that's when you learn that you're only there because…your eldest sibling was given to them. The only reason you're alive is because they gave up their lives for you."

"Not that they had a choice," I blurted. "I presume we don't get told."

She shook her head, her lip still trembling. "I didn't know he was going to take Gemma that night. I just woke up in the morning and she was gone. I-I hate him for that. He panicked after that night when we caught you…"

She turned to face Noah for the first time since she entered the shop and I'd noticed he'd shrank back at the sight of her.

"They have to be virgins," she said to no one in particular but still staring at Noah. "When you hand them over, they have to be virgins or else they're…rejected."

I placed my hand over my mouth. "We were right. That's what happened to Gemma. They rejected her."

She nodded again. "So, you must be the famous Noah."

Noah's eyes filled with tears and he hiccupped a sob.

"You're the reason she was killed so horrifically and the reason her body was dumped as a message to the rest of the town." She stepped so she was stood in front of him. His shoulders were now shaking from sobbing.

"You're also the reason…" Mrs Jones held her head high, "why my daughter was so happy."

His head snapped up in surprise.

"She got to experience something that no one should miss out on," she continued, tears falling onto the breast of her dress in a steady stream. "We couldn't have predicted the end for her but…she was very happy in life. So," she forced a smile, "thank you, Noah. For loving her."

Noah was now crying hard and Mrs Jones pulled him into a hug. He gripped her tight as though clinging on for his life. Clinging to the familiarity of Gemma and also experiencing the embrace of a maternal figure, something he lacked at home because of his own mother's resentment of him. I thought back to the knowing smile of Mrs Jones as she spotted Noah in the garden after he'd shouted up his marriage proposal to Gemma. She could have easily hit the roof about that and put a stop to the relationship. All she had to do was tell her husband and it was as good as over, but she didn't.

Although I always liked Mrs Jones, I was now starting to view her in an even more favourable light.

"I'm sorry," Noah cried. "I never wanted to do anything to hurt her. If I'd have known…"

"I know," she whispered, stroking his hair. "It's okay. How were you to know? You loved her."

I felt a tear slide down my face and Cassius squeezed my hand again.

Denzil cleared his throat. "Excuse me, sorry to interrupt your moment, but this doesn't make sense." He glanced around and Mrs Jones pulled away from Noah but kept hold of his hand. "I'm the first-born and I've not been collected by the Queens."

Mrs Jones shook her head. "No, you have to be presented by a parent and…you lost yours." She smiled sadly. "I think you were…forgotten. You must have passed under the radar."

"And that's why no one came for me to swear in the Rules," he said, piecing it together. "First-borns never get to swear in the Rules."

"Like me," I croaked and everyone looked at me. "I'm not meant to swear in the Rules. The ceremony I got an invitation to...it's a fake invitation."

Cassius took me by the shoulders. "No way, Lib. I won't let anyone take you anywhere. If your parents come anywhere near this shop, there'll be hell to pay."

"So, does this mean my brother…" Noah looked shocked. "My parents took my brother to be killed?"

Cassius hadn't taken his eyes off me, and I saw the realisation cloud his vision as it dawned on him that his sister had suffered the same fate. His parents were killers, too.

Mrs Jones looked sad. "A lot of parents just can't handle the guilt and end up walking themselves, which is what's happened to you poor boys. Either that or they have another baby to try and ease the pain which is why there aren't many only children in Blackbrooke."

"Gemma was," Denzil blurted. "You didn't have another baby."

"He didn't want to," she said softly, but there was a hint of bitterness in her words.

I thought about my mother. This explained the depression. It was getting closer and closer to the time I needed to be taken and not even the arrival of a 'replacement' child could dull the pain. I wanted to feel sorry for her but I felt nothing but anger.

"I'm the only one at risk here," I nodded, "at least that's something."

"No, it isn't," Noah snapped. "We're not losing you."

"What about leaving town?" Cassius asked Mrs Jones. "We could get Lib out of here."

"And Oscar," I said quickly. "I'd need to take him with me."

Mrs Jones shook her head. "You'd never get past the border, Lib. It's on the town computer records that you're a first-born. Plus, no one leaves Blackbrooke until they've sacrificed their first-born. If you never decide to have children or for some reason you're unable to have children, then you're never permitted to leave."

I closed my eyes.

All of the plans Gabriel and I made about seeing the world.

Pointless. Even if we'd decided to run away, they'd never let us out. I'd never be able to leave Blackbrooke because my fate had already been determined. I was destined to be a prisoner in this town until my death.

My knees buckled and I groped for the chair again.

Cassius moved quickly and sat me down. "Someone get some water for her," he called to the others.

Mrs Jones appeared at my side, and took my hand. "I'm so sorry, Lib."

"January," I said so quietly I wondered whether anyone could actually hear me, "four weeks left until I turn eighteen."

"Like I said, Lib," Noah said, his voice loud, "you're not going anywhere. We'll figure this out."

"Jonathan put out a notice," Mrs Jones said, placing her hand on her chest absently, "right after we found you and Gemma with the boys at the house. The whole town was sent a notice asking to remain vigilant in monitoring the relationships between boys and girls in case they were having sex. People panicked and I think that's what happened with…" her cheeks coloured and she avoided my eye, "Gabriel's parents."

I nodded. I'd say they panicked. It wasn't even forty-eight hours after the night in question and they threw him at the Queens. Months before his eighteenth birthday in June.

We could have had him for all of that time.

Months of Gabriel.

I would have done anything for just a second more with him.

"Please don't cry." I heard Mrs Jones' voice but I hadn't noticed the tears. There had been so many in recent weeks that it felt unnatural not to cry at times.

"I hate this town."

"Me, too," Cassius muttered, looking angry.

Mrs Jones removed the lid from the box she'd placed on the counter and pulled out the stack of photographs. "When

Gemma was born, I tried to figure it all out but I was alone and it was tough. The newspaper stopped reporting walk outs in case under-eighteens started trying to piece together the puzzle. A paper trail of newspaper reports were thought to have made it too easy. For that reason, the clippings I collected are from a really long time ago." She placed several down in front of her, smoothing them out.

I stood slowly and frowned at one, picking it up.

TEEN PARTY RESULTS IN TRAGEDY

I blinked at the grainy black and white image under the headline of a garden in complete disarray. "It's the thing Mr Fuller was talking about. This is the night his friends died."

Denzil picked up the clipping. "Lucas Fuller?"

"Yes," Mrs Jones and I said in unison.

Denzil tapped the clipping and frowned in the thought. "I remember him. We used to smoke dope together. Hung out with his group of friends a couple of times as well. Called themselves the Vigilantes. I thought it was pathetic."

Mrs Jones absently flicked through the photographs. "Yeah, I remember them, too. They had a reputation for wanting to conquer the Rules or something. That's why I kept the clipping. They stuck in my head."

"Did they all die then?" Denzil squinted at the text trying to read it.

"Mr Fuller survived," I said quickly. "He was the only one. They tried to have a party at night but the Crits got to them."

"No way," Denzil nudged Mrs Jones who looked up at him. "Would you buy that? Knowing the type of people they were."

"What are you saying?" Cassius asked.

Denzil curled his lip. "This lot were quite serious. They wouldn't have had a party, no way. They used to come in to the shop when I first re-opened it and buy stacks of books and weapons and stuff. I even sorted them out with a couple of guns from the Outside. No, they meant business. I used to nickname them the Scooby Gang when they came in but they didn't like that very much…"

I exchanged glances with Cassius and Noah. "We need to talk to Mr Fuller."

"Why?" Noah asked. "All of his friends got killed. What help is he going to be?"

"I don't know, but he knows his stuff, maybe he was just scared to try anything else after what happened to his friends."

We were quiet for a moment.

Noah's stomach rumbled loudly and everyone turned to look at him.

"Sorry," he said, placing a hand on it.

"Bloody hell," Denzil muttered. "Does that mean I have to feed you lot as well?"

***

A gurgling sound woke me up the following morning and I sat up from my makeshift bed on the sofa to see Mrs Jones in the kitchen.

"What are you looking for?" I yawned, padding over and almost stepping on the sleeping body of Cassius.

She stood up from crouching at one of the bottom cupboards. "Just seeing if he had any sugar in this place."

"Canister on the counter," I pointed out.

I watched Mrs Jones with interest as she pulled two cups off the mug-tree. She was wearing pyjama shorts and a vest top and her hair was loose and brushing her shoulders in soft blonde curls, hiding the bruise on her eye. She looked a lot younger than she usually did when with her hair scraped back tightly and heavy make-up caked on her delicate features.

"Can I smell coffee?" I frowned.

"Mmm-hmm." She held up the canister of sugar and I

shook my head. "I found a machine buried away in the back of one of the cupboards. Knew he'd have one, he used to love coffee…"

I looked into the living room. "Do you know where Noah is?"

"I think he might be in the shower. Den had to go and pick up a delivery from the border but should be back soon." She eyed me for a second. "Are you going to go and see your dad at some point?"

I shrugged. "I don't know."

"We can come with you," she offered, "and we can go during the day so he can't take you anywhere."

"I know," I said reluctantly. "I miss Oscar but I'm… scared."

She smiled sadly, stirring milk into the drinks. "I understand. I was scared for a very long time."

"Would you have taken her?" I asked and she froze.

"I'm afraid I was going to be a coward…" Her face flushed red. "I wanted to walk with Gem. Just head to the cattle fields at dusk and wait for the Hunters."

I nodded slowly, my eyes wide.

"It's a harsh reality to face up to. Very overwhelming. You don't feel like it's real and then all of a sudden, your baby's seventeen."

"I hope I can figure something out. For the sake of the rest of the town," I said, taking one of the drinks. "I mean, Henry Waterhouse struck the deal in the first place. Perhaps there's another deal to be struck…something that'll put a stop to the first-born rule for good."

I wasn't really talking to Mrs Jones as much as I was thinking aloud. Another sleepless night saw me blinking up at the ceiling as my mind whirled around the possibilities of how we could overthrow the Rule. I'd reached no solid conclusions, only that I wanted to speak to Mr Fuller and find out how his friends really died that night. They called themselves the

Vigilantes and wanted to conquer the Rules. What they did clearly didn't work, and I needed to know what that was so as not to make the same mistake again.

One thought that kept running around my head was the prospect of having to stand in front of the Queens and bargain with them. To my knowledge the only person who'd managed to do that successfully was Henry Waterhouse, and he'd killed an army of children for their entertainment and handed over his son on a silver platter.

I gulped and shook my head.

Mrs Jones reached out and rubbed my arm. "You were always very bright, Lib. One of the special kids in this town. I have every faith, plus," she smiled and her blue eyes sparkled, momentarily drawing attention away from the ugly purple bruising, "you have us to help you. We may not be as clever as you but we'll do everything we can."

I felt my cheeks colour and I looked away. I'd been told my whole life that I was clever but I never really believed it and it never seemed fair. I barely had to try and I got good grades at school whereas I'd watch Gemma struggle to the point of tears on a number of occasions.

Mrs Jones mirrored my pose of leaning on the counter and sipped her drink. "I know I've said it already, but I'm sorry about Gem. I know how close you were. She was a lot closer to you than she was with me. You really were like sisters."

"It's fine," I croaked. "I'm sorry I didn't do more to stop her from sleeping with Noah. If I'd have known–"

"No," she looked at me but I couldn't meet her eye, "I meant what I said yesterday, I'm glad she got to experience… you know. In truth, Liberty, I don't think anyone anticipated that kind of reaction from the Queens. It was nothing short of…barbaric. And to think they placed her on Noah's doorstep…"

We were quiet for a moment. I had no doubt Marie was thinking the same thing I was. Trying to imagine seeing the person you love more than anything in the world in that mess. On the doorstep of your home.

I eyed her discreetly. Was she thinking of Mr Jones?

Or Denzil?

I winced at the words I was about to say. "Denzil said you and him used to go out."

"Oh…yeah," she laughed, colour creeping onto her cheeks. "We were very young, before I met Jonathan."

"Were you in love with him?" I asked before I could stop myself.

Her eyes flicked over my face. "Very much. I think he hates my guts these days."

I smiled, hearing my own words echoing back to me whenever I was quizzed about Cassius.

He hates me.

I shook my head. "No, I don't think he hates you. In fact, I may be young and only had one boyfriend so feel free to ignore me but I think…the way he talks and the way he looks at you…it's like he never really got over it."

She smiled forlornly. "I hurt him badly."

I know the feeling, I thought.

We both jumped as the door to the flat flew open and hit the wall causing Cassius to grumble and turn over in his sleeping bag. Denzil breezed in, his cheeks flushed from the cold, carrying a large box.

"Right," he said, setting it down on the table. "Lib, I've got that thing you ordered." He pulled out a carrier bag sat on top of the box and handed it to me.

Mrs Jones frowned in interest and moved so she could see what else was in the box.

"I've got…" Denzil said, reaching in, "some more guns."

"What?" Mrs Jones asked, her voice high with shock. "Real guns?"

He raised an amused eyebrow as he pulled his dreadlocks off his face and into a ponytail. "Yes, real guns. I don't think water pistols are going to do much to protect us, do you?" He unzipped his black coat and shrugged it off. "Can I smell coffee?"

Mrs Jones nodded and busied herself in pouring one for him.

"Bloody hell," I whispered, pulling a large axe out.

"Splitting hatchet axe," Denzil declared proudly, crossing his arms over his chest. "Oh, be careful when you reach in for the machete, it doesn't have a cover."

I turned the axe over in my hands and inspected the head. "I think I like this more than your gun." I held it up as though practicing a swing.

Cassius sat up, his eyes immediately widening at the sight of me wielding an axe. "What the hell's going on?" he croaked. "Are we going to war or something?"

"It's a possibility," Denzil said matter-of-factly, pulling out a flail. "Want to be prepared if those Crit Queens come knocking. Or if we decide to knock for them."

Cassius peered into the box, rubbing his white hair which was stuck up in all directions. I resisted the urge to reach up and smooth it down. "Bloody hell, is that a machine gun?"

"Yeah," Denzil said nonchalantly, sipping his drink, "the fella who sent it wants half of my stock in return but it's worth it. It's amazing the lengths people go to on the Outside. They can't get enough of this craphole."

The bathroom door unlocked and we turned to see Noah walk into the room.

"Can I smell coffee?" he asked heading for the kitchen.

"Yes, do you want me to…" Mrs Jones trailed off as she caught sight of Noah wearing nothing but a towel around his waist, his perfectly toned and athletic chest and large upper arms on display. She cleared her throat and looked away. "Shall I pour you one?"

"Please," he said, nonchalantly, reaching for his bag of clothes.

I folded my arms and raised an eyebrow.

Any excuse to show-off his body. He'd been no different when our group hung out.

He whistled to himself as he picked up a t-shirt and held it up to inspect.

I eyed the others with interest and watched Cassius look down at his skinny frame in dismay and Denzil place a hand on his stomach and pinch at the flesh.

"I'll take it in there with me while I get dressed," Noah said, smiling as he took the cup. "Thanks Mrs J."

Still whistling, he disappeared back into the bathroom. I looked at the floor to try and hide my smile.

"Well…" Mrs Jones breathed, "my daughter had impeccable taste…"

I sniggered and quickly bit my lip as Denzil and Cassius scowled at me.

Denzil, still rubbing his stomach, curled his lip. "I used to have a body like that."

Now it was Mrs Jones' turn to snigger.

He slowly turned to her. "What's with the laugh?"

"Nothing, sorry." She held up her hands defensively. "Ignore me."

"No, come on." He narrowed his eyes at his ex-girlfriend.

She exchanged an amused glance with me. "I just… remember your body."

Cassius grimaced at the exchange and turned to sit on the sofa.

"And you're saying it didn't look like that?" Denzil pointed in the direction of the bathroom. "I had a great body."

I was now trying desperately not to laugh.

Mrs Jones raised her eyes to the heavens in thought. "It was nice but…oh come on, Den. It wasn't…you know, like *that*."

"That's because I didn't do sports," he pointed at her.

"Well, there you go then," she laughed.

I sat next to Cassius.

"This is like listening to teenagers," he whispered to me.

"I know, fascinating isn't it?" I shot back, not taking my eyes off them both.

"Anyway," Denzil continued, "I never heard you complain."

"I didn't," she shrugged, "I suppose we all lose our figures in the end."

"What? I'm exactly the same!"

"Oh, come on, Den. You've filled out a little bit." She unconsciously eyed his stomach and pressed her lips together. "As have I. I did have a baby, after all."

"You look the bloody same."

She shrugged and sipped her drink. "Yoga."

"You still do yoga?" he asked, surprised, edging closer to her.

"As you can see," Cassius whispered, "two old people coming back together after all this time, in their natural habitat…"

I nudged him. "Shhh."

"Yes, I certainly do." She cocked her head to one side. "Why so shocked?"

He looked momentarily annoyed. "Just didn't think you'd be arsed about anything like that after marrying him."

"What's that supposed to mean?"

He yawned dramatically and placed the axe back into the box. "Just because you went a bit straight-laced and boring. Can't imagine him being too impressed with anything remotely spiritual."

"Denzil, that doesn't even make sense." She plonked her cup down on the table and folded her arms. "My husband has nothing to do with methods of exercise or how–"

"Oh shut up, Marie," he snapped, surprising us all. "Forget I said anything. I don't even care anyway. You made your choice."

"Uh oh." I exchanged a worried glance with Cassius,

getting the feeling this was rapidly turning ugly.

"Yes, I did," Mrs Jones said, her voice low and full of warning.

"I mean, forget love!" Denzil bellowed, causing her to wince. "Forget all of the plans we had to get the hell out of here, the hours we'd spend just talking. Forget the fact I loved you one hundred times more than that old man ever could!"

"That's not fair," she said softly, looking at the floor. "You don't have a clue."

"Don't have a clue?!" he spat. "Of course I do! I didn't have a penny and he had it all. Ready-made life just waiting for you. I mean, forget actually having to work for something. Why would you do that when you can stroll into a life with some jumped-up teacher with a big house? Become the bloody first lady of Blackbrooke!"

He waited for her to respond, breathless from anger.

She didn't look up.

"I want an answer," he growled at her. "You owe me that. One day we were a couple and then you just don't speak to me and I have to hear from some arsehole we used to go to school with that you were getting married. I was in the supermarket, Marie. That's when I found out!"

He interlocked his fingers behind his neck and turned away trying to compose himself.

Noah walked out of the bathroom, now dressed, and looked confused at the exchange between the couple.

"What's going on?" he whispered, sitting on the other side of me. "I heard him shouting."

"Don't ask," I shot back.

"This is what my parents used to be like when I was little," Cassius muttered. "I'm four again."

Denzil looked at Mrs Jones glued to the spot. "We could have got married straight away," he said, more softly this time. "I would have worked my arse off for you to give you all of shit he did. You could've chosen me and still led the same life."

This time, her head snapped up. "How could I? How could I have done that, Denzil?"

He opened his mouth to speak but she shot him down.

"How could I have married you? I was in love with you. More in love than…" she trailed off shaking her head, tears now falling onto her cheeks as Denzil just watched. "You were my soulmate. I loved so much that I felt pains here." She placed her hand on her heart. "I'd have died for you, Denzil. How could I have married you knowing we'd have to give up a child?!"

Denzil frowned and his mouth fell open as the reason behind her marriage to Mr Jones became clear.

"When I swore in those horrific Rules," she shook her head, "I knew I couldn't be with you anymore. I loved you too much to subject you to that. And, stupidly, I thought that by marrying someone I didn't love then…it wouldn't be as difficult to give up our child." She smiled sadly. "I didn't expect Gemma to be so wonderful. I didn't think Jonathan and I could produce anything so amazing. That was a surprise."

She placed her hands over her face and sobbed. "I loved you, Denzil. I'm so sorry I hurt you. I thought it was for the best. I thought I was saving you from something terrible."

Denzil reached out and touched her elbow gently, pulling her into a hug.

"Softy," Noah whispered as I wiped a stray tear away.

The situation made me sad. Mrs Jones was my age when she made the decision to leave the love of her life to protect him from heartache, despite it breaking both of their hearts in the long run.

Denzil stroked her hair and let her melt into his arms, still crying hard.

"Sorry." He pulled back and placed his forehead against hers while he brushed her tears away. "I'm sorry. I had no idea."

She nodded quickly and pulled away from him, gesturing to the three of us sat on the sofa. "I think we've made the kids feels awkward enough for one day."

For some reason, I couldn't help but think that, had Noah not been sat on one side of me, I would have entwined my fingers with Cassius. I stole a glance at him, his jaw tight with intensity as he looked on at Denzil and Marie. He saw me looking and flashed a small smile.

I collected the bag containing my item from the Outside. "There's something I need to do. I'll be about thirty minutes." I cleared my throat. "Mrs Jo…erm, Marie, will you be able to help me?"

She dabbed at her eyes with the bottom of her pyjama vest. "Yes, of course."

Denzil clapped his hands together, turning to the boys. "Okay, you two. I need some help with the delivery downstairs and there's a coach party due."

Denzil gave Marie's shoulder a squeeze on his way out and she watched them leave before turning back to me. "Okay then, Lib. What can I do for you?"

I unwrapped the small box and she looked at it and then back at me, surprised. "Really? Are you sure?"

I nodded and walked into the kitchen, pulling out an item from the drawer and holding it up for her to see. "Going to need these as well."

***

"Gentlemen," I heard Marie's voice from the other side of the door, "may I present to you, the new Liberty Connor!"

I winced and stepped through onto the shop floor.

The three were unpacking boxes and stopped what they were doing to look up at me. Marie was holding her arms out, as though presenting me like a prize on a game show.

"Bloody hell…" Denzil uttered, staring.

Noah whistled and Cassius' mouth dropped open.

I grimaced, waiting for someone to say something. After all, Marie and I had spent the best part of the last hour working on it.

"Is that what you requested from the Outside?" Denzil stepped closer, inspecting me.

I nodded and absently touched my hair.

It was short now. Marie had been nervous cutting off so much but I wanted it no longer than my chin. And I now had a fringe. Not something I even thought about but Marie got a little scissor happy and I had to admit, I quite liked it. The drama wasn't in the cut though, not wholly anyway. It was in the colour. I'd requested hair dye from the Outside. Something about the item I read about concerning Blackbrooke females dyeing their hair really annoyed me. Why shouldn't we? It's our hair.

Plus, Gemma had been bugging me for the best part of the last year to let her loose on my locks to make me a redhead. Since her death, I desperately wished I would have just let her.

So, there I stood in front of my astounded friends with flame red, bobbed hair. An extreme departure from my brown bun.

"That's crazy." Noah smiled and shook his head. "I always knew there was something crazy about you, Lib."

I smiled back and looked at Cassius expectantly.

He did the same as Denzil and stepped closer, inspecting it. He looked intimidated by me and that was fair enough seeing as he'd only ever known me with long, brown hair since we were small children.

"You look really…" he blinked and tentatively touched a strand of it, fascinated, "grown up."

"Gemma would have loved it," Marie blurted, smiling but letting out a shaky sad breath at the same time.

Noah nodded enthusiastically in agreement. "Tell ya what, Lib," he winked, "that's fighting hair."

I laughed, already feeling better than I did when I stood staring at my lifeless reflection in Marie's mirrored wardrobe the day before. Plus, Noah was right. I wasn't going down without a fight and I at least wanted people to believe I was strong and defiant, even if I was quaking in my boots.

"Well," Cassius said quietly, still transfixed by the cartoon-red hair, "if you weren't expelled from school before, you certainly are now."

I looked him in the eye and the corner of his mouth twitched into an amused smile. My heart leapt in my chest.

"Ahem!" Noah coughed as an indication for Cassius to step away from me. "Hey Lib, have you got any dye for him? He could do with some colour."

Marie flashed Noah an unimpressed look and he shrank back. "Sorry, Mrs J."

She nodded. "Thank you. And please call me Marie."

"Okay," I clapped my hands together, "now we've gotten over the excitement of my new 'do, how can we help?"

"Erm…" Denzil scratched the back of his neck and looked around at the boxes, "I think you might have timed this right because all we need to do is break down the boxes."

"Result!" Marie looked out of the window and frowned. "Lib, isn't that your parents' car that's just pulled up over the road?"

Everyone immediately craned their necks to see.

"Oh crap," I said, throwing a worried glance at Cassius who moved in front of me instinctively.

"Is the door locked?" Noah asked Denzil sternly.

I watched out of the window as Dad got out of the car. He looked tired and pale. My heart skipped a beat as he opened one of the back doors, unclipping Oscar from his seat and lifting him into his arms.

"Go upstairs, Lib," Denzil said under his breath as he watched Dad approach.

"I can't," I whispered. "I want to see Oscar."

"That's why he brought him," Cassius shot me an apologetic look, "that's how he knows he'll get to you."

Dad tried the door and knocked loudly, peering through the door glass at our surprised faces.

"Let him in," I said resolutely. "I want to hear what he has to say."

Denzil turned to Noah. "Go upstairs and get one of the guns." I gaped at him and he raised an eyebrow. "I don't intend to use it. It's just in case he makes a move for you."

I nodded begrudgingly and Noah shot out of the room, the sound of his footsteps thundering up the stairs.

Dad hammered again.

"Alright!" Denzil shouted, unlocking it and taking off the bolts and chain.

Dad burst through the door before Denzil could finish, causing him to stumble backwards.

"Where is she? Where's my daughter?"

"Right here, Dad," I said, raising my hand.

His eyes scanned past me for a split second before snapping back.

"Bloody hell, Lib," he gasped, "what have you done to your hair?"

Oscar frowned at me as though looking at a stranger before it dawned on him who I was. "Libeeee!" he shouted, smiling widely.

Dad set his squirming body down and he dived over to me. I scooped him up and squeezed him tight.

"I missed you!" he shouted in my ear so loudly I winced.

"Right, Lib," Dad put on his best authoritative voice, "get your stuff, we're leaving."

I shook my head and Oscar leaned his head against mine while we both eyed Dad. "Can't do that. I'm not leaving," I said, trying to be strong but I heard my voice wobble. "I-I know everything Dad. I know what you're going to do."

He looked momentarily taken aback. "That's impossible,

no one's allowed to talk about the Rules and–"

"She figured it out for herself." Marie stepped forward and Dad recoiled in shock as though seeing her for the first time. He probably wasn't used to the sight of her dressed down in jeans and a t-shirt, with her hair loose.

He rubbed his chin. "Listen, Lib…if there was something I could do…"

I hoisted Oscar up even more onto my hip. "There is."

He blinked expectantly. It was then I noticed his face was unshaven and his jumper and jeans were creased.

"You can leave."

He opened his mouth but I shot him down.

"Leave me here, and Oscar, too."

"No," he said quickly, making a move towards me.

"Stay there."

Noah was now stood at the doorway pointing one of the larger guns at Dad.

Cassius moved and laid a gentle hand over Oscar's eyes so he couldn't see what was going on.

"What the hell?" Dad held up his hands and let out a shocked laugh. "Are you going to shoot me, kid?"

"Take one step closer to her and I will," Noah replied, not missing a beat.

Dad looked to me to put a stop to it but I stared back. As hot-headed as Noah was, I trusted him.

"What are you going to do?" he asked and this time looked at Cassius. "Do you think you'll be able to change things? You won't. Then they'll come and take you themselves, and the rest of your family." He nodded towards Oscar and I gripped him tighter.

"I have to try," I whispered.

"Do you think you're the first person to try and change things?" he demanded. "You've got no chance and–"

"Dad!" I shouted.. "Enough. I have to. Leave me to try."

We stared at one another.

"Can your friend at least put that bloody gun down?" Dad asked, holding his arm up.

I nodded at Noah who begrudgingly lowered the gun.

"Thank you," Dad said sarcastically. "I'm not going to hurt her if that's what you're all thinking."

"You will though," Noah shot back.

"Seriously, who is this kid?" Dad jerked his thumb at Noah. "Because he's speaking like he's your boyfriend, Lib."

"Even if he was," I said, indicating for Noah to stay quiet when I saw him open his mouth to protest, "it would be none of your business. Noah's my friend and he's just looking out for me. Besides, don't you recognise him from Gemma's funeral?"

"I was the one carrying the body," Noah growled, "in case it had slipped your mind."

Dad closed his eyes and rubbed his temples as though struggling to keep up. I could tell from his expression this was his last shot. "Liberty…" he flashed a self-conscious look at the others before clearing his throat, "when we had you…we didn't think it would be this hard. We didn't even think we wanted kids that much."

I leaned Oscar's head against me and pressed a hand over his ear so he couldn't hear what Dad was saying.

"You've been so great, Lib," he smiled and cocked his head to one side, "a real star."

"This isn't her obituary," Cassius snapped, the anger in his voice surprising me.

Dad carried on. "I have to say that your mum knew you were going to be special before you were even born."

I took in a shaky breath.

"She said you'd be just fine. Said you'd be free. That's why she named you Liberty." I noticed his eyes pink with tears. "She was so sure of it."

More tears fell down my cheeks as I swayed back and forth, soothing Oscar who seemed to be falling asleep.

He looked at the floor. "If I leave you here, Lib, I might never see you again. Your mum seems to be getting better as the days go by," he continued. "I think it's because she knows you're fighting."

I gulped at the memory of that one word she uttered when I bumped into her in the hallway.

Fight.

"If Oscar stays here with you, I'm really not sure whether that's going to help her mental state right now." His eyes were appealing. "She's been spending time with him."

"Really?" I stroked Oscar's hair and nudged him. "Is that true, Osc? Have you been chatting with mummy?"

Oscar blinked at me and his little lips curled. "Yeah, we drew pictures and played dinosaurs and she did…" He kissed his hand and blew it. I joined in with his laugh. When I was little, Mum and I used to blow kisses at one another and pretend they were butterflies that we had to catch. I couldn't recall her ever doing this with Oscar before.

Dad nodded.

The others were silent as though they didn't dare to breathe and interrupt us.

I cleared my throat, setting Oscar down and kneeling in front of him. "Listen to me," I whispered, placing my hands on his cheeks, "I've got some work to do at the shop, really important work which means I won't be home for a little while, okay?" Oscar nodded and I reached up and smoothed down his carrot-coloured hair. "I want you to go home with Daddy and do me a big favour…"

"What?" he breathed, blue eyes wide.

I whispered in his ear. "I want you to give Mummy a big kiss from me and say 'Libby loves you'. Do you understand?"

I could practically hear the cogs turning in his brain as he committed it to memory.

"Okay," I patted his backside and rose to my feet, "go on, to Dad."

He ran over to Dad who lifted him in the air. I approached them both and rubbed Oscar's leg.

"Bye, Dad." I smiled up at him.

"You be careful, Lib," he whispered, hastily wiping his tears before Oscar could see them fall. "I love you and…I'm sorry."

I stood on my tiptoes to kiss him on the cheek. "I love you, too." I swallowed and took a deep breath. "There's um, some money in a jar in my room for…you know," I nodded at Oscar, "Christmas."

I wrapped my arms around my body as I watched him open the door of the shop. A gust of cold air wafted in and I shivered.

Dad flashed me one last pained look. "Good luck." he glanced around at everyone's faces, "all of you."

I felt Marie take my hand. I didn't take my eyes off Dad as he walked across the road and back to the car with Oscar in his arms, talking excitedly. No doubt about his little mission to deliver my message to Mum.

"It's for the best, Lib," I heard Denzil say, "you couldn't have gone back with them."

Dad started the car and pulled away slowly. I watched until it was a speck in the distance.

"I know," I said eventually. "I'll just miss them."

CHAPTER XI

"I think the guns are a little extreme," Cassius mumbled as we walked through the Blackbrooke Academy gates.

I rolled my eyes and walked backwards to address him and Noah. "Keep yours out of sight, Noah." I pointed up to one of the snipers who was eyeing us warily as we walked in without our school uniform on. I think my bright red bob was drawing some attention, too. We walked through the playground as several groups of students stared at us, nudging one another and whispering.

"Stare away," I muttered under my breath, "some of you might survive because of us."

I could feel the small gun weighing heavy the back pocket of my jeans, and I looked at Noah and winced to see the outline of the gun clearly visible in his coat.

Cassius wasn't armed. He was probably right not to be, I didn't anticipate us getting much trouble from Mr Fuller against the three of us. Noah was armed because he was still concerned my parents were going to snatch me, despite my father and I saying our goodbyes.

I gulped at the thought of us bumping into Mr Jones. Especially after Gemma's funeral. The fact we broke into his house and practically stole his wife also made the chance of running into him quite daunting.

"Let's find out where he is," I said, striding ahead once we entered the building, towards the school's reception.

"Wait." Cassius wrapped his fingers around the top of my

arm and pulled me back. "If we go to the Academy office, we'll get thrown out straight away. We need to find Mr Fuller ourselves."

Noah nodded and straightened his white t-shirt. Several girls walked past and wolf-whistled him. He flashed them a dirty look. "He's right. Let's go."

I followed Noah as he led the way down the busy corridor.

I felt out of place in my skinny blue jeans and yellow t-shirt, with Marie's trench coat, not to mention my red Converse, in contrast to the sea of grey school uniforms.

Cassius looked more at home in his black skinny jeans and buttoned into his long grey woollen coat. He buried his chin into his black scarf as we walked, his white hair and translucent skin more striking than ever.

I felt an overwhelming urge to grab his arm as we walked. Now that my trust in my parents had been rocked to the core, Cassius felt like my only true family. We'd grown up together – laughed, cried, argued, even slept in the same bed.

As I looked at his frowning determined face, I realised something.

I loved him just as much as my family.

"Are you okay?"

I blinked to see him peering at me.

"I'm fine." I looked away and felt my cheeks colour.

Noah pushed open the door to the boys' part of the Academy and I felt nervous as I'd never set foot in there. The walls were darker, a light grey compared to the soft yellow on the girls side and the old iron radiators were painted in gun metal. We walked past a trophy cabinet and I looked into it, but then had to jog to keep up with Cassius and Noah who breezed past without so much as a glance after seeing it hundreds of times before.

Like the girls' side, there were photographs framed on the walls of past pupils who had achieved either excellent grades or achievements in sport or the arts. I recognised a few of the faces and suddenly wondered whether my picture would grace the halls on the girls' side one day.

An image of Mr Jones flashed through my head and I shuddered.

Over his dead body.

We stopped outside one of the classroom doors and Noah peered through the round glass window. "He's not there." He turned to us. "This is Mr Fuller's home-room."

Cassius nodded. "Could be in one of the Language rooms?"

"No." Noah rubbed his chin, deep in thought.

Several boys who looked like they were in third or fourth year walked past and their mouths dropped open at the sight of us.

"Holy crap, is that Liberty Connor?"

"When did she get hot?"

"I'd break the Rules to get in those knickers."

"Hey Liberty! Do you wanna come here and–"

I gasped as Cassius strode into the middle of their group pushed one of them roughly against the wall. "Shut your mouths!" He flashed a look at the rest of them.

Noah and I exchanged glances and my lips curled into a small smile. How the roles reversed over the years. I could still remember the feeling of pinning someone against the wall when they bad-mouthed Cassius. My bodyguard services clearly weren't required anymore.

The pupils looked at Cassius in fear and scurried away. He walked back towards us, scowling. "Feel sorry for their parents."

"I feel sorry for their future wives." I stared after them.

Noah looked at the floor still trying to recall Mr Fullers location. "It's supposed to be Spanish this morning but I seem to remember the classes were moved to another day. Just can't recall why."

"I know," Cassius said, snapping his fingers. "It's the

Christmas concert. Doesn't he conduct the choir or something?"

Noah flashed me a look. "Starting to realise why you want this one around."

Cassius shrugged. "Come on. Let's head to the auditorium."

They broke into a run and I followed, my trainers squeaking on the floor. The auditorium was in the boys' part of the school and separate to the assembly hall. It was a formal theatre where the school performances and graduations took place. The Blackbrooke orchestra would rehearse in there, as well as the drama group. It was grand with red velvet seats and an ornate stage and one of the older parts of the Academy that had remained despite the constant regeneration work that went on around it.

Cassius and Noah were ahead of me and bolted up a staircase on our left, I struggled to keep up with them. Noah's athletic prowess and Cassius' long legs put my short, unexercised legs to shame.

"Come on, Lib!" Noah leaned over the banister several winding flights of stairs above me. "Hurry up!"

"I'm trying!" I shouted back, breathlessly.

I heard them burst through some doors above and when I finally reached them they were waiting, both holding one of the double doors open and looking unimpressed.

"About to send a search party." Noah stuck his tongue out.

We walked down a quiet corridor and I eyed some of the signs on the doors, indicating music and drama rooms. We stopped at another set of double doors and Noah placed his hands on the handles.

"Let's hope he's here."

He pushed them and we walked in at the top of the auditorium. A sea of seats descended to the bottom where the stage was. The first thing that struck me like a lightening bolt was the sound of the choir singing on stage. It was an all-male choir, made up of first year boys and there were about fifty of them all stood in perfect rows. They were singing a familiar Christmas carol and the beautiful sound of their voices momentarily took my breath away.

I craned my neck and saw, at the bottom of the stage, Mr Fuller with his back to us, conducting the choir enthusiastically, the sleeves of his cream shirt rolled up to his elbows.

I stepped forward between Noah and Cassius. "Come on."

We descended the steps which ran down the centre of the auditorium slowly, our eyes on Mr Fullers back.

"A thrill of hope, the weary soul rejoices…"

Several of the boys in the choir looked up at us and confusion flashed on their faces as they sang.

"For yonder breaks a new and glorious morn…"

They nudged one another and pointed up at the strange mismatched trio as we advanced towards them.

Mr Fuller stopped conducting and turned slowly, a frown on his face.

"Fall on your knees…"

The confusion was replaced with realisation as we stopped halfway down the stairs. I stepped lower leaving Cassius and Noah several steps above me, and placed my hands on my hips, glaring back at him.

"O hear the angel voices…"

Mr Fuller nodded slowly in understanding. "One minute," he mouthed.

***

"Alright." Mr Fuller entered the empty classroom where we were waiting. He flashed a look at me perched on the teachers desk, Cassius stood leaning against the wall next to the door and Noah pacing up and down the rows of desks. "How can I help you, kids?"

I reached into my pocket and slapped the newspaper cutting about his friends on the desk. "We want some answers."

He closed the door and folded his arms defensively. "Oh? To what questions?"

Noah let out a laugh. "Where do we start?"

"I understand you're upset about your friends and it's made you do some…" Mr Fuller eyed my hair, "crazy things, but I'm not sure what you want from me."

I strode up to him, stopping about two feet away. "We know all about the first-born rule."

His eye twitched but he didn't say anything.

"We also happen to know you were part of a group who called themselves the Vigilantes when you were younger." I held up the cutting and he turned away, pained. "Were these the Vigilantes?"

He sighed. "What do you want?"

"The truth," I said, feeling bold. "I want you to talk to me about the work you did with your group and why you failed."

"They didn't fail," he snapped, looking angry. Noah and Cassius moved closer to me and Mr Fuller glanced at them both. "Well…not really."

I frowned.

"Let's sit down." Mr Fuller sat on the chair behind the teachers desk. "Grab a seat."

We did as instructed and pulled chairs around the desk.

"Before I start," he interlocked his fingers under his chin, "I just want to say that whatever you're planning, whatever difference you think you're going to make…forget it."

Noah shook his head defiantly.

"I'm serious, kids. I'm sorry to be negative but when it comes to the Crits, believe me when I say, there's no negotiation or reasoning. Nothing that won't result in loss of life anyway."

We waited for him to continue.

"To answer your question, yes I was part of a group called the Vigilantes, and yes they were…it was them who unfortunately died that night. We started the group after figuring out the first-born rule. Someone let something slip they shouldn't and we were terrified. A couple of our circle were first-borns and we became obsessed with the idea of saving them. Thought we'd figure it all out." He shook his head angrily. "I made it my mission to learn as much about them as possible and I managed to get hold of some information." He looked at me and smiled. "You were right to be interested in the story of Henry Waterhouse. It's a fascinating case and we all picked it to pieces, I mean, as you pointed out in the class," he gestured to Cassius, "he sacrificed those boys in front of the Queens and they just watched. He traded his son. The question has always been, why? I don't suppose we'll ever know what was going on in that particular circumstance but…it told us one thing about them - it was possible to talk. Bargain with them in some way, find out what they want, see if we can... accommodate." Mr Fuller spoke more quickly. "It could be something simple, something we use every day that we don't attach any value to. Anything. Of course, we knew it was a risk. We thought it would be worth it to go into the woodland, a group of us and ask them why they needed the first-born and whether we could…help them with anything else. In truth, we hadn't given much thought as to what they might ask from us, or whether they would even ask. Because there were several first-borns in the group, we went with the possibility in the back of our minds that they might not return. We didn't really expect anyone to return, but we wanted to try."

I heard my own words echoing in Mr Fuller's.

Have to try.

"You wanted to go to the woodland?" Cassius asked, sliding the cutting closer to Mr Fuller. "You didn't get very far. Didn't your friends get ripped to shreds in a garden?"

Mr Fuller looked at him for a second before standing up abruptly. "That's enough, kids. I've already told you more than I should have. I have to…"

Mr Fuller trailed off and stared from me to Noah as we immediately pulled the guns out of our pocket and pointed them at him. Mine unloaded, but conscious Noah's was.

"Don't be stupid," Mr Fuller said quietly. "Don't do something you'll regret."

Boldly, Mr Fuller continued to make a move to leave but Noah sprang to his feet and pulled something on the gun that made a sound resembling someone cracking their knuckles.

The two eyeballed one another.

"Sit down," Noah ordered, pointing the gun at the chair Mr Fuller had just risen from. "This is the second time I've had to do this in the last day and I've gotta say, I'm getting a bit bored of not pulling the trigger."

"Ah, just do it, Noah." Cassius interlocked his hands behind his head and leaned back casually in his chair. "He's no use to us anymore. Plus, everyone will just assume he's walked. I mean, it's not like anyone will miss him. Not his kids or his wife or–"

"Alright," Mr Fuller snapped, holding up his hands, "fine." He walked back to the desk and sat down roughly.

Cassius and Noah exchanged triumphant glances and Noah placed the gun back into his pocket.

"The party." Cassius tapped the cutting. "What happened?"

Mr Fuller's body language shifted completely and he slumped. He looked like a suspect sitting across from the police.

"They weren't killed in the garden," he whispered. "They were killed in the woodland. The Queens just…dumped their bodies in the garden as a message. In the same way Gem…" he trailed off and flashed an apologetic look at Noah. "It was a message and the town received it loud and clear."

I shook my head. "Doesn't make sense. Didn't *you* go into

the woodland with them? How are you still alive and they're all dead?"

He squeezed his eyes shut. "I did go with them. We took weapons but kept them concealed. We didn't expect we'd ever win in a battle with them but it made us feel better. We set off at dusk and went straight for the woodland, to where the Queens were and we just waited…" He looked up at us as we leaned forward, our mouths open, waiting for him to continue. "There were eight of us altogether and we were pumped, ready for anything. We thought we were going to change the world, or at least Blackbrooke, forever. We'd said our goodbyes to one another and entered that woodland as fighters, not friends. We'd promised we wouldn't be friends that night," he said the last sentence through gritted teeth. He ran a hand over his shaved head and his wedding ring glinted in the light. "We stood and sure enough the Queens emerged from their caves and underground tunnels."

"How many?" I breathed.

"A lot. We didn't count. They saw us…." his eyes flickered over the desk in panic, "and they stared at us. My friend Joseph stepped up to them and spoke – he was so confident, especially for a first-born – he explained why we were there and they just…stood in the same spot, looking at us. I was scared and stood at the back like a coward."

I couldn't imagine Mr Fuller ever being cowardly. He had such a domineering presence when he stood in front of us in classes.

"The Queens," Mr Fuller frowned in thought, "they don't talk but they can…speak through people."

"What do you mean?" Noah narrowed his eyes.

"They picked one of the girls. I don't know why. They picked her, literally, into the air and hauled her over to them and spoke through her. It didn't kill her, she was just frozen in her own body and her voice…was like nothing I've ever heard."

I heard Cassius gulp.

"It didn't make sense at first, as though it was…Latin or something, but then she spoke and that's when they asked…"

"What for?" I whispered.

He raised a shaking hand up and pointed at himself in the chest. "Me. They wanted me." He looked at each of us, his bottom lip trembling. "They'd never seen someone like me before…my skin…Blackbrooke is traditionally a white town, you must be able to see that." Mr Fuller unfolded one of his sleeves and used it to dry his face. "I was a prize to them. You see, the thing I've learned about the Queens is they're quite similar to magpies. They collect shiny things. What they do with them…we're still not sure, but they like rare things and, at that point, I was rare."

I felt my breathing quicken.

"I was frightened," he nodded, "but when they spoke I knew what I had to do. They said they would…" He looked pained to say the following words. "They said if they had me, then they'd award us with time."

"I don't understand." I turned my palms upwards. "Time to do what?"

"Not time to do anything with." He smiled. "Freedom. Fifty years of freedom for first-borns. For me, they wouldn't require a first-born for fifty years, we could drop the Rule and then reinstate it again five decades later for anyone born after that date. It was…invaluable." He now looked as though he was struggling for breath and rubbed his chest. "I became mesmerised by them and I stepped forward. It would have been so easy – let them take me and free the town. I'd have been a hero. Me, Lucas Fuller, would have saved…possibly hundreds of young people. But," he swallowed and shook his head, "my friends…they forgot what we agreed…they wouldn't let me go. They cried and dragged me back to them. The reality set in and they chickened out and they wouldn't give me away."

Cassius frowned. "Why didn't the Queens just take you themselves?"

"Because, as spectacularly twisted and powerful as they are, they can't take something that doesn't belong to them. The first-borns, they belong to their parents for seventeen years, if they're not presented by their eighteenth birthday then they revert to being their property and they have every right to take them whenever they want. It also buys them the right to take the entire family, too, if they please, as a punishment. Everyone else, they have no rights to, unless they're given as a gift. The only exception is…" he placed his head in his hands, "revenge."

I bit my lip.

"And that's what happened to my friends. They refused to let me go, idiots," he spat. "Held me back, shouting at the Queens they couldn't have me. I was screaming at them to let me go but they wouldn't. If they'd have just let me go!" He slammed his fist down on the desk and stood up turning away from us. "The Queens were angry. It was like dangling a golden carrot in front of them and then snatching it away again. It caused enough rage for them to reap revenge." He turned back. "They ripped my friends to shreds in front of my eyes. Tore them to pieces, taking out organs, peeling off skin..."

Noah stood up abruptly, all colour drained from his face. He kicked the leg of the desk roughly.

I watched as Cassius stood in front of him and placed his hands on his shoulders. "I know this is hard, just try not to think about her."

Noah was shaking his head as though he couldn't stop and Cassius leaned into his face and whispered. "Come on, you can do this. Be strong for her. If we listen, we might be able to save Lib."

Noah looked back at him and nodded, slowly returning to his seat.

Mr Fuller shot him an apologetic look. "It's tough to hear, I know, but try seeing it. I closed my eyes and the next thing…I woke up in the kitchen of the house, the patio doors open and the remains of everyone all over the garden." He leaned on the back of the chair and eyed us. "Even though they wanted me more than any other 'possession' they'd been given previously, they couldn't take me because it was my friends that angered them. They saw I wanted to go and knew I'd been held back so, they had no right to me. They moved me though, to the house. It must have killed them to have been so close to having what they wanted and then having to walk away…"

I blinked, fascinated as he looked angry again.

"If my friends would have just handed me over, not only would they have all survived, but they'd have saved so many lives." His voice dropped to a whisper. "It's been torture to get my head around the fact I'm still here at the expense of so many others and I wanted to hand myself over for a while afterwards but then…well, I met Eddy and fell in love and suddenly it all felt worthwhile again." He eyed us nervously. "I think I know what's going to happen."

I raised an eyebrow.

"I've been waiting for this moment for a long time. You're now going to take me to the woodland and finally give them what they've been wanting all this time."

I shook my head. "No, we won't."

"Really?" He looked sceptical. "Isn't that why you're armed?"

"Yeah," Noah stood up again and to my horror pointed the gun, "that's exactly why. You're our hostage now and tonight we're going to take you to the woodland and give those Crits what they want."

I opened my mouth to protest but Noah started to bellow. "She would have been alive if they'd have gotten you!" Noah's arm was shaking as his finger wrapped around the trigger. "A loser like you! The reason why my friends are dead! Why Gabriel's not here! Gemma!"

"Noah," I touched his arm, hearing the panic in my own voice, "put the gun down. We're not taking Mr Fuller anywhere."

"If taking him," Noah was still practically screaming, "saves you, then he's going!"

"Please, Noah," I pleaded. "Mr Fuller has children! There has to be another way, we can't–"

"There's no other way!" he cried, closing one eye and aiming the gun. "I'm going to shoot him somewhere that won't kill him and then take him."

I grabbed his arm again. "And how are we going to get him out of here? You haven't thought this through and it's not ethical."

"Ethical?!" he spat. "Ethical! Piss off, Lib. I don't care about ethical. Think about Gabriel!"

I shook my head trying to prevent thoughts of Gabriel creeping in. Weakening me.

Mr Fuller had now backed away and was pressed against the white board, his eyes wide and his hands up in surrender.

"I'm gonna do it!" Noah pushed me away roughly and I stumbled over the chair and fell hard on the floor. He aimed the gun at Mr Fuller's legs.

Mr Fuller closed his eyes, waiting for the impact.

"Stop!"

I looked in horror as Cassius jumped out of his seat and in front of the gun.

Noah recoiled and dropped the gun onto the floor in shock. "What the hell…"

"Just stop a second," Cassius said sternly.

I picked myself up and brushed off my clothes.

"Okay," Cassius exhaled deeply, "Mr Fuller isn't going anywhere."

"But we need to–"

"Noah, just…hear me out a second." He pressed the tips of his fingers together, touching them against his nose as he paced back and forth. We watched, waiting for him to speak. "Lib's right, Mr Fuller has a family and we'd be causing a lot of pain for them if we took him anywhere." Noah opened his mouth to protest again but Cassius held up his hand as a signal for him to stop. "Plus, we don't even know if the Queens would still want him. I mean, they've had Xiang so it's not like Mr Fuller is the first ethnic minority they've received."

I noticed he was avoiding my eye. Anxiety started to build in my chest, and I had a funny feeling I knew exactly what Cassius was going to say.

"But," he sighed, "I doubt very much…"

My heart leapt.

"I doubt very much," he repeated, now turning to me, "they've ever been presented with–"

"Don't say it," I whispered, looking away.

"An albino."

I shook my head. "No way."

Noah exchanged glances with Mr Fuller.

"Not. A. Chance." I felt my body start to shudder.

"Lib." He shook me gently. "Look at the bigger picture. You heard Mr Fuller's story. I could save people."

Noah frowned. "What are you talking about, mate? Have you lost the plot?"

"No." Cassius turned to address the others. "Remember the letter in Mr Jones' house – the one that said I was high-risk because of the albinism? I was the only one on that list." He inhaled and looked momentarily angry, I presumed he was still reeling about being lied to.

Mr Fuller looked thoughtful and waved his finger at Cassius. "I often wondered about that. I've done a lot of research on the Queens and the theories about them practising witchcraft. There's quite a lot on albinism and how valuable people with that condition are." He folded his arms and eyed

Cassius. "I thought you were. I always suspected but figured it was none of my business."

"Well," Cassius sat down, "I think the whole town knew, or at least suspected, apart from me. I'm now starting to think I might be a valuable commodity and if I can save Lib's life and a few more by giving myself up then I will."

"No," I folded my arms, "you will not. I won't allow it."

Noah frowned to himself as though trying to process all of the information.

"Lib," Cassius sighed and I scowled, "please just try and acknowledge that I might be able to provide the solution to a…horrendous rule."

I didn't look at him.

"You need someone to present you to the Queens," Mr Fuller pointed out. "You'd need to be taken there."

"I know," Cassius nodded seriously. "Noah's going to take me."

"What?!" Noah and I cried in unison.

A wave of horror passed over Noah's face. "You've got to be kidding."

"Nope." Cassius smiled. "Noah, I know you'll do it because it'll save Lib's life."

Mr Fuller folded his arms as he perched on the desk. "Speaking as your teacher and in a position of power, I can't condone what you're suggesting at all."

"But…" Cassius continued Mr Fuller's sentence for him.

He sighed. "But, if I could have handed myself over that day, I would have. Even though there wasn't a lot I could do about it, I still feel so much guilt."

Cassius stood up straight, forcing a smile. "There we go then, it's settled. We'll go as soon as possible. Try and save as many as we can before Christmas."

"Got it," Noah said tightly, the colour drained from his face, "makes sense."

"Don't you care what I think?" I pointed at myself, getting

angrier by the second. "That's it? You all agree that he just hands himself over? What about me? Why the hell does this have to be the final solution?"

Cassius moved but I stepped back and moved my hands up before he could reach out and touch me. "Get away from me."

I turned on my heel and stalked out of the room before anyone could say anything else. I couldn't condone this suggestion. It was ludicrous, and there was no way I was going to let it go ahead. Mr Fuller, our teacher, had practically given a ringing endorsement to throw my best friend to a pack of monsters.

I stalked down the empty corridor and let out a sob, covering my mouth with my forearm as my face crumpled into a cry.

Cassius.

My pale, white-haired friend who I worked tirelessly to protect when we were children. That same friend now wanted me to agree for him to be taken as a sacrifice so first-borns could live.

So I could live.

I pushed open the double doors to the stairs and started to run down them. I needed to get out of Blackbrooke Academy and speak to Denzil. There was no way he would allow this.

Or Marie.

They were my only hope.

"Lib!" Cassius shouted from the top of the stairs. I looked up to see him peering down. "Wait!"

"No!" I shouted back, trying to run faster. "Leave me alone, I don't want to hear it!"

"Just…slow down!"

He started running and I cursed that my legs weren't long enough to be able to descend two steps at a time without breaking my ankles.

"Go way!" I hollered.

I could hear him approaching and it was only a matter of

seconds before he was by my side and then in front of me, halting me in my tracks. He placed his hands on my shoulders. "Lib…stop…." he said breathlessly.

My cheeks were hot from the exertion and my skin tight from where my salty tears had dried. "I *have* stopped."

"Well," he leaned down and placed his hands on his knees, "in that case….give me a minute."

I clamped my hands on my hips unimpressed.

"Okay," he stood up straight again and cocked his head to one side, "please hear me out on this."

"I can't," I looked away. "It's insane."

"It's not," he said softly. "You know it makes sense. At the moment, we don't have any other options."

"We haven't even given it that much thought! We've only just found out about the stupid bloody Rule. If I knew we were at the planning stage, then I'd have thrown some ideas in the hat before we all opted for a Cassius suicide mission."

"You saw the letter." His voice remained annoyingly calm. "You saw I was high-risk. I'm the only albino in town. I might be the only one in the history of Blackbrooke." His brown and blue eyes scanned over my face and I found myself unable to stop shaking my head. "Hearing Mr Fuller's story just shows that we can bargain with them. We might change history, Lib."

"I don't care. I'm not losing you. Not again."

He shrugged awkwardly. "You'll be fine."

"Fine?" I let out a laugh. "How the hell can you say that? I need you, Cass."

"You don't."

"What?"

"You don't need me. You've lived without me before…you can do it again."

My mouth dropped open in shock. "There's a big difference between going a few years not being friends to an entire lifetime of–"

"Eight," he cut in. "It was eight years. Not a few."

I frowned. "Well…so what?"

"Sooo," he chuckled, "that's half of your life. You moved on, found another friend. Christ, you even got a boyfriend, Lib. The harsh reality is," he rubbed the tops of my arms, "if you hadn't lost Gabriel, then you and I would never have come back together."

"Goodbye, Cassius."

"Wait!" He stepped in front of me as I tried to bolt again. "You know it's the truth, Lib. All that time…you got on with your life and found other people to share it with and that's what kept you going. You know what kept me going?"

I narrowed my eyes and he ploughed on.

"What kept me going was seeing you, hearing you laugh," he gestured to the heavens, "knowing you were happy."

I curled my lip.

"I know it's cheesy and I'm sorry but the truth is…" he now looked deadly serious, "you can forge a happy life without me in it, but take you out of my life and…it's not worth living."

"No," I protested, placing a tentative hand on his chest, "you're stronger than that. You've got so much to give."

"Not without you." He leaned closer and planted a soft kiss on the crown of my head. "You saved me when we were kids. Over and over again. I've been saying to you for the last couple of weeks that it's my turn now, you've just not been listening to me."

I froze as he spoke into my hair.

"Besides, it's written in the stars. You're Liberty, meaning freedom. I'm Cassius, named after Cassius Clay, the greatest fighter…" He let out a small laugh. "I always thought it was an unfortunate name given that I've never been one for confrontation but…I get it now."

"You want to fight for me," I breathed.

"Fight for you and…to fight for the freedom of first-borns.

I can do this, Lib." He wrapped his arm around my neck so we were in an embrace. "Let me do this."

I pulled away and furiously wiped away my tears. "Can I ask you a question?"

He nodded, mirroring my action and mopping his tears with the sleeve of his coat.

"If our names have such strong meanings, does this mean Noah's going to build a big boat and gather up the animals two by two?"

Cassius' mouth twitched in amusement but he nodded seriously. "I believe there is a monsoon due any day now."

"He did always ace woodwork class," I said, deadpan.

We let out a laugh but quickly stopped and eyed one another.

The school bell sounded and the roar of hundreds of pupils being let out of their classes hit us like a huge tidal wave of noise.

The staircase filled with the bodies of the identically dressed Blackbrooke pupils all chatting and laughing excitedly as they shoved past us.

Not that we noticed.

We remained rooted to the spot, taking in every last drop of one another while we still could.

***

Denzil whistled while Marie stared at us, open-mouthed. "You can't be serious."

"Oh, I think they are." Denzil looked from me to Cassius sternly. "You're off your heads, all of you. I knew I should have gone with you to speak to Lucas. I knew he'd poison your heads with that Vigilante crap. If you hadn't noticed, kiddiewinks, his bright plans and ideas ended up getting all of his friends killed!"

We were back and stood on one side of the shop while

Denzil and Marie eyed us from the other.

"I mean, have you completely lost the plot?" Denzil narrowed his eyes at Cassius.

"No," Cassius frowned, "you have to admit it makes sense, it's the only idea we've had. Doing this might save Lib's life, it's at least worth a try."

"Yes, but," Marie stepped closer, her maternal mode kicking in, "the problem is, this isn't something you can just try. If you fail then you die. And so does Noah."

"I'll go," Denzil piped up, a determined look on his face. "If you're insistent on going forward with this crazy-ass plan then I'll go with you."

Noah opened his mouth but Denzil held up his hand.

"There's no point in another young person losing their life," he puffed out his chest defiantly, "I've lived my life."

Marie looked away, pained. "No, I'll go. I've lost everything."

"You can both get lost," Noah piped up angrily. "I'm going, I've decided."

"Well, I really don't think you're in the right frame of mind to make that decision."

"What?" Noah spat.

"Please listen!" Marie grabbed Noah's arm. "If anyone's going to go, it's me. I owe it to Gemma."

"Forget it, Maz!" Denzil barked. "Not happening."

"Don't tell me what to do! I've just left Jonathan who did that for eighteen years!"

"Oh, I wondered when his name was going to crop up."

"I lost my best friend and my girlfriend. *I'm* going."

Cassius and I exchanged hopeless glances as the three of them continued their bizarre argument about who was most deserving of death. Cassius winked and I flashed him a small smile.

It felt strange that after a childhood of it just being he and I together, there were now three other people who wanted to be with him when he died. They wanted to be the ones to hand him over. The ones to stand by his side at the end.

It was wrong.

"I'm doing it."

Everyone stopped arguing and turned to stare. Cassius shook his head in warning but I lifted my head high. "When I've finished talking, there won't be another word on the matter. Nod if you understand and then I'll begin." I folded my arms, feeling like a teacher stood in front of a classroom of unruly pupils. None of them nodded so I carried on regardless, "Cassius is my best friend. We grew up together and we…care a lot about one another. As friends," I added as I noticed Noah glare at him. "If Cassius insists on doing this there's nothing anyone can do to stop him and there's nothing any of you can do to stop me accompanying my friend and giving him to the Queens. Absolutely nothing. And no one will join us."

"Beg to differ." Noah shook his head. "You'll kill me before I see you go out there and face those things."

We glared at one another.

Cassius and I weren't the only stubborn ones. I knew that well enough after having Noah in my life for as long as I had.

"Fine, Noah and I will take him." I pointed at Denzil and Marie. "You two will stay here, you've only just found each other again…You deserve some happiness."

"Lib, you're seventeen." Marie ignored my comment and took both of my hands. "We've lived our lives and you–"

"No," I withdrew my hands, "you haven't lived your life, Marie. You gave up your life to protect the person you loved from pain. Both of you have sacrificed enough."

She bit her lip.

"Please," I appealed to her, "let me do this."

I deliberately echoed Cassius' words to me in the school corridor and he lowered his head in defeat.

"We'll come back." I nodded, my throat feeling dry. "Noah

and I will come back unharmed. The Queens will bring us once they have what they need."

Denzil didn't look convinced but nodded. "Fine. Whatever you say, Lib. You're the boss."

I forced a smile. I supposed I'd always been the boss in Tales from the Crits. I'd visited the place week after week and practically demanded friendship from Denzil, and I'd certainly demanded the job. Denzil eyes softened and I could almost see him shaking his head in exasperation at me as he so often did.

Cassius stared but didn't argue.

"So, when are you planning on executing this amazing plan then?" Denzil raised an eyebrow.

"Tonight." I nodded resolutely and heard Noah gulp.

Denzil curled his lip. "No way, kids. Not a chance."

"Why?" I mirrored his pose, folding my arms.

"Because it's too soon."

"What if a kid gets taken tonight?" Cassius piped up. "We might have been able to save them."

We fell quiet and Denzil shook his head. "No. At least, have tonight. Let's go crazy, have a party or something. I don't know, but you should give yourselves one night of fun." He clicked his fingers at Noah. "What have you always wanted to do but never allowed yourself before?"

Noah shrugged. "Dunno."

"Come on!" Denzil grew animated and I saw Marie smile in amusement. "There must be something! Let's have a party tonight and each do one thing they always wanted. One thing that…." he trailed off and his smile wavered.

He didn't need to finish his sentence. We knew what he was trying to say.

We should do something we'll probably never get the chance to do again.

Not for the first time, we fell quiet.

Marie coughed and raised her hand. "I know something I've always wanted to do…"

"What?" Denzil asked excitedly, clearly relived someone had broken the silence.

She ran her fingers along one of the glass jewellery cabinets. "It's more what Gemma and I wanted really, when she was little. I was with Jonathan for so long and our social gatherings were…boring at best. Gemma always wanted a fancy dress party for her birthday, every year, but he wouldn't allow it. I suppose I just always wanted to do something silly for her. Remind her that she was a child but it always ended up being a boring gathering of all of his friends with poor Gem sat in a corner…" she trailed off realising she was rambling.

I knew what she meant. Gemma's birthday parties saw her don a pretty dress but sit up in her room with me, playing with her new toys while we listened to the adults laugh and clink glasses downstairs.

"Done!" Denzil said pointing at Marie. "We'll head out and get you a costume for the night. Which," he raised his finger in the air, "helps with the thing I want to do."

We looked at him expectantly.

He glanced to the heavens dramatically. "Me? I've always fancied myself as a pirate."

I sniggered and I saw Cassius shake his head.

Noah raised his hand self-consciously. "Mine isn't a dressing up thing but," he gestured to his perfect athletic body, "I've always eaten all the right things and worked out. I'd quite like to just eat crap food and get drunk for the first time."

He had a point. For as long as I knew Noah, he'd only eat fast food whenever he had a long day on the sports field. Every other occasion, it'd just be protein and vegetables. As for alcohol…well, it rarely passed his lips.

"I will grant you that wish, Noah young sir!" Denzil announced loudly, nodding like a genie. "I'm the master at bad food and liquor. How about you, Liberty Bell?"

I chewed the inside of my mouth. What I wanted more

than anything was to see the world but I knew that wasn't about to happen any time soon.

A past conversation with Gemma suddenly flashed into my head and a grin spread over my lips. "Gem and I always used to talk about the graduation ball." I shrugged. "She was so excited about getting a dress and feeling like a princess. It'd be nice to do that for her."

"Okay, I have no idea how to grant that wish but I'm sure our good friend, Maz, can be of some assistance with that one," Denzil said quickly, on a roll.

Marie winked at me.

"Which just leaves the man of the hour." Denzil stepped towards Cassius and rubbed his hands together. "What can we do for you tonight? What do you want more than anything?"

Cassius shifted on the spot awkwardly and the tiniest hint of pink crept onto his cheeks. "Um…what I want isn't really possible…"

"Try me, kid. Tonight I'm your personal Jesus."

"Can you make me normal for the night?" Cassius asked, a sad smile on his face. "Not albino for just one night?"

"Okay, you're right. I can't do that." Denzil winced. "Anything else? Anything at all?"

Cassius let out a laugh. "No, it's fine but…" he looked at me, "seeing as Lib is going to give me away tomorrow, I think I owe her a date for tonight's graduation ball."

I quickly threw a look at Noah, expecting him to be scowling at the suggestion but he looked serene. The battle was clearly over.

"Great," Marie clapped her hands, "it looks like we've got some shopping to do."

***

"Lib, please come out!" I heard Marie's voice on the other side of the bathroom door for the third time.

"Erm…I'll be out in a sec." I grimaced at my reflection again in the mirror over the sink.

I'd been in there for a while, attempting to put on some make-up and re-brushing my hair. Gemma was the master at make-up. She'd be able to apply it subtly for school without the teachers noticing and then vamp it up for when we saw the boys at lunchtime. She didn't even need a mirror, she had it down to a fine art.

I, however, was completely useless. I rarely wore it as my skin was too pale to get away with it, but tonight I'd coated my lashes in black mascara and drawn black rims under my eyes. I'd even branched out and rifled through Marie's make-up bag to find blusher and pink lip-gloss.

I looked down at the dress and buried my head in my hands. "I'm not sure about this, Marie."

"Oh, Lib," I heard her chuckle, "I'm sure it looks amazing on you, just come out and let me see."

Amazing was not the word I would have gone for.

Marie picked out the dress after growing frustrated with me looking at the floor-length, long-sleeved variety in Blackbrooke's only formal dress shop, which we had precisely thirty minutes to dash around before it closed. I would have been much more comfortable in a black, traditional prom dress that was plain and boring but she wasn't having it. So, now I was standing in a short lemon-yellow, one shoulder number in taffeta material which flicked out in a tutu style skirt. She told me it suited my age better and would really set off the new red hair.

The special added touch she was yet to see was that it was teamed with my red Converse as I didn't own a single pair of high heels and it hadn't occurred to me to buy any.

"Come on, Lib!"

I tentatively unlocked the door and pulled it open.

"Wow!" we both said at the same time, inspecting one another's outfits.

Marie looked me up and down. "Lib, you look adorable."

"You look…" I shook my head and smiled, "like a superhero."

Marie had opted for a black skin-tight all-in-one satin cat suit, complete with black cat ears and painted on whiskers. "I'm a cat," she shrugged, "it's silly."

I pulled her into a hug, remembering the ill-fated pet kitten, Portia. "Gemma would have loved it."

We could hear music blasting from the shop as we made our way down the stairs. I let out a shaky breath. "Have you seen any of them?"

She rolled her eyes and padded, cat-like over to the door. "No. They've been more secretive than us."

As silly as it was, I was feeling determined for this night to be as enjoyable as we could all muster. I still couldn't get my head around the decision Cassius had made and a large part of me was convinced I'd be able to think of another solution before the time came. Despite the fact I'd failed so far.

I heard Noah laugh loudly at something and the aroma of takeaway pizza wafted into my nostrils causing my stomach to rumble. We entered the room and saw Noah sitting on the shop counter and tucking into one of the largest slices of pizza I'd ever seen in my life. He did a double take. "Wow, look at you two."

I tucked my hair behind my ear nervously as Denzil and Cassius appeared. I sniggered at the sight of Denzil dressed head to toe in a pirate get-up, complete with eye-patch and fake parrot on his shoulder. "Arrrrrgggggg!" he declared, holding up a toy sword. His face registered with delighted shock at the sight of Marie. "Good lord."

She looked away. "Ignore the black-eye and all is fine."

"Forget the black eye…" he said quietly.

I inspected my shoes awkwardly and Marie cleared her throat and gestured to me.

"Oh, hey Lib." He grinned. "Looking fancy."

"Thanks." I rolled my eyes and noticed Cassius for the first time. I let out a small laugh and cocked my head to one side as he approached.

He winced at my reaction and gestured to the black tuxedo he was wearing, complete with bow tie.

"Very nice." I nodded. "I imagine that's killing you seeing as you never even liked wearing the Blackbrooke uniform."

"I know, but at least this one makes me feel like the world's first albino James Bond." He moved his fist to his hip for me to link him. "Would you like to take my arm and we'll head into the ball?"

I placed my arm through his, looking up at him as we strode in a circle back to where we started, stopping in front of Noah.

Cassius raised an eyebrow at him. "Looking a bit underdressed for the most important night on the Blackbrooke Academy calendar, my friend."

Noah shrugged and reached to his side for a bottle of beer. "I'm just going to enjoy from the sidelines."

"Noah," Denzil turned around, still lingering around Marie like a magnet, "you need to move onto the whiskey, mate. You've not lived until you've had a shot of the good stuff."

"I put a shot in my beer." Noah tapped the bottle. "Is that okay?"

Denzil stared at him for a moment before shrugging his shoulders. "Whatever floats your boat."

"I think," Marie glanced at Noah before returning her eyes to Denzil, "there might be some more spirits in your kitchen upstairs, perhaps we can mix a few cocktails for them? Nothing too alcoholic of course."

Denzil grinned at us. "Excellent idea!"

The pair hurried out of the room, upstairs and I turned to Cass. "Kids…"

"I hear ya," he nodded, seriously, "they grow up so fast."

"Wow." I looked around the shop floor for the first time at the multi-coloured balloons and decorations placed everywhere. I also noticed all Crit-related paraphernalia had been completely removed from sight.

Cassius saw me looking, "We're going to try and be normal teenagers tonight. Forget about the Crits."

I looked at him sadly and Noah let out a loud burp.

"Sorry," he said, rubbing his chest, "this beer is more gassy than I thought."

I walked around the counter to flick through Denzil's CD collection. "If this is a party then we need some music."

Noah curled his lip. "None of that horror film crap though."

"As if," I shot back, pulling out all of the CDs. I spread them on the counter and Noah scooted himself around to see.

"No…no…no." I grimaced in disgust at some of the titles.

"Hey, that's a good one," Cassius interrupted, tapping his finger on one of them.

Noah and I flashed him a look and he raised his hands up defensively. "Hey, I like Bob Marley."

"No way." I frowned as I continued flicking through the discs. "Too chilled out. How about…Greatest Driving Songs."

Noah looked confused. It was clear by his pink, bleary eyes the drink was taking effect. "But…none of us drive."

"No, I know that, Noah, but…" I trailed off impatiently as I saw him scratch his head like a clueless ape. "Forget it. You know what?" I held up another, more familiar case this time. "We can't go wrong with–"

"Best of the Eighties?"

I scowled in response to Cassius' tone.

"Best of the Eighties it is!" he said brightly. "Erm…Noah, are you going to share any of that pizza?"

Noah looked horrified and grabbed the box, hugging it to his chest. "It's mine. It's the first pizza I've ever had."

I touched Cassius' arm and eyed him with warning. "I

think there's other food for us upstairs in the kitchen." I flicked my eyes to Noah who was devouring another slice and bobbing his head to Tainted Love by Soft Cell. "Leave him with the pizza. He's happy."

Cassius gave it one last longing look before sighing. "Come on then, let's go and get some to bring down to the party. I haven't eaten all day."

Noah didn't seem to notice us leaving and swigged the beer without even swallowing the food in his mouth.

I followed Cassius up the stairs and stopped abruptly as he turned, placing his hands in the pockets of his smart black trousers. "I didn't want to say in front of the others but…you look really pretty."

I immediately looked down at my trainers which were probably the same colour as my face.

"I mean, not that you don't always look pretty," he said hastily, wrongly assuming he'd offended me. "You do, every day but I just…it's not often you wear…."

I looked up, now amused.

"Forget it." He continued climbing the stairs. "You look pretty."

"Thank you," I mouthed to his back.

We pushed open the door to Denzil's living room and froze in the doorway.

My mouth dropped open.

"Oh shit," Denzil cursed, jumping up from the sofa and frantically buttoning his shirt, his pirate hat askew. Marie sat up and bit her lip, adjusting the headband with the cat ears. Her dark lipstick was all around her mouth.

And Denzil's.

Cassius folded his arms and stood up straight, like a figure of authority. "Thought you were coming up to make cocktails?"

"We were," Denzil grinned, "but we got…talking."

"I'll say," Cassius shot back.

Marie ran her fingers through her hair which looked like it was knotted at the back of her head. They were both breathless.

My cheeks went even hotter.

"Well, I'll be heading back down," Marie said overly-brightly. "Catch you down there. Oh, and trust me, Lib," she whispered, glancing at Denzil and then at the sofa, "the irony of you walking in on…that isn't lost on me."

She hurried past and Cassius and I both immediately looked at Denzil who was gathering bottles of spirits out of one of the cupboards, whistling happily. "What?"

"You make me sick, Denzil," I tutted, shaking my head dramatically.

"She's a married woman." Cassius pursed his lips. "Not cool."

Denzil grinned wickedly, passing several bottles to Cassius to carry. "That's where you're wrong. It is cool. It's very cool."

I rolled my eyes. "Could you at least do it behind closed doors next time? Say in the privacy of your bedroom rather than the living room."

Cassius nodded in agreement.

"Get some glasses, Lib," Denzil instructed as he walked towards the door to the stairs. "Cassius has the bedroom tonight anyway."

"Me?" He frowned. "Why?"

"Because…" Denzil trailed off.

It's your last night.

I watched him squirm at the unsaid words hanging in the air.

"Because," he said, more resolutely this time, "you're too tall for the sofa and too bony to kip on the floor again." He kicked open the door and hoisted up the bottles in his arms. "Come on, let's go and have a drink."

***

"I'd like to propose a toast!"

"Oh Jesus..." I rolled my eyes and begrudgingly raised my martini glass full of a lurid green cocktail in the air.

Denzil pulled himself up so he was stood on the counter and stooped so his head didn't touch the ceiling.

"How many more toasts?" Cassius called up to him.

"One more!" Denzil swayed. "I've forgotten what I said in the first one."

"You said..." Noah pointed at him drunkenly from his vantage point on the floor, his back pressed against the jewellery cabinets. "You said in the first one that Mrs Jones had the best body you'd ever seen."

"Yes!" Denzil clicked his fingers. "Moses, you're like my brother."

"It's Noah."

"That's cool with me, brother," Denzil pointed at himself, "if you want to change your name then you have my full support. Anyway!" He raised his glass. I grimaced at him stumble, getting visions of him going crashing through one of the glass cabinets. "I'd like to make a toast to new friends."

I exchanged glances with Marie who shrugged hopelessly.

I had to admit, this was one of his better ones.

Marie was leaning her elbows on the cabinet Noah was sitting in front of, looking up at Denzil.

"This time last month..." Denzil began.

Cassius appeared at my side and held up his glass, I smiled and did the same.

"I had one friend in the world and that was little Miss Liberty Bell." I placed my hand over my face in embarrassment. "I bloody love that kid. She figured it all out, the clever little sod. And she brought all of you amazing people into my life..." He looked thoughtful. "Some are coming back at long last." He smiled at Marie. "Some are just entering my life." Noah grinned up at him drunkenly. "And others," he shifted round so he was looking at Cassius, "are heading off early."

I felt a burning sensation in my throat and quickly took a sip of the cocktail to prevent it getting worse.

"To Cassius," Denzil said softly, "the bravest kid…no wait, the bravest man I've ever met. So, with that!" He once again raised his glass, sending his drink sloshing up the sides and down onto the counter with a splash. "Everyone raise your glasses to Cass. He'll save us all. Single-handedly making Blackbrooke history."

"To Cass!" Marie and Noah chorused.

I nudged him. "To Cass."

"Ahem!" Denzil jumped down with a thud and stumbled. He pointed at Cassius. "Speech!"

"Yeah speech!" Noah shouted, now looking like he really couldn't focus on much at all. Denzil topped up his glass yet again.

"Aw, no." Cassius grimaced.

"Come on." I patted his arm, enjoying watching him squirm. "I think that'd be nice."

"Public speaking is not my idea of a good night," he mumbled, despite conceding defeat. "I'm not getting up on the counter." He cleared his throat. "Right, erm…well, thanks everyone for coming to this year's Blackbrooke Graduation Ball…"

Marie let out a small laugh. Denzil moved so he could slide his arm around her waist as he finished his drink. Clearly, both were feeling bolder after having a drink and Marie looked as though she was finally letting herself have a bit of happiness after the horror of the last week.

"But seriously," Cassius looked at the floor, "I know we're having a laugh tonight and I'd just like to say thank you once again to Denzil who made us play charades for that uncomfortable fifteen minutes earlier…"

Denzil shrugged. "It's not my fault you lot don't know the rules."

“Anyway,” I noticed Cassius was nervous as he reached up to his bowtie unconsciously and pulled on it as though it was restricting him, “I’d just like to say that…” He looked at me seriously and I felt my breathing quicken. He licked his bottom lip and seemed to change his mind and instead raised his glass. “Life’s been a blast and I’ll be waiting for you all on the other side. With a slightly better drink than this.”

“Here here!” Denzil shouted.

“And just a word to Lib.” He swallowed. “Even though you’re serving me up as an appetiser to the Queens tomorrow…” I stuck my tongue out at him and he winked. “You’ll always be my best friend.”

“I’m gonna be sick…”

“Oh Noah.” I frowned. “For God’s sake. Cassius was making a speech about–”

“No,” Noah stumbled to his feet and made for the door, “I’m actually going to be sick.”

Marie flashed Denzil a horrified look and moved quickly, grabbing Noah under the arms before he could slump onto the floor. “Quick, help me get him upstairs and to the bathroom!”

Denzil moved to the other side of a now green-looking Noah whose head was rolling from alcoholic stupor. I watched them leave and grimaced at the sound of them stumbling up the stairs with him still making heaving noises.

The room suddenly felt very quiet after getting used to the drunk booming voice of Denzil. The Best of Eighties CD was playing quietly in the background and I noticed it was one of my mum’s favourite songs, *Time after Time* by Cyndi Lauper.

“Crazy night.” Cassius fiddled with the cufflinks of the shirt and eyed him like a complex puzzle.

I smiled and took his arm, turning it over to help him. I unhooked them from the buttonholes easily and placed them onto the counter.

“Thanks.” He rolled the sleeves up and I found myself

looking at the paper-white skin of his forearms. He caught me looking and coughed nervously, starting to roll the sleeves back down.

"No, don't," I touched his hand and looked up at him, "you don't have to do that. Not with me."

He shrugged. "Sorry, I just get used to covering up and I sometimes forget…"

"Forget what?" I frowned. "That your skin is pale? It's nothing to be ashamed about."

He turned away. "It's just…ugly, isn't it?"

"Of course it's not."

He didn't meet my eye and I grabbed his hand, pulling him into the centre of the shop floor. "Come on, dance with me."

A wave of horror passed over his features. "Lib. No…"

"Come on." I pointed at the floor. "This right here, is the Blackbrooke Graduation Ball and you're my date, which means by law you have to dance with me."

I raised my eyebrows, daring him to argue back.

"Fine," he muttered, "I can't dance though."

"Neither can I," I said happily, stepping into his arms. We clasped our hands together and he placed his other hand on the small of my back.

"Good God, Cass, you can get a bit closer. I'm not a bomb."

"Really?" he shot back, without missing a beat. "Funny because I'm always waiting for the next time you're going to go off."

I hit him on the shoulder and he laughed as we moved slowly to the song. I leaned the side of my head onto his chest, enjoying being near him for as long as I could. I could hear his heart beating and licked my lips, feeling tension in my arms and legs all of a sudden.

"Are you imagining him?"

My eyes flicked open. "I beg your pardon."

Cassius looked over my head, refusing to meet my eye.

"Him," he practically spat while we still attempted to dance. "I bet you're wishing it was him you were with right now rather than me."

I wanted to wrench myself out of his arms and hit him but I stayed, determined not to fall out with my friend tonight of all nights. "Why would you say that?"

He didn't respond and scowled at a spot in front of him.

"Come on." I tried to shake him but his body was rigid. "Why?"

He shrugged, his attitude clearly taken a turn for the worse. "He was your boyfriend."

"And you're my friend. I'm here with you."

"Only by default."

"Oh, for goodness sake." I pushed both palms into his chest which only resulted in me pushing myself backwards. "What do you want from me? What do you want me to say?"

He glared for a second before his features softened. "I'm sorry, I just…"

I stepped closer.

"I'm just…" He let out a nervous laugh. "I suppose you could say I've always been a bit…jealous of him."

I didn't say anything, waiting for him to continue.

"I mean, you only had to look at him and then at me…" He smiled sadly. "I knew there wasn't ever a chance for us when I saw you with him the first time."

I frowned in confusion before the penny dropped. "You thought you and I…"

He winced. "Yeah, I suppose I did."

I felt shocked. Cassius and I had always been close but I didn't for a minute think it was anything more than a friendship from either side. Or had I? I had to admit that I'd been feeling an increasing need to be close to him recently. To touch him. But that was normal I was quite sure.

"I remember the day I saw you kissing him at the edge of the sports field and I just…knew." He raised his hand to his chest, over his heart. "I don't blame you. He looked like he'd stepped out of a bloody Gap advert or maybe even spot cream or something. No wait, not spot cream but maybe one of those ones for…"

He trailed off as I reached out my hand and gently slid it underneath his, still unconsciously resting on his heart. His heart was now racing under my hand.

Alive.

Beating for a little bit longer.

"Cassius."

"Yes?"

I licked my lips. "Did I break your heart?"

After a moment, he closed one eye, wincing. "Maybe just a little bit."

My eyes were trained on his pale hand over mine. "I had no idea."

"How could you? You didn't feel the same."

I blinked up at him.

"You didn't." He shrugged. "That's okay."

I tried to let the information seep into my brain but I couldn't get my head around it. All of those hours playing as children. Feeling the way he did. Probably expecting us to come together at some point down the line but then watching me fall in love with someone else. Not just anyone else but Gabriel Moretti.

Perfect Gabriel.

I rested my forehead onto our hands.

"That's why tomorrow's fine," he whispered into my hair. "There's never been anyone else and there never will be…it's like…Kermit and Miss Piggy."

I drew back and his eyes widened in horror at what he'd just said. "Or perhaps a more glamorous partnership that just doesn't spring to mind right now."

I returned my head and heard him sigh with relief.

"I've never wanted anyone else. I'm not interested."

I opened my eyes again. "Have you ever kissed anyone, Cass?"

He froze for a second before coughing nervously. "Erm... yes, of course."

I flashed him another of my famous unimpressed looks.

"No." He avoided my eye. "No, I haven't."

I could feel his breath on my head and now it was the turn of my heart to start to hammer. I looked up at him and moved my arms so they were around his neck. Slowly I pulled him down so his lips could meet mine.

I kissed him softly, tasting the sweet alcohol we'd been sipping all evening. I felt his hands grip my waist and to my surprise he pushed me away gently, setting me down from standing on my tiptoes and taking a step back. His cheeks were tinged with pink and he looked pained.

I smoothed down my dress. "I kissed you," I said stupidly, feeling embarrassed. "I know you haven't done it before but you're supposed to at least move your mouth a little bit and maybe don't push me away..."

He avoided my eye. "You didn't have to do that."

"I did it because I wanted to," I snapped.

"Well, I can't!" he shouted and causing me to recoil. "I'm going to the Queens tomorrow."

"Yes, I know that!" I pushed him hard. "I'm taking you, remember?"

He stood straight and we glared at one another.

"If I kiss you," he said softly, "I won't want to go tomorrow."

I nodded slowly in understanding.

"I'm going to bed," he mumbled, walking past me to the door. "If you want to bunk in with me then you're more than welcome." He shrugged. "I don't think there's anywhere else for you to go."

I imitated him and shrugged nonchalantly. "Whatever. I'll see you later."

He stalked out and closed the door behind him.

I walked to the cabinet Noah was sitting in front of earlier and plonked myself down onto the cushion, the skirt of my dress puffing out like a cupcake around me. I picked up Noah's half drunk cocktail and sipped it.

"To Cassius," I whispered, bitterly.

***

I knelt down and picked up a perfect, smooth pebble from the bed of the stream. I picked it because it was a brilliant white colour, offset by the surrounding dull browns and greys.

The water flowed around my ankles, which were thankfully encased by wellies. I inspected the stone and dried my wet hand on the skirt of my dress. The water was freezing and my skin prickled from discomfort as I pressed my fingernails into my palm scrunching my hand as tight as I could for warmth.

On closer inspection, the pebble wasn't really white but more pearlescent with swirls of pink and green which became apparent when a beam of sunlight from between the treetops shone down onto it.

"What have you got?"

I blinked up at Cassius stood on the bank of the stream, on a grassy hill. He was about seven years old and wearing jeans and a loose white t-shirt. He yawned loudly, looking bored. I held up the pebble for him to see. "It's really pretty."

He curled his lip. "Just looks like a stone to me."

I returned my eyes to it, turning it over in my hand again. "It's much more than that."

Cassius stuffed his hands into his pockets. "We should go. Your parents will kill us when they realise we're in the woods."

I ignored him.

"They still think we're playing on the park," he appealed, biting his lip nervously. "We're not supposed to be in here, Lib."

I didn't answer and waded further down the shallow stream looking for more pebbles.

Cassius sighed and crouched, sliding down the hill on his bottom. He took a tentative step into the icy water and winced from the cold as it immediately soaked the bottom of his jeans and probably leaked into his trainers.

"This is a bad idea," he mumbled, splashing through the water behind me.

I turned to face him and he stopped abruptly.

"Cassius," I huffed, "if I hear another word out of you then I'll have no choice but to push you over."

"Like to see you try." He stretched himself to try and be taller. "I'll pick you up by your feet and dip your head in."

"Don't be stupid." I placed my hands on my hips. "You'd kill me."

"No, I wouldn't," he muttered as I turned back around and carried on walking.

"Where do you think you two are going?"

I froze.

The unmistakable voice of my mother.

"Liberty Amber Connor, get back here right this instant!" And now my father. "You're in a lot of trouble."

I closed my eyes and turned around, stepping in front of Cassius. "I'm really sorry," I started, my mind whirling. "But we were playing and…"

I trailed off as I looked up at the top of the embankment at my parents' unimpressed faces.

Only it wasn't the faces of my parents looking back at me.

There, dressed in clothes I'd seen parents in countless times as a child, stood Gemma and Gabriel.

"I told you we shouldn't have let them go and play on their own," Gemma snapped at Gabriel, the voice of my mother coming from her mouth.

Gabriel removed the glasses of my father from his face and rubbed in between his eyebrows in frustration. "I love that this has now turned into my fault."

"It *is* your fault!" Gemma shouted, getting in front of him and gesturing wildly like Mum would. "I ask you to do one thing. One!"

"Oh, give it a rest, woman," Gabriel spat.

Were my parents always this mean to one another? I wondered, frowning to myself.

I felt the familiar feeling of fear from their arguing bubbling in my chest and my bottom lip trembled.

"It would have been just brilliant if we'd managed to get Cassius killed as well!" Gemma screamed like a banshee.

They glared, their faces red with anger.

Gabriel looked past her and right at me.

I felt my heart leap in my chest at the feeling of his eyes on me again.

"Gabriel…" I whispered.

He frowned at me in confusion and reached out and touched Gemma's shoulder, pointing at me. Gemma turned around exasperated and they both stared at me, still stood in the river.

"Oh, Lib," Gemma said, sighing, "look at you."

I shivered and blinked up at her.

"What's that in your hand? Lib, that doesn't belong to you, put it down," she ordered, shaking her head at me.

"I found it," I said, my voice child-like. I gripped the stone harder in my hand. "It's mine."

Gabriel placed both hands on Gemma's shoulders, looking at me with his beautiful brown eyes. Eyes that surveyed me like a father would look at his daughter, not a lover.

"Lib, your mum's right, put it back. It's not yours." He pointed at me. "Look at the state of your dress."

My breathing quickened. Slowly, I looked down at myself.

I wasn't a child anymore. I was in my yellow dress from the party, and I now stood taller in the river, the water soaking into my Converse. I gasped at the streak of dark blood on the bottom of my dress.

I felt something move in my hand.

My body started to shudder.

I tore my eyes away from my skirt and forced myself to look at my hand, which had been holding the pebble.

There, sitting on my cupped palm was a bloodied heart. Torn arteries were hanging down from it, dripping with blood which fell into the stream. The heart jerked and pumped slowly as though a creature struggling for breath. I let out a small cry and placed my free hand over my mouth but realised that was covered in blood too and I'd smeared on myself.

Gabriel placed an arm around Gemma and they both looked at me sympathetically. Gemma ran her fingers over her collarbone in the same nervous gesture Mum used to do. "Listen to your father. Put it back now, Lib. It's not yours."

I could even feel the hair on my head shaking as I turned to look at Cassius. I couldn't get my breath and stared to hiccup.

Cassius was back to being eighteen again, stood in the river in his tuxedo, towering over me. His odd eyes were wide and horrified and a trickle of blood ran out of the side of his mouth.

I forced myself to look at the huge gaping hole in his chest, veins and flesh spilled out onto his crisp white shirt, turning it a dark purple.

The heart pounded in my hand.

"Lib!" Gemma shouted. "Get out of there."

Cassius tried to say something, and a bubble of blood escaped from his mouth as he took a staggering step forward. I instinctively drew back and looked down as I felt myself slip on the bed of the stream.

The water was now too dark to see through. And it was thick.

Thick red blood, flowing and lapping around our legs.

"Lib..." Cassius choked. He dropped to his knees and

clutched at his chest, flashing me one last appealing look before falling face down into the river of blood.

The heart in my hand started to slow. It let out several more laboured pumps before stopping and slumping in my hand.

"Oh Lib…" I heard Mum's voice from Gemma.

I turned around and instead of on the bank of the stream, they were stood about a foot from me in the water.

Their eyes were red and their mouths curled into demented and distorted smiles that took up most of their faces.

Gemma cocked her head to one side. "Now look what you've done."

I screamed.

***

I jerked awake, my head hitting the jewellery cabinet. My fringe was stuck to my forehead, damp with sweat. I pulled myself to my feet, still shaking from the nightmare and gripped the cabinet to steady myself. I couldn't help but glance down at my dress and smoothed down the skirt when I saw it was free from the sticky blood in my dream.

Leaning my head down onto the cabinet, I started to cry, letting the tears fall onto the sloping glass, like tiny streams, gathering at the bottom.

"Cassius…" I whispered.

I made for the door, reaching for the handle and missing it completely, groping thin air instead. My breathing quickened in panic and I wrapped both hands around the handle and pushed it, scrambling for the stairs.

I burst into Denzil's flat which was completely dark and I made out the sleeping forms of Denzil and Marie cuddled together on the sofa. I let my eyes adjust to the dark, before springing into action and making for Denzil's bedroom.

Cassius was in bed and facing away as I let myself in, but

quickly sat up and switched on the lamp. "Lib? Are you okay?"

I shook my head, my back pressed against the door.

"What's the matter?" He peered at me. "Where were you?"

"Downstairs. I fell asleep…I had a nightmare."

He yawned, his hair sticking up at all angles. He peeled back the covers on the other side of the bed and gestured for me to get in. "Come here. It's over now. It's not real."

I walked over slowly and crawled onto the bed, ignoring the covers he'd pulled back and kneeled in front of him, sitting back on my feet. "It's not over. And it *is* real."

Cassius cocked his head to one side and reached out to stroke my face. "Come on. You need to get some sleep."

"Have you slept?"

He smiled. "Not a wink."

"I'm…struggling, Cass."

"No, Lib." He mirrored my pose, kneeling in front of me. "You can't. You have to be strong."

I felt tears continue to roll down my face, over his fingers.

"Do you promise?" he asked sternly.

I looked away.

"Lib!" he hissed. "Seriously, you need to promise. Think about Gabriel and Gemma. Let's make sure they didn't die in vain."

"I promise," I croaked eventually.

He clenched his jaw as his eyes flicked over my face. I reached up, gripping the back of his head roughly and pulling him so our foreheads were touching. I ran my fingers through his hair as I cried and heard his breathing quicken. He swallowed and did the same, stroking my bobbed hair.

I raised my eyes to his. "I love you."

He didn't say anything and just looked back.

I choked on a sob and gripped his hair tighter causing him to wince as I pressed into him. "I'm in love with you, Cassius."

He recoiled immediately and took me by the shoulders, holding me at arms' length. "Lib, I think you need to get some sleep. You been…drinking and–"

"No," I took his face in my hands, my vision blurred from tears, "I love you so much. I didn't know I did but I-I feel differently around you now."

This time he pulled my face into his, kissing me.

Really kissing me this time, instead of just letting my lips dance on his like earlier. I closed my eyes and wrapped my arms around his neck as he moved his to my waist, squeezing me tight.

We pulled back and eyed one another in shock.

I could taste him on my lips and shimmied closer, reaching down to the bottom of the white t-shirt he'd changed into.

"Lib…" he whispered in protest, looking away.

I ignored him and lifted the t-shirt over his head and we both looked down at his brilliant-white chest. Me with wonder, him with shame.

I couldn't help but think of Gabriel's body, dark and practically dewy with health. Cassius sat in front of me, afraid to meet my eye and his cheeks pink with embarrassment at his white skin which looked like chalk. I reached out and placed my hand in the same place I had earlier, over his heart, half expecting it to leave a powdery residue on me.

I swallowed with nerves and reached to the back of my dress and found the zip, starting to pull it down. He watched as I slid the one shoulder the dress possessed down my arm with a shaky hand. I wriggled out of it and kicked off my shoes, so I was kneeling in my underwear in front of him. I was sure he must have been able to see me trembling.

He pressed his lips gently onto my stomach. "You're perfect," he whispered, kissing my creamy skin, covered in goosebumps.

"Cass…" I breathed as he moved so I was lying down with him on top of me. I ran my leg up the side of his and he pressed into me, causing me to dig my fingernails into his back as we kissed.

He pulled away and lowered his head next to mine, his lips brushing my ear as he caught his breath. I could feel his heart hammering on me and I was sure he'd be able to feel mine as well.

"We can't do this," he uttered eventually between breaths. "I definitely won't leave tomorrow if we do." He looked at me. "I very much doubt I'd ever leave this room."

I kissed him quickly. "You don't have to."

"Yes," he shifted so he was sitting on the edge of the bed, "I do."

I leaned up on my elbows. "Did I do something wrong?"

"You? No way, of course not." He glanced at my body and groaned, placing his head in his hands. "God, you're amazing. I've been imagining this moment forever. I never in my wildest dreams thought it'd happen. This is either the best decision I've ever made, or the most stupid."

I wrapped my arms around him, nuzzling into his neck. "Can I tell you something?"

He turned his head. "Of course."

I kissed his skin. "I was petrified anyway."

He let out a laugh and turned to face me. "Let's just get in bed and try to sleep. Maybe even kiss again…a little bit."

I pulled him into a tight hug, not wanting to let go.

"I'll miss you, Cass," I whispered.

"You too, Lib."

We got into bed and lay facing one another, looking. I reached up and traced my finger down his straight nose.

"Where's Noah?" I whispered after a moment.

Cassius pulled me into a sideways hug, our foreheads leaning together again. "He's in the bathroom. He passed out and they couldn't move him."

I sniggered and Cassius opened his eyes, watching me.

"I will love you, Lib." He took my fingers in his hand and kissed the tips of them softly. "Doesn't matter where I am. I'll love you."

CHAPTER XII

We performed an awkward waltz the next day. None of us left the shop but we managed to completely avoid speaking until the afternoon. Marie spent most of the day sitting on the bathroom floor with Noah who was sick from a hangover. She visited the kitchen every now and again to fetch a glass of water or dry piece of toast for him, her face grave.

Without a word, Denzil dished out paracetamol to the rest of us and I took one gratefully. I hadn't realised I'd drunk quite so much until I opened my eyes in the morning to Cassius' smiling face and felt the immediate impact of a dull headache and dry mouth. It made me feel even more grateful that he'd quickly put a stop to the antics the night before. I groaned at the memory of myself boldly removing my dress and straddling him on the bed.

I felt so embarrassed, much to Cassius' amusement.

"Beer goggles, eh?" he'd mocked when we were lying in bed that morning. I'd started to protest but he silenced me with a kiss, which I returned, despite the morning breath.

The kisses soon stopped, and now I hugged my knees to my chest on the sofa, brooding over whatever we were heading out to face that night. I looked over at Denzil stood in the kitchen, re-adjusting his dreadlocks for what must have been the fifth time in as many minutes.

The tension in the air was stifling and Cassius was sitting next to me, staring at the TV showing a black and white Christmas film. I could tell he wasn't paying any attention to it, just like I wasn't. He'd perfected pretending to be interested when he was a small child and I made him watch Disney films with me.

He let out a shaky breath and I took his hand, squeezing it.

The bathroom door opened and we turned, expecting to see Marie again but this time Noah emerged, looking bleary-eyed but better than he had that morning.

"Why the hell do people drink?" he asked, his throat gravelly. "It's not worth it."

Marie walked out of the bathroom, looking tired from playing nurse all day. She placed the empty glass and plate she was carrying in the kitchen sink before following everyone else's look to Noah.

He stretched his arms over his head and frowned at me and Cass. "Have you two sorted out what weapons we're taking tonight?"

We stared back in surprise.

"Well," he clapped his hands, "chop chop, we need to get everything sorted. There's not much time."

We nodded and stood abruptly, relieved to be doing something. Noah being unwell made us worry about whether we'd need to postpone. And, even though no one dared to articulate it, I knew we were all thinking the same thing.

Let's just get this over and done with.

It was agony. Goodness knows what it must have been like for Cassius. To his credit, he didn't seem to be afraid. Nervous and apprehensive, but there was no fear in his eyes.

I was feeling strangely fine, still quite sure I'd be able to bring back both of my friends alive. Not sure how, but holding a strange hope in my heart.

Denzil disappeared into his bedroom, returning with the box of weapons. We gathered around the table and peered in.

"I want the axe," I said quickly. "I want that and I want a gun."

"I want a gun, too," Noah jumped in.

"Wait a second," Denzil held up a hand, "let's think this through. I mean, have you even got a plan? What time are you going?"

"Dusk," I said resolutely, folding my arms. "We'll be at the woodland for dusk. We shouldn't encounter any of the other Crits as long as we avoid the cattle fields."

"But you have to cross the sports field," Denzil pointed out. "There's a chance your scent might linger and if the Hunters pick up on it, they'll follow it to the woodland and might find you before the Queens can even be bothered making an appearance for the night. And then there's the Lurkers…"

"What do you suggest?" Noah narrowed his eyes.

Denzil sighed. "Let me at least drive you to the edge of the woodland."

"No, absolutely not. I'm not sure I trust Mr Fuller not to tell anyone what we're doing and Mr Jones probably wants blood…" I flashed Marie an apologetic look. "I think everyone in town's going to be looking for your van to see if it appears at a funny time of night. We can't risk it."

Cassius nodded. "She's got a point."

"Fine," Noah pulled a large gun with a shoulder strap out of the box and slung it across his body, "then we'll go early and just wait in the woodland."

"We need to wait until the Academy closes," I said. "Wait until the snipers have finished for the day."

"Which is dusk!" Denzil said, pulling at his hair. "We're back where we started."

I sighed. "This is dangerous …It's a risk from start to finish. If the Hunters or Lurkers pick up on the scent and follow us into the woodland then…" I reached into the box for the axe and pulled it out, turning it over in my hands, "we kill them. That's what the weapons are for."

"You've got no chance..." Denzil muttered.

"Oh?" I raised an eyebrow. "Ever seen me with an axe?"

Cassius sniggered and Noah smiled proudly.

"Denzil, I get it. You're worried. We're young and you feel like you should be taking our place out there. We won't let you, blah, blah, blah...." I smiled and he looked away angrily. "You need to trust us when we say we know what we're letting ourselves in for. We're prepared for it but...if you carry on telling us we don't stand a chance then I'm afraid it'll be your fault if we lose our bottle in front of the Crits."

He nodded slowly. "Let's get you lot loaded up then."

"Wait," Marie raised her hand, "you kids go and get yourself ready while I fix you some food. Then you can sort the weapons out." She turned away and started inspecting the contents of the cupboards. "You can't leave without having something to eat."

Denzil shrugged hopelessly at us. "You heard the lady. Off you pop."

I looked down at myself, still in my pyjamas. Marie had a point, I didn't want this to be potentially the last outfit I ever wore.

"Mrs J's right." Noah looked like he might be sick again at the sight of the vomit splatters on his t-shirt. "Let's go."

I took a stack of my clothes into the bathroom and turned on the shower. I listened to the water hit the bottom of the bath for a moment while I stood naked, hands clasped together under my chin from the cold. I eventually stepped under the hot water.

I let it run over me and looked down at my body.

You might die today, I thought.

I inspected my skin, now turning pink from the heat and wondered whether the Crits would rip into it. Whether, in a matter of hours, this very body I was looking at would be in several different parts, scattered over the woodland.

Or perhaps I'd be strung up in one of the Queens tunnels for days while they picked me apart piece by piece, like they most likely did with Gemma.

I forced the thoughts out of my mind and reached for the shower gel, squeezing some into the palm of my hand. I had to stop thinking the worst because no matter how bad the end could be for me, it probably wasn't a patch on the fate Cassius would suffer. His value to them, if our suspicions were true, was like nothing they've ever received before. I doubted they'd just kill him.

I shuddered at the thought of them keeping him alive like a pet. Feeding on him now and again.

I closed my eyes.

My mind was reeling, stuck on thoughts of Cassius. If I wasn't thinking about him being killed horribly then I was thinking about the night before.

My heart started to pound again as I remembered us kissing and undressing on the bed. I licked my lips which tasted like bitter shampoo and grimaced, turning around and letting the water run over my face and into my mouth. I leaned my hand on the tiled wall and bowed my head so the water ran down the back of my neck.

I could still feel his hands on my waist, his lips on my stomach, the weight of his body on mine.

I reached for the dial and turned the temperature down as low as it could go, gasping at the blast of icy water on me. I left it for as long as I could stand it before turning it off completely. I stood still, while the water dripped off my skin, now coated in goosebumps.

I stepped out of the shower and wiped the steam from the mirror, inspecting my reflection. My cheeks were flushed and lips parted.

"Lib!" I heard Cassius shout from the other side of the door. "Are you ready?"

I blinked at my reflection and watched my cheeks flush even more red at the sound of his voice.

"Yes," I called back, looking myself in the eye. "I'm ready."

Chapter XIII

"Okay, I'm only going to say this once," Denzil said as he paced up and down in front of us on the shop floor. "What you're about to do is risky, stupid even, but…it's bloody brave."

He avoided our eyes, clearly emotional. Marie stood behind him and rubbed his shoulder. "Listen, I made just about as many speeches I could possibly make last night so I'll keep this brief and say…you all look absolutely terrifying."

I let out a relieved laugh and looked at Noah who winked and stuck his tongue out playfully.

Here we were.

Three teenagers looking like we were ready to go and join the frontline.

In a way, we were.

Although the humans of the town weren't battling the Crits, it was undoubtedly a war and it was a war the Crits had been winning for far too long.

Every human in this town was guilty for letting it happen.

Every human besides the poor defenceless kids who were handed over, practically gift-wrapped to the Queens before they even got the chance to live their lives.

I adjusted the strap from the gun that went over my head and sat between my breasts.

"Take the automatic!" Denzil had whined earlier when I picked up the shotgun.

"No," I'd responded coolly, examining the double-barrel shotgun and holding it up in front of me. "I could take a head clean-off with this thing."

"Yes, but you need to have a good aim!" He'd practically been on his knees, begging for me to reconsider.

"I have fabulous aim," I'd whispered.

I looked down at my hands. I was holding the axe that I'd been so taken with as soon as I saw it. Around my waist was a belt containing a large machete. I licked my dry lips and looked up.

Denzil's eyes were on me.

"Little Liberty Bell, all grown up," he said, folding his arms.

I nodded and returned his smile. I suppose I was.

"She would be grown up if she wasn't wearing that dress," Noah muttered.

I shrugged.

"Don't you want to reconsider?" Cassius joined in, frowning.

I looked down at the yellow prom dress from the night before, teamed with my red converse again and my black leather jacket. "I've never felt prettier than I did last night."

We eyed one another. Me in my mismatched outfit standing at five foot three in front of my pale, white-haired friend who towered over me at more than six feet tall, wearing his trademark skinny black jeans and long coat.

If it wasn't for the weapons, we'd have looked like two relatively normal teenagers.

Cassius had a shotgun in his hands. It was the only weapon he wanted to take. He too believed he had great aim.

He nodded his head towards the door. "We should go. It's getting towards dusk."

"Wait!" Marie piped up loudly as we shuffled to the door.

We turned as she walked towards us, tears brimming in her eyes.

"Noah," she croaked, "I-I have something…"

Noah frowned as she reached into the pocket of her long

brown cardigan, pulling out a small box. She held it in her shaking hand for him to take.

"Open it," she wiped her tears with her sleeve.

Noah obeyed and removed the lid of the box.

"I bought it for her," Marie blurted, more tears flowing down her face as she watched Noah remove a beautiful gold necklace with a heart-shaped locket hanging from it. "I bought it for her to wear when we…Anyway, I didn't get the chance to give it to her."

Denzil rubbed her shoulders, now looking dangerously close to tears himself.

"She'd never have forgiven me," Marie cried, "but I just wanted her to wear this and know…" She stopped to compose herself.

Tears ran down my face but I made no move to wipe them away as they rolled down my chin onto my neck.

"I wanted her to know," Marie repeated, after taking a composing breath, "that I'd…always be with her."

Noah nodded quickly, turning the locket over and over. I could see there was some writing engraved on it. Noah squinted and started to read the inscription out loud. "If there ever comes a day when we can't be together…" he choked on a sob, "…keep me in your heart…I'll stay there forever."

"It's Winnie the Pooh." Marie smiled. "I used to read it to her when she was little."

Denzil lowered his head and rubbed the side of his face on her cardigan, drying a tear.

Cassius moved the gun he was holding onto one hand and used the other to squeeze me tight as I cried, planting a kiss on my forehead.

Marie took several deep breaths to try and recover herself. "There was another line in one of the Winnie the Pooh books that I'll always remember. I have no idea why it stuck in my head but now…standing in front of you three, I understand."

She looked directly at me.

"The line was…" Her eyes were the same I remembered looking into when I was a child. Kind eyes. Sad eyes. "You can't stay in your corner of the Forest waiting for others to come to you. You have to go to them sometimes." She motioned her hands to the door. "So go. You must go now."

Cassius pulled the door open. I felt a cold blast of air hit my face and noticed the sky had turned a beautiful burnt orange.

"Noah." Marie pulled him into a tight hug. "Keep her in your heart; she'll always be with you."

"Let's go," I said, hiccupping. "We need to get out of here."

This was hard for all of us and now we were just torturing ourselves.

"Cass." Marie folded her arms and took a step back, sensing he didn't want to be reminded that this, for him, was most definitely goodbye. "Best of luck."

He nodded seriously. "Thank you."

He walked outside without a glance back.

"Okay," I sniffed, trying to regain my composure as Noah followed Cassius. Denzil and Marie looked at me expectantly, waiting no doubt for me to say something profound. I walked, the axe weighing heavy in my hands. "I'm expecting we'll get to the Queens quickly, then there will be negotiations…." I looked behind me at the other two waiting on the pavement outside, not speaking to one another. "Noah and I will be back no later than nine." I forced a smile. "Have some food ready, we'll be starving."

I didn't give them the chance to respond as I stepped outside and closed the door behind me.

Goodbyes weren't an option.

Not for me.

Not for Noah.

If we said our goodbyes then we were as good as dead already.

I didn't even want to accept that Cassius probably wasn't

going to come back.

"Let's go." I strode ahead of them, down the street. They were quiet and walked behind me. The metal sound of the weapons we were carrying, clinking together was all that could be heard.

Our mood was sombre and it wouldn't do. Battles weren't won this way.

I turned around and they both stopped abruptly in their tracks. Noah had his hands stuffed in the pockets of his pale blue jeans and he looked cold in just a white t-shirt but had refused to wear a coat as he said it would hinder him.

I glared at Cassius who looked even paler and his eyes were wide with fear.

"When I was seven I saw a Crit," I blurted, eyes flicking to each of their faces. "A Hunter on the edge of the woodland at the school field. It was daytime, it shouldn't have been there but I shouldn't either. I wanted to have the best hiding place…"

Cassius narrowed his eyes, clearly remembering our games of hide and seek.

"Anyway," I continued, adjusting the strap of the gun over my body, "the Watchers shooed it away from me and I always wondered why but now I know. I was the property of the Queens. The Hunter should have killed me that day but it couldn't take what didn't belong to it." I stood up straight. "Let's make sure that after today, none of the children of Blackbrooke belong to the Queens."

I wasn't sure why I mentioned my encounter in the woodland all of those years ago, nor the connection I was trying to make, but it seemed to have the desired effect.

Noah inhaled deeply and stepped so he was at my side. "Let's kill them all."

"That's the spirit." My mouth curled into a smile as we continued walking.

Blackbrooke Academy loomed in the distance.

I remembered my first day at school clearly. I'd made this walk with Mum, holding her hand and skipping down the street. She'd taken me for out breakfast as a treat and I was so excited. I had seen Cassius enter the school gates with his mum and we'd waved furiously at one other, standing proudly in our new uniforms. We were four.

I turned my head and looked at the Cassius I knew today.

He returned the look and, like on many occasions previously, everything felt okay.

"Do you need a leg-up?" Noah asked when we reached the school gates. I looked up at them in the same way I did after Gemma's funeral. That already felt like a million years ago.

"Yes please," I replied, not taking my eyes off the gold cast iron B and A lettering on each gate. "No looking up my skirt this time, Cass."

"Bigger fish to fry, Lib," came his amused response.

I looked up at the sunset, and a purple cloud rolled lazily overhead. "Glad to hear it."

Both Noah and Cassius helped me up so I could pull myself over. I was more careful coming down on the other side this time and lowered myself as best I could before artfully landing on my feet.

I brushed at the skirt of my dress as the others climbed over. Noah, with athletic ease, and Cassius using his gangly height to his advantage. His landing was more of a crash and I had to help him up.

"Thanks," he said genuinely.

Noah was already walking in the direction of the playing fields and I ran to catch up with him.

"Where shall we go?" I asked. "We can't wait in the usual place, under the tree. We'll be like sitting ducks."

Noah pulled the two guns on straps further onto his shoulder. They made a hollow metal sound as they knocked together. He had loaded himself up with as much as possible and we'd laughed at the sight of him grabbing a random flare that was at the bottom of the box after we'd removed every thing.

Birds flew overhead, squawking loudly. I watched them disappear in one of the trees at the side of the field. They were getting out of the way for the night.

Even the wildlife of Blackbrooke knew what happened when the sun went down.

Noah pointed to the far side of the sports field where there was a small dirt track for farm vehicles. Over the track was the woodland. There was a huge electric fence we'd have to tackle but if we managed to get over it then we'd be deep in the woodland rather than the edge where the other Crits would likely find us first.

"We really haven't thought about this fence," Cassius mumbled.

Noah grinned. "Not a problem."

I exhaled and hoped I was right to trust him.

We walked fast across the field and my eyes kept darting around at every little sound. The sun was almost down and I remembered it was around this time the Hunters made an appearance.

"Maybe we should run?" I suggested.

Noah looked up at the sky and pulled one of the guns from off his shoulder, ready to fire. "Ever seen one of these in action?"

"No." I raised an eyebrow, tightening my grip on the axe. "Have you?"

Noah's crazed grin wavered. "No…but I bet I'd be able to take out a fair few of those dogs if they appear."

Cassius flashed me a worried look and turned back to Noah. "There's no harm in us maybe just having a jog over to the trees. I feel a bit exposed."

"Come on, then." Noah broke into a run and we followed.

Cassius stayed at my side even though he could have easily ran ahead. He grabbed my free hand and pulled me along with him. I couldn't help but cast glances over my shoulder to see whether there was anything there.

"Stop looking!" Cassius hissed at me. "You're slowing us down."

"Sorry," I shot back.

We reached the trees and stopped for a minute, catching our breath.

"Right." Noah turned to face us. Annoyingly he hadn't even broken a sweat. "When we get to the fence, we need to just fight through the electric shocks and get over the thing."

"What?!" Cassius and I cried.

I walked up to Noah so I was stood practically toe-to-toe with him. "I hope you're kidding. The shock alone will kill us!"

"Sshh," he scolded, raising his finger to his lips.

We stopped for a second to listen for any movement.

A bird flapped in a tree above us and we ducked before slowly recovering and standing straight.

I lowered my voice to a whisper. "Please tell me that isn't your grand plan."

"Lib," Noah uttered, looking annoyed. "The fence isn't going to kill us."

I opened my mouth to protest but he interrupted me.

"It wasn't put there to keep humans out of the woodland." He flashed Cassius a look. "It was there for the cattle so they don't go wandering in there."

"A cattle fence." Cassius frowned questioningly at Noah. "Are you sure?"

"Positive. I've climbed it. Plus," he bent down to tie his shoelace, "before the whole town turned veggie, my dad and brother used to slaughter cattle. My dad used to tell me they'd sometimes find cattle dead in the woods because they'd fallen over tree roots and broke their legs." He shrugged. "It was a waste. They put up the fence. It gives a small shock which isn't nice but it won't kill us."

Bizarrely, I now felt more nervous at the prospect of having to climb over an electric fence than I did facing the Crits.

"Guys," Noah scratched his head, looking pained, "if the Queens decide they're going to speak through me, like Mr Fuller said they did with his friend….I mean, if it looks like it's hurting me can you," he gestured to the gun in Cassius' hand, "do the honours."

I rolled my eyes and stalked past them both, through the trees and down onto the farm dirt track. "Oh yeah, of course, Noah. I'll shoot you in the face as soon as the Queens use you as their glove puppet."

"I just don't want–"

"Noah!" I whirled round. Trees lined the track on either side and the sound of distant bird song rang through the air. The last of the day's sunlight shone through the gaps in the trees, casting distorted shadows over my friends' faces. "Can we please not talk about putting one another out of our misery? Can we stop assuming the worst is going to happen all of the time?"

"Lib–"

"If we think negatively," I walked backwards, "then bad things are going to happen. Am I right, Cass?" I placed my hands on my hips, blinking at him. My smile slowly faded as I saw a look of horror flash over his features as he remained rooted to the spot. My eyes flicked to Noah and I watched him slowly raise his gun up in front of him, aiming it at me.

My body started to shake as I turned my head to see what was behind me. Cassius shook his head in warning and held his hands up as an indication for me to keep still. My breathing became shallow as I felt the warmth of something behind me.

Another living thing.

I saw movement from the corner of my eye and let out a whimper.

Noah was furiously opening the barrel of the gun, looking

like he was struggling to get it to engage. My fingers gripped even tighter around the handle of the axe.

Cassius started to raise his gun up slowly.

Another movement in the corner of my eye.

Don't look, Lib, I warned myself. I could feel my face start to tremble.

The thing moved into my vision, stepping in front of me. Looming so tall and hunched. My mouth dropped open into a silent scream.

The Lurker looked down, cocking its head to one side, seemingly fascinated by the sight of me. Its neck was bent into an s-shape and it stooped so low that its face was on the same level as mine. It opened its grotesquely wide mouth and I saw what looked like hundreds of tiny razor sharp teeth bared at me.

I jumped back as a loud gunshot rang out.

The Lurker stood bolt upright and turned to Cassius and Noah, making a low growling noise.

Cassius fired again and it stumbled.

I couldn't move from the spot I was standing in and just watched in horror.

Noah was still struggling with his gun and he cursed and threw it on the floor in frustration, reaching for the other one immediately and artfully manoeuvring it in his arms, letting off several shots at the Lurker. Each gunshot caused it to stumble but wasn't enough to prevent it from advancing on them as they continued to fire.

The creature was draped in a long brown cloak that looked like skin rather than clothing and its sparse stringy hair was teaming with cockroaches that crawled all over its head.

"Aim for the head!" Noah shouted to Cassius as they shot at it.

Cassius nodded and frowned in determination as he let off another shot.

Noah fired his next shot straight at the Lurker's oversized

head and it fell to the ground in a heap, the sound of bones breaking rang out as it hit the floor and it let out a scream before falling still.

We stared in horror.

Noah and Cassius lowered the guns, breathless from adrenaline. The mist from their laboured breath rising up in front of their faces.

They looked at me.

I nodded. "I'm okay."

Noah gestured to join them and I edged around the dead Lurker as carefully as I could.

"Nice shot, Noah." I forced a smile as I stepped up to them. "Looks like the head shots are where–"

I didn't finish my sentence and all I saw were the shocked faces of Noah and Cassius as I was hauled into the air and sent flying back onto the dirt track. I landed on my back, winded, and the Lurker, which was still very much alive, was upon me, baring its teeth and screaming in rage. It crawled over my body and I used all of my might to try and kick it off me. It hissed and shifted its weight so I used the opportunity to turn and scramble to my feet to get away.

It moved, too, and I felt an excruciating pain in my arm as its clawed fingers dug into my flesh. I let out a scream as I felt the skin and flesh on my arm starting to pull away from the bone as it used me to haul itself back onto its feet. Hot waves of adrenaline kicked in as my skin started to tear on my forearm as it slowly pulled me towards it, a demonic grin on its face.

I eyed its contorted and spindly neck. Without giving it a second thought, I gripped the axe tighter and with a scream of exertion, swung it as hard as I could.

I let out a cry as the Lurker's head disconnected cleanly and dropped onto the floor with a dull thud. The body, still standing, twitched and purple and grey sludge started to ooze from its neck in a steady river. The body toppled in the opposite direction to the head and I heard a ripping sound and searing heat shot up my arm.

I frowned, unable to comprehend the sight in front of me. A large area of skin from the top of my forearm was missing and I looked calmly at the body of the Lurker and saw my skin in its claws, like a creamy torn sheet.

I returned my eyes to the exposed flesh on my arm, feeling myself instantly break into a cold sweat.

Why isn't it hurting, I wondered, starting to see black spots dance in front of my eyes.

"Lib!" Cassius sprung into action, followed by Noah and they immediately ran to my side.

Cassius hastily removed his scarf and shook his head in horror at my arm. "I'm sorry, Lib, but this is going to hurt."

"I can't feel anything," I whispered, staring at the head of the Lurker. I stood, swaying.

Cassius winced, wrapping the scarf around my arm. "I just hope it doesn't fuse to your flesh."

"Shhh…" I said, staggering away from him. I picked up the axe in both hands. My injured arm felt strange, as though the casing for my muscles wasn't there anymore and everything was sloshing around, even with the scarf wrapped tightly around it.

Cassius stepped towards me, but Noah reached out and touched his arm to stop him.

I looked at the head of the Lurker. It was making small, strangling growling sounds and its eyes looked up at me, still alive. It bared its teeth and snapped them at me again, its own decayed blood bubbling out of its mouth.

I didn't say a word as I raised the axe and brought it down hard in the centre of the skull which cracked open into two parts. I shook the axe and one side of the head slid off it. I raised it up again and brought it down on one of the halves, cutting it open horizontally underneath the small hole of its nostril.

It stopped making a sound.

There were blood splatters on my dress and I pursed my lips. My arm had now lost all feeling and I turned to look at the others.

"What now?" I pulled my injured arm close into my body as though wearing a sling,

Noah's mouth curled into a grin. "That was the most amazing thing I've ever seen."

Cassius moved to my side as my knees buckled and I sat down on the dirt track, exhausted. Noah knelt next to me and placed a hand on my shoulder.

"We need to get over the fence. We'll help you as much as we can, Lib, but you need to be strong."

I could see the gold chain of Gemma's necklace poking out of the collar of his t-shirt.

I exhaled and started to pick myself up. "I'm okay. If I can handle one Crit, I can handle them all."

Cassius smiled. "That's my girl."

"Right," Noah placed the strap of the gun over his shoulder and gestured to the trees behind me, "let's get to the fence and…."

He trailed off and we all frowned at the strange noise we could hear in the distance. It was a rumbling, like an earthquake.

Strange as the noise was, it wasn't wholly unfamiliar.

Noah and I exchanged glances.

Hunters.

It was the same sound we heard that night when I found Noah on the playing field. Hundreds of paws hammering on the ground.

We moved up the small embankment at the side of the dirt track and looked across the school field where we'd just come from. I saw them straight away on the other side. A mash of brown and grey. Little dots in the distance, getting bigger by the second.

"They're heading this way," Cassius flashed us a worried look. "Why are they coming to the woodland? The cattle fields are the other way."

"They heard the guns," Noah said calmly, not taking his eyes off them. "They know we're here. Come on, the fence."

We ran across the dirt track and into the trees on the other side. I clutched my arm to my stomach and winced as the pain started to kick in. The fence was made up of concrete blocks, topped with thick wire which held the electric current. I could hear it fizzing.

"Cass, you get over first," Noah ordered. "I'll help Lib over and then I'll–"

"They'll follow us in here," Cassius interrupted, looking defeated. "If the electric fence can't stop us then it certainly won't stop them. There's no rules against them coming into the woodland, they'll have us in a matter of seconds."

"No…" I said without conviction. "They won't be able to find us in there, we'll hide."

"They'll smell us," Cassius whispered.

It was now almost completely dark and the sky had turned a light purple.

Cassius looked calm. "It's over guys. We tried."

Noah frowned at him, his jaw clenched.

The sound of the paws thundering on the ground grew louder as they approached. I estimated we had less than a minute before they were upon us.

"We need to try," I appealed, looking from one to the other desperately. "We need to just get over there and try. We can't just stand here and wait to be…We can't and I-I won't."

Noah pulled Gemma's necklace out of his t-shirt and clutched the locket. "Cass is right, they'll smell us."

He raised his hand before I could argue.

"You two…" his voice broke and he coughed, trying again. He stood straight and forced a smile. "You two get your weedy arses over that fence and I'll go round a different way…throw them off the scent."

I stepped towards him. "Which way? What other way could you possibly go?"

He didn't say anything.

I shook my head in confusion and looked at Cassius who was staring back at Noah, shocked.

It took a moment for it to click into place what he was trying to say.

"No!" I said quickly, making a grab for his hand. "No, Noah you can't."

"Lib," he said softly, taking my hand, "there's no other way. You two get over there and find the Queens, sort all this shit." He gestured over his shoulder. "I'll sort this lot out."

My eyes filled with tears. "You don't stand a chance."

He looked away.

A sob escaped from my mouth and I started to feel desperate. "Please Noah, don't do this. I need you."

He wrapped his free arm around me, the other still clutching his gun. "Please let me do this," he whispered to me. "I need to be with her."

Suddenly I felt hot anger and I pushed him roughly, catching him off guard. He stumbled back but I was upon him again, shoving him. "Why do you have to do this, Noah? Why do you have to be so stupid all the time?" I demanded, tears running down my face. "You're stupid. You've always been stupid!"

"I know," he said softly.

"No!" I wiped my nose roughly and rocked back and forth on my feet as though ready to pounce. "You're stupid. With your stupid smart-arse remarks at school. Your stupid sports. Your stupid love letters to my friend." I sensed Cassius was behind me now. "Your stupid decision to sleep with her."

He was crying now, not taking his eyes off me, just nodding in agreement at everything I said.

"And now this! You're stupid!" I clenched my hands into

fists and hit him hard on the chest, ignoring the pain shooting up my injured arm. "You're so stupid. You can't do this. Please don't do this. Please don't leave me."

He placed his hands around me lightly as I sobbed into his chest.

I pressed into him and felt the locket between us.

It was like when the three of us clung onto one another at Gabriel's funeral.

"Okay…I won't."

I pulled back and looked at him. He smiled warmly and brushed some hair back from my face. "I won't leave you, Lib."

I was about to place my head back on his chest when I caught him flash a look at Cassius. Before I could react, Cassius wrenched me out of Noah's arms, placing one hand over my mouth and the other around my middle. He lifted me away as I kicked and thrashed.

"NO!" I tried to scream. "Let me go!"

I watched with horrified eyes as we ran in the opposite direction to Noah, who was stood in the same spot. He opened the gun and checked the bullets and closed it again. He pulled the flare out of his pocket.

"Get over the fence!" he called to us. "Be quick, I don't know how long I'll be able throw them off."

I watched Noah reach for the locket and raise it to his lips, kissing it softly. Then he was gone, bolting into the trees towards the school field.

"Noah!" I gagged. I pulled my leg back into Cassius' groin and he immediately let me go, letting out a howl of pain. I didn't look back and headed in the direction of Noah, calling his name as I hit branches out of my way.

"Lib!" Cassius called after me in panic. "No, Lib! Come back!"

I was convulsing from sobs now and looked around frantically. I ran back to where we'd come from. Crying, I clambered up the embankment to where there was a clearing in the trees so I could see onto the field.

"Noah!" I screamed.

He turned, his eyes wide with horror. He'd managed to run to the centre of the field and was surrounded by Hunters. Several of them looked in my direction, just as frightening as I remembered with their big hulking bodies and blood soaked fur.

Cassius appeared at my side but I moved away, not trusting him. "We need get out of here now, Lib."

I watched Noah raise his gun and turn in a circle. Some of the Hunters shrank back when the gun passed in front of them. It was clear he was outnumbered though.

One dived and knocked the gun out of his hands and he automatically reached for another but there wasn't one there. He looked over at us and shook his head. "Get her out of here! Don't let her see this!"

I screamed again as Cassius lunged for me and I punched him in the face, buying myself some time. "Noah, run!"

I knew it was hopeless as I watched the pack of Hunters close in, prowling around him. Some, attracted by my screams were making their way over but I didn't care.

Noah on the other hand did. "Hey!" He pulled at the bottom of the flare and it ignited in his hand. He waved it furiously, bright flashes of pink light illuminating the field around him, making the eyes of the Hunters to shine like rubies. "Come back here if you're man enough!"

The Hunters who were heading for us now turned back and Noah let out a manic laugh. "Yeah, that's it. Come on, you worthless dogs, lets be having ya!"

I reached out my hand, tears blurring my vision.

Cassius too was rooted to the spot.

Noah stopped waving the flare and just stood still with it raised in the air.

I couldn't help but remember him stood in Gemma's

garden shouting his love for her.

The image of her pressing the pillow into her face from excitement.

He smiled and reached for the locket again with his free hand. He closed his eyes and whispered something.

Something we'd never hear.

I clamped my hand over my mouth as the Hunters circled in so close I could barely see him anymore. Occasionally, between their bodies as they walked, I saw him still looking down at the locket.

"We need to go, Lib. Right now," Cassius said softly.

I nodded and furiously wiped my eyes and he didn't hesitate in grabbing my hand to get me away from the horrendous scene about to unfold.

Noah's screams echoed around the woodland and I clamped my hands over my ears as we fled to the fence.

I stepped onto Cassius' interlocked fingers. I stopped at the top of the fence and let out a small yell at the shock.

"Come on, Lib," he urged. "Just throw yourself over it."

I ignored the jolts of electric current through my body and swung my legs over before dropping down onto the other side.

Cassius appeared at the top of the fence, wincing from the shocks and lowering himself next to me.

"This way," I whispered pointing into the woodland. I got two steps before I fell forward onto my knees and started to vomit. Cassius knelt next to me, rubbing my back.

"We have to get this right," I whispered. "What just happened…it can't be for nothing."

I saw Cassius nod from the corner of my eye and I pulled myself back to my feet. We walked quickly through the trees, not saying another word.

"Do you know where they are?" Cassius broke the silence and jogged to keep up with me as I stepped over tree roots quickly, trying not to fall over.

"No," I said honestly, "but I think the further we head in

here, the more chance we have."

We walked a little further into the dark woodland and I stopped abruptly. "Noah died."

"I'm sorry," was all Cassius could say.

My face crumpled into a cry. "They'll say it's a walk out."

"Hey," he took my face in his hands and forced me to look at him, "we know better than that. Noah's a hero."

I nodded, gasping for air between cries.

Tentatively he leaned down and kissed me softly. I tasted my own salty tears as I returned the kiss. Sick with grief but grateful for his contact. Cassius moved the gun so it was around his back, and I dropped the axe onto the floor so I could place my arms around his neck.

The sound of a howl in the distance caused us to pull back.

"Better keeping moving." he said breathlessly.

I retrieved the axe. "Let's go."

Further into the woodland, the trees became denser, leaving less room for us to walk, the air thinner. I pulled my leather jacket around me with my free hand and cursed for deciding to wear the dress. Not only was it too cold to be walking around at night in a short dress but the woodland was full of weeds and I found myself wincing at the occasional thorn scratching my leg or the irritating sting of a nettle leaf.

"I don't feel like we're getting anywhere," Cassius whispered from behind me.

I didn't answer him and ducked under some hanging branches.

The mist coming from my breath was now even thicker and I was quite sure my lips must have been blue over my chattering teeth.

My thoughts were dreamlike which made me think the pain from my arm was making me delirious. I kept getting visions of Gemma and Noah. At the wedding they'd never have.

Him feeding her wedding cake as she laughed heartily.

Their first dance.

Guests showering them with confetti.

I shook my head to rid the thoughts and started to walk faster.

Cassius caught up to me and touched the elbow of my hurt arm causing me to wince. "Shall we stop and try to figure out where we are?"

My eyes had now adjusted to the dark so I could make out his frightened features. "No, we can't afford to stop. We'll know when we get there."

"Get where though?"

I turned back around, clawing more branches out of my way. "Let's just go."

A large cracking of broken twigs sounded behind me.

I sighed impatiently. "Bloody hell, Cass, alert the whole wood we're here, why don't you?"

"That wasn't me," he whispered.

I stopped and turned slowly. He stood still, his breathing heavy. He didn't look at the twenty or so Watchers stood several steps behind him just staring at us. Their red eyes glowed bright in the dark and I could see their skinny tails swishing from side to side in apprehension.

I stood at the side of Cassius, nudging him to turn around.

Slowly and carefully, I knelt down so I was at eye level with the creatures who just stared at me.

"We're here for the Queens," I said shakily, looking around at their blank faces. One of the Watchers smacked its mouth and one made a low grumbling sound. I lowered my voice even quieter. "Take us to them."

I stood up in an attempt to look authoritative.

"Take us to them," I repeated, with more conviction this time.

One of the Watchers turned its head and started to lick and gnaw at an area on its back.

I reached out and took Cassius' hand.

“I…” I took a deep breath. “I have something for them.”

Now I had their attention.

One let out a strangled cry, tilting its head back at a freakish angle, before turning and trotting off into the trees. The others slowly got up and padded after it. I could hear their ancient bones cracking and groaning as they moved.

“Come on.” I pulled Cassius gently.

We followed the Watchers, staying about ten feet behind them. Just following the noise of their movements and low growls and cries. Occasionally, one would stop and turn to check we were still there, fixing its beady red eyes on us warily.

“Are you okay?” Cassius whispered to me eventually.

“Are you?”

“You didn’t answer me.” I heard the amusement in his voice.

“Neither did you.”

The trees were soon so dense that we had to walk single-file to get through them and I begrudgingly let go of Cassius’ hand, taking care walking over the large tree roots, not wanting to fall and injure my arm even more. It had now started to burn as though it was on fire and I clenched my teeth, trying not to think about it.

“I think this could be it,” Cassius said from behind me.

I looked up and saw a large clearing ahead. The trees had been chopped down, leaving small, flat stumps sticking out the ground that looked like stools in a picnic area. It seemed freakishly light and I stared at the bright moon shining down, directly above us.

The Watchers walked into the centre of the clearing and stopped, sitting down on their bony bottoms.

Cassius and I stood side by side, not knowing what to expect. He clasped my hand and raised it to his lips, planting a soft kiss on my knuckles. A strange rumbling started from under our feet.

“There,” Cassius pointed to a large mound of earth on the

other side of the clearing, "that's where they come out."

My bottom lip started to tremble.

"It'll be fine." He nudged me. "I promise you, Lib."

I felt my whole body start to shake again.

Come on, Lib. You killed a Crit tonight. You're supposed to be the brave one. The protector.

I thought of Denzil and Marie waiting pensively back at the shop, hoping we'd come back. I felt like I'd already let them down by losing Noah. I pulled myself to my full height. I didn't want to let them down again.

We both watched as the mound of dirt started to move, its sides collapsing and small stones that made it up, rolled down the side. One of the stones hit my shoe and I instinctively kicked it away.

A Queen crawled out from the ground and slithered its way out of the dirt. It rose to its feet, which were disguised by the cloak of skin, and shook off the stones an soil which showered the floor around it.

Although we'd encountered the Queens only a few nights ago, their appearance was no less terrifying. Its neck looked weak, like all Crits. Its head bobbed from side to side, clumsily and its long, feather-shaped dead eyes stared at us.

I didn't dare to breathe as another Queen dragged itself from the ground. This one more human-like in its mannerisms as it brushed the dirt from its robe with its long bony fingers.

It was followed by another.

Then several more.

We watched as more and more Queens crawled from the earth and congregated around the two scared teenagers before them, standing tall and cocking their heads in interest.

The Watchers were nonchalant and some even appeared to have gone to sleep underneath their masters. A slight breeze whistled through the trees and I watched in horror as it whipped stringy grey hair over the faces of the Queens.

When no more appeared I turned to Cassius who nodded at me. I took at step forward, feeling like my knees were going to buckle again.

They can't kill you. They can't kill you unless you're given. You're safe.

I licked my lips before forcing my eyes up to look around their faces.

"I need to talk to you," I said at last. "I need to be able to speak to you."

The Queens exchanged glances and looked over to Cassius.

I shook my head. "You can't speak through him." My breath caught in my throat. "You can't use him because it's him I need to speak to you about."

One of the Queens, who I noticed was slightly larger than the others and wore the hood of its cloak of over its head, slithered forward. It looked me up and down, inspecting me as though I was some kind of specimen. It then looked beyond me at Cassius and I saw its eyes narrow. It reached its arm up in his direction. The others followed its look as though seeing Cassius for the first time.

"I need to be able to speak to you about him," I repeated.

The main Queen lowered its head as though nodding. One of the Watchers yawned loudly and the Queen's eyes snapped to it. Without hesitation, it grabbed the Watcher around the neck and it let out a strangled cry, feebly trying to claw and escape.

It squeezed the Watcher, causing its eyes to bulge grotesquely. I covered my mouth with my hand in disgust, fully expecting its eyeballs to pop right out and roll and hit my shoe like the stone earlier.

The sound of the Watcher's neck breaking, like a too-dry twig snapping under foot, echoed around the clearing. I squeezed my eyes shut, before slowly opening them and seeing the Queen holding the creature at arms-length towards us. It adjusted its grip around its neck and the flesh ripped as it pierced its skin with a long, sharp thumbnail.

A waterfall of grey and red coloured blood splattered on the floor below its limp hanging body.

The other Watchers stared, their tails twitching from excitement.

The eyes of the Queen's victim were wide and full of terror, frozen in death. Its jaw dropped open and its throat made a strange rumbling noise.

I instinctively stepped back and felt Cassius' hands touch my shoulders.

Its mouth moved, lifeless like a puppet, letting out a strange series of noises sounding like words.

The Queen, its hollow eye sockets still on me and Cassius, squeezed the Watcher's throat tighter.

"Whhaaaaaaaaa…."

I winced at the noise.

"Whaaaaaaat…."

The Queen shook the Watcher, the other Queens loitering behind it, glaring at us.

"Whaaaat do you want?"

I gasped at the bizarre voice from the Watcher's mouth.

"What do you want?" The Queen looked at me and cocked its head to one side. "Liberty Connor."

I tried not to react at the mention of my name. I took a step forward, trying to appear bold. Not wanting them to see how utterly terrified I was. "I'm here to do a deal."

The Queen's eyes narrowed again. "We don't do deals with humans."

"Yes, you do. I'm here to…" I looked down and could feel Cassius' eyes burning into my back, willing me to continue. "I'm here with Cassius Godwin. He's an albino…" I trailed off, closing my eyes. "The only one in Blackbrooke. Possibly the only one in Blackbrooke history."

The Queen moved closer, past me, and circled Cassius who remained rooted to the spot. Still holding the Watcher out in front of it while the other Queens looked on longingly at the white-haired pale-skinned boy in front of them. "Cassssssssssius," the Watcher hissed. "We know you…"

I nodded quickly. "I'm here to do you a deal."

"Oh?" The Queen moved to me, its movements fluid, and stopped so the Watcher was inches from my face. I could smell rotting flesh on its breath and turned my head away. "What deal is this, Liberty Connor?"

This is it, I thought. Get it right, Lib.

I took a breath. "I'm here to ask for first-borns to be spared…forever."

The Queen recoiled in shock. "Never."

"In exchange for Cassius," I said quickly.

The Queen stared at me. The others moved so they were either side of it. Like the frontline of an army, facing us.

"For the boy…" the Watcher whined, "we'll spare your life."

I shook my head. "Not just mine. No way."

The Queens exchanged glances and bobbed their heads together as though conferring with one another, despite making no sound at all.

I looked at Cassius.

"Do it," he mouthed, his eyes wide.

"Not just for me," I mouthed back.

It might have been enough for *him* to save my life, but it would have been a disaster for me.

"How many years?" the Watcher asked eventually.

I clenched my jaw. I hadn't been expecting to have to put a number on it.

"A million," I whispered, not removing my eyes from him. The corner of his mouth twitched into a sad smile. "Even that's not enough. To me," I returned my look to the disgusting creatures, "he's priceless."

"How many years?" Clearly, the Queen was undeterred by my sentiment.

I inhaled deeply. "Five hundred."

"Nonsense." I could have sworn a heard a strange laughter from the Watcher. "Fifty years."

I shook my head. "No. I know you offered fifty for Lucas Fuller and Cassius is worth more."

They looked, surprise registering on their faces.

"Liberty Connor," the Watcher hissed, "you *did* do your homework…"

The Queen turned to the one stood directly by its side and seemed to bow its head in understanding before turning back to me. "One hundred years."

"That's it, Lib," Cassius whispered from behind. "That's the deal."

My mouth moved, trying to form words. To argue. To continue the negotiations. To stall for more time but I knew it was futile.

We'd just bought the town of Blackbrooke and all first-borns one hundred years of freedom.

In exchange for one amazing human being.

I closed my eyes. "It's a deal."

The Queens didn't move.

"You need to give him to us," the Watcher said, lustfully. "You need to say he belongs to us and the deal will be done."

"How do I know you'll keep your side of the bargain?" I asked tightly. "What if I hand him over and first-borns continue to die?"

The Queen cocked its head to one side. "You must trust our word, Liberty."

A tear rolled down my cheek but I made no move to wipe it away. "I don't," I whispered.

"Lib…" Cassius warned from behind me but I didn't turn around.

"I need to know I can trust you." I swallowed.

The Queen nodded slowly.

"Liberty," it started, the eyes of the Watcher still

dangerously close to bursting from its face. "We will keep our word. And after the deal has been made, you may leave this town forever."

I blinked in surprise.

"Leave and never return."

I shook my head, feeling another tear run down my face. "They won't let me out…at the border."

The Queen nodded. "Yes…they will…"

My breath came rushing out of my mouth in a whoosh and I momentarily felt winded. I would be free after all. I could leave this town.

See the world.

Just like Gabriel wanted.

Cassius appeared at my side, taking my hand again. "You know what you need to do."

I let out a sob and returned my look to the Queens. "Please…can I say goodbye to him before I…"

The Queen didn't say anything and moved backwards, away from us.

I turned to Cassius and he took my face in his hands, leaning his forehead against mine. I could feel his hands were trembling.

"I want to ask what's going to happen to you," I whispered, looking into his eyes.

He shook his head. "Sshhh, no…you don't."

"I can't believe I'm letting you go again," I cried, squeezing my eyes shut. "There's only so much pain we can take. Being free doesn't matter…"

"It does," Cassius said quickly. "Lib, look at what you've done. You've set this town free. *You.*"

I felt hot tears run over my lips. "No, you've saved this town. If it wasn't for you, we'd never be able to do this. You're so brave. You're the bravest person I've ever met."

"Right back at ya, Connor." He winked. "You go out there and live the life you always wanted to live. Be seventeen. Be eighteen," he laughed, his eyes wet with tears, "be every age. Live for all of us. Live for all of them and whatever you do," he took the hand of my good arm, "don't forget that I, Cassius Godwin, loved every inch of you."

I choked on a sob.

"You're the best friend anyone could ever ask for." I leaned my head on his chest as he spoke into my hair. "Now," he placed both hands on my shoulders, holding me at arms length, "let's get this over and done with."

"Are you scared?" I asked before I could stop myself.

He moved his head and kissed my hand on his cheek. He looked serene. "No."

I squeezed him tightly for the very last time. "Okay," I sobbed, nodding my head and pushing him away gently. I turned to the Queens. "I'm ready now." No sooner had I spoken the words, I sank to my knees, paralysed with grief. The Queens glowered down at me and I wondered whether they were used to these kind of displays from the parents who'd visited them over the years. "Please don't hurt him… please…" I wailed placing the palm of my good arm on the floor in front of me and grasping at the soil. "Please don't hurt him…"

"Liberty," the Watcher rasped, "do we have a deal or not?"

There was an edge to the voice and I remembered what Mr Fuller had told us about the rage and revenge enabling them to exact any kind of punishment they wanted.

I nodded, still looking at the floor and watching fat tears plop onto the ground before me. "Yes…we have a deal."

"Say the words, Liberty." The Watcher sounded feverish with excitement. "Tell us he's ours. Tell us you're giving him to us."

Cassius had now placed the gun down onto the floor and removed his coat so he was stood casually in his jeans and long-sleeved t-shirt, hands in his pockets. He smiled at me.

He looked like he had hundreds of times before. A

beautiful mosaic of memories swept through my head.

Him as a boy, holding up his hand to show me the butterfly that had landed.

The sad glance at me over his shoulder at his mother's funeral.

His laughter in the kitchen with Oscar when I ruined Sunday dinner.

His hand clasped around mine when he saved me from my own walk out.

Dancing in Denzil's shop.

Kissing.

"I love you," I mouthed to him. I turned back to the Queens and rose to my feet.

I closed my eyes.

Exhaled.

Opened them.

"I, Liberty Connor," I began, my voice authoritative, "bring Cassius Godwin for you to take…forever. In exchange, you're granting Blackbrooke one hundred years of freedom for first-borns." I swallowed before continuing, "You may take him right away. And I'll leave Blackbrooke and never return."

The Queens bowed formally in front of me and I watched in surprise.

"We accept your proposal, Liberty Connor."

My breathing quickened as the Queens moved past me and advanced on Cassius who stood and waited. I didn't turn around to watch what they might do to him.

"Can I leave now?" I choked.

"Yes." The sound of the Watcher from behind me.

I heard a struggle and what sounded like cloth tearing.

I let out a whimper.

"You may leave, Liberty. You will be safe up to the border."

I nodded, more tears now flowing down my face and falling onto my chest. I picked up the axe and walked directly ahead of me.

Another sound. This time, a cry.

A human cry.

I couldn't stop myself from turning around. I couldn't see Cassius, just the backs of the Queens huddled around him.

One of the Queens whirled around and glared at me.

"LEAVE!"

Chapter XIV

I turned, slipping on some damp tree roots as I scrambled away before I angered the Queens any more.

I clawed my way through the trees, crying hard. My chest hurt and I was sure it was the feeling of my heart breaking in two. A clean break, right down the centre.

I stopped in my tracks.

There was no way I could live without Cassius.

I couldn't. I had to go back.

You're too late, Lib, I thought and leaned my head against one of the trees in front of me.

I now just needed to get out of the woodland quickly.

I half-ran and half stumbled, not having a clue what direction I was going. The trees soon became more spaced out and I recognised the electric fence looming ahead of me. I walked along it for a while until I found a tree that I could climb and use to hoist myself over. I didn't even wince at the shock this time and landed roughly on the other side. I stood and made my way over to the dirt track and up onto the sports field.

I gasped and stopped in my tracks as soon as I set foot on the field.

Hundreds of pairs of red eyes glared at me in the darkness.

Hunters.

It looked like every single Hunter in Blackbrooke was stood no more than thirty feet away from me.

No doubt waiting for the perfect moment to pounce and

devour me until nothing was left. Like they had with Noah earlier.

"Come on then," I called to them in defeat. Their ears pricked up at the sound of my voice and I plonked myself down so I was sitting on my backside on the grass. "This will be the perfect end to a perfect evening. Do it. One of you has been waiting ten years for this moment."

They didn't move a muscle.

"What the hell…" I narrowed my eyes.

One of the Hunters eventually rose from its lying position, and walked over slowly. Its shoulder blades stuck up high from its back and seemed to grind together as it skulked towards me. I braced myself as it stood two feet away. Its huge hulking body looked wet with blood, like the Watcher's, and its teeth were bared.

I nodded as an indication for it to hurry up. Feverishly wondering whether it was the same Hunter who happened upon me when I was a little, finally able to kill me as it pleased.

It leaned its face close to mine and I squeezed my eyes shut, waiting for the first bite. That one had to be the worst. I very much doubt I'd feel any others.

Its nose was wet as it touched my neck and I winced.

It nudged me.

My eyes flicked open.

It nudged me again and made a low grumbling sound. It looked me in the eye and then turned its head to the other side of the playing field. The other Hunters were now behind it. All staring at me.

Slowly and tentatively, I stood and looked around at their faces.

The leader of the pack nudged the back of my knee causing me to stumble forward. It walked ahead, looking at me expectantly.

"You will be safe to the border."

The words of the Queens popped into my head as I looked on in disbelief. They were going to walk with me to the border.

I slowly started to follow the pack of Hunters.

I eyed them as they surrounded me.

Some in front. Some either side. Some behind. All with their heads bowed and walking in step with me. I raised my head as the Creatures and I walked together.

I didn't know whether it was some kind of spell from the Queens or whether the Crits could communicate and this was some kind of strange agreement.

I didn't care.

I was leaving.

They were taking me to the border and I wouldn't be coming back.

"Please forgive me, Denzil," I whispered to myself. "Dad… Oscar…Mum…"

They'd probably never know what happened to me. My parents would think it was a mass walk out with Noah and Cassius. No one would know how brave those boys had been, what they'd sacrificed for this town.

I was still alive and for that I was lucky but I'd sacrificed, too. I'd now lost everything.

I continued my march through Blackbrooke, not shedding any more tears.

The gun I was wearing clanged on my back and I flexed my fingers around the handle of the axe, staring straight ahead of me, down the main road out of Blackbrooke.

Lights loomed ahead.

Lights of Border Control.

Not lights for us. Lights for Outsiders that drove up to the Border who would be quickly turned away from the town.

I licked my lips wondering how Border Control were going to react when they saw me with the Hunters.

Would they shoot me?

As we got closer I saw the gates were wide open and the kiosks, usually manned twenty-four hours a day were empty. Empty in an eerie way, as though they'd just been abandoned. I could hear the sound of a television coming from one of them and a crackle of a radio.

"Come in, Blackbrooke Control....Can you hear me, Blackbrooke Control..."

I stopped before I could step through the gates.

This was it.

I looked down at the Hunters either side of me.

One nudged me forward.

"Don't worry," I whispered. "I'm leaving."

I took several steps forward and the Hunters remained rooted to the spot, watching with interest.

The gates lurch into action and started to close behind me, locking the Crits back in.

And me out.

As they clanged closed and a bolt locked into place, the Hunters immediately started to growl and one threw itself against the gate, trying to get to me. Another did the same and they barked frenzied, their teeth bared, looking like they desperately wanted to rip me apart.

Definitely a spell from the Queens.

Some kind of hypnosis until I was safely over the border.

I slowly turned my head to look down the road leading away from Blackbrooke. Lights shone brightly all along it. The smooth tarmac looked wet and the light bouncing off it was eerie yet quite beautiful at the same time. It was so quiet.

Peaceful.

I walked several steps forward.

"Excuse me, miss."

I turned to see a man step into the middle of the road, gun in hand, looking confused. "I erm...I think I must have fallen asleep or something...I don't know what happened," he said, more to himself than to me. "Listen, you can't be here. Where have you come from?" He frowned back at the gates where the Hunters were still barking and howling. "It can't have been from there," he jerked his gun in the direction of Blackbrooke and narrowed his eyes. "Did you walk all the way up here?"

I glanced down the road again before returning my eyes to him.

He stepped closer. "Is that an axe? What were you going to do, hack your way into Blackbrooke?" he chuckled. "Do you know how many I get up here just like you every night? Too many. Now, I suggest you get yourself out of here before I call the police. Do you have somewhere to go?"

I looked back at the fence.

Only this time I didn't see the Hunters.

I saw the faces of my friends staring at me.

Gabriel.

Gemma.

Noah.

Cassius.

Their fingers wrapped around the wire.

I blinked and they were gone.

"Miss?" The man was almost upon me now, looking concerned. "Do you have somewhere to go?"

"Yes," I said eventually.

"Is there anyone I can call?" he asked, still frowning.

"No, it's fine. I'll just…" I felt my mouth curl into a smile. "Walk. I'll just walk."

He stepped away from me, watching as I turned and started down the road.

"Christ, is that a real gun?" he called.

"No," I shouted back, "it's a replica."

"Thank God for that," he yelled as I got further away.

I let out a laugh as I walked down the street to my freedom. I outstretched my arms and threw my head back.

"I'll live for all of you," I whispered to the heavens. "I swear."

I passed an old and faded sign and saluted.

Thank you for visiting Blackbrooke! The residents of Blackbrooke and the Creatures wish you a safe journey, wherever you come from and wherever you're going…

Chapter XV

The road leading out of Blackbrooke was long. I felt like I was walking for miles but I didn't care.

I didn't have anything.

Knew no one on the Outside.

Had no idea what was going to happen next.

I didn't even know what time it was.

The moon, still bright, had now moved to the other side of the sky. Trees lined the road but I wasn't scared. I wasn't scared of anything anymore. I'd seen it all. I was leaving the Crits behind, caged in Blackbrooke.

I wondered to myself how the town would learn of the new first-born rule being abolished. Would it be when the next distraught set of parents took their child? Would the Queens send a message?

I knew I'd never find out. It wasn't my problem any more. I'd done everything I could. We all had.

Bright lights flashed up ahead of me and I saw a truck coming down the road. I shielded my eyes as it approached and moved to the edge of the road so it could pass. It must have been a delivery truck for one of the shops or restaurants in the town. Denzil said the goods started arriving through the night and stored at the border until the morning.

I frowned as the truck started to slow when it got near, its engine chugging loudly as it came to a holt.

I stopped too, still shielding my eyes.

The driver and passenger door opened at the same time and two dark figures stepped out.

"Miss Liberty Connor?" An official voice sounded.

The shadowy pair stopped about ten feet away from me. I couldn't see their faces because of the bright headlights behind them.

"Yes?" I called, my heart starting to pound. I immediately regretted saying yes, wishing I'd have said another name. Anything.

"Miss Connor, you're going to have to come with us."

"Who are you?" I walked backwards.

"We can't discuss that here, miss."

I swallowed, starting to feel dread in the pit of my stomach. "I'm not going back there," I blurted, my voice wobbling. "You can't make me. I'm free now."

"Miss, please try to calm down. You're going to need to step into the vehicle."

I didn't hesitate for another moment and turned to run.

"Hey! Stop!" I heard them start after me.

I choked on a cry as I headed into the trees hoping to lose them. All feelings of elation and relief, gone in an instant.

"Leave me alone!" I screamed back at them. "Leave me!"

"Stop!"

I heard a gunshot and screamed, dropping to my knees as a jolt of pain spread across my back.

They've shot me, I thought, falling onto my injured arm before I could stop myself. My breathing quickened as my face pressed into the grass.

They shot me in the back.

I'm going to die. I'd survived the Crits and now I'd been shot in the back by a human.

My eyelids started to grow heavy as I heard footsteps approach.

"Are you sure you shot her?" I heard one say to the other.

"Yeah definitely. Look at the state of her."

"We need to get her back..."

I felt hands under my body haul me up and I now couldn't

open my eyes at all. My head rolled forward as they tried to pick me up.

"I think she's gone…" One of them said.

"As good as."

My eyeballs rolled to the back of my head as I finally lost consciousness.

***

"Her arm is a mess…"

"What got her?"

"Lurker, judging by the torn skin."

"Will the arm be okay?"

"I think so. She might need a skin graft though."

I could hear the conversation going on around me.

Am I dead? Surely death was pleasant. This wasn't. My arm was hurting, my back ached and my head felt like a lead weight on the pillow I was resting on.

No, this wasn't death.

Unless it was hell.

I groaned and tried to open my eyes.

"Here she is…" A familiar voice, although I couldn't place it. "Liberty. It's okay, you're safe now."

"Someone shot me," I croaked. My throat was so dry.

I felt a hand smooth down my hair. "Shhhh, try not to speak."

"My back…" I moaned. "Can I walk?"

"What?" The voice sounded amused. "Of course, you can, Liberty. You were shot with a tranquiliser dart. It was supposed to hit you in the backside."

They had my full attention now. I forced my eyes open and immediately closed them again, blinded by the bright white light.

"I don't like the look of that arm…" the other voice sounded.

"Who's there?" I cried out.

"Liberty," the protective hand on me again, "you need to relax and wake up when you feel ready. Rest assured, you're safe here."

Why was that voice familiar? My brain couldn't function properly. I probably wouldn't have even been able to recall my own name if I hadn't heard the man saying it over and over again.

His accent wasn't English.

Who did I know who wasn't English from Blackbrooke?

I felt my brain drifting away again, slipping out of consciousness.

Wait.

My eyes flicked open. My head snapped to the side to see a startled looking Guilo Moretti, Gabriel's dad, recoil at the sight me. I sat bolt upright in bed. All pain now replaced with the strength of fear. My eyes frantically scanned the room and landed on Mr Jones stood at the end of my bed.

I was in hospital.

Blackbrooke Hospital.

I was back.

"No!" I screamed, peeling back the scratchy hospital sheets and diving out of bed. I felt a tug in my arm and immediately ripped out the IV drip, letting out a yell.

"Liberty!" Guilo held up his hands. "Calm down. I know this must be a big shock but you need to listen…"

"Listen?!" I repeated, pacing up and down like a caged animal. I looked down at my injured arm which was wrapped in something that resembled cling film so I could see exposed flesh through it. I grimaced in horror and looked back up at the two men, eyes settling on Mr Jones.

"You!" I pointed. "I might have known you'd bring me back!"

Where Guilo looked afraid of my outburst, Mr Jones looked merely unimpressed. "Calm down, Miss Connor. I can't speak to you in this state."

"Speak to me about what?" I screamed. "Speak to me about how I saved the first-borns of Blackbrooke and finally escaped and you pulled me back?!"

Mr Jones rubbed his chin. "Liberty, relax…you're not in Blackbrooke."

"What?" I glanced around the room impatiently. "Yes, I am. I'm in the hospital…and *you're* here. Please don't insult my intelligence."

Guilo looked down, seemingly embarrassed, and Mr Jones let out a laugh. "Liberty, trust me, I wouldn't insult your intelligence," he started out of the door and turned back. "That's the reason you're here after all."

I stepped towards him but he held out his hand and gestured to Guilo.

"Get her some clothes and then send her to me."

He disappeared from the room and my head snapped to Guilo. "What the hell's going on, Dr Moretti?"

"Please," he swallowed, picking up the end of the IV that I'd ripped out, "call me Guilo here."

"Where's *here*?" I demanded.

"I'll go and get your clothes." He hurried out, not meeting my eye and I sat on the edge of the hospital bed, my whole body shaking. I was wearing a hospital gown. How long had I been there? I reached my arm behind me to rub my back where they'd placed a large cotton wool swab.

Why did they have to use a tranquilliser?

Guilo returned and begrudgingly handed over my dress and shoes. All were dirty and stained in Lurker blood. A doctor's nightmare.

"More clothes are on their way. Just be careful with the dressing on your arm," he muttered, the Italian twang in his accent even stronger when he was nervous. "I have more work to do on it."

I scowled as he left the room. I couldn't even associate him with Gabriel in that moment. I was too angry and confused at my whereabouts.

I quickly dressed and let myself out of the room, clutching my arm to my chest. Mr Jones was waiting outside, looking at a notice board on the wall.

Although the room looked like a hospital, now I was out here, it looked like a school building, or offices. The floors were carpeted in black and the walls were painted grey breezeblocks. Despite how simple it looked, something about it seemed expensive and official.

"Follow me…" Mr Jones started down the corridor, glancing at some of the things on the walls. It was mainly displays about Blackbrooke – history, artwork, maps.

Mr Jones led the way into a room and opened the door for me to go through, flicking on the light. It looked like somewhere the police would interrogate suspects and I eyed him warily.

"It's okay." He nodded for me to sit down on the plastic chair on one side of the desk. I slowly did as instructed and didn't take my eyes off him as he sat opposite me.

"Do you know why you're here, Liberty?"

I raised an eyebrow.

He smiled tightly. "Liberty, I need you to try and keep up with what I'm about to say. You're sitting in a very sophisticated facility dedicated to Blackbrooke. It houses a team of around two hundred and fifty who work solely on researching the town and the Creatures that live in it. You see, Liberty," he paused after every sentence, "Blackbrooke, as you're well aware, is an…interesting place. You know a fair few things about it, and you've figured out some amazing… solutions."

"Solutions? Are you talking about Cassius?" I swallowed, feeling myself get angry. "Are these 'amazing' things you talk about those that involved me sacrificing my friends?"

Mr Jones looked me in the eye. "Yes. Liberty, what you

did…it's nothing short of unbelievable. The bravery…"

"Did you know?" I stared at a spot on the table. "Did you know Cassius was the answer?"

He shook his head. "No one knew. Lucas had never told anyone about what happened to him. Not until he told you."

I chewed the inside of my cheek. "Then how the hell do you know? He only told me, Noah and Cassius that information."

Mr Jones' lips twitched. "How is my wife?"

My mouth dropped open and my heart felt like it had stopped. "No. Marie wouldn't do that to us."

"Oh Liberty." He stood up, leaning on the back of his chair. "Of course, she would. Why do you think she was staying there with you?"

"She loves Denzil," I blurted.

The smile fell from Mr Jones' face and he looked distracted. "Well yes, I'm aware her little mission is somewhat…clouded by old feelings."

"Mission?" I whispered in disbelief. It couldn't be. Marie was so warm and loving. She helped us.

I thought back to her pained expression behind her smiles, assuming it was grief for Gemma but now sure it must have been guilt from spying and ratting us out.

"Yes, a mission," he leaned down. "After that day you and your little friend were snooping around my house, I decided to put her to good use. She didn't like it. Took some convincing."

The image of Mrs Jones pushing her hair from her face to reveal her black eye made me look away in disgust.

"Oh Liberty," he chuckled, walking behind me, "get a grip. You really need to start looking on the bright side. You did a wonderful thing tonight – you saved first-borns."

"Only for a hundred years," I muttered, more to myself than to him. Still wracked with remorse. "Cassius was worth more than that."

"Still," Mr Jones shrugged nonchalantly, "it was a feat in human perseverance and intelligence. You're a special girl, Liberty."

"What do you want from me?" I couldn't remove my eyes from a spot on the table, now feeling like the world was spinning out of control on its axis and I couldn't get a hold of what was happening.

"Well, my dear," he placed a gentle hand on my injured arm, "your brain, your determination. You've proved that you're head and shoulders above your peers at school and all of the work that went into tonight was…exquisite."

I clenched my jaw, unable to take in his words.

My mind was jumping around wildly. "How could you have taken Gemma without telling Marie?"

His smile fell. "My wife is a weak woman. She wouldn't have been able to do it. I think you've seen the perfect demonstration of how weak she is having witnessed disloyalty. She's been disloyal to both of us, Liberty. Not a nice feeling, is it?"

I leaned my face closer to his so we were practically nose-to-nose. "Whatever is going on in this place, I will not be a part of it and you can't make me. I'm free."

Mr Jones let his head drop down, looking defeated. My moment of smugness was short-lived and I let out a howl of pain as he dug his fingers into the flesh of my exposed arm and dragged me closer to his. "Listen here, you jumped-up little shit," he spat, "if it were up to me, you'd be as far away from here as possible. Hell, I'd happily throw you to the Crits, you trouble-making whore."

I cried at the pain, now completely rendered disabled and seeing hot flashes of red dance in front of my eyes. "Stop…" I choked.

"But no," he rasped, digging his fingers deeper. "they all want you here, say you're a valuable commodity. I didn't think you'd survive tonight but here you are. You just. Won't.

Fucking. Die!" He threw me backwards and I immediately clutched at my arm, rocking back and forth on the chair crying as pools of hot, dark blood shot up underneath the transparent film.

He wiped the spit that had escaped from his mouth, and pulled the door open roughly. "Someone will be here to collect you and take you to where you'll be staying for the foreseeable future."

My shoulders were shaking from crying. "It's prison."

He let out a snide laugh. "Enjoy being on the QT."

I looked at him questionably.

"QT." He curled his lip. "Queen Team." He nodded to my arm. "You really shouldn't have pulled at the dressing on your arm, now look what you've done. I'll get Guilo to come and fix it."

The door closed and I lowered my head onto the desk and sobbed.

I wished the Hunters would have killed me tonight.

Or maybe the Lurker I encountered at the start of the night. Then Noah and Cassius could have done the rest.

I cried for what felt like hours, alone in that room with its blank, sparse walls and no windows.

Sophisticated facility dedicated to researching Blackbrooke?

Queen Team?

It was too much to take. How much research was needed on the dreaded things? They weren't bothering us. Especially not now.

This couldn't be happening to me. It felt like a bad dream. Like the final kick in the teeth after everything that had happened.

The door opened and I looked up to see a young woman with short black hair and a friendly smile, blinking at me. She glanced at my outfit in horror at the bloodstains.

"Hi, I'm Angelica," she said at last. "I'm here to take you to your team."

I nodded, defeated but eager to get out of that tiny room and grateful to see someone who wasn't Mr Jones.

"Wow, that's nasty." She nodded at my arm as we walked.

I shrugged and followed her into a lift at the end of the corridor. "You should have seen the state of the Lurker."

She laughed, thinking I was making a joke, but stopped abruptly and gulped when I didn't join in. I eyed her in the lift. She was wearing what looked like a uniform of black leggings and a black shapeless sweatshirt. Probably about the same height as Gemma and even more dainty, she didn't peel her eyes off the small screen in the lift that said we were travelling upwards.

The lift pinged at floor five and the doors opened to an identical corridor. Angelica strode ahead and turned back every now and again to flash me a reassuring smile. I could tell she wanted to talk but was under strict instructions not to as she was practically bursting.

I rolled my eyes as she smiled at me yet again before stopping at one of the plain grey doors on the corridor.

"Okay," she let out a breath, "behind this door is where you're stationed with some of the Queen Team. Please don't worry about the lingo," she added quickly. "It's not like the army or anything, it's just what we say. I'm on the Hunter Team."

I nodded, not caring in the slightest.

"Anyway," she hurried on, "each team gets a research room which is what you'll see when you walk in and it can be a bit overwhelming but there's a living area in there as well that's a bit more relaxed. Kind of like University digs, or so I'm told anyway…"

I glanced at her hand on the door handle and then back at her.

"Oh, sorry." She shook her head. "I'll leave you to it from here. I'll see you around, Liberty."

I watched her walk away and felt my stomach dip. I didn't

know the girl and in the brief time we'd met, she irritated the hell out of me but now I didn't want her to leave me on my own.

Not that I planned on staying anyway.

I'd be getting the hell out of there as soon as I could figure out how.

I opened the door and was greeted by a large room with black walls and a black ceiling. In the centre was a huge, backlit 3D map of Blackbrooke, I tentatively stepped further into the room and looked up at the dozens of TV screens covering the far wall. I leaned closer, observing that some of them looked like live CCTV footage taken in various areas of Blackbrooke.

"Hello."

I whirled round to see a man, probably a couple of years older than me, eating from a box of Chinese food.

"Sorry." He placed the box down onto the flat roof of the model Blackbrooke Academy and wiped his hands on his jeans. "You must be Liberty. Apologies, I was just grabbing some supper; it's been a long day."

I took his hand which he held out for me to shake. He looked like one of those cool arty types I'd seen in magazines, the type who would go to school in London and bum around in coffee shops, reading poetry. His purple t-shirt practically hung off one of his shoulders and his trilby hat was set at a jaunty angle, coupled with his beard, framing his long, pointy face. "I'm Jeremiah." He smiled warmly and outstretched his arms. "Welcome aboard!"

I looked around the room. "Erm…is it…just us?"

"No, there's another. He's been working a late shift in the lab but is heading back any second." He nodded enthusiastically. "So, I hear you've been in a battle tonight? I mean, I can pretty much tell by your clothes."

I blinked at him.

"Oh." He scratched the back of his neck. "Sorry, I didn't

mean to bring it up. It's just that…" His outgrown bleached blonde hair stuck out from his hat, a stark contrast to his almost black facial hair and dark brown eyes. "Well, the rumours have been flying around that you were going to go out and fight tonight. Quite a formidable force by all accounts. Not like me. I'm just some softy they drafted in from the Outside…"

I looked down at my feet, unable to deal with his excitement. "I'm tired."

"Of course!" Jeremiah jumped into action. "I'll show you where we sleep and I can talk you through all of this tomorrow."

I nodded and followed him without a word.

I needed to sleep and despite the pain from my bleeding arm, I was quite sure I'd be fast asleep as soon as my head hit the pillow.

The door to the room opened behind us and I sighed thinking it must be Guilo coming back to inspect the damage Mr Jones inflicted on me. The damage I'd have say I'd done myself in a fit of rage. I averted my eyes, already embarrassed about having to lie to Dr Moretti, whom I always liked and respected.

"Is she here yet?!"

I felt my breathing grow shallow as I slowly turned around at the familiar, excited voice. I gasped and covered my mouth at the sight in front of me.

"Gabriel…" I whispered.

There he was.

Gabriel Moretti. All five foot ten of him. The same beautiful dark eyes, thick brown hair.

His body draped in a lab coat.

"Lib…" he breathed.

"I-Is it really you?" I was rooted to the spot, already starting to shake.

He ran towards me and scooped me into his arms. I let out

a breath that was more like a sob as we both sank to the floor, holding one another.

I reached up and ran my fingers through his hair.

His hands found my face and he smiled before closing his eyes and kissing me, stroking my cheek.

"Oh my God." He squeezed me. "I can't believe you're here."

"How…" I croaked, uncontrollable tears running down my face as I buried my head into his shoulder.

"I'm erm…." Jeremiah muttered awkwardly. "I'm going to….yeah." He turned and hurried away.

I pulled back and took Gabriel's face in my hands again, inspecting it, sure it was some kind of trick. "Am I asleep? Am I dead?"

We remained this way for a little while longer, just taking in the sight of one another again, laughing occasionally at the absurdity yet exhilaration of the situation.

His smile fell when he saw my arm and then his eyes dropped to my blood-stained dress, "Oh God, Lib…what happened tonight?"

My bottom lip trembled. "Oh Gabriel…I'm sorry,"

"Sssh," he soothed, pulling me into his chest and stroking my hair, letting me cry. "It's okay. I'm just glad you're here."

I gripped him hard. "We lost Noah."

He sucked in a breath.

"I'm sorry," I repeated, now wailing. "I tried….I-I didn't want him to…"

"Lib," Gabriel took me by the shoulders, "please don't blame yourself."

"I had to give away Cassius to the Queens," I sobbed, my breathing erratic. "Two of my friends died…they were so brave…"

"It was amazing what they both did." He forced a small smile. "What you did was amazing, too, Lib."

"They're dead."

"But look at what you've achieved." He shook me gently. "You're incredible. You figured it all out. When Mr Jones addressed us today and told us what you were planning…" he trailed off and his face flushed red, "I was so scared. We had to just wait and see if you showed up."

I looked at him as he spoke, drinking in every detail of his face. "I'm sorry, this is just….I mean, I thought you were dead. I went to your funeral."

"I know." He nodded gravely. "I felt…awful. I-I didn't know what was happening. I just got brought here one night. They told me it was because they needed someone who was gifted in maths and science to look at the biology of the Queens and analyse their movements…" he trailed off, staring into the distance. "It was only after a couple of days they told me that the whole of Blackbrooke thought I was dead." He blinked and a tear rolled down his face. "It's awful, Lib. The way they did it…my mum doesn't even know."

I thought back to Consuela's distraught face at Gabriel's funeral and her words to me.

I knew there was no way someone could have acted that.

He took my face in his hands again. "I desperately wanted to get a message to you but I couldn't. It was like torture. I saw you…" He glanced up at the rows of CCTV cameras. "In the Academy with Noah and Cassius yesterday," he reached up and touched my short red hair, smiling, "I saw this and thought 'wow, look at my girlfriend'. She's beautiful."

I nuzzled into him so he couldn't see my face. My smile fell.

Girlfriend.

Cassius popped into my head and I squeezed my eyes shut, trying to get rid of the image of us kissing and undressing on the bed at Denzil's flat. Pressing my body lustfully into his.

I sat up straight, unsure of what to say next, settling for something generic. "This is amazing."

"I know, I can't believe how lucky I am. I feel like I'm

getting you back." He reached up, grabbing the back of my neck and moving his lips on mine hungrily. I felt his tongue in my mouth and abruptly pulled back.

"What's the matter?" He frowned, recoiling. His eyes surveyed my face and I noticed hurt instantly registered on his features.

He knew.

"Nothing. I'm sorry. I'm just…overwhelmed. I…" I winced before I said the words. "I *mourned* you, Gabriel. Now here I am, kissing you…"

I found myself having to look away, unable to meet his eye while Cassius was on my mind.

"Lib?"

"Mm-hmm."

"Can I ask you something?" He cleared his throat, sounding stern and I bit my lip nervously. "Is there anything I need to know about–"

He was interrupted by a loud siren going off. I immediately clamped my hand over one ear and tried my best to do the same with the hand of my injured arm.

Large lights on the walls, that looked like the ones on top of police cars, flashed on, bathing the room in red light.

Gabriel jumped to his feet, rushing to the CCTV screens and pressing some buttons on the control panel. He narrowed his eyes at one of the screens.

"Gabriel!" I shouted over the alarm. "What's going on? What is that?"

"I'm trying to see." He looked closer at one of the screens and then recoiled. "Impossible…" He flashed me a panicked look and made for the door. "Stay here."

"What?" I jumped up. "What's going on? I want to know."

He looked down at my hand wrapped around his arm and then back at me.

Jeremiah appeared in the doorway. "Is this an S Code?"

Gabriel nodded, the colour drained from his face.

"S Code?" I repeated, watching Jeremiah follow Gabriel out of the door.

I ignored Gabriel's order and followed them, running as fast as I could as they bypassed the lift and made for the stairs.

My heart was pounding, a feeling of dread descending down on me. I caught sight of the back of Gabriel's lab coat flapping behind him as he ran around a corner after descending several flights of stairs.

Gabriel swiped a plastic card that was hanging around his neck on a pad which opened a door, and him and Jeremiah rushed through it.

"Shit!" I cursed, running as fast as I could before it shut completely. I jammed my fingers into the door and winced in pain as I threw it open and hurled myself through. I stopped at the top of another set of stairs, this time metal and looked down into a large room that was the size of an aircraft hanger.

I gasped in shock at the hive of activity going on below me and slowly made my way down. It was undoubtedly a lab of some kind and there were cages and mortuary slabs everywhere containing dead Crits.

I raised my hand to my mouth as I remembered Dad saying the bodies of Crits were always returned to the woodland or wherever they came from.

As I looked around the room, that was obviously untrue.

I reached the bottom and walked past a table that contained a dead Hunter, lying on its back and its torso cut open form its neck to its groin. Its rib cage was pulled apart and several of its organs were sitting in dishes around the table.

The table next to it contained a similar sight, but this time a Lurker.

My back pressed against something. I turned around just as an angry looking Watcher launched itself at the glass I was leaning against. I looked at it in horror as it paced up and down the tiny tank, saliva dropping out of the side of its mouth.

I turned to where the group of lab workers had congregated. A truck was there, like the one that had picked me up earlier. On closer inspection, it looked more like an ambulance. I could hear people shouting.

"Step away from the gurney!"

"Keep your distance!"

"How the hell…?"

I pushed through several people and ran straight into the arms of Gabriel who looked shell-shocked. He pushed me back.

"Lib, I told you to stay where you were."

"What's going on?" I asked, trying to look over his shoulder.

I heard a toe-curling scream from the centre of the crowd.

Gabriel and I locked eyes. His full of horror and warning.

I pushed him roughly. "Get out of my way!"

I beat my way to the front and saw several doctors, including Guilo, hunched over the bed they'd just taken out of the truck.

"Everyone please, step back!" Guilo shouted angrily, turning around and holding out his arm. He was wearing a surgical mask. He saw me and his eyes widened.

"Someone remove this girl!" He pointed and the people surrounding me immediately sprang into action.

"No!" I screamed. "Get off me!"

"Lib!"

I stopped squirming in their arms, my blood instantly running cold at the voice calling my name.

Several gasps could be heard from around the room and, in a state of shock, the people let me go so I could lurch forward again. This time I reached the gurney and shrank back at the sight in front of me.

They'd almost completely scalped him. Most of his head was pink and mushy and only a small patch of hair remained.

One of his eyes was missing too, leaving a gaping hole. His nose was bloody and it had dried all over his face and down his neck.

His entire torso was covered in blood and it continued to ooze out all over the gurney and dribble onto the cold concrete floor.

Barely alive, but alive nonetheless.

My voice broke as I whispered his name.

"Cassius."

THE END

PART II OF THE EXPLOSIVE BLACKBROOKE TRILOGY IS COMING SOON...

3535363R00221

Printed in Great Britain
by Amazon.co.uk, Ltd.,
Marston Gate.